Avengers of Light:

The Curse of Asmodeus

By

Elijah Howe (Elijah Jubilee Howe)

Table of Contents

Dedication

For the Dyers. Every family has stories that only they know.
Since our adventures are endless, thanks for all the sequel ideas.

Acknowledgments

First and foremost, I thank God for making this book possible by His grace and for His glory. Without my Lord and Savior, Jesus Christ, whose grace and mercy I'm completely dependent on every single day, I could never have written or published this book. From Him, though Him, and to Him are all things, and I hope my efforts bring Him glory.

I'd like to thank my parents for always believing my work would come to fruition. You never seemed to care if your daughter was more interested in books and boxing gloves than makeup or dresses, and I love you both dearly.

I'm grateful to my father for giving me books to read instead of electronic devices when I was a little girl and for my early Biblical education.

And thank you to my mother, who taught me to slow down and enjoy the journey whenever I got stressed about the goal. Thank you so much for all the support and love in this endeavor.

I want to thank my eldest brother, Nicholas, for always being there for me and setting a high bar for the way I should act. You taught me there's no such thing as an overnight success. Your youngest sister loves you and thinks the world of you.

Thank you to my sister/best friend/partner in crime, Hannah. Life has been so much more fun getting the privilege of going through it with you as my sister in Christ. Thanks for being the first one in my family to read and fall in love with this book.

To my brother Jordan for always seeing the bright side of any situation and for contributing Micah's drawings with your artistic talent. Thanks for being part of the original party—love you.

To my brother Gabriel, thanks for all the stories/games, good and bad, you were a part of when we were younger. Remember, all the fighting means we forgave more than most.

A big thank you to my friends Cora and Paige Gascon. Thank you both for your great work on this book cover/back. Without your help, Cora, my magic system might still be a mess! You're both a blessing, and I pray great things are in store for the two of you.

A thank you to Karen Kostlivy. You encouraged me to write a middle grade, and I would have been flying completely blind into this crazy publishing journey without your help. Getting to work with you in a friendship/partnership has been a tremendous blessing.

Thank you to my editor Sally. It was a tough choice choosing what developmental editor to go with, but I don't regret going with you one bit.

Thank you to the editing team of the Amazon publishing agency for working with me every step throughout the process of this book's publication.

I want to thank my friend Lindy Vincent for always believing I'd be a published author and for being my unofficial photographer on the publishing journey.

In conclusion, thank you to all my brothers and sisters in Christ who supported or encouraged this project over the last few years. Whether you helped knowingly or not, in thought, prayer, word, or deed—I appreciate you. I hope you enjoy this book and the world I've created.

About the Author

E. Jubilee Howe is a Christian author born and raised in Northern California. When Jubilee's not writing, inhabiting coffee houses, and listening to music or sermons, she's binge-watching anime or spending time with her family. While most other children were being given technology, she was reading and writing books. Jubilee loves to weave Christian values along with the battle between good and evil into all her works.

Jubilee's website, "The Howe Sisters' Guide to Writing," which she has with her sister Hannah explores their perspectives on films, books, concepts in creative writing, and more.

Prologue

Do you ever look at the world and think, 'I'm nothing like them?' Does trouble follow you wherever you go? Do you feel like the celestial being up there is writing you a troubled story, and you have no idea why? If you see horrible creatures or things in dark corners you can't explain, you might be one of the 'commissioned.' If this isn't you, and your life isn't a freak show like ours, then maybe you can enjoy this story like any other alleged work of fiction. Read it, put it away, and pretend it's just a warped fairytale. However, if your life does sound like what I've described, I won't have to convince you, the forces of darkness won't leave you alone forever. My family learned that the hard way. When that happens…come find us.

Don't believe me? Maybe I should tell you the whole story. I can trace part of it back to the same `dream I've been having for three years. I was ten years old back then. We lived in our little one-story house with soft carpeting in the hallway and the three bedrooms close together. We'd been playing in the living room - my siblings and I - while our mom made dinner. The smell of food was amazing as always; enchiladas, rice, and beans were all cooking while Mom rolled dough for flour tortillas, her thick dark hair tied back in a bun.

Dad was reading in an easy chair. Everything about the night was as normal as possible, including the fight we had while playing with each other. Dad stepped in to fix it, and we all said grace before having dinner. By the time we were done, it was late, and there wasn't much time before we were supposed to be in bed. I remember being annoyed over not getting to do as much in the game we played or that I got talked over at dinner. Little stupid things! Now I look back and wish I could freeze that evening, just to enjoy those simple things one more time.

After dinner, Mom tucked my sister and me in, put my stuffed Pooh bear in my arms, and brushed my hair behind my ears like she always did. Dad was in the doorway, visible because of the dim hallway light. "Goodnight, my precious. Sweet dreams."

1

I was half asleep. I put my head on the pillow and caught one last glimpse of my parents through the thin slit in my eyes. Just then, I heard my mother say to my father, "We need to talk…."

Dad put his hand to Mom's face affectionately and said, "I know." Then he took one last look at Emma and me before shutting the door. Emma, my sister, put her arms around me like a pillow and went to sleep.

For a few hours, everything seemed fine. Our bedroom window was cracked open, and the wind was blowing the tree outside in our front yard. A strong gust of wind rattled the blinds, causing me to sit up. There was a light creeping through our door from the hallway. It wasn't yellow like the hallway light; it was…purple and red. Since then, it's been hard for me to tell if I imagined it, but I recall the smoky colors illuminating the carpet clear as day. I slipped my feet out of bed as Emma yawned.

"Elsha, what are you…."

I hurried to the door, putting my hand on the knob—and froze. My hair stood on end as the wind from outside began to whip violently, knocking the blinds loudly back and forth. Everything on our windowsill fell to the ground. Emma rushed to close the window, and I turned, looking at the sky. The clouds outside were a thick thundering color, covering our whole block with terrifying images of dark blue and purple.

Lightning broke through the sky outside our window. The explosive sound forced me to swallow my fear and turn the knob. As I stepped out of my room, a shockwave of force knocked me down in the hallway. The sound of violent winds beating against our home was so loud that I had to cover my ears. My eldest brother, Galahad, rushed out of the room at the end of the hall.

Galahad put his hand on my arm, helping me up. "Are you okay?"

"Mom…Dad…." I rushed to the master bedroom, but the door was already open. The sheets on the bed were pulled back like they'd gotten up. Their wedding photo that should have been on the nightstand was gone. I hurried down the hall as the sound of my siblings talking behind me echoed in my ears. Something was wrong. I got to the living room and stopped. Amidst all the chaos, something else was very off. All the photos that had been on the furniture were gone. Everything in the living room had been knocked over and tossed about like a twister hit. The front door was hanging off the hinges like the storm had broken through it. Galahad rushed forward and reached for the bat our Dad put behind the front door for protection. It wasn't there. The storm outside had quieted as quickly as it had started, and then the panic came.

There's no way to describe everything we felt after that: panic, confusion, worry, sadness. All of them hit my siblings and me at once.

Just like that, we were alone. And I haven't seen my mother's face or heard my father's voice since. If not for Galahad, we probably would have ended up in a gutter somewhere. My middle-brother Killian wanted to go out and look for our parents. Micah and I were panicking, and Emma was trying to talk everybody down. Galahad called the police and told them what had happened. Then the next strangest thing occurred. The police searched our house but found no record that we ever had parents. The photos, bills, mail, everything was gone. They couldn't even find our birth certificates. It was a long and grueling process of losing our home and everything we had except for a couple of bags of what we could grab before childcare services took us. Then, just like that, the Dyers never even existed. We were the only proof of it, and to the world, we were no one.

I'll save you the details of how many therapists, childcare agents, and foster care representatives came by to discuss what to do with us. If we went into the system, they all made it very clear we could be adopted separately or sent into different foster homes. Galahad said that wasn't an option. We ended up at what I like to call jail for kids *cough* or…Blech's Boarding House in Sacramento.

3

Chapter One

Meet The Dyer Family…What's Left of It

What's a boarding house? A place of torture if you ask me, but according to the adult world (what they tell themselves at night so they sleep better), it's a place where kids without parents can get the schooling they need until they're adopted or find their original families. Boarding Houses get money from the state so they can provide for children, but ours was run by Satan—not literally; we deal with him much later— a.k.a Mr. Scratchet Blech. The main classroom in the Boarding House was always cold. Miss Michum said children being cold made us tougher—only she was always bundled in layers of clothing. I couldn't 100% blame her for the chill. The building was brick, three stories high, and massively outdated. Our classroom was on the second floor, overlooking the back alleys of buildings where a lot of homeless lived.

I sat by the window in the small wooden chair, not because of the wonderful view—but because I'd rather freeze than be in the center of the classroom. The center of the classroom for me meant being the point of attention. There are few things I hated more than that. On the list were spiders, the black plague, death, the gruel Blech's served at lunch….you get the idea.

With our complicated history, my siblings and I were already the subject of bullying. The last thing I wanted was the opportunity to be noticed.

My head was crouched, and my elbows on my desk. I wore a Tshirt and my sweatshirt over it with a knit cap. I always overdressed, but today the cold weather gave me an excuse. My pencil was beyond dull. But if I wanted to sharpen it, I had to get up and walk past Miss Michum to the sharpener in the wall and risk being called to the board or laughed at. It happened literally every time before, so don't judge me. I struggled to write the math problem she was covering on my thin-lined piece of paper.

Emma was next to me. Her pencil wasn't dull. Emma sharpened it in class—she was always the bold one. Miss Michum moved through problems fast and erased them before all the kids could get them down. She didn't really seem to care if we learned it or not. How do I know this? Because Miss Michum said, "It's not my problem if you don't learn this—none of you are going anywhere in the world anyway!" She loved saying this to all the orphans, but I was her favorite. I've wondered since that time if Miss Michum was in fact a demon....but let's keep going. As usual, I struggled through the class with my head down. The one time I tried to ask a question, I stuttered—Miss Michum *hated* stuttering. She brought the ruler down on my desk.

Whap!

The ruler grazed my fingers, and I bit back a yelp.

Emma straightened, steamed.

When this kind of drama happened, Micah usually stayed back because he was as much used to it as we were. I glanced back over my shoulder to see Micah drawing on his sketch pad, but he'd frozen. Killian was there as well, seated farther back. He'd barely slipped in. Killian did that a lot. Sat by the window so he could slip out in class and come back when it was nearly over. He looked confused.

I let my hair hide my face; it was pressed against my cheeks because of my hat being pulled down.

"You didn't have a right to hit my sister's hand! If you didn't go so fast, then maybe…" Emma began.

"Silence! Since you both like being so active in class, you can stay after and clean the classroom! And as for you, Mr. Dyer…." She looked at the back of the class. Killian was looking back and forth between Michum and me. I wanted to be mad at him, but he couldn't have done much if he'd been here. Emma's eyes didn't have as much mercy for Killian. She was shooting him death looks. Micah was glancing around between all of us. "Since you can't bother showing up, you'll spend part of your lunchtime helping them!"

Killian gripped the sides of his small wooden desk, looking down, "Oh, bite me…"

Miss Michum's face twisted with anger. She gripped her pointer and marched down the aisles to Killian. Murmurs went around the room. We all stared aghast. Micah was waiting to see what our brother would do with more excitement than fear. Miss Michum smacked Killian on the back of the head.

Emma stood up and clenched her fists. "Don't touch my brother!"

Michum aimed her pointer at Emma. "Stay right where you are! I'm your educator and…." She had one hand rested on Killian's desk. She let out a scream. "—AAAH!"

I was leaning out of my chair, looking back at them, when Michum grabbed her hand, dropping her pointer.

Killian had bit her. She snarled as a small echo of laughter went over the classroom.

"You….." Michum looked like she wanted to release a lot of foul words that probably weren't good for ninth graders. "YOU DYERS ARE THE MOST DIFFICULT WORTHLESS LITTLE MONGRELS I'VE EVER BEEN UNFORTUNATE ENOUGH TO TEACH! I'M NOT SURPRISED NO ONE'S ADOPTED YOU YET! ALL OF YOU ARE STAYING AFTER CLASS AND CLEANING THIS ROOM SPOTLESS, EVEN IF IT MEANS YOU MISS LUNCH!"

***

Emma and Killian only argued for a little while when we cleaned out the classroom. Killian biting Miss Michum had earned him some brownie points even though he'd skipped class. Micah tried to lighten the situation with humor while we cleaned under the desks and swept. I was doing everything not to cry. Killian was mumbling under his breath as the four of us left the classroom and walked down the dusty wooden hallway to the cafeteria. The building was so old the ground creaked beneath our feet. Micah was congratulating Killian for biting Michum. Micah showed him some of the drawings he'd made in class while Emma talked to me. I was trying to listen to my siblings, but every time a door closed or a window shudder blew, my hair stood on end.

I tried to calm my heart rate.

Everything was normal.

Emma put her hand on my arm as the boys pushed open the double doors to the cafeteria. "Hey, everything's okay, Elsha. It's only 12:30, so we didn't miss all of lunch. Maybe we can go over what's next in our story," she encouraged. The cafeteria was loud as always, but Emma didn't need help being loud—she had a strong voice.

I nodded, looking up at her. Emma was much prettier than me. She reminded me of our mom. She had a heart-shaped face and blonde hair that barely reached her shoulders. Today she was in a pink sweatshirt and sneakers, very worn, but she made them work. It was difficult to describe our mom after all this time, but I remember she was beautiful. Emma knew that the best way to pull me out of a tough life situation was to talk about our stories together. We don't have a lot going for us, but one thing the Dyers have is imagination. Killian and Micah had their own games they played with the pictures they drew. Emma and I had a similar game together—we only had salvaged a few Barbies from our old home, and we constantly made up adventures for them. It took our minds off the real world. But right now, it was hard not to think about the gag-worthy smell coming from the cafeteria, the throbbing in my fingers, and the rest of the horrible classes I had ahead of me.

Emma bit her lip as we got in line for food. "Galahad is supposed to be back from volunteer work for lunch."

My expression brightened slightly, and the muscles in my face relaxed at hearing the mention of my oldest brother. "That'll be nice," I said at last. Emma leaned down to hear me because Killian and Micah were talking loudly in front of us as they got their food.

Galahad was farther ahead in classes than us, so we only saw him at lunch and recreational time now. Oh yeah—you're probably wondering about the age gap between my siblings and me. I was 13, Micah was 14, Emma and Killian were 15 (twins) —and Galahad was 16. We were all born close together. Blech's had classes for varying ages, and Killian should have been where Galahad was, but cutting class and talking smack about the teachers held him back.

The cafeteria was packed with metal tables and kids of various ages. Some bigger and others smaller than me. I searched the crowd of empty faces for Galahad when a girl nearly knocked me over. I put my hands on the side of the sneeze guard over the food to steady myself. Emma took me by the arm and glared at her, "Watch where you're going!"

The frizzy-haired girl glanced down her nose at Emma and then acknowledged me. "Oh, I didn't see anyone there." She rushed off to sit with her friends, and I cast my eyes down.

Emma nudged me encouragingly, and I looked up. Through the crowd of kids rushing and eating, I saw a familiar boy with a crew cut in a sweatshirt and jeans jogging over. If I'd seen only his walk from a distance, I'd know him in anywhere.

Galahad.

He clutched his backpack a little out of breath as he rushed over. Security was by the doors watching all of us like a prison guard and glanced at him. Galahad broke into a smile, scooping me up in a hug. I smiled as he swung me in a circle before setting me down. I straightened my knit hat and adjusted my sleeves laughing. Galahad leaned down to meet my gaze, "Elsha, it's great to see you guys," he looked at Emma and gave her a hug too.

Killian smacked Galahad on the arm as a form of greeting, and Micah smiled.

"Do you think after school maybe we could all do something fun together?" I looked up at Galahad with a hopeful smile. He was generally the orchestrator of any group activity or game with my siblings. It was always he or Emma that got us together. If left to our own devices, Killian and Micah would play their games, and Emma and I would do our own thing. When Galahad talked, my other siblings listened. I had less authority over them, partially because I was the youngest and the most quiet.

Galahad smiled, holding me more tightly with his arm, "Sure. When I get back and we finish our homework, we'll all play together. I'm sure with the combined imaginations of Emma and your brothers, we can come up with something."

My mood improved almost instantaneously. Maybe today wasn't going so badly after all.

"Mr. Blech didn't keep you doing community service all through lunch like last time?" Emma said as she paused before the lunch lady. The lunch lady dropped a spoonful of what was allegedly cream of wheat in her bowl.

Galahad moved his head thoughtfully, walking with me down the lunch line. "No, not right now. But I do have some service at the library down the block after lunch." He put his hands in the pockets of his sweatshirt.

Emma looked at him in surprise, "But that's during the recreational time! They don't have a right to keep you all day!" she objected as the lunch lady served me. "I don't see why you have to be out doing that instead of here with us…"

Galahad shrugged and walked with us over to an empty table, "It helps me out with Blech. Besides, I like keeping busy."

As we all approached the table, a large boy with a smashed nose slid into the seat spreading his arms. He flattened his torso over the table and looked up at us disdainfully, "My seat!"

Killian raised an eyebrow. "Is that what you're trying to tell us?"

"Yeah!" Bryan, the smash-nosed boy, grinned.

Micah shrugged, "And here I thought I was reading too much into things."

A few other unsavory-looking kids came over and slid into the seats next to Bryan. "This is our table, freaks!"

"Oh yeah…" Killian stepped forward, but Galahad held out an arm halting him. Galahad's eyes went over to the security guard. He was watching us. "What are you doing? Let's pummel these guys!"

"There's no need for that," Galahad cautioned, looking back and forth between Killian and Bryan who stood up. Bryan was a large boy—much too big for a fifteen-year-old. He was known for beating up smaller kids and picking on pretty much anyone he met who didn't have the spine to stand against him (like me). Galahad was six feet tall, so he scared him off occasionally, but sometimes Bryan tested how much he could push my brother.

"What's the matter, Dyer? Too *nice* to fight back?" Bryan said.

Galahad held his gaze.

I was looking up at him. The rest of my siblings were staring at him too; he was our circumstantially appointed leader (he was the oldest, so he basically assumed the responsibility/last say in all family disputes and decisions). It was a painful few seconds as I studied my oldest brother's eyes—he was thinking, deciding, and finally, he spoke.

"C'mon guys, let's get another table," he walked past Bryan, who snorted and laughed uproariously. Killian held out a hand in the confusion following us as we sat at an uneven metal table across the room by the garbage cans. Somehow that was always where we ended up. None of us spoke for a few seconds as we ate.

Eventually, Killian slammed his hand on the table. "What the heck was that?"

All our bowls shook.

Galahad rested his elbows on the table and looked at Killian, "What was *what*?"

Emma, Micah, and I exchanged glances because we knew what was coming.

"Fight, fight…" Micah whispered jokingly as he doodled in his notepad while he chewed.

Emma smacked him lightly on the arm, "Micah!"

Micah shrugged and put in his ear pods. They connected to a small iPod that only played a few stations. Emma's frown deepened. Those were one of the few things left from home Micah had, so none of us liked to bother him about them. Galahad always told him it wasn't respectful to have them in while we were eating as a family or having a serious talk. It annoyed the rest of us occasionally, but we accepted Micah was in his own little world.

"You could've laid Bryan out right here in front of everybody! Why didn't you?" Killian leaned forward. "He's a no-count bully, loser…"

"And what good would that have done us? Gotten us in more trouble so the girls wouldn't even get lunch? Don't think I didn't notice; it's half past, and you guys were barely in line. You got in trouble in class, didn't you?" Galahad pressed.

Killian scoffed, "Oh yeah, assume it's all my fault…"

Galahad let out a breath, "I didn't say that. But if you came to class *on time* …you could help the girls and Micah. Then maybe, they could pass."

"There's no point! Miss Michum and all the other teachers here don't care what happens to us!" Killian argued.

Emma, Micah, and I looked back at Galahad to see what he'd say.

"So, I guess we just quit and encourage them to give up?" Galahad said.

We looked back at Killian.

"You're so full of…"

"Killian!" Emma snapped.

"You have to stop taking off and start taking responsibility," Galahad said.

"What? Are you afraid I'm gonna leave and not come back like our parents?" Killian said.

We gasped. That was off-limits. Killian, in all his argumentative nature, knew our parents weren't to be talked about. Even mentioning it was enough to cast a dark shadow over all of us.

I cast my eyes down a moment, and when I looked back up, Galahad's glare had deepened at Killian. "Could you not mention that? You're just going to make everyone upset." I knew Galahad well enough that when he said *everyone,* he really meant the most sensitive in the group: Emma and I.

Killian crossed his arms, slouching back in his chair.

"Now, enough of this; stop arguing and eat your food," Galahad said, drinking his water. He never ate as much as the rest of us, even though I imagined he should since he was older and larger.

I tugged at Galahad's sleeve after we ate in silence for a few moments. "Galahad, why didn't you make that guy move?" I knew he was probably right in the decision, but I didn't understand why.

Galahad thought a moment, "Because he wasn't worth it. If I'm going to get in a fight with somebody, it has to be over something worthwhile. And a table, that's not worth it. If I submit Bryan, I promise it'll have to be over something important." He moved my hat affectionately on my head, ruffling my hair, and I laughed.

For the moment, the drama was over. Micah showed Killian the artwork in his book, and they began to talk. Emma started talking to Galahad about the next story she had planned for our dolls, and he listened attentively as always. I began to relax, growing immersed in the conversation and being between Galahad and Emma. I finished my plate, and Galahad encouraged me to go get seconds. At Blech's, only one portion was customary, but Galahad said it was fine. Initially, the idea of getting up and walking over was terrifying because I had to pass all the mean kids. Emma offered to go with me seeing my hesitation. We both stood up, and Galahad turned to talk to the boys.

As Emma and I talked walking over, I caught a glimpse of something in the glass on the double doors to the cafeteria.

I froze mid-step.

The noises in the cafeteria seemed to fade: the clinking of glass plates, plastic forks, choking and gagging of kids, and the loud, obnoxious noises Bryan was making all slipped into a blur. In the glass, I saw a face: ghoulish, green with wrinkled flesh and prominent sharp teeth. Its eyes were like black holes sunken into its bald head. The head and face looked like melting green wax with fangs sticking out of the mouth, and the wrinkles in the skin were deep. It was as real as anything else in the cafeteria... It was looking right at me. I caught my breath.

Emma leaned down to meet my gaze.

"Elsha, what is it?"

She had to see it. It was right there. And Miss Michum might be ugly, but she didn't look like that. That thing didn't even look human. I tried to speak. I raised my hand to point. This was one of those things I was always seeing that none of the teachers believed. It was the reason I got called crazy or a freak. My heart hammered in my chest. Bryan was getting up with his friends to get seconds. They walked in front of Emma and me pointing and laughing at us for no reason. I was too scared to care about why.

Suddenly my plate wasn't in my hands.

As my breath left my mouth, my plate flew from my hands across the cafeteria, shooting right at Bryan and his friends.

13

Emma's mouth dropped open, and the sound of glass shattering filled the air.

Chapter Two

The Family That Fights Together Stays Together

One second, I was staring at an image of a ghastly figure in the glass on the doors with a plate in my hands. The next, the plate had flown right into the doors and shattered the glass. I hadn't thrown it. I swear!

I was frozen, trying to form words; the students were mumbling and scuffling, half of them were laughing, and I had no idea why. My eyes fell on Bryan and his friends. They were crouched on the floor in front of me, the doors with shattered glass behind them.

Bryan lifted his head, "She threw a plate at me!"

"N-no, I didn't!" I choked out. My siblings ran to my side. Galahad wanted to know what happened, and Bryan was insistent that I threw the plate. I said I didn't. My siblings believed me, even though the rest of the kids seemed to say I did it. I still got a strong reprimand from the security guard. Galahad argued with the guard for me, but it didn't do any good. I wasn't allowed dinner privileges that day because of my alleged plate throwing (apparently in Blech's dinner was a *privilege*).

I just kept my head low through the next classes. I wasn't going to risk getting in anymore trouble. I didn't see any monsters, I hoped to keep it that way. Micah was mostly silent through all the drama which—I won't lie—bothered me. I appreciated Micah's jokes when things were tough, I really did. But when things got serious, I never heard a peep from him. He just retreated into his drawings or his little crafts. We didn't have many toys from the old house, but Micah kept all bits and pieces from the ones we did. He searched through the garbage for useful action figure pieces to make his own characters. It was a real gift. But the only one of us Micah really strove to communicate with was Killian. Micah sat next to me in Blech's recreational park on a swing. It was a small park, not the cleanest in the world with a spray-painted slide and creaky swing. I was staring down at my sneakers as I moved slowly back and forth. There was a chain link fence around the recreational area and outside it the Boarding House garbage dump. We had a view of the sketchy alley leading out to the street. Blech's was surrounded by buildings around it that blocked out most outside light or people—it always made me feel caged. Like I couldn't see anything outside that terrible place. Emma was sitting on the ground next to us looking through a small bag of material. She liked to pick up stray pieces to make clothes for our dolls.

Galahad was off doing volunteer work at the library down the block. He rode his bike there (he and Killian were the only ones with wheels, and it took some doing but that's another story) and he never told me exactly what he had to do. But he always looked tired when he got back. Killian was across the playground with other kids getting ready to play freeze tag. Even with how other kids looked down on us, Killian was fast and athletic enough to impress them when he played sports. Galahad was great at sports too but rarely played with the other kids. I'd see him out on the basketball court by himself shooting hoops and dribbling. He'd ask me to play but I was never good at anything athletic. If I played, I'd probably embarrass myself, so I never tried.

Micah wasn't one for athletic games either. Killian had constantly messed with him for it but they were still friends. I looked at Micah wondering what he thought of all this: Miss Michum hitting me, Bryan accusing me of throwing a plate, me seeing a monster etc. He wasn't looking at me. He just drew and kept looking up at Killian.

"Do you…even care about any of this?" I forced out. I didn't want to sound harsh, but he said so little to me I really had to wonder.

Micah lifted his head a little guilty. He shrugged, "I guess I try not to take any of it too seriously."

I raised my eyebrows. "Is there a funny side to *any* of this?"

Micah turned his notepad to me, "Maybe this will help." On the sketchpad was a cartoonish image of Miss Michum with Killian sinking his teeth into her hand. Miss Michum had an overexaggerated head and all the students in his picture were laughing. Micah put himself in the image screaming "JUSTICE!" It was good cartoon art. Micah was talented, whether the teachers or Blech saw it or not.

I laughed.

That clearly pleased Micah, he smiled proudly closing his eyes. Micah had a round face with buzzed short brown hair, he always wore a red t-shirt tucked in and sneakers. Whenever Emma or I laughed at his jokes, he always brightened.

"Killian would like that," I tried to control my laughter.

Micah looked even happier at that. He looked down at his sketchpad turning the page. "So…what did you see this time?"

I swallowed hard. Micah and I had a thing going. Whenever I saw something out of the ordinary, I'd describe it and he'd draw it. Often, he used the monsters I described in his picture games with Killian. They both drew creatures and made them characters they could use or role-play with. It was less expensive than video games or toys. I started to tell him about it. Micah drew as I spoke, and when he was done, he turned the picture to me.

"Something like this?"

It was scary how accurate he was. I nodded. Emma looked over our shoulders at the image of the grotesque face. She pulled her head back in disgust. "Ew! What is that thing?"

"This is what Elsha saw," Micah said.

"Why do you have to draw all those freaky things? I know you guys use them in your games, but that's the last thing Elsha needs right now. And the teachers already think we're nuts…"

"Look on the bright side," Micah puffed his chest out. "Now we can officially be the kids that are too cool for school because we're over here alone claiming this part of the playground."

"Or…we're over here because nobody wants to play with us," I said. Killian was across the playground racing other kids and winning, of course. The game ended and all the kids separated, catching their breath. The playground supervisor separated the kids into teams. Killian was over there, so I wanted to play. Even if I wasn't good at it, it still looked like they were having fun. Maybe all the kids wouldn't judge and laugh at me. There was always a chance….

Emma noticed me watching and gave me a nudge. "Did you wanna…" she gestured to the game and back at me.

My face grew hot. She and Micah were looking at me, the sound of the supervisor calling names. The dreaded last sounds of "Any lastminute joiners?" echoing in my ears. If I didn't speak up now, I wouldn't get to…

The whistle blew. And in another second, they were playing the game. I let out a breath. Half disappointed in myself and half relieved. I guess I could always play next time. Emma was looking at me sympathetically. She perked up with a smile and pulled something out from her slightly worn pink backpack. We all had backpacks that were from the Salvation Army. That was all Blech's could afford. Not that I could complain, a small beat-up backpack was better than none. Emma held out my favorite (and only) doll that I salvaged from our old home and brought to the orphanage.

"Tada!" Bella (my doll) was in a new outfit; a patched pink top and a white skirt with cloth wrapped around her feet like socks. "What do you think? She's ready for the runway?"

I took the doll and lifted her arms, imagining what character she could play when Emma and I got the chance, "I love it! When did you get so good with clothes?" Other girls made fun of Emma for it, but I thought she had a real talent. The doll even had small, freshly picked flowers tied around her waist like a belt. Emma had a love for flowers. Some of them she tried to grow in pots on our windowsill, but everything she made died. None of us could figure out why. Killian said they committed suicide. Micah said everything was destined to die in Blech's. Neither of them was exactly wrong….

Galahad responded by getting her a book on flowers from the library.

Emma shrugged, putting her hands in her pockets, "I don't know, Blech's throws a lot of stuff away; I fish what I can from the garbage with Galahad and Killian's help. The gate is too high for me to get over."

I looked over at Killian playing with other kids. He climbed in the garbage to help Emma get clothes for my dolls. Even though he skipped out and played with other kids that didn't like us, he was still one of us. "Thank you," I held my toy tightly. It wasn't much, but it was from home. I knew other kids thought we were too old for toys, but it was a way of making a world of our own.

Three girls from the cafeteria walked up to us from across the playground. Hayley, Jenny, and Meryl. Or as Emma liked to call them: skinny, nosy, and whiny. They took any excuse to laugh at my siblings and me. When we were separated, they saw us as an easier target, and now we were missing two heavy hitters: Killian and Galahad.

"Look who chickened out of playing with us," Hayley scowled.

"Good thing too; if baby fat had played with us, we'd have lost for sure," Meryl scrunched her nose like a pig and looked at me. I looked down at the toy in my hands, which was much prettier than I was. My eyes were already moist, but I wouldn't cry in front of them.

"Ever heard of the three stooges?" Micah studied the girls.

They both glared at him.

Micah shrugged. "You could take beauty tips from them. I'm just saying…"

Emma broke out in a laugh. The sound of her laugh stiffened my upper lip.

"You shut up, skippy!"

Micah frowned at the nickname. He liked to run around and walk quickly when he was thinking; people saw it and thought something

19

was wrong with him. They'd given him the rather un-endearing nickname, and it was now the butt of many jokes. Micah never showed it bothered him, but I knew it did.

"Oh, knock it off, Hayley! Everybody knows you only pass your tests because you cheat off Emily's paper!" Emma snapped.

The teacher watching the kids play wasn't looking at us, but they would be soon enough. Killian was running when he paused and looked our way. His expression shifted from laughter to concern, his dark hair half over his eyes.

"I'm not the one with the crazy sister and the lame brother! Tell us, Elsha, what did you see in the hallway the other night?" Hayley said.

"You're one step away, Hayley…" Emma snarled.

"I…I saw a woman, old, with a long nose, warts and…." I began. "A tall hat?" Hayley raised her eyebrows before laughing. "Maybe we should tell Miss Michum what you really think of her!"

Emma sneered, "How about I say what I think of *you* instead!"

"Why you….!" Haley raised a hand, but now more people were looking. Her boyfriend, Bryan, the jerk of jerklosovakia, hurried over and Killian was close behind.

Hayley snatched the doll right out of my hands and threw it in the sandbox.

That did it. Emma shoved Hayley on her butt with both hands. Then everything happened quickly. The playground security was yelling and trying to make sense of what was happening. Bryan had run over and come to Hayley's aid; he grabbed Emma's arm. Micah started hitting him on the side with his sketchpad, Killian jumped on Bryan's back. Hayley grabbed Emma, and now they were wrestling on the floor. I stood up and pulled at Bryan's arm, trying to get him to stop. He threw Killian off his back and shoved me in the gut knocking me to the ground. Emma had the top mount on Hayley, but her two friends were trying to pull my sister off.

"Leave Emma alone!"

I grabbed a bucket full of sand from the sandbox and threw it on the girls making them step back and wave their hands frantically. "SHE GOT SAND IN MY HAIR!"

I looked up, darting my eyes around the lot. Galahad was riding up on the other side of the chain link fence by the garbage where the bikes were parked. Galahad got off his bike and came in through the gate in a matter of seconds. I was waving and calling to him, hoping he could solve the chaos. Killian and Micah were both trying to stop Bryan, but he was larger than both put together.

Bryan shoved Micah and Killian front-kicked him in the gut. Bryan went to hit Killian, but I ran in the way, "Stop it!"

It wasn't a smart move. Bryan's fist almost connected with my face. Even Killian shouted, "Elsha, No!" But before Bryan's fist hit me, Galahad grabbed his arm and twisted it behind his back. He shoved Bryan face-first on the floor in front of us, and that fight was over. Killian put his arm around me protectively.

The playground security came over and pulled Emma off Hayley.

Galahad looked up at us, "Are you guys okay?"

Micah was breathing heavily; he gave a thumbs up and nodded.

The playground security sneered, "...DYERS!"

***

Blech's Office was colder than the rest of the building (which was impressive). My siblings and I stood in a row before Blech's desk. We were arranged from oldest to youngest, not because Blech demanded it but because it was a force of habit. The glass windows behind Blech's desk were rusted and cracked in a jagged fashion. The old trees outside his window had long spindly branches like claws that blew in the wind. His office was layered with dust, like he didn't care

21

how clean it was or about the temperature. I rubbed my arms, staring at Mr. Blech's long bony hands on his black wooden desk. I didn't want to meet his gaze. I'd done that before, and it made my hair stand on end.

"So…. you all have time to start fights on the playground, do you?" Blech said in a deep empty voice. He looked like a skeleton with wrinkled fake skin on his bones, and he was balding. His suit was well-pressed, but that didn't help him.

"Sir…if I can speak for my siblings…" Galahad stepped forward with his hands in front of him.

Blech held up his hand. Galahad looked down and realized he'd stepped on the expensive rug in front of Blech's desk. The rest of us were on the wood floor farther back. Galahad stepped back with forcible calm.

"That rug is worth far more than any of you, Mr. Dyer," Blech said.

Galahad's expression twisted. He wanted to get us out of here with minimum punishment, not make things worse. He bit his tongue and swallowed his pride like I'd seen him do so many times. "A boy on the playground and his girlfriend started a fight with my brothers and sisters; it wasn't their fault."

"And your siblings are always truthful, are they?" Blech lit a long cigar and sat back in his tall leather chair. He blew a long puff of smoke, making some of us cough. "Miss…Elsha, is it?"
I forced myself to meet his gaze white as a sheep. "Y-yes sir?" I said, barely audible.

"What exactly did you claim to see in the cafeteria?" There was an awkward silence for a moment. I pulled at the edges of my sleeves before crossing my arms over my stomach. "I saw….it looked like…."

Blech had Micah's sketchpad on his desk. He flipped it open to the most recent drawing and held it up for us to see. "Like this?"

I nodded.

"And what exactly is this?" he asked, tapping the end of the cigar in the ashtray.

"A ghoul," I said at last. My siblings looked at me in surprise. I didn't know why that was the first thing that came to my mind. It was bald, green, and wrinkly with fangs, but how I knew the name was beyond me.

Blech nodded, looking at the image, "A creature from one of your games, no doubt?" he flipped the sketchpad shut.
"No, I saw it, I swear!" I said, my voice rising.

"And do all of you believe her?" he gestured to my siblings.

Galahad looked at my siblings, then back at Blech, "Yes sir, we do."

"Elsha doesn't lie!" Emma argued.

"If she says she saw it, then she did," Killian said.

Blech frowned at me, "Do ghouls...*exist*? Horrible ugly creatures, that live to torment mortals?"

Micah was staring at Blech, "Well, when you put it that way, sir...."

Killian nudged him in the arm. Micah cleared his throat, "Uh...never mind."

I looked down, "No...they don't."

"Do all of you still believe her?" Blech looked at Galahad. "Keep in mind your next several hours of community service will depend on your answer."

Galahad let out a breath, "...Yes, we do."

'Then all of you will suffer the consequence of her lies," Blech tossed the sketchpad back at Micah, and he caught it with urgency. Micah held it to his chest tightly. It was his most prized possession. Galahad already had scuffs on his hands like he'd been working. The last thing he needed was more chores. "It seems we need your spare time to be filled with more constructive activities," Blech knit his long bony fingers. "The garbage cans were knocked over by some cats this morning—clean them. You'll have to pick up the trash and take it out first, of course. The kitchen floor could use a good mopping and waxing; the dishes need washing after dinner, the bathrooms need cleaning, and then...."

"We can get to work?" Micah interjected.

Blech grinned wickedly at him, "Levity will not spare you the rod in this case, Mr. Dyer. And as for you, Galahad, you can forget about those extra portions for your siblings this month. I think we've been a little too generous with you."

I looked at Galahad. I didn't know what Blech was talking about, and clearly, neither did Emma. We were always told by Galahad we could go back for seconds at mealtime. I assumed it was okay; I never thought that he might be doing extra community service to make sure we could. We nodded and went to the exit, not wanting to be in the ice-cold room with that man for any longer than necessary. Galahad stayed a moment; I heard him behind me. "Please, you don't give kids in this school enough not to starve as it is. My brother and I will work as late as you want; just let me...."

"If the children starve, then we have fewer to feed, and thus grocery bills will decline—I fail to see the negative, Mr. Dyer," Blech said casually.

Galahad waited a moment before responding, "Do you even have a soul?"

We all looked back. Kids didn't speak to Blech that way. My mouth was hanging open in shock, I looked back over my shoulder, and first, I meant to look at Galahad. He was standing before Blech's old wooden desk, looking down at him. But something else caught the corner of my eye. In the glass, more like a reflection than an actual person, I saw the hag. Not Miss Michum and not the goblin; this was someone else. She had a long nose with a ghoulish skin color and warts along her chin. Her hair was stringy like wires, and her eyes were swirling like a black hole. Unless I was mistaken, she was looking at me. She had long, sharp fingernails that seemed to be scraping into the cracked glass window behind Blech's desk.

Emma took my arm, "Elsha, are you okay?"

I probably looked like I'd seen a ghost. No, Micah had drawn her before when I'd seen her—a witch. It was a witch. I knew it wasn't possible, and they didn't exist, but she was there.

I looked at Emma frantically, "You…you see her, right? She's right there!" I pointed urgently.

Blech grinned. I tried to form words, but a ball was in my throat. Killian now had his arm around me and was asking what was wrong.

Blech tilted his head, "See anything interesting?"

Galahad rushed in front of me and took me by the arms, but I was still staring at the hag. "Elsha, what is it? What do you see?"

"I…there…in the glass…." I said weakly.

They all looked. Galahad's expression was concerned; he'd been through this before with me. He looked back over his shoulder at the window, then at me. "Elsha…there's nothing there."

Chapter Three

Finally—I'm Not The Only One in My Family That Sees Things

Finally, we finished cleaning the garbage, waxing the floors, and all the other cruel and unusual punishments Blech invented to break us. We made our way down the old hallway to the lounge/game room. The cafeteria was closed off to us because of my alleged platethrowing. As we reached the doors, Micah read the sign.

"Game room is closed for the night…. great," he frowned. "All day lifting barges and toting bails with nothing to show for it."

Galahad shrugged, "We'll get in tomorrow."

Killian huffed. "Sure—unless we're too busy scrubbing floors."

Galahad looked down at him. "Don't make things worse, Killian."

"Why are you picking on me— because Blech took away your right to provide for us? You thought if you kept doing work down at the library, you'd make sure we're all happy? We're not! Things have been just as horrible as ever!" Killian contended.

I didn't understand that about Killian. Best efforts, good intentions, and all other sacrifices didn't matter when he got angry. Galahad had been biking to the library and working because he had a deal going with Mr. Blech to get us more privileges. Now, because things had gone poorly anyway, this was somehow all Galahad's fault.

"I've been trying my best to make it as easy on all of you as I can…"

"Why don't we just run away from here like I've always said?" Killian said.

Galahad raised his eyebrows. "Do you think your sisters can survive out there? Or are you just thinking of yourself, like usual?"

Once again, Emma, Micah, and I were in the middle, looking back and forth between these two.

"What's your plan, fearless leader? We stay here and work our fingers to the bone till we die or get separated?" Killian said.

"What?" I said, suddenly concerned. The thought of being separated from my family was a terrible one. As much as we frustrated each other, when I thought of losing them, our harsh little life seemed better. We had to be adopted together. We were the last family we had.

Emma frowned. "You don't know that! You don't know everything, though that may come as a shock to you!"

Killian pulled his head back in surprise. "What's that supposed to mean?"

"Alright enough," Galahad stepped towards him. "Killian, you're not helping anything by scaring them."

Killian ran his hands through his hair, frustrated, "Why do you always take their side? Why?"

Galahad replied calmly. "Because you're supposed to take some responsibility."

Killian crossed his arms. "What like you? Making us stay together? I don't think that's gonna work..."

"It's worked so far. There's no reason to be angry just because someone other than you came up with it," Galahad said. Me and Emma figured that finished the argument, but Killian kept going.

"You want to act like you're so in control of the situation, and it's all a lie! You couldn't keep Mom and Dad with us! None of us could! You were a helpless kid just like us!" Killian said.

Even when we'd had a horrible day, and the last thing we needed to do was fight— it was like he *had* to get the last say even if it meant upsetting everyone. The thought of Mom and Dad leaving all five of us hit me. My eyes grew moist.

Emma took immediate notice and looked at Killian, "What's wrong with you? You should be thinking of ways to make things better, not worse! And worst of all, you're making Elsha upset!"

I wiped the corners of my eyes, turning away. I thought if my hair covered the side of my face, no one would see me crying, but deep down, I knew they did. My eyes grew puffy when I was sad. When Galahad noticed me turning my face away, he was less happy. He grabbed Killian's arm and looked him dead in the eye, "Apologize for upsetting your sisters—*now*."

Killian looked at me, and I could see the regret in his eyes, then slight fear when he looked at our eldest brother. Killian hung his head, "...I'm sorry."

"Dyers!" Miss Rickman, the head of the adoption department, called to us down the hall. We all turned around to look. Killian pulled his arm out of Galahad's grip and dusted off his sleeve. Miss Rickman was on a sharp pair of heels, tapping her pointed toe loudly on the wooden floor. "Try to stay out of the rec room while it's closed off, children—I know it *pains you* to obey the rules but force yourselves. Emma, Killian, Galahad, Micah," she looked down her sharp nose.

Emma looked at her strangely, "Elsha's here too."

Miss Rickman looked surprised, "Oh…I didn't see you there."

Typical. I wasn't the type to be seen unless I was shouting at the top of my lungs. I was the kind of person who was easy to overlook or to talk over. Miss Rickman did it all the time. It was hard to blame her. I was a forgettable person, all things considered. Miss Rickman smiled. "I have good news!"

"I won the lottery," Killian said.

Miss Rickman frowned, "No." Killian snapped his fingers in response, mumbling, "Darn it." Galahad gave him a look, and he was quiet. "One of you has been chosen for adoption!"

"One?" I frowned.

"Yes, and honestly, I am a little surprised at the choice…" she began.

"Killian, they want you," Emma said.

Killian shook his fist at Emma.
There's no way they want me.

"No, Miss Dyer, they want him," she said to Micah, surprising all of us. "They said you were the most innocent looking." Killian shrugged, unable to argue. "Come with me, please," she gestured for him to go.

All of us looked at Micah. He followed her to the door to her office, where he stopped and saluted us, making Killian roll his eyes and usher him out faster. As he left and the door shut, we all exchanged glances, tense as if we didn't know what would happen. A few moments passed, and Killian threw up his hands.

"I knew it! He ruined it!"

"Calm down, Killian. He knows the plan; if we don't get adopted together, we don't go," Galahad said. After a few seconds passed, we heard a commotion coming from her office. We went up to the door and pressed our ears to it.

I heard a woman's voice I didn't know. "He seems like a really bright boy…"

"Oh yes, he's very…*different,* "Miss Rickman said awkwardly.

Emma huffed, and so did Killian.

Killian whispered urgently. "He's a freaking genius is what he is!"

"Shh!" Emma pressed her ear closer. "Blast these thick old doors! I can't hear…"

The door opened, and we all fell forward. Miss Rickman glared at us as three caregivers (really guards intended to keep kids in line) tried to carry Micah out. He was kicking dramatically as they transported him through the hallway.

"Please! You don't want to take me! I have deep-rooted issues!" Micah said, fighting.

Killian nodded. "It's true, he does."

"Get him out of there!" Miss Rickman said.

"We're not so sure..." the two parents in the office said as they watched Micah.

"No, wait...FREEDOM!!!" Micah yelled.

Galahad facepalmed.

The parents hurried out of her office and looked at us skeptically, "Are they his siblings?"

"Yeah—Elsha's crazy, I'm a pain, and Emma's pushy. Still interested in adopting him?" Killian crossed his arms.

The parents looked horrified, "On second thought...we'll keep looking. You can keep him!" they hurried down the old hallway and through the exit doors. I should have been offended by what Killian said, but after having Micah back with us, I wasn't.

Miss Rickman looked at us, horrified, before taking off after the couple. "PLEASE WAIT! HE'S REALLY *NOT* THE WEIRDEST ONE IN HIS FAMILY!"

The caregivers set Micah down, and he walked up to us with a proud grin. "And that's how it's done."

We all broke into laughter and gave Micah a group hug. It didn't matter if we'd been fighting two seconds ago or that we'd been angry, we were together. And as usual, Galahad was right—that was the most important thing. And we'd stay in that horrible place if it meant staying together.

***

The girls' rooms were just as crowded as the boys in Blech's. After our brief happiness in the hallway passed, I was met with an uncomfortable bunk bed lined up with several others by a cracked

30

window. Twelve girls stayed in one room that was nowhere near large enough. I was by the window on the second level and couldn't sleep. I kept seeing the scary faces in my mind. Emma must have known it because when the other girls had gone to bed, she came up to my bed. She slept below me. She had both of our dolls and crawled under my blanket. We got lost in conversation. My eyes drifted to the window as she talked. There was a gentle rapping on the window. Emma and I both nearly jump at the sound. We sat up and saw Micah flattened against the window, mouthing words like, OPEN THE WINDOW BEFORE I FALL!

Emma and I quietly climbed out of bed and opened the window. "Micah, what are you doing?" Emma whispered, rubbing her arms from the cold.

"Hey, ladies, Galahad says we're gonna get our playdate after all. Get dressed and grab your stuff; meet us downstairs in the lounge in ten!" he said in an urgent whisper.

I leaned out the window and saw the boys on the next balcony already dressed. I smiled. "What is this, you guys?"

Galahad had his backpack over one shoulder and shrugged, "I promised you we'd do something fun together. I'd never break my word to my little sister. We'll see you downstairs—and keep quiet."

Emma and I got dressed and took our couple of dolls in our backpacks, sneaking downstairs. It was a scary thing for me, sneaking out of our room at night. If we were caught, it could mean a hundred other chores. But now I was going with this—we'd sneak downstairs and have fun for once in a long time. The Boarding House was eerie, but when Emma and I made it to the lounge/rec room and found our brothers in there, everything got better. We flipped on some lamps. Galahad was creative and came up with a way for us to use all our gifts in our games. He wrote characters for all of us. Killian and Micah were orchestrators as well and jumped right in with all their imagination. In that dimly lit room, we had more fun than I can remember having in a while, and in the worst of places, it was one of the best memories of my life. After we got through the toy portion, we

31

came up with a tag-like game. The wind was beating on the glass windows in the lounge as we played.

We ended up chasing each other around the lounge. We left the lounge with our things and ran down the hall into the conservatory. I kept getting frozen and un-frozen, but it was good for a laugh. Killian was trying his hardest to catch us, and because he was too fast, Galahad kept asking him to dial it down. Me, Micah, and Galahad got frozen, and Emma and Killian were circling against each other.

"Can someone unfreeze me, please?" Micah yawned.

"Hang on, as soon as I beat her…" Killian said.

"What makes you think you can?" Emma said.

As they were talking, I got the strangest feeling. Like we were in danger. That feeling you get just before something bad happens. I looked in the dark shadows in the conservatory and saw the shape of the plants as something else; they looked like robed people. The hanging leaves looked like ratty tangled hair, the points like a hooked nose.

I swallowed hard. "Uh, guys…"

Killian rolled his eyes. "Elsha, I'm trying to concentrate."

"I see something scary down here," I forced out.

"I'm about to win…" Killian began.

Galahad walked over to me. "Time-out, somethings up with Elsha."

Killian groaned. "He always stops games right when I'm about to win… What is it?"

"It's late, and she's probably just scared," Micah said.

An ear-piercing cackle echoed around us. A ghoulish hag with wrinkled skin flew out from behind a tall shadow of the plant in the corner of the room. All of us stood together in a circle, with Galahad at the front defensively. She flew around the room near the ceiling in a circle, and Killian raised his eyebrows in shock. Now they couldn't deny it; they were all seeing what I was seeing. I felt a heavy wind around us; she flew and cackled.

Emma let out a louder ear-piercing cry, "IT'S A…A… WITCH!"

Killian covered his ears, "Okay, Elsha, it's not just you! What is she screeching about?"

"She's calling more," I said, though I had no idea how I knew that. I just sensed it. As the words left my mouth, it was no sooner than the glass windows around the conservatory shattered, and several flew in on brooms with gusts of wind trailing behind them.

"Everyone together!" Galahad said.

"Any plans beyond that leader?" Killian's breath quickened.

I had a plan. Panic. That's what I was doing as all of them flew around us cackling; one swooped down, and Galahad pulled us all to the ground in a crouch. I wasn't insane. I knew that now—but that wouldn't save us. As we were all down close to the floor, I saw lights outside the glass wall of the conservatory, headlights. A car was out there. I nudged Galahad, who looked up. The room swelled with smoke and wind as they flew. It whipped around behind them in a thick poisonous fog.

"Move!" Galahad pulled us towards the left side of the room, and we broke into a run as the hags came towards us. I heard the car outside rev up. It came crashing through the wall, squashing the witches on the hood where they were knocked aside like street cones. I looked up through my hair, which I now found annoying being over my eyes.

I had really seen that.

The driver-side door opened. A man with slightly curly brown hair, combed back, and scruff leaned out wearing a camo jacket and a wife beater. He was muscular and looked ex-army. He had a tattoo on his forearm of black notches. "Are you kids 'getting' in the car, or do you wanna hang out with the hags some more?"

Chapter Four

I learn it's Not Easy to Kill a Witch

Normally, getting into a car with a strange man who looked like an ex-convict was on my list of NEVER TO DO'S. It was the opposite of a bucket list (yes, I don't have an actual bucket list of hopes and dreams; I only have a list of bad things that, if I can avoid, I'll consider my life a near success). I wrote down things I hoped to go through my whole life without ever doing. Some things on the list were: go sky diving, ride a bike, get a tattoo, talk to strangers, get in a car with a guy who looks like a violent offender, you know—typical unsafe stuff. But when the only other option was to get killed by fanged hags on brooms...the violent offender seemed a lot less scary.

My siblings and I ran like chickens without our heads scrambling to grab our backpacks as the witches flew around us.

"Let's go!" Killian said ever fearless.

"Wait, let's think about this..." I said.

Killian threw his hands up. "If we don't, we'll die!"

"It's on her list," Micah said, making Killian roll his eyes.

Emma took my hand and looked me in the eyes. "We gotta go, Elsha, it's gonna be okay, but we won't last here! C'mon," she said encouragingly. A hag with a long hooked mouth and hair-thin tall fangs came at us cackling. She was going to bite my head off; I just knew it.

My heart stopped.

Galahad grabbed a large glass vase with a plant and threw it directly in her long-crooked mouth. The vase shattered, sending her and the broom spinning. It was insane how quickly the witch recovered—it was like that broom was on a motor as it whipped around, coming right back at us. Her eyes were blazing wickedly as she shot in our direction. He grabbed my hand and took me to the car opening the back seat and helping me in. "Let's go!"

"Finally, a kid with some sense," the man driving said as he looked to the left and right at the witches coming towards us. One flew directly at the driver's window, and he pulled a huge revolver from below him and fired off three loud shots at the witch, hitting her in the face and body. I turned away, hiding my face as I heard the witch scream along with a sound like fruit being smashed. He dropped the weapon below him and put both hands on the wheel. There was glass on the floor as well as a green liquid and a snapped broom (I didn't want to think what the liquid was). I climbed in the very back of the car with Emma, Killian, and Galahad. The driver began to pull out of the conservatory as Micah grabbed the door. Micah was forced to jump through the open window as he pulled out of the lot, the driver's side door hanging partially open. "Micah! What are you doing?" Emma screamed as she tried to buckle herself and me in.

Micah struggled to hold on. "WHAT DOES IT LOOK LIKE I'M DOING? TRYING NOT TO FALL TO MY DEATH!"

Killian was squished in the back with the rest of us, but he leaned forward between the two front seats and grabbed Micah by the arms, "Get in here!"

He pulled him inside, making Micah narrowly avoid getting smashed against the conservatory wall. Micah sat back and breathed heavily, "I saw my whole life…pass before my eyes…."

"It wasn't much, was it?" Killian said, making Emma smack him.

Micah shook his head, "No, it wasn't…what's happening? Where are we going?" he turned and looked at the large tattooed driver in the army cap. "Who….AAAAHHH! Who is this? I thought we were running away from the dangerous people? Wasn't that the point of getting in the car?"

Galahad checked our seatbelts. "He just saved our lives, Micah!"

"Where are we going? Are they going to follow us? Who are you?" Emma asked all her questions quickly as the driver violently backed out of the Boarding House lot running through bushes and destroying shrubbery.

"Ooh, we're gonna get punished for that...." Micah looked at all the damage.

"Sorry, kids, my first priority was to get you out alive—not neatly," the driver swerved the vehicle in a circular fashion so that the front end of the car was headed for the tall black gate around Blech's. The gate was closing fast, and I could feel the driver speeding up. "Come on, come on...." He mumbled under his breath.

My heart was hammering as the sound of the witches cackling and gaining on us was close behind. We weren't even out of the Boarding House grounds yet. I put my hands by the window and felt my muscles tense. The vehicle seemed to move under me, like it jolted forward.

The black metal gates were closing.

Killian was looking back behind us and in front, "Step on it, man!"

Emma covered her eyes. "Oh, No!"

The car lurched forward, and the driver said a four-letter word. The gates closed, scraping across the back end of the vehicle. Our front end made it out unscathed somehow. The tall gate closed on the witches behind us, causing them to scream.

I sat back in my seat, breathing heavily. "Oh my, Go..." I mumbled under my breath.

The driver interrupted me, "I'd be careful with your mouth, kid. Headmaster, where we're going, doesn't like kids being *casual* with the almighty's name."

I swallowed. I wasn't going to argue with the scary man who currently held our lives in his hands as he drove.

I looked back behind me and saw the figures flying around the Boarding House like smoke. Blech's seemed to get smaller in the distance as we passed other buildings and made it to the highway. From far away, it looked like a house of horror. My window was partially rolled down and the cold city night air hit my face, I breathed it in, almost feeling less suffocated by being farther away from the horrible place.

"That was freaking awesome!" Killian said, putting his hands on the back of the front seats and leaning forward.

"We ain't out of the woods yet," the driver glanced behind him as he passed vehicles and switched lanes making my stomach do flips.

"What are those things?" Galahad said.

"Your sis had it the first time—witches, and they don't like kids," the driver said swerving the car into the fast lane. "They've been casing that place for weeks, trying to get a hold of kids like you."

"Witches?" we all questioned.

"Like us?" I had no idea what he was talking about. Orphans? None of this made any sense.

"Losers?" Micah posed.

I heard the cackling follow us; it got louder. I stuck my head out the window to look behind us and saw the witches flying after us like some Halloween nightmare on their brooms.

"They're following us!" I said, making the driver glance behind his shoulder.

The driver cursed, reaching down in front of Micah and grabbed a dark wooden crossbow. He was holding the steering wheel with one hand and the weapon with the other, so we were swerving around the dark road far too close to cars. I grabbed the sides of my seat instinctively and froze.

"Somebody back there got my lighter!" the driver said. Killian grabbed it from the backseat flap and gave it to him.

"Don't give him more things to hold while he's driving!" I objected, more afraid he would kill us in a car accident than the witches would. The driver lit the end of the crossbow with the lighter and leaned out the window.

"Take the wheel," he said to Micah.

"Oh Go-," I stopped myself as the driver arched his head to me. My stomach grew sicker with every change in the situation. Micah had a petrified expression, but he grabbed the wheel and the man leaned out with the flaming crossbow. I felt the car going faster as my fear grew. I wanted us to be as far away from danger as possible and the car seemed to be listening. My heart beat faster as the car seemed to be pushing forward, barely touching the ground under me. It must have been the excitement of the moment. The driver shot the witches closest to us with the flaming crossbow and an ear-piercing shrill cry filled the air. I looked out my window and saw the witch catch fire like she was soaked in gasoline. The other witches swerved through the air, trying to avoid her; the witch crashed into a traffic light sending sparks flying.

Other vehicles on the road were honking loudly at the commotion. I wondered if I was going to be on the news the next day as the girl in the violent offender's car committing illegal crimes on the road. My reputation didn't need it that was for sure.

Micah's hands were shaking as he leaned over and struggled to hold the wheel steady. "Guys, for the record, this is the most dangerous thing I've ever done!"

We drove past the fast lane and took an exit onto a country road. Most of the lights of other cars faded behind us. Two witches were left, and they followed us. The driver shot down one more, causing her to land in the field with flames. He reached around for more ammo and said another word I wouldn't repeat. The driver reached behind his seat and grabbed a shotgun leaning out the window and firing at the witch. She caught up with the car. I heard something land on top of us. The driver looked up. "Everybody get down."

The driver shot at the roof of the car, making all of us cover our heads. The shotgun blew a hole right through the roof and pieces from the top of the car stained in green goo sprayed down on us.

Emma and I screamed.

A shrill cry came from the top of the car and the witch tumbled off the side, landing on the country road. The driver stopped the car, "Anybody dead?"

We were all too scared to respond, so he said again in a voice that could have been used to scare marines, "I said—IS ANYBODY DEAD!"

"No! We're fine!" we all shouted.

The driver put the car in reverse. "That's more like it."

"W-what are you doing?" I said, trying not to tremble.

"Lesson number one, shortstop—when you kill a witch," he backed up over something, and I heard a broom snap. It sounded like we'd crushed a watermelon under the wheels. Micah stuck his head out the window to look under the wheels. "Make sure the hag is dead."

Galahad knit his brow. "Who are you?"

The driver looked in the backseat. "Name's Kaine, gym/demonology 101 teacher and expert witch hunter for the Manor of Raziel."

"The what?" Emma said, as clueless as I was.

"You'll see. The kids got an eleven o clock curfew, so I'm gonna get you back before that to get settled," Kaine put the car in drive.

Emma looked at the clock in the car, "It's fifteen to eleven and we're out in the middle of nowhere. How are we supposed to get there by then?"

Kaine studied her as if she were a strange sort. I wasn't sure why since it was a perfectly sensible question. "Blondie has all the questions, doesn't she?"

"That's not my na…" Emma began.

"You wanna know how? I'll tell you how—I'm driving."

"We're all gonna die," I said.

"Hang on," Kaine said. And then he slammed on the gas, leaving a trail of green ooze on the road that glimmered eerily in the moonlight.

#

I was so sick by the time we stopped; it wasn't even funny. Emma was yelling at Kaine the whole time to slow down. He pulled up to a large lot up a series of hills, and a tall bronze gate was open waiting for him. We drove up to the front of a broadly spread mansion that was still lit up. It was beautiful, like a classic English Manor you'd see in an old movie and at least three stories high. There was a long driveway leading up to it, and if I wasn't mistaken—there was a large plot of land behind it that had other buildings on it. There was a huge lawn with torches lining the driveway up to the stone steps of the mansion. There must have been a lot of people inside because even with my stomach sickness, I could hear the commotion. As we pulled up to the driveway, I saw a boy standing there in a dark midnight blue shirt that had a collar up to his throat with a thin slit in it. He wore black dress pants and matching shoes. Kaine wasn't slowing down, and we all became scared he'd hit him.

We all started screaming at once.

"Get out of the way!"

"Run for your life!" Micah yelled.

"Stop the car!" Emma was yelling as she shook Kaine by the neck.

"Oh my gosh, oh my gosh, oh my gosh…" I braced myself. The car came to an abrupt stop as if it heard my concern for the boy's life.

It stopped an inch away from the boy.

Shockingly, he didn't move. The boy's expression didn't change. He simply looked down at the vehicle and tapped the dented fender that was covered in witch goo with his boot.

"WILL YOU KIDS LET GO AND STOP FREAKING OUT!" Kaine said.

"Sure, yell at the top of your lungs—that's one way to pacify the situation," Emma got out of the car and rolled her eyes. I stepped out, trying not to throw up. Micah fell out and kissed the ground— literally. Galahad helped me out and made sure Emma and I were okay. Kaine walked up to the boy.

"A mission accomplished with your usual finesse, I see," he said in a completely detached manner.

"Who's the stiff?" Killian rested against the car and made sure all the movement was in his limbs.

Kaine wiped some green blood off his shoulder. "If the Headmaster didn't want them brought my way, he shouldn't have sent me."

"Tulken was most likely hoping you would curb your natural brashness—unlike him, I was never convinced of that outcome," the boy said.

"Dashiel…" Kaine began in a cautioning tone. Despite the way my brothers (the ones who weren't kissing the ground and saying: where have you been all my life?) were sizing Dashiel up, my sister had a very different reaction. Emma definitely noticed the boy and it wasn't because he was stiff or strange (even though I found him to be both of those things). She had that look in her eye whenever cute boys were in the adoption center; nervous but interested.

"The headmaster requests that the new additions to the Manor be admitted to their quarters as soon as possible. He will speak with them later. If you had arrived on time, occurrences may have been different," Dashiel said.

"We had a little car trouble," Kaine said crossing his inhumanly large, tattooed arms.

Dashiel swiped a finger across the side of his boot to examine the blood. "Witches I see," Dashiel cleaned his fingers off.

"But I want to know…" Emma began.

"Just like Emma has to talk, and talk, and talk…" Killian rolled his eyes. Emma frowned deeply and elbowed Killian behind her making him grunt.

"Ow," he said, grabbing his gut. "This is my favorite shirt…"

"Isn't that your only shirt?" Micah said.

Emma adjusted her hair and ignored Killian stepping forward. "I'm sorry but can I ask the question all of us are thinking?"

Dashiel looked up when she spoke. His expression thought about changing. Around my sister, I didn't see how he couldn't—granted, she was covered in dust and her clothes were stained and her hair was messy from the drive, but she was still cute as ever. Dashiel responded momentarily, "If you find it completely necessary."

"Where are we? And what just happened back there? Kaine said something about going to a Manor or Razors…" Emma began.

"The Manor of Raziel, young lady, and you're looking at it," he said, even though, at most, he was only a year or two older than her.

"All I'm looking at is a world of dizziness…why are there twenty of you?" Micah blinked and wavered on his feet in front of Dashiel.

Galahad stepped forward. "We got the name. My sister wants to know what it is."

Dashiel narrowed his gaze thoughtfully at him.

"All of your questions will be answered when the headmaster allows it," Dashiel said.

"What assembly line did he pick you up off of?" Killian said.

"Killian, knock it off…" Galahad warned.

Dashiel looked at him, "Unless you are unaware, assembly lines are not how humans are procreated."

"And what does that have to do with you?" Killian crossed his arms.

Dashiel narrowed his gaze, "Is that intended to be dehumanizing to me?"

"Yeah," Killian said flatly.

Dashiel tilted his head thoughtfully, "Hm. Follow me." He said, and then he turned, leading us up the stone steps into the Manor. I didn't know what we were getting into but at least we were alive. Kaine had saved our lives and brought us here…the question was: where was here?

Chapter Five

We're Not the Weirdest Kids in the World—But If These People Die....

As we walked up the front steps of the Manor, there was too much for me to look at. The Manor itself seemed to stretch out for a long while and different parts of it were lit up. The tall trees around and behind it blew in the night breeze and there were lights on the land behind it like lamps reflecting off them. The front porch of the Manor was lit by two elegant lamps on each side of the steps. I held my old backpack tightly and my siblings did the same with theirs.

We'd gotten very far from the Boarding House in a very short amount of time and these were the only possessions we had. The sound of children playing, people talking and arguing was coming from inside even before Dashiel pushed open the doors. The first thing that hit me as I scrambled in behind my siblings (trying not to trip or walk into them) was the large living room. There was a chandelier on the ceiling and a dark green rug with gold thread across the center of the living room. A large sectional couch encircled a flatscreen TV at the center of the room, where kids were running around and trying to grab the remote from each other.

Three women in maid's dresses were dodging the kids and vacuuming under the furniture. That caught my eye before anything else. A feather duster was working on the bookshelves around the room and one of the maids was calling to it loudly, "Don't miss the top shelf!"

My mouth was hanging open. I was peeking out from behind Micah's shoulder and trying to see if I imagined things. To the right was the kitchen. I smelled it. There was a swinging wooden door with steam coming from inside and a loud commotion like people were working. There was a large room to the left with double wooden doors. A lean man with dark hair slicked back in a collared shirt was walking back and forth in the entryway reading. The sound of steel colliding was coming from behind him. Occasionally he said, "Beat," then "counter parry." As my siblings were walked forward, I took the place in. The room behind the lean man was lit with lamps and there was a row of boys and girls in tall boots and dress shirts with vests holding swords. I hoped they were fake swords, but by the sound, they weren't. This was more people in one home than I'd had around me in my entire life. But as usual, no one talked to me.

"Are you guys some kind of a group home?" Emma asked as Dashiel walked us into the center of the living room.

Dashiel didn't look behind him as he answered, "You could refer to us as something like that—yes."

The thin hungry-looking man closed his book and grinned, walking over to us. "Kaine…you managed to bring them back alive. You can't appreciate the momentous nature of that now children, but trust me, returning unscathed with Kaine is something to be treasured," he said in a husky British accent.

Killian blinked, "The momentous nature of not dying? I think we can appreciate it."

The thin man laughed, holding his book of Shakespeare's poetry in front of him. "The young man has wit—I think he'll be positively brilliant here."

Killian looked at Emma and mouthed *Brilliant?*

Emma smacked him on the arm.

"If you'd had any real trouble, my friend, you have just given me a call, and I'd have helped you out…." The English man continued sardonically, causing Kaine to sneer.

"No thanks—shouldn't you be over there with the swordsmen making sure nobody gets stabbed?" Kaine gestured to the large hall to the left where the young boys and girls were practicing motions with their swords.

"Now, if no one suffered an injury, how would they ever progress in the skill set?" he turned to us. "Young ladies, gentlemen, I'm sure your belligerent cabbie failed to introduce himself. The man you've had the prodigious but requisite chagrin of meeting is the Manor's gym teacher—Kaine. As for myself, whom I promise you'll find a supreme delight academically and personally—my name is Paris Percival. Teacher in the art of the sword and in the dramatic arts of the theater...."

He sounded like he could have gone on much longer, and I didn't understand half of what he said as it was.

"Why don't you pull out your biography and tell them all about while they're tired, freaked out, and oh yeah—don't—care," Kaine raised an eyebrow, frowning.

"Okay..." Emma looked back and forth between the two of them.

Percival smiled, glancing down at his book. "You know I speak...only in jest, my friend. Tulken was expecting your full report, by the way. He wanted to know if the place the children came from was anything for the rest of the Commissioned to worry about."

Kaine cracked his neck from side to side and groaned, "....Alright. Where's H.M.T?"

"Last I recall? Maddison...said he was taking a walk in the courtyard with Professor Clash," Percival's tone changed ever so subtly when he said the name Maddison. He gestured to double doors at the back of the living room with his long hand, and Kaine huffed.

"Dash is gonna show you kids around—try to stay out of trouble," Kaine walked away.

"But wait you still haven't told us..." Emma began.

"No need to be fraught with concerns tonight young mademoiselle," Percival looked down at Emma. "--Oh and Kaine," he said in a more cautioning tone.

Kaine paused and glanced back over his shoulder, "—Yeah?"

"Tell your boy when I say no magic in my bouts—it's not to be ignored," Percival said coldly.

Micah looked around at us confused, "No magic in his what?"

Kaine rolled his eyes, "He's not my…" he stopped and let out an annoyed breath. "I'll have a talk with the kid." Kaine went out the sliding doors at the back of the living room.

Percival looked after him till a couple of seconds had passed, and his smile faded. He broke his gaze away," Dashiel, would you show these young protégé's to their rooms? It's late and most likely the Headmaster won't be explaining their predicament tonight."

"Yes, Professor Percival," Dashiel nodded, putting his hands rigidly behind his back.

Percival walked away, going back into the room where the kids were sword fighting.

My siblings and I were still standing at the center of the living room like a group of clueless dunces looking around. No one had explained where we were, and we were all too shocked or scared to ask. My eyes had been frozen on the large hall where the kids were using swords. They were practicing thrusts and slashes, only in one quick motion at a time.

My eyes fell on one boy. He was tall, attired all in black, with knee-high leather boots. There were complex laces from his toe to knee (which I imagined took time to tie) and his leather vest was buckled shut over a long sleeve elegant black shirt. He was practicing moves with another boy when he raised a hand and the boy's sword flew out of his grip.

Emma was talking in the side of my ear at Dashiel. "I still want to know what's going on here! We almost got killed by witches, and now we're supposed to believe this place with the floating cleaning utensils is safer?"

"The Manor of Raziel is one of the safest places for the Commissioned, Miss Dyer," Dashiel said.

The sword that flew from the boy's hand came out of the hall and shot right at me.

My heart stopped. I survived witches only to die by flying sword. How was I supposed to move? I was too slow to dodge. Galahad yelled at me "Elsha, move!" But I'd already accepted my fate. I always knew if there came a moment when something physical was required of me to save my own life I'd die.

The sword came within an inch of my face—and stopped. It didn't fall; it stopped in midair. As it floated before me, I saw a hazy green light like very dim flames lingering over it like a slowly moving liquid. I blinked and thought I was seeing things, but it was still there. A low hissing sound echoed quietly as the green flames moved. Percival sternly said, "I told you magic wasn't to be allowed in this session boy...."

I caught my breath as Galahad ran to my side. I was frozen. "Are you okay? Don't ever just stand there if something comes at you."

"Is she alive?" Dashiel said.

Galahad put his arm around me. "Of course she's alive!"

"Then there's little cause for concern. Let's continue..." Dashiel said, making Emma scowl at him. I knew there was only so much cute armor a guy had with my sister and Dashiel was using his up fast. He didn't seem intentionally insensitive or rude, just practical to an inhuman degree.

"That's impossible..." I stared at the floating sword as the shifting colors of green faded in and out of view. I reached out my shaky hand to touch it. The flames around it brightened; it flew away from me and into the hand of the tall boy I'd been watching. His eyes flashed a brighter emerald green as he closed his hand around the hilt and the flames around the blade disappeared. He blinked, his eyes returning to a slightly less emerald color.

The tall boy looked at the sword and then at Dashiel, "New students?" he said with casual interest.

"An accurate observation," Dashiel said plainly.

"You'll have to forgive Dash; he isn't the best at making people feel welcome," the tall boy put one foot over the other and rested against the doorway. I couldn't help but notice the adornments on his uniform: he had silver rings on almost every other finger of various designs. One looked like a claw, the other a snake, and his green eyes seemed to shift between dark and light.

"A sword at my sister's head? Is that your idea of welcoming?" Galahad held his arm around me protectively.

"Vaniah, stop pestering the new students and get back here!" Percival called.

The boy frowned momentarily, "In a moment, Professor Percival." The boy bowed slightly, looking back at me, "I apologize for that…" he waved his long hand as if waiting for my name.

Moments like that made me extremely uncomfortable—when people said something to me and expected an answer.

I was uncomfortable a lot, okay?

Emma looked at me and mouthed *he wants your name.*

I spoke barely above a whisper, "…Elsha."

"What?" he gestured his head towards me. He was about to walk over. Fear of that forced me to speak louder.

"—Elsha," I tried not to sound too shaky, but he walked towards me anyway. I stepped back but forgot that Galahad was there. I looked around for an escape, but it was too late. The boy with the near curly hair, almost black, that fell slightly beside his eyes walked up to me. He had long sharp features and olive skin like he had some European descent. He was about fifteen. He sheathed his sword and bowed at the waist.

"Dante Vaniah, a Knight of Valor in training at your service, Elsha," he looked up at me while still bowed.

My mouth was parted, but nothing was coming out. I probably looked like a bloated terrified codfish. Killian spoke for me, "You might grow old waiting for a response she doesn't talk much…"

Dante glanced at him curiously before he looked back at me. I wasn't going to let Killian be right. I swallowed hard, "…How did you do that?"

My siblings all stared in shock; Micah took in a dramatic gasp.

Dante studied me with a smile, "Years of practice. Welcome to the Manor of Raziel."

Emma put her hands on her hips. "Everyone keeps saying that and we all have no idea what it is!" Dashiel was about to open his mouth, but she interrupted him, raising a hand. "And don't tell me I'm looking at it because that doesn't explain anything!" Dashiel looked at her curiously and stepped back, accepting her warning.

"Didn't Dash tell you?" Dante tilted his head. "You're all gifted."

Killian huffed "Please—I am clearly but these people…" he gestured to us.

Emma turned to him, "Shut—up, Killian!"

"He's right. We're all kind of weird and honestly unlucky. Emma talks a lot, Killian's full of himself, likes to argue. I'm not that great at anything and we fight all the time. And Elsha…she doesn't talk. Totally weird family," Micah said.

I nodded unable to argue.

Emma moved her hand as if weighing the truth of that statement. "Yeah, we kind of are…"

Dante was staring at us with a completely confused look. "Being gifted doesn't mean all of you will be the strongest, smartest or instantly the most talented right away."

"Oh good, 'cause we're not," Micah said. Emma smacked him on the arm.

"It means that all of you have a gift, whether it be magic, skill, sorcery, or ingenuity, and that because of your gifts, you were called to be a defender of the innocent—a hunter of evil in the Manor of Raziel. Your Commission is to fight monsters so that the rest of the world can live their lives in ignorant peace," Dante said. I could have sworn I heard the bitterness in his voice. But what he was saying was so insane that I didn't have time to focus on how he said it.

We all stared at him.

Galahad told Emma to stop smacking people.

"As always, you have to abduct the spotlight—the Headmaster wanted to explain everything in the morning," Dashiel said.

Dante spread his hands, "Sorry, Dash, but I thought they needed a little answer now. Not having one isn't fun—take it from me. Enjoy your stay." Unless I was mistaken, Dante looked at me last before returning to the Hall. I saw Percival waiting for him with his arms crossed, tapping his foot. Percival raised an accusatory finger and reprimanded Dante. He must have been the boy Percival was telling Kaine about. The rest of the kids in fencing class looked like they were taking some enjoyment in his reprimand. I looked away, not wanting to eavesdrop.

"Monsters? Like, more of what attacked the car on the way here? There's more?" Micah said as we followed Dashiel to the stairs by the kitchen door.

Dashiel began to walk up. "Of course—thousands."

Micah mouthed the word, Thousands, with a look of horror and turned to run out the door when Killian grabbed him and pulled him back.

"I have a million questions…" Emma began.

"That's not new," Killian leaned on the banister.

"How does this place work? Do the kids here have parents? Do you teach us a basic curriculum? Do we learn about these monsters here? How do you know we're called? Is this school dangerous…" Emma said quickly, making Dashiel stop and turn to face her on the stairs.

"Young lady—all of your questions will be answered by the headmaster in the morning in Orientation if you decide to stay."

"If?" I said. "We have a choice?"

Dashiel looked at me curiously, "You're not prisoners here. This is an institution, and while it might be the safest place for all of you—we can't force you to be here. Now logically, after you've learned the truth, I don't understand why it would be such a strenuous decision of whether or not to remain….but then I've never understood the reason behind decisions men over the course of history have made."

My siblings and I exchanged glances with each other. "What do you mean…men have made?" Emma asked cautiously.

Micah poked Dashiel in the arm with his finger. "Are you like….a monster or something? Alien?"

Dashiel knit his brow, looking down at Micah's finger, "Alien? Creatures believed by humans to exist on other planets. A work of fiction designed by men who don't wish to accept that God chose earth as the only planet capable of sustaining life. An interesting but indefensible theory." He paused a moment like he was thinking, "—Hm. Oh, forgive me—I didn't answer your inquiry. No, I am not a monster."

Micah whispered to me, "I'm not ruling out the alien theory!"

Dashiel turned to Emma. "As to your first query, this school is completely safe…." Before he could finish his statement, the swinging door to the kitchen next to the bottom of the staircase blew open. Fire and hot liquid flew out and we all moved back. The hot brown liquid landed on the banister near us and we all retracted our hands.

Everyone in the living room yelled and the maids began rushing over.

I caught a glimpse of Dante when it happened, and he wasn't unsettled at all. He laughed quietly to himself and turned away.

"Hm—someone let Dori in the kitchen," Dashiel assessed.

There was smoldering hot gravy on the rug and the furniture outside the door. The kids out in the living room started laughing and said, "What can you expect with those two?" Seconds later, a small dark olive-skinned girl with wild curly hair that was tied back in a bun came out. She was about my age and had large hazel eyes. She had on an apron and was holding a pot. "Dante! I was trying to make Gumbo, but Dori took the explosive potion cause she thought it was a spice and…." The girl stopped when she caught a glimpse of my brother Killian giving her the eye. She looked at him a moment and her eyes grew slightly large. Killian paused his laughter a moment when he saw her, but he quickly recovered with a smile. She straightened defensively—with all the liquid in her hair, it was hard to take her strong stance seriously.

Killian laughed, "Are you sure you weren't trying to make hair products? Cause that's where it all went."

The girl's face turned pink. The sound of the kids laughing in the background made me think Killian shouldn't have made it any worse than it was by teasing her. "What is that—your cool look?"

Killian's grin faded and he pulled his head back in surprise; Galahad suppressed a laugh. Micah didn't suppress anything: he laughed uproariously. Killian regained his cool quickly, "Hand me a tissue. I'm torn."

"Is he related to you?" she said. After a second, I realized she was talking to me.

"Yeah," I said quietly.

"I'm sorry," she said, turning her nose up and walking past Killian. Out of the kitchen next came a girl my age in a pink t-shirt, jeans with a bob of brown hair and abnormally large eyes and teeth.

"Addie! Addie, come on! I was trying to help! I thought it would make the food spicy; how was I supposed to know explosive meant literally explosive?" she said in a very high-pitched cartoonish voice. She sounded like someone who should have been voicing a cartoon squirrel. "Do you still think we'll get a passing grade in Collins's class?"

"Dori let it go!" Addie, the girl with the pot, said. The maids from the other room ran in with sponges and scrubbers. Dori went back into the kitchen and came out with an ax and a firefighter's helmet.

"Get out of my way!" she said, causing Dante's smile to turn into a look of terror. He ran and grabbed the axe from Dori. A grown woman came out of the kitchen door with a blue apron drying her hands. She looked like Addie: her hair was curly black, and her eyes large hazel.

"Dori, put that down and come help me clean up the mess you made!" she looked at us briefly before turning and going back through the swinging door. "You kids better make this spotless or else you're helping with kitchen duty for a week; you got that!"

The teacher Percival didn't look bothered by any of this as he stood in the hall with the kids practicing swordplay. He was resting against the wall, reading his book, uninterested in the chaos. I wondered if this was a normal Tuesday night at this place.

"On your left!" a group of kids running down the stairs said. We all put our backs against the wall and let them run by us. They were carrying crates full of jars with strange things in them. It looked like insects and organs. One of the kids was carrying a giant python around their shoulders. "Let's see if Cleo can scare the professors by showing up in the garden!"

"Hurry up, the slithering thing is freaking me out!" one boy said as he was holding the reptile at arm's length. The snake looked very uncomfortable and was slithering and hissing as the boy trembled, gripping it wherever he could.

All of us froze with terror except Killian, who thought it was cool.

At the sight of the snake, Percival gestured to Dante, and I saw his mouth form the words, "Handle that!"

The kids with the snake ran past Dante, who stopped them. Dante looked strangely offended as he took the serpent from them, "Leave Cleopatra out of this, okay? Clash isn't gonna like it," Dante took the long snake gently out of their arms and onto his shoulders. The snake coiled partially around his arm and rested its head against his in what almost seemed an affectionate gesture.

The kids stepped back when Dante approached and shot each other fearful looks. They murmured and frowned at him as the snake coiled around his shoulders. I was trembling, and I was nowhere near the creature. What confused me is they looked at Dante like he may as well have been the snake. Dante held it like the thing was a kitten. And even kittens were somewhat frightening to me because they scratched.

The kids who ran down the stairs mumbled to themselves, "Easy for reptile boy! Snakes and him are practically related!"

Dashiel's expression didn't change as all the kids passed us.

"Come on guys, we're ready to make the ghoul acid!" they all said, running into a different room.

"You're not supposed to make acid from ghouls—it's against Collins's no dark magic policy!" one girl said.

Dashiel started up the stairs again and stopped when he realized we weren't following, "Is there a problem?"

The five of us were frozen in a row on the staircase, looking like a horrified remake of the Brady Bunch. The house was beautiful and kept up; even the wooden stairs were lovely and hand-crafted. But I was beginning to wonder if magic kept this place so neat with all the madness that went on inside. As we were pressed to the walls, I noticed paintings and art on the walls. If I wasn't mistaken, they were Biblical depictions—angels and saints. Joan of Arc, the archangel Gabriel and Michael were there. The only reason I recognized them was that at Blech's, we had looked through art in History class one time. I took notice of all these details in a few seconds before Micah responded to Dash.

"No, we love exploding kitchens, ghoul acid and swords that fly through the air—it livens things up," Micah said sarcastically.

"Hm—interesting. Typically, new students are alarmed by such things. Come along," Dashiel said. We walked up the stairs after him. There was a long hallway of rooms and a large loft in the center of the second floor. The loft was a wood floor with a soft carpet. A group of students were up there in what looked like a study group. One boy was standing at the center, walking back and forth reading aloud in front of the others. He had a white collared shirt and dress pants with neatly clipped straight brown hair combed back. If it hadn't been for his age I would have thought him a professor—but he couldn't have been more than sixteen, if that. Despite the neat attire, I could see the veins in his neck strain as he turned his head to us. He must have been an athletic kid under all the fancy clothes. That wasn't what caught my attention—on his arm was perched a beautiful falcon with golden eyes. Its feathers and rich colors were beautiful, but I confess the bird had me slightly startled.

"What are those who become aware of and accept the existence of the commissioned referred to as?" the boy walking back and forth said with the falcon perched on his arm said.

"Proselytes," the boys and girls on the couches in the loft echoed. They looked like they were all dressed for some private school. Sitting perfectly straight. The boys and girls both had collared shirts. The girls were in skirts to the knee and had impassive expressions.

"What is the term for those who seek to convert the blind world to the knowledge of the commissioned called?" the boy standing asked.

"Zealots," they echoed.

"Did we interrupt a class?" Emma said as we walked past them.

"What is the term...." The boy stopped. His gaze zeroed in on us and it wasn't a welcoming expression. His brow knit a moment and his eyes gave us a once-over distastefully. Maybe he thought we interrupted his study session, but Emma hadn't spoken loudly.

Emma raised a hand to wave with a small smile, "Hi, we just got here and...."

"I didn't speak to you," the boy interrupted coldly.

Emma's eyes grew large. The only reason a snappy retort didn't leave her mouth was pure shock.

The boy didn't even look at Emma; he turned to Dashiel. "Could you ensure they keep their voices down? Some of us are trying to prepare for the start of a new term," the boy said. The falcon made a noise in agreement. The boy put his head to the birds for a second affectionately before looking away from us. "It's alright, Nicodemus, we'll continue the lesson momentarily..." he spoke to the bird more softly than his own class.

Emma pulled her head back in surprise. "What did he call that bird?"

"They just arrived, Uriah. And under the circumstances, I suppose some disorientation is to be expected," Dashiel said.

Uriah picked his head up and looked at us condescendingly, "....The last time I checked the Commissioned weren't bringing the blind we rescued to the Manor."

"Blind? What does he mean..." Emma began.

Dashiel turned his head to her, slightly softening his tone, "That will be answered in due time." He arched his head slightly back to Uriah, "...Headmaster believes they are Commissioned," Dashiel said more coldly.

Uriah arched an eyebrow and looked us over. He didn't say anything else before returning his gaze down to his book and continuing to ask questions. The other kids with him hadn't looked at us pleasantly either; the girl was sneering at Emma and me. I didn't have very high standards for other people after dealing with kids at Blech's, but they were downright snobby. I frowned, wanting to walk by them as quickly as possible.

"Wow—they really roll out the welcome mat," Galahad glanced back over his shoulder at the study group.

"Who are the stuck-up Jehovah's Witnesses?" Killian said.

Dashiel paused and looked at Killian curiously, "...It's been a long time since one of them has been Commissioned."

"He was kidding," Emma said.

Dashiel blinked, processing humor like it was unfamiliar. "....Oh. Ah, I see. That was Uriah Canaan Hark. He and his sister have been studying here for some time. They are Commissioned, I promise."

The snobby kids looked at us as Dashiel led us down the row of rooms. This floor was the students' bedrooms. There was an aged staircase at the back corner of the hallway with a deep black wooden door covered in cobwebs. It was latched. A chill went down my spine at it.

"Where does that lead?" I said.

Dashiel glanced behind his shoulder at me, "The door leads to a tower connecting to the Manor. You needn't concern yourselves. It is forbidden for any non-Faculty to go up there."

"Why?" Emma said.

"What does it matter if it's forbidden?" Dashiel said.

Micah shrugged. "If it doesn't matter, why can't we know what it is?"

"If it doesn't matter, why do you want to know?" Dashiel tilted his head, genuinely perplexed.

"Well I don't care about knowing things that matter because everyone knows them—but if no one knows them and it doesn't matter I wanna know what other people don't know," Micah said.

Killian turned to his brother. "What the heck are you talking about?"

"—It—is—forbidden," Dashiel said, stopping at a wooden bedroom door. The caution in his normally detached tone was the most emotion I'd heard him use. He opened it and stepped aside, "You will have this room and your sisters will be down the hall."

"No, we want to be next to each other. Do you have an adjoining room?" Galahad said.

I was grateful he said it because I didn't want to be separated from my family, even by a few feet. Especially not in a place this chaotic. I was afraid if I opened a bedroom door acid, snakes, swords, and God only knew what else would fly out.

"If you insist," Dashiel said, gesturing to the next door down.

We all went to it and stepped inside. Galahad closed the door behind him. The bedroom was spacious, which was foreign to us. It had twin beds and a terrace with a full-body mirror by the restroom. And the door to the adjoining boy's room was on the right. It had a soft tan carpet and a bookshelf with a couple of chests of drawers. The bed pieces were white, and the quilts were peach and a pale purple. Clearly a girl's room. It was far nicer and warmer than anything I'd had in three years. I had to admit I wanted to relax here, but there was still so much we didn't know.

Galahad checked the windows and looked around to make sure we were alone—and that nothing would explode, that was my request.

Emma and I sat next to each other on one of the beds and finally set down our backpacks. Killian and Micah sat on the soft carpet dropping their things as well. Galahad ran a hand through his hair pacing a moment. Finally, he came to a halt. "…Family meeting."

Chapter Six

We Meet the Headmaster

The only thing that was keeping me sane as I sat in a very strange Mansion with some even stranger people was Emma sitting beside me, brushing through my hair. It was warmer in the room, so I took my hat off and ran my hand through my hair; I put it on quickly after. Emma asked Killian to open the window on the terrace to cool the room and he did. Micah sat on the small lounge couch by the mantle and Killian lurked by the terrace with his arms crossed.

Galahad put his thumbs in the pockets of his jeans, "Okay…this is…"

Micah rifled through his backpack. "Crazy?"

Galahad nodded, "Yeah. But those witches and then the kids downstairs…they just said everything Elsha's been seeing…."

"Really exists," Emma said, unable to hide her surprise. She looked at me apologetically. "I'm sorry, Elsha, but…it was all so crazy to believe. We should have listened sooner. Did you hear what Kaine said? Those witches were casing the Boarding House. We could have been killed long before tonight!"

Galahad shifted his weight slightly on his feet in thought. "So why weren't we?"

"I mean, should we really complain…." Micah dug his arm deeper into his bag.

"What is so important you have to get it out now?" Emma arched her head at Micah accusingly.

"My sketchpad! I had it with me when we snuck downstairs…."

Emma rolled her eyes. "So what? We just spend the night in this mad house?"

"Right now, we don't have a choice. They know more about what's been happening to us than we do. It's not safe to go back to the Boarding now and I'm not sure it's what we should do. But we need to learn more about who they're saying we are and why those monsters wanted us," Galahad said.

"That other guy said something about us being called to fight monsters—there's no way..." Killian snapped.

Emma frowned, "Clearly, there must be some reason those witches wanted us dead, Killian! Why would they attack us if we were nobodies?"

"In case you haven't noticed—we are nobodies! We're five orphans whose parents never existed and can't go one day without getting in trouble! They've got the wrong kids," Killian said.

Galahad arched his head to him, "We don't know that. We'll stay the night and talk to the headmaster in the morning. Or would you rather hitchhike back to Blech's and spend the rest of the night scrubbing floors as punishment for wrecking the conservatory?"

Killian scoffed, "I never said I wanted to go back there."

"Well, I wish you'd offer helpful suggestions once in a while instead of just finding things to complain about," Galahad crossed his arms, turning away from Killian, who glared at him.

"You know what, *sir Galahad*...." Killian snarled it like an insult.

Micah looked up, "—Uh oh."

Killian spoke loudly, making Galahad turn to look at him again. "I may be a *knucklehead,* but I know better than to think anything those freaks down there said is true. This family wasn't called to any destiny, and I'm not about to be some private schooled chump like those losers upstairs."

Galahad tried to keep his voice calm but firm like he usually did when Killian began to lose his temper. "Okay, there's nothing supernatural going on here. Then how do you explain what we saw?

If you could think past your own opinions and look at facts for once…." Galahad stepped towards him and stopped releasing a breath. "You've got your complaints—everyone here knows them. Now *ease off,* and let's consider for a minute we are like these people."

"Oh, for the love of God, stop it!" Killian closed the gap between them and glared up at him like they were about to come to blows.

Galahad didn't move. "—Stop *what?*"

"Stop acting like there's some divine reason we're all so screwed up!" Killian said.

"Your sisters and Micah are *not* screwed up," Galahad said. "If you wanna play the brooding edgy guy, go ahead, but this isn't all about you! Your brother and sisters don't need you to make things worse by labeling them!"

"Don't tell me what I can and can't say!" Killian snarled.

I put my head on Emma's shoulder, hiding my face. I could never hide how bothered or sad it made me when my family argued. Her shoulder was a comfort from all this madness. I didn't know what to think. We'd seen the proof in the pudding: I really had been seeing monsters and the things those kids were doing downstairs…It made my mind go back to the plate I sent flying in the cafeteria. No, there was no way. There had to be some other explanation. Those kids downstairs were using magic. I was getting ahead of myself…

"Galahad's right," Emma pushed my hair behind my ears.

"Of course, you agree with him! It means I'm wrong," Killian said.

Emma moved her head. "You usually are so…"

Killian opened his mouth to interrupt her. Galahad shot him a glance and started in a dangerously low tone, "Killian…."

My pulse jolted. The fight was only getting worse. I hated speaking up, but I felt the need to step in and defend Galahad.

I picked my head up, taking Emma by surprise.

"What about what I've been seeing at the Boarding House? This might be the explanation…." I began weakly.

"You've got a point," Emma said.

I opened my mouth.

"You just want to take her side," Killian snapped like it was so typical.

"You don't have to snap at her," I said.

"You're not even a part of this," Killian said, turning to me. "Stay out of it."

My face grew hot like it did before I cried. What was he saying? Because I was quiet, I wasn't part of what was going on? I stood up, and Killian looked shocked, "Just because I don't let everyone know what I think all the time like you doesn't mean I don't care!"

Galahad's voice softened as he spoke to me, "Elsha, no one is saying that…"

"He's saying it!" I pointed to Killian.

Galahad stepped past our middle brother dismissively, "Ignore him!"

"Hey!" Killian objected.

Micah broke through the conversation holding up his sketch pad, "I FOUND IT!"

We all looked at him.

Micah looked cluelessly at all of us, "…What? Are we still arguing?"

Like I said, he was in his own world. I envied his obliviousness; he was the only one not angry now.

Micah retreated slightly, "Too soon?"

Killian ignored him and turned to me. "Just like Galahad, you want to act as if our parents ditched us for a reason, and maybe this commission is real—well, it's not! We're not like these kids, we don't belong anywhere, and it's about time you accept it!"

I felt tears welling up in my eyes. Why did he have to push too far every—single—time? I stood up, wiping the corners of my eyes. "Elsha…"Emma began before snapping at Killian. "See what you did?! Why do you have to be such a jerk!"

Galahad groaned, "Emma, that's really not helping."

"It's not fair she gets to be upset, and then suddenly it's all my fault!" Killian argued as I went to the restroom.

"IT IS ALL YOUR FAULT!" Emma said.

"Enough! For once you need to stop Killian," Galahad said behind me.

"Guys, we barely survived the night, can't we just…" Micah said, trying to pacify it.

Killian and Emma were hurling insults. I put my hand on the bathroom doorknob and stopped. I couldn't take it. I couldn't bear hearing all the arguing. There were times like this in the Boarding House. I could only listen to the arguing for so long. I turned and shot for the bedroom door instead. I heard Galahad call behind me, "Elsha, don't go out by yourself….."

The last things I heard from inside that room was Emma saying, "Do you see what you did, you fathead!" And Killian's tone softened right before I stepped out and closed the door behind me, "I didn't mean to hurt her…." Was the last thing he said.

Too late.

Warm tears streamed down my cheeks. Some words were better left unsaid. Once they were out, you couldn't take them back. The students that had been in the loft had gone to bed. I hurried past all the bedroom doors down the stairs hoping the first floor would have a place to hide till my family got a hold of themselves. Even with everything that had happened tonight, it seemed no supernatural occurrences could make us get along.

#

I hurried down the stairs to see most of the kids had cleared out or gone to bed. There were noises coming from the kitchen door, like there were some people inside cleaning. I stopped at the foot of the stairs and put my hand over my mouth to cover my trembling lips. The fire had been blown out, and the kids with the swords in the hall across the room were putting their weapons away. They'd walk out into the center of the living room soon enough and see me. I couldn't deal with that. I got off the staircase and walked around behind it, hoping there was a closet or something below the stairs. A nice little corner to have a helpful, therapeutic, small breakdown—yes. That was what I needed.

Dante stepped out of the large hall where they'd been practicing. He was talking to a small girl with jet-black straight hair and a round face. She had her hands in the pockets of a loosely fitting leather jacket and was wearing biker boots. I heard Dante call her Jasmine. Dante caught a glimpse of me before I turned and hurried to the first door below the stairs. It wasn't a closet; the door was much too nicely crafted. I opened it and went inside.

I closed the large wooden door behind me and sunk against it in a seating position. I closed my eyes, letting the tears fall freely. My chest was aching, and my breathing wasn't steady. I held my knees and sunk my head in my arms, wanting to disappear from the world forever. There were many times I wished I could step out of my own shoes and not be in my life—this was one of them.

I blinked back some tears so I could see the room more clearly.

It was a large office with a hardwood floor and a rustic feel to it. There were bookshelves lining the left wall and next to the window seat across from me. Beige curtains hung next to the window seat and a wooden desk was on the right side of the room. A wooden cabinet

67

set was behind it and there was a stack of books and papers on the desk. Flowers sat on the window seat and a small clay pot with a purple flower was on the desk. It was a lovely office and had a comforting air. It wasn't like the Boarding house—which looked straight out of the bad place (we go there later, but it's a lot hotter than Blech's office).

My observations were interrupted by a light knock at the door. I tensed up. If I stayed silent for long enough, maybe whoever it was would go away. But they knocked again.

I locked the door, expecting it to be Killian.

"Who is it?" I forced a strong tone. It wasn't my office and I had no right to lock anyone out, but I wouldn't let myself be seen like this. "Dante, we met downstairs, remember?"

I recognized his voice. I desperately hoped he was alone. I wiped my nose, "Yeah...I remember. What do you want?"

"Well, I'd settle for knowing you're okay." I heard something against the door, like he was leaning on it. I had to wonder why he took such an interest when he didn't even know me. No one at the Boarding House had ever cared when I was upset besides my family members.

"I'm fine," I lied.

He laughed lightly under his breath, "Right—you realize that's the worst level of okay on the list? It goes terrible, awful, in mortal agony, and fine."

I couldn't help but crack a smile through my tears. "Go away," I said, less sad.

"Is that what you really want?"

"What do you care?"

"What if I told you I could help?"

"You couldn't possibly understand what's going on. Just leave me alone."

He let out a breath, "You're right—I can't. But I can get you someone who can, someone better at me than understanding other people's problems."

"You can't…it goes farther back than me, my family…it's nice of you guys to offer us a place to stay but nothing is going to fix everything we have wrong with us. I'm too screwed up," I said honestly.

He laughed lightly, "For this guy… *nearly* no such thing. Don't go anywhere."

I heard his boots on the hardwood. He'd walked away. I wondered who he was going to bring. *He wouldn't bring Kaine and have him threaten me* I hoped? I wiped my eyes one last time and stood up, unlocking the door. If he brought a teacher I couldn't hide in here forever. I paced, trying to compose myself, when I eventually rested on the leather window seat. I looked up not even realizing the bookshelves were so tall they reached the ceiling. I couldn't imagine someone being old enough to read all those books.

There was a knock at the door a few moments later. I sat a little straighter.

"May I come in?" a slightly deep man's voice said.

"I unlocked it," I said as sort of an apology for taking hold up in there.

The door opened, and a man in his late thirties wearing a dark beige suit stepped inside. He had short dark brown hair and a strong jaw, handsome for an older man—a little bit like Galahad, only much older and slightly weary. His eyes were pale blue and he looked at me with something I hadn't often seen in adults—not pity, but compassion. Like he read the situation and was deciding what to do. I guessed if he was a teacher, he was used to dealing with temperamental kids. Dante was leaning in the doorway behind him with his arms crossed.

"Dante, would you go find Elsha's siblings and let them know she's safe and in my office? They'll be looking for her most likely."

"Yes, H…" Dante stopped when the man met his gaze. "…Sir," he said at last before turning and leaving.

The man shook his head. "Children…it's so difficult to convince them that things won't always be the way they are now. But then that's the beauty of life as a mortal. We experience everything so fully because it only happens once—but we can't imagine ever being past the immediate moment. It truly is a gift."

"And a curse," I said, thinking how I would give anything to be out of the present moment.

He moved his head thoughtfully as he walked over to me, "Yes, almost every gift is a curse in some way. But good things wouldn't be appreciated without some trial to make them more treasured." He pulled one of the chairs before the desk near the window seat and sat in front of me.

I hung my head. "Not my family, they're just cursed. So am I."

He grabbed a tissue box from the desk and held it out to me. "How so little one?"

I took a tissue and blew my nose. He set the box down beside me before leaning forward slightly to meet my gaze. "Our parents left when we were younger, what's left of my family fights all the time…. I'm no good to anyone because I'm not special. And now we come to this place, and you people tell us that we're gifted... We can't even solve our own problems," I held my arms uncomfortably. "…We're not called to anything great. We're just rejects."

He knit his brow. "Who told you that your family wasn't gifted or called to anything great?"

"My brother, Killian. He thinks we're just losers the world doesn't want who'll never do anything because our own parents didn't want us," I looked down.

"That's truly hard to grow up without those figures in your life. I never had attentive parents, so I can understand part of where you're coming from. But to have no parents at all….I'm very sorry. As to your not being Commissioned….is your brother the authority on what you and your siblings were born to do?"

"He thinks so," I huffed.

"I'm afraid the position of designing your life purpose was fulfilled long before your brother was born," he said.

I looked up at him, "…It was?"

He nodded with a small smile. "Oh yes. And not just your purpose, but mine, your family's…we all play a role in the grand design that is this confusing, messy, painful world. But no one here can dictate what that is. You're frustrated because you can't see your gifts right now, not because they aren't there."

"What gifts? I don't have anything special about me, I'm not smart, tough, or…"

He stood up, shaking his head, and walked over to his desk. He picked up a beautifully sculpted clay pot with a purple flower in it. It was a tulip, and it had a beautiful blend of colors. He walked over and held it out to me. I wondered what he wanted me to do. I wasn't normally allowed to touch expensive-looking things. He seemed to read my mind and said, "It's alright; you can hold it."

I took it and looked at the vase. It was deeply engraved with several intricate lines. "It's really pretty," I had personal envy for pretty things. They were so unlike me.

"Do you know how it's made?" he sat again, resting his arms on his knees.

"No," I hoped it wasn't a quiz because I didn't know the answers.

He opened a drawer of the desk and pulled out a bowl of crumbly grey powder. It wasn't very pretty, and it had an odd smell. "This is that beautiful vase you're holding."

"But it doesn't look anything like it."

"Maybe, but it's made of the same substance. This is clay; it just hasn't had all the materials added to it that it needs to be molded. It becomes a mud-like substance that can become anything. It's all up to the maker what that is. But either way, it needs time. Now with time, faith, and care it could be a beautiful fixture by Michelangelo, or it could be a soggy lump of mud like my art projects in school."

I laughed.

He smiled, "And the flower…well, that was just a seed. But with time and care, it becomes something beautiful. You're just like that, Elsha. Now no one expects a pile of clay powder to be a vase overnight; or for a flower to be its most beautiful when the seed's been planted. You are special because you're a child. And just like that clay, a child can become anything. The possibilities are endless." "Is that why you run a house for weird kids?"

He laughed, "They are peculiar, I suppose—but I find that term is just coined by a world that wants to force everyone into conformity."

"What's that mean?" I hoped I didn't sound stupid.

"It means they want you to be like everyone else. And no one who followed the trends of the world ever changed it—believe me. I love being able to watch all these peculiar children become who they were meant to be."

I couldn't help but ask. "You don't have any kids of your own?"

His expression shifted to curiosity, like he was thinking. "…No, I don't." He said it like he hadn't been asked that often. He shook his head with a slight smile, "I believe I'm more fit for teaching than parenting. I try to give them all the consideration I can. What makes them different, special, that's inside of them. I don't give any of these children or you, worth. You have that no matter what you do. I just try to help them become people who can truly believe in it."

Here I'd been thinking no one cared I existed my whole life—except for my family, of course—and this guy was looking after a ton of kids just like us. No one made him care, no one asked him to, but he was doing it just the same. Maybe, just maybe, we weren't as alone in the world as we thought. "….And you want to help my family and me?"

"Yes, now dry your eyes. Childhood is a terrible time to be spent crying. As hard as that is to believe, trust me, there will be time for tears when you grow up," he handed me the tissue box. "Now what happened?"

I blew my nose, "My brothers were fighting, and I tried to stop them. They said some things…."

He let out a breath, "They always do at that age."

I told him what we had argued about. He listened. It was strange having an adult listen to me. I felt it was hard enough getting a word in edgewise through to my family, let alone to someone that much older than me. He asked the occasional question but never interrupted. When I was finished, he let out a breath and straightened. "Well…it sounds like you have very opinionated siblings. But it also sounds like they love you. If they do, they should be here…" he looked at his watch. "…now."

As he said it, the door to the Office burst open, and my siblings ran in, stumbling over each other. They were all talking at once and Killian was trying to get his opinions in as always. Emma was telling him to shut up and Galahad was trying to keep order. Micah only interjected to crack a joke or pacify the situation, which made Killian angrier. They stopped when they saw I was talking to someone.

Killian let out a breath, "Elsha, I'm sorry…"

"Now if only you could have said that before all the other harmful things you let out in the moment," the man stood up.

My siblings all exchanged looks and then looked back at him.

Killian raised an accusatory finger. "Look, old man, could you leave us alone with our sister?"

Galahad shot Killian a cautionary look.

"Killian, you're being rude!" Emma said.

The man looked down at me, holding the flower, "Keep it. Consider it a gift."

"Thank you," I smiled.

"I don't see why I have to apologize if she's not even gonna listen…" Killian began.

The man crossed his arms and looked down at Killian. "Ah—I see. You're a young man who doesn't mind everyone knowing your thoughts even before you've thought about the consequences. I would think about how what you say affects other people. Maybe if you did that more often, you'd be slower to speak and quicker to listen."

Killian looked at him curiously. "….Why would I want to do that?"

"Do you want to upset your brothers and sisters?" the man asked.

"No…" Killian said.

"Then think before you speak."

Micah laughed, "Killian, not arguing—add that to the wonders of the world…"

Killian glared at Micah.

The man looked at Micah. "And you find relief in jest, I see? That is a gift. But be careful. Our jokes are a relief unless they are at anyone else's expense. It might help you to find humor in everything but we're told to mourn with those who mourn. Enjoying ourselves while others are hurt isn't right. If your family isn't at peace, you won't always be able to avoid it by joking."

Emma nodded assertively at Micah. "You see! You should have at least tried to be involved in the argument and then maybe...."

He looked at her, "And you..."

She looked up. "Me?"

"You're very quick to correct others in their faults, be careful your own mind is clear. Otherwise, even condemning wrong actions could be done with prideful intentions—a gift as well as a curse young lady," he said.

"Give it to her," Killian said.

"And you enjoy the idea of being right far too much—but you feel very strongly about things and that's a gift as well. It just needs to be restrained," The man said, cautioning.

"I'm sorry, Sir, but as much as I'd love to hear you make my siblings have more respect for each other—we're here to see our sister, and you still didn't tell us who you are," Galahad said.

"Oh, forgive me—my name is Edward Tulken. I'm the Headmaster here at the Manor of Raziel. After we give Killian a moment alone with his sister, the rest of you can apologize for whatever you said in anger during that argument."

Chapter Seven

A Dangerous Discipleship

Killian apologized to me (and everyone else). Tulken was right about that: Killian loved me. He just didn't always have the best way of showing it. Emma and Micah apologized for the things they said. Galahad stood by the door of the office with Tulken.

Killian had his arm around me apologetically, "I love you. You know that, right? Your brother can just be…really dumb sometimes," he said of himself.

"Oh, we know…" Emma began, but I shot her a look. She swallowed, "…All of us can."

"Now that's settled," Tulken came over to us with Galahad. "Calisto was still awake, and I asked her to make some cookies for the little one."

"Who's that?" Emma asked.

"Addie's mother, the cook," Tulken walked over to the burgundy leather chair behind the desk. He sat down and knit his fingers, resting his hands on the desk. "I believe all of you had some questions that couldn't wait till tomorrow."

Emma was skeptical, "You'll answer anything we want to know?"

Tulken straightened something on his desk before looking up at her. "To the best of my ability. Ask away."

Galahad was the first to speak, "Things haven't exactly been made clear by your faculty. Were gifted to fight evil? Are the rest of the kids in this Manor like us?"

"In a way, yes, they are. They've all been called to be what are known as the Commissioned. An elect group of people given what we here call True Eyes," Tulken said.

We all blinked.

Micah was the first to say what we were all thinking. "Uh…sir, I don't mean to be rude, but we all have eyes."

Tulken smiled. "Many have eyes, but they don't see."

"Is that why the boy upstairs called us blind?" Galahad said.

Tulken thought a moment before shutting his eyes and putting two fingers to his temple, "…That would be Uriah. He's been here quite some time. The common term for the non-Commissioned is blind, not to demean them like some do—but because it isn't their fault they don't see. Blind can't accept our Commission because they aren't aware it exists. To resent or judge them for that, it's like being angry with a deaf person for not hearing you. I was blind before I was given true eyes."

Emma swallowed, "Accept our Commission? What exactly is that?"

Tulken Continued, "Every monster or dark creature you thought was real is. There are people called to bear the burden of knowing their existence and fighting them. Everyone here is being raised up to fight on the side of light in this dark and depraved world—that, young lady, is our Commission."

My mouth was hanging open because I still didn't understand. Tulken must have seen it wasn't sinking in. His eyes rolled up slightly in thought, "Hm…maybe I should start from the beginning to make this simpler."

Galahad looked around at our clueless expressions. "Simple would probably be best, sir."

"Very well, in the beginning…."

Killian raised a hand, "Is this gonna be a long story?"

Tulken tilted his head at him. "It'll take less time if I can tell it without interruptions. In the beginning, before the creation of man— Lucifer the bright and morning star, led a revolt against God. He was defeated and cast out of heaven forever. But when Lucifer fell, he took a third of the angels with him. Those angels are now known as demons and live as enemies to God. Over the centuries Lucifer has made followers of many lost souls in this world, and it has given way to thousands of evils. Dark magic, demonic possession, witchcraft, you've already seen some of them. Those evils lurk in this world at every corner, but not everyone can see them."

Killian ventured carefully, "So wait…if I can ask..."

Tulken nodded.

I was dumbfounded. Not just by what Tulken had said, but also that my middle brother had asked for permission to speak. You could have knocked me over with a feather.

Killian went on, "All that stuff we heard when we were really young in church…"

"Oh yes, all true. Well, depending on the church you attended. Some prioritize truth over others but in general, you'll hear more there than you will by listening to those of the world," Tulken said. "God created everyone with a purpose. Were any of you made to read catechisms?"

We were. It was vague but we all remembered that.

"Yes," Galahad said.

"And what is the purpose of life? Why do we exist?" Tulken rested his elbows on the desk and looked at Galahad expectantly like he was supposed to know the answer.

I was glad Galahad was the oldest, adults looked to him and that was way too much pressure for me.

"To….glorify the lord and enjoy him forever," Galahad said.

Micah sighed in relief, "Oh good, because I didn't remember…."

"Micah!" Emma shushed him.

"That's right, Galahad. But within that answer, each of us has a specific calling here on earth. The commissioned are called to defend the world from demon, black magic, and the forces of darkness."

Emma raised a hand. "Uh, how exactly are we supposed to do that?"

"Our missions take many forms. Sometimes they can be as simple as retrieving a piece of information, a book, or a scroll. Many Commissioned take it as their duty to make the blind world aware of the truth, depending on the Manor, that can be the main priority. Other times we'll be called to arms," Tulken said.

I raised my hand.

Tulken nodded in my direction.

"Y-you, don't expect us to fight witches and stuff like your gym teacher does? I mean, we're just kids. None of us have ever been in a fight that wasn't outside the Boarding House."

Emma bit her lip, "Yeah…and fighting bullies is a little different from monsters."

"It's understandable that you're afraid. The unknown is often frightening. But I don't think of it as putting you and the other student's here at risk. By preparing you, I'm protecting you. I'd be doing everyone here a disservice if I raised them to believe the world would never hurt them. The challenges you'll face will, in fact, reveal your strengths. Whether or not you want to prepare for these challenges is up to you."

"You mentioned black magic, I saw the maids and some kids out there doing it…"

Tulken shook his head. "There are many kinds of magic; Collins teaches the fundamentals of it in Magic 111. He has a….unique passion for the topic. Not all of it is dark. The witches, they use black magic and as you've probably noticed it's taken a toll on their…appearance."

"They all look like this?" Micah held up his picture of a witch he sketched for me some time ago. It was cartoonish but eerily accurate. Micah would do that. Stay completely out of a conversation till something applied to him.

Tulken pulled a pair of a slim brown rectangle-shaped glasses from his pocket and put them on. He leaned forward, looking at the sketch and smiled. "Yes…. Micah you're quite the artist."

Micah smiled broadly.

Tulken looked at Killian. "What was that about your family not having any gifts?"

Killian looked at the floor ashamedly.

"So, who's Raziel?" Galahad said.

"Ah, we have his picture on the wall by the staircase out there. Not that we can know exactly what he looks like of course but that's based off Commissioned testimony," Tulken gestured outside his door.

I recalled the paintings of angels outside by the staircase, but I hadn't had a lot of time to study them in detail.

Tulken continued, "After the forces of evil became more rampant, an angel named Raziel was commissioned to find those who'd been given holy gifts and give them a haven. Raziel made this Manor, but a different Angel was sent to establish each one," Tulken said. "In places where the forces of darkness are most strong, a Manor was formed."

"So basically, you're saying my siblings and I are going to be risking our lives in this…battle?" Galahad said, going with the idea for a second.

"Every day you step out that door. The world seeks to corrupt everything it touches. Evil lurks at every corner, even in ourselves. But we have a gift, to know the truth and defend it. To suppress the pull towards darkness and choose light. I don't have to tell all of you about darkness, Kaine tells me you came from quite a terrible place. You can stay here, but you will have to make a decision," Tulken said.

Killian had been standing back with his arms crossed for a while. He spoke up at last, "How do we know for certain that we're really….called? Is it possible it could have been a mistake?"

Tulken shook his head. "No, the council of elders was very clear about the five of you."

"Who are they?" I said.

"My…superiors, you might say. I run this Manor, but they're in charge of which headmaster goes where. I was given the opportunity to teach here with some of my friends like Kaine. Each of you has a special gift, we just have to find it."

"But we're losers. We don't fit in with anyone and all we do is get in trouble," Killian said.

"You don't fit in with the world because you aren't meant to. You were meant to protect it. And that calls for a special sort of person," Tulken said.

This was beyond a LOT to take in. He expected us to fight evil and none of us, as far as we knew, had any gifts. One question prodded my mind. I wouldn't dare assume I was gifted, but if it really was true our lives had been plagued with monsters, did all our family have the same fate?

I couldn't have been the only one thinking it. When I raised my eyes from the rug, Galahad was looking at me. Studying me. It was no secret to him I had always had the most trouble accepting our parents' absence. Galahad didn't talk about it much. All this information had me wondering…

"….Headmaster?" I said barely above a whisper.

He met my gaze expectantly. "Yes Elsha?"

I was afraid of my family's reaction. If I asked, maybe Killian would snap, Emma would freak out—I didn't know what to expect.

But I had to at least know if it was a possibility. "Would your superiors know if our.... family was Commissioned?"

Tulken put his hand to his mouth lightly in thought. He waited a moment. "The Commissioned are not always guaranteed to come from a family with true eyes. Sometimes those with the truth aren't related by blood. As for your parents...I can't say."

"But...Kaine said monsters were watching us at the Boarding House. Isn't it possible they had something to do with our parents' disappearance?" I said. "If your bosses found us, couldn't they find our parents?"

Emma's expression had saddened. She looked away. I knew I was reaching, but if our whole lives were designed this way then I had to know what role our parents played.

"My superiors only have knowledge of things related to the Commissioned. Your parents...may or may not have played into the equation."

He said it carefully, but we all knew what he meant.

Galahad let out a breath, "So...you'll only be able to help us find out more about our parents, if something unnatural was involved?"

"Yes, if intervention demonic or divine involved them....I may be able to help. But I can't say anything for certain," Tulken said.

Above all the things he'd told us, the possibility of understanding what happened to our family held the highest place in my mind.

Tulken sat back, "It's late. Calisto has prepared you something in the kitchen, so feel free to help yourselves to some of her divine cookies before bed. If you haven't left by morning, then I'll explain our curriculum and everything else tomorrow. Whether you decide to stay or not, you can tell me everything you know about your parents. Perhaps, some of us here might be of service."

"Thank you, Sir," Galahad said. Tulken gestured for us to leave the office. We followed Galahad out the door and Tulken followed us.

He closed the door to his office, and we all walked past the staircase to the swinging kitchen door.

As the door swung open and we stepped in I smelled a variety of smells. There was the strong smell of spice (most likely from the gumbo the girls had been making earlier) and now chocolate. The mess had been cleaned up and there wasn't any more hot liquid on the door or the walls. As we stepped into the kitchen, the three maids marched past us to the door muttering to themselves.

"Children don't appreciate what it takes to clean up a mess...." One with curly blondish brown hair said as she clutched a broom tightly. Her two mops marched behind her (yes, they marched without anyone holding them). "I've told you a hundred times Tulken and I'm gonna tell you again...I clean floors and carpets! I don't clean exploding gumbo off the walls or the ceiling!"

Tulken nodded, standing by the kitchen door. "I understand Leena and we're all very grateful for you going above and beyond the call of duty."

She paused in front of him and stood on tiptoe to look him in the eyes. "Well don't expect it all the time! Do you remember the other thing I don't do?"

Tulken let out a slight breath, "It's been a while since I read the list you made me, so no."

"I'll tell you—I don't pick up messes in the children's bedrooms! So be clean!" she gestured at us. Her floating mops nodded behind her.

The other one had a pixie cut, and she had the feather duster floating beside her. "And because of these little miscreants, we're going to miss our next episode of Gilmore Girls!"

The last maid was carrying a box of cleaning supplies and looked at us timidly. She waved in a friendly manner. "Hello, children! Welcome to the Manor..."

The pixie haircut nudged her on the shoulder. "Don't be nice to them; they're potential mess makers!"

"Where did you find the sisterhood of traveling maids?" Micah said to Tulken as the women shuffled out of the kitchen.

"Leena, Cheryl, and Joyce—they're practitioners of household magic. We were friends at our old Manor and then at the academy. When they had their choice of what Manor to be stationed, they requested here," Tulken said.

"Is it because they knew and respected you as a teacher or something?" Emma asked.

Tulken looked down at her, "No, it's because I was the neatest in college."

Emma blinked, "Oh…"

The kitchen was large with wood floors. Cabinets lined the walls above smooth granite countertops, and a large wooden table was at the center of the room. The woman with the black curly hair was standing over that table stirring thick chocolate dough. The two girls who'd run out of the kitchen before were cleaning the counters with rags.

"I appreciate you staying up to bake something for the Dyers Calisto," Tulken said.

We walked over to the stools by the table where the woman was working. I sat down and put my hands on my lap. Micah and Killian scuffled over a stool and Galahad stood back with his hands in the pockets of his jeans.

"I have some things to tend to. But I trust you'll see that these five are taken care of?" Tulken gestured to us.

Calisto smiled, "Of course, Headmaster! It's no trouble at all! Plus I've got these little helpers here." She gestured to Addie and Dori. "I'll save you some cookies for you and the other professors to have with breakfast!"

"Thank you, that's very kind of you." Tulken turned to us, putting his hand on the door, "I hope to see you all in the morning. Don't stay up too late."

When he left, the two bickering girls, Addie and Dori, came over to us.

"I told you I was trying to make it spicy…." Dori began.

Addie rolled her eyes before approaching us. "Hi, I don't think we had the chance to really be introduced. I'm Addie, and this is my mom the Manor chef."

Galahad introduced us.

Dori's large eyes narrowed in on my brother and she grinned an impossibly broad smile. "Well hello….I'm Dorine but my friends and lovers call me Dori."

Galahad's expression was extremely uncomfortable which Killian found amusing.

"What do your enemies call you?" Micah said.

"Doriana, the queen of the rubber fighting ducks at Malibu," Dori grinned.

Addie nodded, "It's true. We play lots of games here and when it came time to make up her villain character in D&D…that's what she picked."

Galahad blinked, "…. Okay."

The timer on the oven rang and Addie went over. She pulled out a batch of cookies, and the rich smell filled the air. "Somebody order a batch of chocolate chunk cookies?"

Killian walked over to Addie and rested against the counter, crossing his arms. "So was the exploding gumbo really an accident or…."

"Ha-ha," Addie said flatly. "It was Dori's fault for not checking that the ingredients weren't magical. Any student here knows that we're forbidden from using magic or spells in food unless specifically asked or assigned."

"I like to live outside the lines, Adelaide—where's your sense of adventure?" Dori spread her arms dramatically.

Calisto put dirty dishes in her hands, "And as penalty for living outside the lines, you can wash dishes inside the sink, honey."

Dori stuck her tongue out, going over to the sink. "Try and put a little excitement into people's lives, and this is the thanks I get…."

"I'm kind of like that," Killian slouched, trying to take on a cool posture.

"Like what?" Addie turned to him slightly.
"I like to live outside the box…." he began.

Micah looked up from his sketch pad, "Yeah—he uses the cheapest hair gel money can buy and that's about as on the edge as life gets."

Addie laughed, making Killian frown. His dark hair fell beside his eyes as he tilted his head down to look at her taking the cookies off the rack. "You made those?"

"My mom and I," she set them on the cookie rack and put one on a napkin for him. "Here, you can try the first one."

Killian pulled his head back, slightly taken aback by the kind gesture. All of us weren't sure how to act to be honest. It had been a long time since anyone had extended hospitality to us. Usually, we were the kids no one wanted to sit with, talk to or even acknowledge. I hoped we didn't seem rude because of how stiff we probably looked. I was sitting with my hands in my lap, looking at the counter where Addie's mom was rolling another batch.

Killian (being the contrary person he was) said just because the cookies looked good didn't mean they were good. He bit into one and his eyes rolled up into his head and he let out a sigh. Emma and Micah laughed along with me and Galahad. Killian took Addie's hand and asked her to marry him.

Addie said no.

This resulted in a sea of laughter by Emma.

Killian raised a hand gesturing to Emma, "You know what big mouth…"

Micah laughed, "You should have seen your face! It was like the commercial with a slogan: how a real cookie can make you feel."

Now everyone, including Killian, was laughing. I was trying to relax, but I wasn't one to push my way into a conversation. Calisto must have noticed my awkwardness. She leaned down slightly, looking at me, "Have you ever rolled cookies before hon?"

"N-no," I said quietly.

"Would you wanna give it a try? You never know you might like it!" she smiled. She had an energetic way of talking and waving her hands excitedly that despite my best efforts was a little infectious. Calisto was pretty with bright red nails and hoop earrings; her large eyes made it obvious she and Addie were related.

Emma raised her hand, "I would!"

Emma walked around and helped roll cookies. She started chatting with Calisto and the tension broke slightly. I listened to the conversation gradually becoming more comfortable. Dori grabbed Galahad's ear and talked to him about all manner of things. Killian was watching Addie, and she didn't look completely comfortable with it. She came over to me and held out a warm cookie on a napkin, "Would you like one?" She had a New Orleans accent like her mom.

The chocolate cookie was the size of my fist. Soft and chewy with walnuts and milk chocolate pieces that I saw as soon as I cracked it open. I smiled weakly, "Thanks…you and your mom are like professional bakers."

Addie shrugged, "Everything I know I learned from her so I can't take credit. That's one thing New Orleans has that I miss, all the cooking."

Micah was on the stool next to me, drawing on his sketchpad as we all talked. But Calisto, Addie and Dori did their best to get him in on the conversation. "Is this...your gift?" I said to them. "Baking?"

Addie laughed, "No, this is just for fun. My mom owned a restaurant before here..."

Calisto put her arm around her daughter, "No baby, I worked in a restaurant and made the sweets. But I never got to have my own shop. It was always a dream of mine, though. But that's part of being a parent. You do what's best for your baby and for Addie, that was coming here."

Something sad crossed Addie's face before she looked back at us. "Yeah...I don't know what my gift is yet. Some kids here think it means I'm not really Commissioned...."

"Like who?" Killian pressed immediately defensive. Addie jumped as he approached behind her.

"I don't want to say anything bad about anybody..." Addie began.

"Mr. Nobody's Commissioned unless they meet my standards Uriah..." Dori mumbled under her breath.

"Dori! So he's a little uptight..." Addie began.

Dori shrugged, "He's cute, though. Wears his collared shirts a little too tight..."

"—Stop," Addie disagreed.

Killian slouched, annoyed, "Uriah doesn't like you? I knew he was a jerk." "

"Why does he have a problem with you not having a gift yet?" Emma asked.

"It's not just him…a lot of the kids don't like anyone coming from New Orleans. It just…it makes them think when I get a gift, it might be…" Addie didn't finish as if it went without explaining.

"….Voodoo?" Galahad said.

Of course, he spent the most time in the library. He probably knew more about the rest of the world than all of us.

Addie nodded. "They aren't wrong; New Orleans really is a hotbed for demonic forces."

"But that doesn't mean you've got anything demonic in you, baby," Calisto kissed Addie on her curly head and fondled her hair. "You just don't listen to them." Addie forced a small smile. Calisto put the last batch in the oven before turning back to us. "You kids have been through a lot. And what you're going through isn't out of the ordinary to anyone here. All of us felt like being Commissioned was a curse at first. But sometimes what seems like a curse is a blessing in disguise."

It was hard to imagine anything in our lives being a blessing. I couldn't see it. But still, they seemed like good people: Tulken, Calisto, Addie and…I wasn't sure what Dori was, but she didn't seem dangerous. Not unless armed with a rubber duck or gumbo. After a little while of eating cookies and drinking iced milk together, all of us relaxed. Emma and I went up to bed and had another talk with our brother's before we went to sleep. It wasn't an easy decision, whether or not to commit to this place. But Killian's interest was piqued. Micah kept his thoughts to himself, but I saw he wanted to know more about this place. Emma and I stayed up talking about it before bed, we tried to sleep in the same twin because it was still a strange atmosphere. Even though we'd almost died that night and learned that the world was full of monsters (not that it was a complete surprise being raised at Blech's, tbh), we felt safer in the house with the whacky kids than anywhere else. Still, there were a hundred questions to be answered the next morning. And the one that was still at the front of my mind, which I'd brought up to Emma in private when the boys retreated to their adjoining room....was if anyone here could help us find out what really happened to our parents.

Chapter Eight

My Family and I Decide *Not* To Survive

The feeling of being in a dream isn't quite like anything else. You're there, and you're not. I was in my own skin, and yet I didn't have control over my movements. The room in the dream was hazy. I was inside a tall black castle. The floor and walls were deep and empty, like dark glass. Smoke and fog moved across the floor, coming from two tall torches by a throne at the center of the room. The throne was jagged and black, like the back of the chair was comprised of sharp blades. At the throne sat an inhumanly pale man; he had a long curved face that was white as milk with jet black hair and a deep red suit embroidered with gold thread. He had black boots that seemed to glow with smoke as he crossed his legs. Even though he gave every appearance of seeming human, I knew he wasn't. He spoke to a woman who stood in partial shadow before him.

She was stepping carefully around a red pool of liquid in tall black knee-high boots. She had a glass tube in her hand that was filled with black sand, and she was carefully pouring it to make some symbol.

"I trust with all the power I've given you that you won't disappoint me, Magdala," the man on the throne said in a hollow voice. "When you begged me to impart the power of sorcery to you above all the other mortals…."

"I said you should choose me because there was nothing I wasn't willing to do," she stepped back and flipped her long curly mane-like black hair behind her. In the flickering light of the pool, I saw she was wearing a purple coat that was tight at the waist like a corset and the length of a short dress. She paused as she stepped back from the flames that were rising in the pool. "And…destroying the competition didn't hurt my resume," she shrugged.

The man on the throne laughed.

I raised my arm, shielding my eyes from the rising flames. Moving my limbs in the dream was like moving underwater; everything was slower. The woman didn't appear bothered by the fire. She crossed her arms and watched the flames. Her face was in partial shadow. But if I wasn't mistaken, she was beautiful. It seemed odd to me she should be in such a dark place with that wicked-looking man on the throne. Despite her dark attire, she seemed out of place with it somehow.

A shape emerged from the flames coated in thick red liquid. The liquid slowly dripped off the figure, revealing a man in wickedly sharp, deep red armor. His helmet was like a Spartan with a crack at the front, but there was only black where the face *should* have been. There was a pair of red eyes in the darkness. His armor looked like something Micah would have drawn for an evil warrior in his and Killian's games.

The woman waved a casual arm, "One Dark Blood warrior…as you requested. And as I'm sure he'll tell you… he's very eager to bring the rest of his brothers to this world."

"YES, MY LORD! THE REST OF MY BRETHREN MUST BE FREED AND SERVE YOU TO WREAK HAVOC AND DESTRUCTION ON THE WORLD OF MORTAL MEN!" The creature in the armor knelt and said in a hoarse but passionate voice. "WE WILL BRING DEATH TO EVERY DOORSTEP! KILL EVERYONE BELONGING TO THE LIGHT AND VANQUISH THE COMMISSIONED….!"

Magdala rolled her eyes and walked over to a chair by the throne, taking a casual seat. She might not have looked threatened by his words, but I was frozen in terror. As the Dark Blood warrior continued going on about all the violent things he and his brethren would do to the world, I saw shadows around the castle cheer, scream and shout. They were inhuman creatures. Some were small and wrinkled with ghoulish skin like the face I'd seen in the window, others large and ogre-like, and some had horns and hooves.

I would have trembled if I'd been able to move.

The cheering and roaring grew louder when the man on the throne quieted them. He addressed the Dark Blood warrior. "The only thing standing between us and our conquest of the world is the Avengers…." His voice grew dim and hollow. It echoed and blurred, so I couldn't hear what he said last. I felt like he would see me somehow. I turned around to run out the doors of the castle, but it was like I was running in mud.

My body shook.

I forced my eyes open. The blurry image of a white window seat was before me. I was in the Manor. It took me a few moments to let that sink in. I sat up, realizing Emma had gone back to her own bed. I was safe. But the images were fresh in my mind. My eyes went to the pink clock on the nightstand between our twin beds.

It was 7:15. I hadn't slept in a comfortable, nice bed in a long time. If not for the nightmare, I could have stayed much later. There was a knock at the door a few moments later. Emma groaned. That was usually what she did if anyone tried to wake her up. I didn't want to answer the door by myself, but I guessed trying to wake Emma might take the better half of the morning. It was Addie inviting us to breakfast downstairs. It was a weekday, so the students at the Manor were on schedule. She wanted to know if we'd like to sit with her.

I told her we'd love to. Two other girls were waiting in the hallway for Addie. Dori and the girl I'd seen with Dante the other night. They walked down the stairs with her, and I woke my sister (which took some shaking). Then Emma got our brothers up. Galahad had been up for hours—of course. Apparently, he'd gone downstairs, touched bases with Tulken, walked around the campus, and already found the best place to exercise. Tulken told him he wanted to show us around with Kaine and answer any questions he could. Kaine and Tulken both taught classes, but not till later in the day, so they'd be able to give us a real tour after breakfast.

Killian and Micah were still asleep, but Emma took care of that. Shouting, "BOYS GET OUT OF BED, OR ELSE WE'LL MISS BREAKFAST!" was very effective. We all got dressed in the clothes we'd worn last night. The maids we'd seen last night were collecting laundry in the hallway from the baskets outside the bedroom doors.

Leena stood with her hands on her hips and looked at the baskets. "Well—we don't have all day! Get yourselves together!" the baskets hopped in a row after her and the other maids. Students were coming out of their rooms and rushing down the hall to get breakfast. I was somewhere in the middle of my siblings as we shuffled out.

Emma was smoothing her wrinkled pink t-shirt as we walked down the hall to the stairs dodging the laundry baskets.

Killian gave her a funny look while he was fixing his dark hair, "What are you doing?"

Emma scrunched her nose at him, "Just because I slept in last night's clothes doesn't mean I have to look like I did!"

"Sure…." Killian rolled his eyes. "Good luck with that."

Emma poked him in the arm with her finger, "Oh yeah? What's with your hair? Why are *you* trying not to look like a mess?" He and Emma were supposed to be twins. They were the same age. But they looked nothing alike. Emma was blonde with a prominent nose and hazel eyes. Killian had jet-black hair, olive skin, and blue eyes. Killian looked like he might be Hispanic, and Emma looked Caucasian as possible.

Killian rolled his eyes, "Unlike the rest of you, I aim to look good, okay?"

"Hence why there's a hair gel shortage in the US right now…." Micah said, making us laugh.

Galahad glanced back over his shoulder at me. "Elsha, you've been awfully quiet. Did you sleep okay?"

"She's always quiet," Killian said dismissively.

Emma wasn't as gracious.

"Oh my gosh, Killian, would you just…!"

I swallowed as we came near the head of the stairs, "Yeah, I just…had kind of a rough night. Did the headmaster say what the plan was if we decided not to stick around?"

Galahad let out a breath resting his hands on the top of the banister. "He said he'd help us in any way he could, but as to where we go from here…the ball is in our court."

"Why don't we remember seeing monsters before the Boarding House? I mean with our…?" Micah began in a serious tone.

"—Watch it," Killian cautioned.

But I knew what Micah meant.

I nodded. "I know you guys don't like to talk about our parents…but maybe they have something to do with this. Tulken said the lives of kids like us were troubled, faced with monsters and stuff. Maybe that had something to do with why they left."

Killian was resting against the banister with his arms crossed, looking down. "Yeah, but don't get your hopes up."

It was cold of him. But no one could argue. Even Galahad didn't say anything at that time. It was a long shot. But I had to at least know if it was possible.

"Whether we learn anything about them or not. I think as a family…." Galahad began.

95

Killian scoffed, "What's left of one."

"—*As a family*," Galahad continued in a cautionary tone. "Staying here is about more than learning our past. We need to decide if we're gonna commit to training and schooling at the Manor. We should take a vote now, just to know where everyone stands."

Micah blinked. "Well, I'm standing by the wall, and Killian is against the banister…."

"This is serious Micah!" Emma nudged him.

Micah grunted, "Okay, okay! I get that. But as far as I'm concerned, this whole thing is insane! Sure, they seem like good people, but who are we kidding? None of us have any superpowers."

"But the only other option is going back to the Boarding House and waiting to be adopted again," Emma said.

"Maybe if we do that, we still have a chance at being a normal family again someday," Micah said. That was Micah. He was comfortable with what he knew. He didn't like change or adventure. I was in the same camp. I wanted answers, but I was no monster fighter. And from what I saw and heard in that dream…

I didn't want to bring it up for fear that the dream might inspire my siblings instead of scaring them like me. It might motivate them to want to train here, and I wasn't ready for that.

"I think he's right. I don't want to be some hero… I just want us to find our family."

Emma was looking at me. She usually always liked to agree with me, but now she looked conflicted. Emma bit her lip, "These people have helped us….still, as much as I want us to have friends, I'm not sure it's worth risking our lives."

"Okay, that's three *no's* to training at the Manor," Galahad said. He wasn't saying his vote, which wasn't unlike Galahad. But it made me think he'd already made up his mind. If he'd agreed with the majority, he would have just said so. "Killian?"

Galahad looked at my middle brother. Killian was biting the inside of his cheek with his arms crossed, glaring down, like his gut was twisting at keeping his thoughts to himself. It ate at him not to say his opinion the moment he had it. Killian was finally (and eagerly) about to open his mouth when Addie stepped out of the swinging kitchen door at the bottom of the staircase, her curly hair bouncing around her head wildly.

She called up to us, "Hey guys come on! The food is getting cold, and Tulken wants us to say grace!"

"GRACE!" Dori called from inside the kitchen.

Micah snapped his fingers, "She took the line right out of my mouth...."

Addie rolled her large eyes, "That's not what he means, and you know it, Dori!" Killian watched her intently as she tapped her foot, looking around and waiting for the other students. He huffed, looking back down, and was silent a moment.

Galahad crossed his arms, "—Killian?"

"...Fine, for *now*—we can stay. But don't expect me to trust these people," Killian glared at our oldest brother. Micah looked at Killian,

Emma shot him a glance. I heard footsteps coming behind us. The group of kids from the loft last night marched towards us. Uriah was leading the way, and they were all impeccably dressed. Uriah had a leather book bag across his shoulder and a dark brown sports coat he was smoothing as he passed us. Trying to be polite, we started to move out of the way. Uriah and the other kids didn't wait.

"Sorry..." I fumbled as they brushed past us.

Uriah was talking and nearly shoved me off the side of the rail as he walked by. Galahad stepped back out of the way, and Killian leaped onto the railing, positioning himself in a nimble squat. Micah plastered himself against the wall at the top of the stairs dramatically as the kids rushed past us. Emma dropped her mouth, fumbling back, and scoffed.

I glared at Uriah when he got to the bottom of the stairs. He talked, and his group listened, nodding like he was the most interesting thing in the world. He was running down a list of classes and times, telling all of them they had to be early and well-prepared. "I take it back. I'm not sorry," I said quietly.

Uriah must have had radar because he paused at my words. He glanced up at me, and I looked away. When I looked back, Addie was still in the doorway to the kitchen. She turned white when she saw Uriah and the other kids. Uriah paused, stopped in front of Addie, and looked at her like I wouldn't have looked at a bug. Without saying a word of greeting or acknowledgment, Uriah smoothed his hair back and walked past her into the kitchen, continuing the conversation. The girl flipped her hair behind her and marched by Addie rudely in the same way. Addie frowned and fiddled with the edge of her shirt, following them in.

Killian was still perched on the railing like Spiderman and didn't look happy. He was looking at the swinging door where Addie and Uriah had been. "Can I kill him?"

"No," Galahad said.

Micah looked at Killian, "I'll give you an alibi." His eyes grew large as he took notice of Killian's position, "Since when could you land like that??"

Killian looked down at his hands and feet, almost as surprised as the rest of us, "Uh…guess I'm in better shape than I thought?" he shrugged.

Galahad looked like thoughts and ideas were coming to him as he looked at Killian. He shook his head finally. "Let's not show these people our gratitude by breaking their banister," he waved a hand. "Off—now."

"WHY DON'T YOU JUST RAM US OFF THE STAIRS, YOU JERK!" Emma called out.

Killian hopped off the stairs, "And you thought I was bad...." Galahad started down the stairs, and the rest of us exchanged glances. He hadn't said his vote. He wanted us to stay. I just knew it. I wasn't going to. I loved, respected, and admired Galahad, but there was no way he was getting me to train here. I didn't want that life. I wanted a home. Killian hurried down the stairs past Galahad and darted into the kitchen. I took a deep breath and started down the stairs by Emma. The images of last night's dream were plaguing my mind. A sorceress, an evil overlord in a dark castle filled with monsters... my siblings and I were safer returning to Blech's after learning what we could.

I'm not staying here, I thought. *I don't need to fight evil, and I'm not gifted... I just want a family.*

#

The dining room was filled with several long wooden tables. The longest was against the wall with a buffet-style breakfast. Breakfast was amazing. Addie's mom made pancakes, biscuits and gravy, and fried potatoes, and there was a chilled tray at the center of the dining room table with fruit. Pitchers of orange juice, milk, and ice water were across the table. Tulken said grace (the right way, not the way Dori had), and we all ate. Killian ate several plates of food. I was too scared to serve myself as usual, so I relied on Galahad and Emma to bring me portions. There were so many kids there I thought it would be hard to single out faces.

It wasn't. I quickly registered who the groups were and how that affected where they sat. Uriah was with the other slightly older, welldressed kids at a separate table. They'd occasionally glance at passing kids but generally acted like they were the only people in the room. A group of athletic kids in exercise clothes who were shoving each other and joking around, they talked about the new ways to kill demons. Surprisingly to us, no one had been sitting with Addie, Dori, and Jasmine. We went there.

Uriah's head turned. I saw him look dead at us with a glare. It was only for a second before he returned his attention to his food.

"What is that guy's problem?" Emma whispered to Addie.

Addie's gaze was down, "It's nothing."

Dori scoffed, "Ha—nothing, as in he and Herodotus think they're better than us because we don't have gifts yet?"

"Who's Herodotus?" Galahad said.

"The uppity twiggy girl he calls his sister," Dori said. Jasmine sat and chewed her food in silence, listening more than she talked. I glanced over at her, but she rarely looked up.

"They treat all of you guys weird because you don't know your gifts? That's so not fair," Emma said defensively.

"That's one of the many reasons," an arm in a black shirt reached over my shoulder to grab a green apple from the fruit bowl at the center of our table. I caught my breath. The fingers were covered in silver rings of snakes and fangs—I would have recognized those anywhere. Dante. Dante tossed the apple up and caught it sitting beside Jasmine. He put his feet up on the chair across from him. I saw other kids staring with disgusted and weirded-out expressions. "That....and the Harks have been here for three years and always knew they were Commissioned. They're one of the few whose family's put them here on purpose."

Emma was shocked. "You mean their parents know they're in a school to fight monsters?"

Dante nodded, eyeing the apple that his hand was laced around, "Yup. They were gifted young, and some of them got parents who were pastors of mega-churches. The rest of the kids in their group have rich parents and stuff like that. Most Commissioned get picked up in the craziest of situations and don't believe it at first; with the Harks, it was a little different."

"How did they get found?" Galahad said.

Dante laughed. "They were waiting in the driveway with all their luggage wondering what took Tulken so long."

Emma rolled her eyes, "Oh, you've gotta be kidding…."

Dante shrugged, "Uriah and the other kids from that group have high standards for what it means to be *Commissioned*. They think when other kids don't have gifts, it's a sign they might not be… truly *righteous*."

Emma scrunched her nose, "I don't remember who made them in charge of who got called…."

Dante laughed, "Oh, what I'd give to have you tell them that…" he took a bite of his apple and chewed thoughtfully. Addie had suddenly lost her appetite. Something told me it was an even more sour subject for her. But I noticed it wasn't just Uriah's group shooting our table offhanded looks. The rest of the kids were glancing over and murmuring. Addie's head sunk lower and lower the more they talked. Dante's expression grew more serious, then he broke into a smile and continued with his apple. The teachers ate at a different table at the head of all the students. The blinds were drawn on all the windows letting the sunlight stream in and light the room.

Micah was nearly seduced by the food, but I told him to stay strong. We, unadventurous people, had to stick together. After breakfast, the students had to run to their classes. My siblings and I were approached by Tulken and Kaine, who offered to walk us around the grounds.

The land was beautiful in the daytime. The lot was so vast it was hard to see everything as we walked. Behind the Manor was vast greenery that stretched farther than my eyes could see. On it were several different buildings. To the right, Tulken explained, were the class buildings. Directly behind the Manor were the gardens and the greenhouse. Professor Clary taught about plant life, flowers, and vegetation, so the lot was kept looking garden magazine worthy. Stone pathways were lined with lamps leading to different parts of the campus, and tall trees were everywhere. We walked on the pathway past the class buildings under the shade of trees as the warm breeze filled the air.

Tulken walked with his hands in his pockets beside us. Kaine was sipping a dark cup of black coffee and walking behind. He wore dark sunglasses as if he hadn't fully woken up and didn't like the sunlight. I still found him a little scary, but I tried to remember despite his tattoos, army cap, and large disposition—he saved our lives.

"You have a beautiful home here," Emma said.

"Thank you," Tulken smiled. "But I believe you all have some questions about what we're doing here. I know you have a very difficult decision before you, so please—tell me your concerns."

"Okay, if we're in danger constantly, why did the witches just barely come after us?" Galahad said.

"The witches serve the head fallen demons. The third of the angels that rebelled in the beginning have seniority over other creatures of darkness. These creatures target the Commissioned—you—because the elder demons do. They search the corners of the globe for the Commissioned because they, like the other believers in this world, are the salt and light. But the demons aren't omniscient. They follow trails, scents, and children with supernatural abilities. It takes them time to find you."

"Why were they spying on us then? And why couldn't anyone else see them but me?" I asked as we walked down a pathway lined with trees towards a field.

Tulken flexed his hands. "I don't know why they persisted in keeping eyes on Blech's for so long. Monsters have scoped out Commissioned before but never with such secrecy. Tell me, were these monsters you saw mostly in reflections?"

My siblings looked at me.

"Yes," I stepped forward so I could walk next to Tulken. I spoke so quietly he probably wouldn't hear me otherwise. "I saw them in glass, mirrors, water…."

"A mirroring spell," Tulken commented, looking down at me next to him while we walked. "When witches or creatures of darkness want to have eyes on others but not actually be there physically—they must use a mirroring spell. It projects their image onto reflective surfaces. Because it's a mere projection, even the Commissioned can't see them."

"Then why could Elsha see them?" Galahad said.

Tulken looked at me a moment. "…I don't know. I've never heard of anyone being able to *see through* spells unless they use magic to do so. Even then, it requires materials, a spell book. It could be your gift; we'll have to do further investigation."

"You said all of us have a gift, and we'd be trained to use it," Emma said.

"Exactly," Tulken looked back at her.

"How exactly would we do that?" Emma said.

"You would take general ed, a list of classes which gives you all the basic knowledge you need. Regardless of your gift, everyone is required to take demonology, magic 111, basic weapons training, and gym. After taking these, our goal is to help a student identify what their gift is, and then specify their classes and major based on that skill," Tulken said.

"And when we do that....we have to stay here and fight evil all our lives like Rambo?" Micah gestured behind us to Kaine.

Kaine smiled at the nickname. "Not all these kids are strictly the fighting type. The commissioned come in all shapes and sizes. Now if you ask me, knowing how to kill a witch is more important than knowing the history of the magic three-legged translator bug, but...."

Micah raised a hand. "The what now?"

Tulken shot Kaine a wary look but continued calmly. "It's up to each commissioned what they want to do. After they've identified their gift and finished their schooling here, they're free to do whatever they choose. Some students stay here year-round, and others with parents return home for the summer. And some of the children, like Addie, have a parent working here. If students wish to pursue further education here, they can continue advanced schooling and transfer to a university like I did."

"And then they can teach at other Manors?" I said.

"Precisely, little one," Tulken smiled.

Emma brightened, "So we could live here all year if we wanted?"

"Yes. Students who wish to advance more quickly stay for summer classes. Dashiel and Dante are both pursuing that avenue. Dashiel wants to be a fencing instructor, and Dante wishes to be a knight of Valor," Tulken said.

"What's a Knight of valor?" I asked.

"It's class of commissioned that strictly gets sent on high level battle centered missions. It's pretty respected as a noble class of Commissioned. Not all the kids are cut out for it," Kaine said.

"Some, like Kaine, belonged to the Hunters. A task force specifically assigned to track down and kill witches. For the Commissioned, whose gifts and personalities are more fit, there are more combative occupations in the field," Tulken said.

"But we all have to learn to fight monsters?" Micah said as if that concerned him the most.

Kaine smiled, giving a single nod. "….Oh *yeah*."

"If we didn't prepare you for the dangers of this world, we'd be sending you into a battle unarmed. It's your choice what part of that battle you wish to fight once you leave here," Tulken said. We passed a large plot of land with what looked like a wooden obstacle course stretched across it. There were stands and seats next to it. I hoped that wasn't for first-time students.

"What about the Boarding House?" Killian said. "Blech looked kind of like a monster, and everybody there seemed like one of the bad guys."

Tulken looked at Kaine. "You were assigned to scope out Blech's because we suspected evil forces. Is Blech one of the enemies?"

"Yeah, but not the kind I'm licensed to kill. Unless you want to amend that law at the next conference H.M.T…." Kaine took his sunglasses off.

"No, Kaine," Tulken said.

"What does that mean? Licensed to kill?" Galahad said.

"It is the sworn oath of the commissioned to only use lethal force on unnatural beings. Demons, witches, monsters, they're no longer human, and their souls are no longer their own," Tulken said.

"In other words, the ugly mugs are already dead. There's no chance we're killing one of the *good ones,*" Kaine said disappointedly.

"Yes, even though this Blech Kaine told me of is a very wicked man…. he is still a man. And therefore, where his loyalties lie may change. He may belong to the fallen one now, but like all men, he might be purchased and redeemed. Killing him… isn't our place," Tulken said.

"Well, that's a bummer…" Killian said.

"You're telling me, kid," Kaine agreed.

Tulken came to a halt at the end of the pathway, where there was a stone patio area. It was on a paved circle with benches and had tall pine trees beside it. I could see the obstacle course and a baseball field beside it. Next to the baseball field was a volleyball court. It really was a beautiful, inviting campus. And the idea of staying here and being taken care of… it didn't all sound bad. Fighting monsters… that part wasn't so inviting.

Tulken rested against the edge of a patio table and put his hands in the pockets of his coat. "Make no mistake, what I'm asking of you isn't easy. And as to your family, I'm looking into what I can, but I won't make any false promises. I don't know that your family was Commissioned, but the five of you are. Now you can leave this place and go back to Blech's. You can wait to be adopted by a normal family that may or may not ever know what you truly are. You may survive… but that isn't the life you were called for. And from personal experience, I can tell you—while we might long to have things in common with people of this world, your real family are the ones who've received the same Commission."

Galahad's hands were in the pockets of his jeans as he looked out at the field.

"What we have here is more than a school, and these people may not be your first choice as best friends or teammates. But you'll learn when dark trials come; you have more in common with the people here than anyone else in the world. We train, learn, fellowship, and grow together. Now no Manor is perfect, but we strive to steep our curriculum and daily life in truth. Church, recreation, study groups...."

Killian raised a hand, "Uh, sir, this family isn't big on Church since our parents disappeared, so...."

Tulken turned to him calmly, "How do you plan on living according to the truth if you don't study it? How can you work with other Commissioned against the enemy if you don't fellowship?"

Galahad bit his lip, "Understand, sir...I've been trying to keep us together for a long time, and I want what's best for my brothers and sisters."

Tulken met his gaze. "I know. You're a conscientious young man. I'd like to speak with you alone before you make your decision, if that's alright."

Galahad didn't object. He followed Tulken and walked beside him towards the class buildings.

Kaine checked his watch, "Looks like the kids are almost done with the first half of classes. I've got to kick some tails in the gym. You kids stay out of trouble." Kaine walked off towards the field with the obstacle course. The doors to the classrooms came open, and kids came out from different buildings, all walking in different directions.

I sat on the patio stone table and held my arms. Emma stood by me while Micah walked around quickly in thought. Killian leaned against a tree and crossed his arms. "Typical, the headmaster would want to talk to our fearless leader…."

"What do you think they're talking about?" I asked Killian. He and Galahad used to be closest before Micah came into the picture. Galahad grew up faster than the rest of us, assuming he had to be the man of the family. When he did, he severed his relationship with Killian, and the two no longer played together. Micah always wanted Killian to think he was cool and play with him. When Galahad got too mature for kid's games, Killian played with Micah. Galahad was willing to play and entertain, but now it was strictly for Emma, and my benefit.

Micah came to a halt and looked at Killian expectantly.

Killian let out a breath, "I know Galahad…and he's already made up his mind. So ready to jump into a routine with these people we don't even know and live by their rules…."

Emma scoffed, "You make it sound like these people are the same as Blech!"

Killian raised his eyebrows, "Different rules, sure, but what makes you think all this care about helping us find our true potential isn't a load of…."

Micah looked up at Killian. "But…this place doesn't seem so bad, and Tulken liked my drawings. That's gotta mean something, right?" Sometimes, the way Micah looked at Killian said he really thought the world of him. Micah joked, but he cared about his approval more than even Galahad's.

"What if Tulken's right?" Emma argued. "If we go back now, knowing what we know…how are we going to have anything in common with a normal family?"

I looked down. I hated to admit it, but she was right. There was no way we could go back to normal because we never were. And now we knew why. How would we live with another family if they didn't know what we did about the world and the battle waging between good and evil? Part of me wished those witches had never broken into the Manor. Now we were here at this new place, talking about the dangers we could get into…I still wanted us to have a normal life.

"Galahad's gonna make us stay here," Killian groaned at last.

Emma crossed her arms, "And what's your alternative solution, *Mr. Know it all*?"

"We ditch all these schools and people who'll probably quit on us like everyone else, and we take care of ourselves! But since I could never make our milk toast by the book, brother agree to that… this is where we're gonna be. In other words…" Killian began cautiously before looking at me. I pulled my head back in slight surprise that he was zeroing in on me. "…Don't ask Tulken about our parents again." I opened my mouth, "But…."

"I know Galahad won't say it. But every time you go back to the past… it's two steps backwards. And that kind of thinking…it isn't gonna help us do anything," Killian snapped. "If we have to stay here, I'm not gonna have us being the whiny kids waiting around for Mommy and Daddy to come back for us."

I forced the tears to stay back. "I'm not going to pretend our parents didn't exist!"

"Tulken is being too polite to say he can't help us find out where they are. Maybe we don't even want to know," Killian's tone was low for once.

"Just because it hurts to remember them doesn't mean we shouldn't," Emma said, defending me.

"I remember they left—not much else sticks," Killian said coldly.

"Yeah, because everything else good they did was just nothing to you," I snapped back. Killian looked at me in surprise. I understood what he was saying, but he didn't have a right to crush my hopes.

Killian looked away stubbornly. Before we could argue further, Galahad came back by himself. Tulken went down another walkway toward the Manor. Galahad had his hands in his jeans pockets and was looking down thoughtfully. We were all silent as he approached. Killian had a look like he knew exactly what our oldest brother would say. At this point, all of us did.

"Is it time for the second vote?" Emma said.

Micah stood by Killian with a resigned expression.

I looked up at him expectantly. "…We never got your vote, Galahad."

Galahad's expression was concerned and firm like there was turmoil going on. He let out a breath, "…We can't go back to our old life. There isn't one. Blech's Boarding House was a prison. Even if we could stick it out there on the slim hope that someday, we might see our real parents again, I can't raise all of you to wait on false hope. You'll never be able to face the world if I don't prepare you for it. Everything else is behind us. We need to look forward, and this is it."

I didn't want to fight evil. But it was looking as if it really wouldn't be up to me. We had nowhere else to go. And being the only one to vote against it would make me look like a whiner.

This is insane. How can he expect us to do this?

"We can't hide from what's out there forever, and it's time we move on. I want more for all of you than just survival," Galahad looked at me last. There was a moment of silence as he studied my expression, then he looked back at my other siblings. "….Anyone opposed?"

YES! I CAN'T EVEN DO A PUSH-UP! HOW AM I SUPPOSED TO FIGHT MONSTERS? I thought as loudly as my thoughts would scream.

But Galahad couldn't read my mind. If I had spoken up and said I couldn't do it, he would have backed out because he couldn't force me. But how he looked at me mattered. And I wouldn't be the weak link.

None of my siblings raised their hands. I bit my tongue and nodded in assent, meeting Galahad's gaze. As we all agreed to shuffle back to the Manor and tell Tulken, I couldn't help but wonder:

Big brother, what in heaven's name are you getting us into....

Chapter Nine

Our First Day at the Manor of Raziel....*oh boy*

The rest of the day was spent figuring out our schedule. Our ages didn't matter in this school (which I appreciated because it meant we could stick together). Despite Galahad being 16, Emma and Killian being 15, and Micah being 14, with me as the youngest—we all had to take the same general ed classes as first-semester kids. Tulken said not to worry about figuring out our gifts too soon because some kids were still searching for them (like Dori and Jasmine). As Tulken showed us the classrooms and went over the curriculum, I kept looking up at my oldest brother with large eyes as if asking: *Are we really doing this?*

But Galahad pushed forward and didn't indulge my pitiful expressions.

How could you Galahad?

Then Tulken walked us past Professor Percival's fencing class. Dashiel was there training. He was wicked fast, and the way steel collided as he fought other students made me shiver.

Tulken said we'd have to take one year of fencing.

I shot Galahad a concerned glance: *We can't really be doing this.*

As always, my brother was immovable. In the field outside near the armory, there were the older kids practicing archery on targets. There was a long wooden weapons rack that had wheels on the bottom. A couple of kids had pulled it out of the armory. Uriah and the older kids who'd been sitting together were going through weapons like lightning. A younger kid was running back and forth to the weapons rack handing Uriah different weapons. He took the bow and arrow and shot a bullseye. As if that wasn't enough, he grabbed a second arrow and fired again.

Split!

The second arrow split the first in half. Uriah didn't take his eyes off the target and held out his hand. The smaller boy ran back to the weapons rack and grabbed a crossbow coming back. He was panting and out of breath, trying to get the weapon in Uriah's hand fast enough. Uriah took the weapon without looking at him and fired another bullseye. He returned the crossbow to the smaller boy, and the cycle continued with several other weapons. I probably shouldn't have had my mouth hung open, but he was so good with all of them. All the kids were good, but he was faster than the rest in how quickly he switched from each tool.

"Is that his gift?" I asked, turning to Tulken. "Uriah, he's an expert with all weapons?"

Tulken glanced over at the training, "No, it's not his gift. Uriah and his sister believe they must be proficient with all weapons. It's something their families firmly encourage."

"Must be nice to have *mommy and daddy* backing them up," Killian said bitterly.

Tulken looked down at Killian. "The Harks and other parents who know their children are commissioned have very high standards. They put a great deal of money and effort into their children's education and expect only the finest results. Typically, the children who know of their calling and come here have Commissioned as parents. It's a rare case, but it does happen. The pressure tends to fall on the children of Commissioned… more strongly than others."

"Rich with two parents—yeah, I feel really bad for them," Killian scoffed.

"—Killian!" Galahad cautioned. "Quit it with the attitude."

"Whatever," Killian averted his gaze crossing his arms. "So,

they've been here since they were…." I began.

Tulken tilted his head in thought, "Hm, a little younger than you."

"Did they fall behind and get forced to stay longer?" Killian said.

"No, Uriah, his sister, and all the others like them are top of every class," Tulken said.

Killian frowned, "…Of course."

"It's their conviction to be educated in all areas historical, theological, magical, and combative—they believe it's a Commissioned true duty. Because of that, they remain in schooling longer," Tulken said as we passed by them.

I felt some relief and pressure. I hoped we weren't expected to do any of that. But Tulken had said it was their conviction, and it wasn't required of all of us. Killian clearly didn't like the attitudes of Uriah and his friends. I hoped he'd want to back out, but he didn't. I lost Emma when she saw the hanging gardens and rose-covered greenhouse. I had hopes that Micah would retreat and be the first to start complaining when we saw the class schedule. Micah was my fellow quitter when things got unfamiliar and dangerous, and I hoped he wouldn't let me down. Then we got to the arts and crafts room…Micah's eyes lit up. There were as many drawings, paintings, and building materials for all kinds of things.

I was shooting Micah a glance as he and Killian looked around the crafts room like they were kids in a candy store.

Stay strong, Micah, stay strong…

Then Tulken showed him the box of action figures and the workshop area.

I lost him.

Micah's eyes were glowing as he looked at all the different figures and pieces there were. With all the wooden crafts and sculptures there, he and Killian could build a whole kingdom for their games.

I let out a disappointed breath. He wasn't going to be any help. I should have been excited for my family to find purpose, but after my nightmare, I was just terrified. We had lunch with the students. Wednesday was comfort food day. Addie's mom made shepherd's pie and potato leek soup for lunch with different kinds of muffins. It was delicious, but I was so scared that I hardly ate a morsel. Tulken said we could start as soon as the next morning. We got all our books and a list of classes that evening. After dinner, my siblings and I only stayed downstairs in the living room for a little while with the other kids.

Tulken read in his chair by the fireplace when he wasn't working. Most of the time I saw him working with the other Professors around the Manor or taking stacks of paper into his office to grade. Addie's mom was cleaning up the kitchen with the help of Cheryl, one of the household magic practitioners. The kids played games, talked, and did all kinds of different activities in the evening. My eyes shot around for Dante, but I didn't see him. I asked Jasmine what he was up to, and she said, "Buried in some magic book." We went to bed early. Not because I was sleepy but because I needed alone time with Emma to get myself together.

I had several dreams that night. In some of them, once again, I saw flashes of the sorceress from the night before. I had nightmares of the witches coming for us at the Manor, of Tulken turning into Blech and this place being a trap, and of Killian arguing with all of us till I got upset again. My last dream was back in our old house— images of it were still hazy in my mind. I remembered the hallways, the carpet, and the small, modest living room with a fireplace. Somehow my memory was better in the dream. I was in our first home, and suddenly it was like I could smell the old carpet; the door to my Dad's office was cracked open, and the musty air was leaking out. I was in the living room, and my siblings were there, but it was like looking through water.

I tried to move towards them, but a woman was in my way.

I caught my breath. Magdala from my dream was standing in the center of the living room. She turned around, and the corners of the house began to burn. I was frozen as the flames enveloped all the images of my childhood home like a piece of paper burning.

"No!" I sat up in bed.

I was sweating, and my hands were grabbing the sheets. I looked around and saw Emma face down on her pillow, groaning. There was someone knocking at the door. It took a moment for me to take in the bedroom and remember that I was safe. The white twin beds, the soft carpet, and the window seat with a view of the gardens and the sun rising outside…the Manor. I was breathing quickly and shaking my head to try and force the images back. These dreams meant something. They had to. But Killian was done hearing about it. If I told my siblings, he would either shut me up or they would think I'm being paranoid. Maybe I was; I really didn't know…

There were another couple of knocks on the door.

Emma picked up her head and yawned before putting her arm over her eyes, "Killian, if that's you, I'm gonna stuff you into a pillowcase and let the Manor's animals sleep on you!" Emma slipped her feet out of bed. Addie had loaned us loose, comfortable sleepwear. Emma's pink t-shirt said COULD YOU NOT? She requested it specifically from Addie's closet.

I caught a glimpse of myself in the mirror across the room on top of the chest of drawers. I had bed hair of the worst degree. Back at the Boarding House, the other girls had called it a rat's nest. Honestly, I couldn't argue. I was a Raggamuffin.

Emma opened the door, "Say *one thing* to me, Killian, and I'll have you for breakfast....!"

It wasn't Killian. It was Dante—standing in the doorway with an amused expression. I pulled my blanket up over my head.

Emma screamed. Dante wasn't exactly a normal-looking boy, but I thought it was extreme.

"Sibling love, it never ceases to amaze me...." I heard him say.

Emma breathed tensely, "Oh, sorry...Dante, right?"

"The man, the myth, and the legend—at your service," he said slyly.

I heard Emma give a half-hearted, slightly annoyed laugh. "Riiight..."

Emma didn't sound flustered at all, which confused me. How she kept her cool in messy pajamas talking to a cute boy was beyond me. I didn't like Dashiel, though, so maybe it was just a matter of taste.

"Kaine asked me to come up and make sure you guys were up and ready for orientation. Didn't you have a sister?" I heard him say.

No.

"Yes, she's...." Emma was probably wondering why I retreated into the blanket. "Somewhere, I'm sure. What kind of orientation are we talking about?"

"Just some videos and tutorials. It starts at 6:15, so…you guys probably wanna head-on down. Breakfast is at 7. Here's the schedule. Tulken always gives first-time students a full outline to keep them on track till they get the times memorized."

"Thank you, we'll be down in a flash!" I heard her close the door. "Elsha!" Emma came over and pulled the blanket off my head.

I shielded my eyes from the light, "What?"

"What are you doing? Trying not to exist?" Emma put her hands on her hips.

"Emma! I didn't want him to see me looking like a ragamuffin!" I said.

"Have a little confidence! Besides, you look adorable! Any boy would be able to tell that….." she stopped and looked curiously at me. "….Why do you care what he thinks?"

I flushed deeply. "I don't!" I shot out of bed and locked the door.

Emma raised an eyebrow, "Uh-huh…whatever. Galahad's probably already up and about. That just leaves the other two miscreants. I'll get them up." Emma walked over to the adjoining bathroom and went inside. She opened the door to the boy's room and stuck her head inside, "GET UP, YOU SAVAGES, OR WERE GONNA BE LATE FOR ORIENTATION! DO YOU WANT US KICKED OUT ON OUR FIRST DAY?!"

I heard bodies fumble and hit the floor in a scuffle. Killian started yelling first, but Emma yelled back, and then all was normal. We didn't have much to get dressed in besides what we'd came in for the first day or so; that would have to do. I groaned and took my clothes, went to the bathroom, and locked both adjoining doors. Emma was arguing with the boys that because we were girls, we should have the bathroom first. I hung my head against the door, wondering how long we'd last here.

#

Classes and times:

6:15 Orientation

6:30 Breakfast

(8-9:15) Natural World Ecology 10, taught by Maddison Clary, a study of the real world, plants flowers, the study of the roles of them in magic, and such. Life, the role of every living thing in the system. An extension of the class happens later, in which the study of supernatural creatures and their roles is explained.

(9:30-10:45) Magic 111 taught by Collins (a beginner's course in the basics of magic where you learn about the nature of it, light and dark, why they use it, what is permissible to use, etc.

(11:00-12:15) Gym, taught by Kaine. Teaches basic physical health and stamina requires the students to pass the obstacle course and is supervised by knights of Valor in training since their regime is more difficult.

(12:30-1:30) Lunch

(1:45-2:30) Commissioned History of Election 111 taught by Tulken. Teaches the basic history of the Commissioned, details of the Manors, different ones, and where they are. How the commissioned are called, the difference between the elect and the normal world.

(2:30-3:15) Basic Demonology 10 taught by Kaine. How to recognize demons, monsters, witches, and such.

The workload didn't inspire me. But the idea of being in all these classes with my siblings and other new kids made me feel a little better. Orientation was a bunch of short videos and some pamphlets on the sports events and dates. We were a little late, but thankfully we got most of the info written down. Book supplies and such were given to us by Tulken the day before. We kept our old backpacks because of sentiment, but having new pencils, crayons, and markers was nice. Dori, Jasmine, and Addie were in Orientation with us, which made me feel a little better. Dori seemed oddly bleak about the first classes, and I didn't get why. I asked her why she wasn't excited about them. She said the kids like Uriah, his sister, and Dashiel, who'd been here longer, looked down on first-time students because the classes they had to take were so basic. Basic sounded to me like *less difficult,* so I wasn't gonna complain.

Breakfast was great, as always, but I didn't eat much. I never did when I was nervous. It must have been bad luck. I was a chubby kid because I was nervous all the time. After breakfast, the students got to scramble and brush their teeth before the first class of the day.

The first class was Natural World Ecology with Maddison Clary. I had to stop and catch my breath as soon as I came into the classroom. It had a slanted floor going down to a long wooden desk, and there were large glass windows that had various vines lining them as the sun streamed in. Hanging plants were on the ceiling above us, and birds chirping passed in and out of the room through cracked ovalshaped windows high on the wall. The vines were intertwined, hanging above us, and flowers were on the main wooden desk below, as well as greenery. I felt like I'd stepped into a hanging garden. Emma's eyes lit up. We had planned to sit together, but there weren't enough seats in one row. Galahad and Emma preferred to be closer to the front, and Micah, Killian, and I sat in the back. Jasmine was in the back, with Dori and Addie sitting in the row directly ahead of us. Killian slouched into his chair, occasionally glancing at Addie.

Emma had never been able to make anything grow, so she was curious about Clary's teachings and methods. I wondered what kind of a teacher she would be since I was used to the worst from Blech's. A pretty, full-figured woman, I assumed was Clary, walked into the classroom in a large beige sweater and torn jeans. She had flowers on the cuffs of her jeans and daisies on her sandals and glasses. She pulled off her daisy sunglasses to reveal flower-tipped pink reading glasses. Her hair was in long blond ringlets highlighted hot pink and sunset orange at the tips; flower pins kept it back. Her tone and attitude were extremely chill, and her voice was overly gentle as she went to the board. Clary's hands spread dramatically, and her eyes slit behind her pink glasses. "And the very nature of plants in the ecosystem…is life. Everything plays a role, and one piece cannot exist without the other. We have a natural connection to plants because, like us, they're alive. Sometimes, we take for granted the beauty nature gives us every day but imagine the world without it. Nature makes the world around us so much better, and yet it never says a word."

I wondered if she was always this calm. Emma was writing everything down and looking up at her.

"Some of us have a stronger connection with plant life than we realize. Nature is alive. And we connect with it by knowledge of it, experience; it helps us to know the flowers, to talk to them," Maddison lifted a small daisy in a pot. "Every flower has a different power when applied in magic or for healing; daisies are for gentleness, roses for passion. So, keep in mind when you pick a flower or cut a vine, it should be with purpose. You can't end a plant's life without reason…."

Micah exchanged looks with Killian and mouthed *end a plant's life*?

Killian shrugged. His attention was on Addie, who was being pestered by another student. I was trying to take notes, but the boy's mean words made me look up. He was trying to take Addie's notebook, and she snapped in an urgent whisper, "Give it back!"

"Or what? You'll use voodoo on me?" he whispered angrily. I'd seen this before, kids being in the back so they could get away with things.

I swallowed timidly, leaning forward, "Could you stop?"

The boy looked over his shoulder back at me, "Or what?"

"Or I'll make you *eat* that notebook, loser," Killian's expression was unmoved.

Addie was looking over her shoulder back at us, and her eyes grew large. She looked surprised someone was coming to her aid. "I don't need your help!" she said to him.

"Let me be the judge of that," Killian stared down the boy.

Clary was still lecturing in a mellow tone as she held a small potted plant. We were so far at the back of the big classroom that it was no shock she didn't see us. "For example…this plant is used in a vision spell. If we pick it to use for the greater good in a spell, then it's alright …."

The boy in front of us tore the notebook from Addie's hands, and she winced in pain. Killian lost it. He reached forward, grabbed the boy by the back of his shirt, and yanked him out of his chair, making a loud noise in the classroom.

"Ah!"

Emma looked back over her shoulder, "Killian!"

Killian practically snarled, taking the notebook back. He pulled his arm back like he was going to hit the boy dead in the face.

Galahad had been towards the front of the class, but now he stood up, coming over. "What's going on here!?" Galahad grabbed Killian, letting the boy fall to the floor. He held my middle brother back, who was fighting like a rabid dog to be let loose, and swinging the notebook down at the boy like it was a club.

Professor Clary stayed calm through it all and, over the arguing, occasionally inserted, "Now children, let's all breathe…."

Killian pulled against Galahad's hold. "He has it coming. Now let me go!"

The boy stood, trying to come at Killian.

Micah pointed, "Look out!"

Galahad extended an arm to keep the boy, who was much smaller than him, away from Killian. Killian pulled himself from Galahad's grip and nearly fumbled against the potted plants on the window ledge, and Clary's eyes grew large, "—NOT THE TULIPS!"

Galahad caught Killian by the arm, keeping him from crashing into them. "Careful! Now what happened…."

Killian shrugged off his grip, "It doesn't matter! I'm fine!"

"Now, children, let's all say something kind to each other…." Clary began.

Killian went back to his seat, saying something not very kind about the boy, and then Galahad. Galahad looked at him, confused, spreading his hands and then shook his head, going back to Emma. Killian slouched in his chair and didn't pay attention to anything in class. He was smart enough to; I knew it. But he didn't have any reason to try as far as he saw it. I felt bad for him and tried to say something, but he wasn't interested in what I had to say.

Magic 111 was next and sounded interesting: there were so many rules of magic and potions I didn't understand them all. This room was extremely different from Clary's: it was large with wooden floors, tall bookshelves lined the walls, and then cabinets full of bottles and vials at the back. Ladders were propped in corners tall enough to reach the highest books there. I hoped the Professor could shed some light. Dante walked in before the start of class, and as always, students shot him offhanded looks and murmurs. I didn't get what their issue with him was. Sure, he was weird— but wasn't everyone here? Dante sat in a chair by the desk at the head of the classroom with his legs crossed, flipping through the course curriculum. A pencil was floating next to him in a circular fashion as he read. His ring-adorned hand was below his chin like he was thinking. I was watching him intently till I caught Galahad watching me. I instantly looked down.

I waited a few moments before I leaned over and whispered to Jasmine, who was next to me in this class, "Have you ever taken

Professor Collins before?" She looked a little surprised I'd spoken to her. She was quiet like me and, therefore, probably overlooked.

She blinked her dark eyes at me before answering, "No, I've heard about him, but I'm a first-time student too. I've only been here since the summer." She'd been sitting with Addie, Dori, and my siblings before, so I guessed she didn't know her gift either. That made me more comfortable talking to her. She began opening up to me. I learned she liked animals and helped their wildlife expert, Professor Clash, take care of them.

Micah was doodling with building a figurine while Galahad lectured Killian about NOT being beating other students with a notebook. Killian nodded, annoyed, "I know, I know…but in case you've forgotten, I didn't get a vote on staying in this place!"

Galahad raised an eyebrow, "So you're just gonna act out till you get your way? Your fifteen, not five—grow up."

Killian leaned out of his chair towards Galahad, making a fist. "Hey, that moron started it, not me!"

"You can't control other people's stupid actions, but…." Galahad began.

"I can control my own, blah, blah—I get it, *fearless leader*!" Killian sat back and put his feet up on another student's desk. Galahad knocked them off, shooting Killian a glare. Killian huffed, "I'm really not looking forward to meeting another nutty teacher."

"Yeah, especially since plant lady bought a ticket to the crazy train," Micah said.

Emma gave Micah an annoyed look, "Would you knock it off? So she's passionate about plants?"

Galahad nodded, "An eccentric nice professor is better than an evil one who lives to make us suffer. Besides, how weird could this next teacher be?"

The door to the classroom burst open, and a gangly man with short black hair in a long blue cartoonish wizard robe slid into the room with his arms spread.

I nearly jumped. Jasmine's eyes grew large. The gangly man spun in a circle and was carrying a tall wizard's hat. He came to a halt in front of the desk. The rest of us were staring open-mouthed, but Dante didn't even look up from the curriculum; he just moved his foot up and down thoughtfully. "I know we have some new students who haven't had the pleasure of taking my course over the summer...." Collins began in a youthful Irish accent. "But for those of you who don't know me, my name...." the man ducked under his desk and took out a long wand swinging it around him dramatically. "—Is Cornelius Codonahough Collins—master of the magical arts and wizardry!" He spread his arms and knocked over a bottle of blue liquid on the table and his coffee cup with it. The cup broke on the ground by Dante. Dante looked away from his papers to check his boots and make sure nothing had spilled on them; after that, he returned his gaze down.

Collins didn't notice the cup falling; instead, he grabbed his coffee pot and poured it on the table where the cup used to be without even looking. "All of you will learn the cost of magic and the most important rules to follow when tampering with the *supernatural*!"

My mouth fell open along with my siblings as the stream of coffee poured out.

Collins held his hands out expressively as the coffee spilled off the table, "Are you prepared to delve into the mysterious, magnificent, magical, and *wonderous!*"

"And you thought Clary bought a ticket to the crazy train...." Killian began.

"This guy owns the whole railroad," Micah said.

"First of all," Collins said, turning to the chalkboard with a coffee pot still in one hand and a piece of chalk in the other. "Let us make one thing clear for all you students who practice the arts or who possess the *rare* gift of sorcery…."

Dante had his hand under his chin with his head tilted down. His hair was slightly hiding his eyes, but he grinned proudly as Collins spoke.

"Magic is only to be used by students in practices, assignments, and exercises allowed by the faculty. Now, this doesn't mean I'm going to follow you around and make sure none of you use magic to cheat on homework or do your chores. But as a *policy,* you're not supposed to use magic to simply make life more convenient. When you graduate here, that's up to you, but magic shouldn't become a crutch—it needs to be a tool like any other that you use when needed for the right reasons. Understood?"

The class murmured in assent. I hadn't heard anyone else say they were gifted in sorcery, so I wasn't sure how many kids it applied to, but the rule seemed to make sense. One of the boys sitting behind me murmured to another, "Why doesn't he tell his freaky teaching assistant that?"

I looked back over my shoulder at the young boy. His eyes grew large at the fact I'd shot him a glare. The boy crossed his arms, looking away. I wasn't one to speak out, but sometimes I'd been told I could shoot people warnings with my eyes.

Collins went on. "Who can tell me the four main restrictions of all magic—in other words, what *can't* magic do?" he waved one arm behind him dramatically and accidentally flung the coffee pot behind him over Jasmine's head.

"Ah!" she ducked low as it hit the wall behind her.

Dante's hand shot straight up—not even noticing that Jasmine was checking her hair to make sure no coffee had gotten on it.

"Yes, Vaniah—would you care to share with the class?"

"Magic can't make something from nothing, it can't bring anyone back from the dead, it can't make anyone fall in love, and it can't change the truth," Dante said somewhat reverently.

I knew what his interests were. Not that I'd ever have the guts to talk about them with him, but at least now I knew.

"Correct," Collins was happy to have an involved student. "Any questions?

Galahad raised his hand, "Um, I understand the first three rules—what does rule four mean?"

"Ah yes, the inability to alter reality: Magic can never truly change the truth. It can only make an illusion that will blur it for a time that eventually will have to be dissolved. Meaning it cannot change what *is*; it can only find a substitution or illusion to make it appear as if it were different. To attempt to do such would be heresy and use of dark magic," Collins said.

"So, if I wanna rewrite reality where I'm rich with a lot of girls…." Killian began.

Galahad groaned. "You *would* imagine that scenario."

"You want to know if such an alternative reality could be maintained," Collins picked up a stack of books and put them on his desk.

"Yeah," Killian nodded. "And if it can, where do I find the stuff?"

The class laughed.

Collins shushed the classroom. "I'll let my finest student answer that question. Vaniah?"

Dante shifted in his seat, "If you want to cast a spell to change the state of reality, it will fall under the shadow of dark magic because it's the attempt to control what is reserved for the divine: God. Any reality which is not the one already predetermined, or part of the grand design—would fall apart eventually."

Galahad raised a hand, "Humor our ignorance…but if magic is such a dangerous topic, why did we see the maids using it to clean? And why is the gift of sorcery so rare?"

Collins put his finger to his mouth in thought, "We have some first years here, so maybe I should dial back a bit—rules and restrictions of magic are very important, but first, there needs to be a clear distinction between what kinds of magic there is and what we have here."

Emma blinked, "I mean, that would be nice…."

Collins held up his hand, "There are three kinds of magic practitioners: sorcerers, wizards, and warlocks. Sorcerers would be those like myself who possess the *gift* of magic. They have a natural connection to the elements as well as time and space. Meaning they can use the art of levitation and telekinesis. Wizards are those who use the *practice* of magic. They have no natural connection to time, space, or the elements, but through the study of books and the use of potions, they can use some magic. The maids practiced what's known as household magic—completely harmless. Sorcerers are naturally more powerful than those who simply practice magic because their powers can always be expanded by further knowledge. But even without that, they'd be dangerous as far as an opponent goes."

Dante's grin grew.

This was his favorite subject, and here was my chance. It was now or never. If I asked a question, maybe, he would be impressed and talk to me about it later—I wasn't sure I was ready for that. But if I thought about it anymore, I'd chicken out. I mustered all the strength, bravery, and courage I had in me....it wasn't much. My shaky voice broke from my throat, "A-and what about warlocks? What makes them different?" I croaked.

I didn't dare to look and see if Dante was looking at me, I tried to stare right at Collins so I wouldn't be too obvious.

Collins' smile broadened, "Excellent question, young lady! Warlocks are what we call those who practice dark magic."

"So, what makes..." my voice cracked a little, and I cleared my throat. Dante's eyes were on me now. I couldn't back out. "What makes the magic dark?"

"Basically, dark magic can provide great power to any individual, whether they're a sorcerer or simply a practitioner—but it *always* comes with a great cost. Light and darkness cannot co-exist ultimately. Only the Commissioned can rightfully use magic either as a gift or a practice—but mortals who long for power stoop to dark forces to give themselves control over gifts we've been blessed with," Collins said. "For example, a blind human might find one of the fallen ones' many servants and strike a deal to obtain a certain amount of power, but it will cost them their life—or worse."

Killian raised a hand, "Uh, what's worse than losing your life?"

Collins' expression grew grave, ".... Your soul."

I shivered.

"Some of the elect play with darkness, make no mistake, but they pay dearly for it in this life. If you're commissioned, and your place is secured in heaven, then no demon can take it from you. But there will be consequences here on earth, and I've seen…lots of terrible ones. Tulken could explain the difference and nature of that in his theology class better than I did. If someone professing to be of the light tries to practice darkness, one will win over. There's really no way for us to know which they belong to until that fight is finished. Sometimes we never know."

Collins cleared his throat and broke into a cheerful smile again, "On that subject— any attempt to tap into powers that belong to God or to use the enemies' means to acquire power falls under the realm of dark magic," Collins said. "Changing fate, bringing people back from the dead, making someone love you, etc."

"In other words, fathead: no money and girls!" Emma smacked Killian on the back of the head.

I bit my lip before forcing out another question. "For the rule that reality can't be changed…if it's possible to do a spell that makes us think things are a certain way? How would we know the difference?" Collins lit up, "Excellent question! For example, let's say Killian did do a spell to give himself wealth and power…."

Killian grinned.

Emma made a face, "Yuck!"

Killian glared at her.

"If he did that, then everyone it affected would be under the thrall of the spell. We would think that things have always been the way the spell or curse makes them appear. But there would be… something off. Little vague hints that reality was tampered with. For example, Killian might be rich, but we wouldn't be able to give a concrete reason where he got the money. People would remember he'd always had it. If he had a lot of girlfriends, they'd remember they were dating him, but they wouldn't recall when or how it started. Fake memories would be in place, but they could only be rooted so deep."

It was a scary thought. To not know what was real. Collins must have sensed my timid reaction because he felt the need to clarify. "But understand, a curse of this caliber could only be performed by the most powerful of sorcerers or magic practitioners. Changing reality is a curse that couldn't be cast without *great* cost. And few are willing to pay the price."

That made me feel a little better. But it also made me wonder…. why I kept seeing that sorceress in my dreams. Who was that man on the throne?

"For us to study, I've chosen volume 3,496: the Rules and Restrictions of Magic. I want you to read chapters one through three and take notes because we're going to have a pop quiz at the end of the week," Collins tossed aside book after book to find the one he wanted. "If you have any questions feel free to attend tutoring with my top student," he gestured to Dante.

The class groaned. Dante didn't appear bothered, just amused.

Collins flipped through books, and Killian was rather bored. I learned a lot. Now I knew Dante was gifted in magic. That was how he used levitation so easily. I read in the book Collins assigned that every time someone tapped into dark magic, a part of them now belonged to it. The thought made me shudder. Then my eyes fell on an encouraging rule from the book: Only light can save someone completely given over to darkness. I underlined it with a pink highlighter.

At 10:45, the class was over, and we had a small break in the rec room before gym with Kaine. I'd met Kaine, and I wasn't looking forward to a class taught by him. The recreation room was a little freer and crazier. Kids were practicing household magic and spells, and some were practicing swordplay. I was worried sick because the last thing I wanted was an obstacle course. I was still wearing a sweater over a t-shirt, a hat, and jeans, so it wasn't the best to do anything physical in. When our break was over, we all walked out of the rec room down a pathway to the gym. It was a building right beside the obstacle course. We approached the entrance to the gymnasium's double doors. Emma was trying to cheer us up, "Look, we've done okay in school so far. Now, it's just a little gym."

"I don't have any trouble with some gym time, but you guys…." Killian began shaking his head.

"They'll be fine. How hard can it be?" Galahad said.

Micah most likely wanted to look brave in front of Killian, so he put his hands on his hips proudly. "Yeah—there's no harm in trying, right?"

We walked up to the gym building, which was connected to the outdoor gated obstacle course. The doors to the gym burst open, and a student flew out the doors past us with a puff of smoke, "AAAAAAAAAHHHHHH!" The student slid out across the field, leaving a trail of flattened grass behind them. Professor Clary was watering flowers when her expression enflamed at the sight. The student gave a thumbs up, "I'm okay!"

Micah froze alongside all of us. He turned around and began to walk away, "But then again, there's no shame in quitting."

Chapter Ten

Kaine Makes an Obstacle Course to Kill Me

Dragging Micah into the gym wasn't an easy task, especially not while he was kicking and screaming. My fighting the whole way didn't help. Eventually, Galahad picked me up and carried me into the gym, promising it wouldn't be that bad.

I've heard that before. I *love* my big brother, but he's pushing it.

Dashiel, Uriah, and the other kids from his group were in the corner of the gym doing up-downs and pushups. No one was making them, so I had to wonder why they were going through the extra warm-up. They stopped and looked at us, catching their breath as we came in. I cast my gaze down immediately as we walked by them. They seemed to be good at everything, and I certainly wouldn't be. Kaine was standing at the center of the gym in a white tank top and army cap with a whistle around his neck as all the students from our class shuffled in. The indoor inside of the gym was huge—larger than any I'd seen. It almost looked like a normal gym at first, with wooden floors, bleachers, and wooden cabinets lining the walls with equipment. Only one wall was lined with bow staffs, wooden swords and daggers, and crossbows; another corner of the room had hanging heavy bags, a large mat, and padded walls. It looked like something for combat training—I didn't like that idea.

That wasn't even the worst part.

The gym's right wall opened, leading out to the obstacle course. I recalled from the sports pamphlet that we'd been given earlier there were a lot of different teams at the Manor: track and field, baseball, basketball, fencing, and horseback riding. I could see bits of those fields out there, but the thing which burned in my mind was the course. It was a wooden structure with moving stairs leading up to a platform. Immediately on it were razor-sharp swinging pendulums, wooden monkey bars with a wall on the right and the left shooting exploding red flames. Then the wooden floor ended, and the only thing to walk on were a series of wooden posts sticking out of the floor, but fireballs were still shooting through, and above were hanging ropes you could choose to swing across to reach the final step: a tall wall with rocks you had to climb.

Killian's eyes lit up as he saw everything, "Wow...this looks...fun." Galahad wasn't saying it, but I could tell his interest was piqued. He and Killian had always been more athletic. Killian was ridiculous: he could eat whatever he wanted and stay lean, he was nimble and quick like a jackrabbit, but he'd never officially played a sport. Galahad studied boxing first and later wrestling because he wanted non-lethal ways to stop attackers. Punching someone in the nose did permanent damage; throwing them over in a headlock was less lethal. Killian paused, glaring at Uriah, who was looking disapprovingly at us.

I turned white, stopping as I came in; other students kept coming in, avoiding me like I was a rock to go around. "You've got to be kidding me...."

Another girl was on the course hopping from one post to another while other kids cheered. Suddenly, a ball of flame came right at her. "Look out!" I screamed, afraid for her life. She turned around, and a scream stopped in her throat as the flames connected with her. She vanished in a blue light.

Emma looked horrified. But no one else was reacting in shock. "They're trying to kill these kids!"

Galahad's eyes shot to the teachers who were talking like nothing had happened, "What the...."

I glanced around to where Galahad was looking. The girl was sitting on the bench next to Professor Collins, who I hadn't even known was here. Collins was dressed in a blue collared shirt and slacks like he was between classes and holding a glowing glass ball that swirled with color. Dante was next to him, leaning forward, resting his arms on his knees in a black gym shirt and exercise gloves—a similar uniform to what everyone else was made to wear for Kaine's class. He was chuckling, and the girl started shaking her fist at him, screaming.

Galahad brought my attention back, "There's a lot going on here we don't understand, but we can handle it. No one's expecting us to do everything from day one. If we try…."

Micah looked at the course outside through the crowd. "Couldn't we quit in shame and keep our lives?"

"Everyone is going to *try*—okay?" Galahad said more firmly. "Besides, this isn't the military. These guys just want us in shape. It's not like they're trying to turn us into marines…."

A loud whistle broke through the air as another girl was thrown from the course. Micah screamed.

Emma and I put our arms around each other frantically. "—What was that?" Emma's eyes shot around.

Kaine took the whistle out of his mouth, "EVERYBODY LINE UP!" All of us turned, standing at attention with the other new kids. Addie, Jasmine, and Dori were with us in the row. The other older kids did the same. Kaine walked in front of us with his arms crossed, "Alright, you sad little excuses for demon hunters—you think you're tough?"

"He's a regular General Patton," Micah whispered to me.

"—QUIET!" Kaine shouted, making Micah straighten. "You little kids think you got what it takes to kill the undead?"

Micah raised his hand, "Uh…I don't."

I knew I didn't, but I was too scared of Kaine to say so.

"If I say you have what it takes, kid—you have what it takes!" Kaine stopped in front of Micah and looked down at him.

Micah raised his hands in surrender. "Okay, I have what it takes."

"Kid…*you* don't have what it takes," Kaine said.

Killian laughed, "I mean, he tried to tell you, old man…."

Kaine shot Killian a glance, "You got something to say, hair gel?"

Killian straightened. "What did you call…?!"

"I'm gonna call you a lot worse if you don't shut your trap and do as you're told," Kaine looked down at him. "—Now answer the question."

Killian's expression tightened, "No, sir."

"YOU ALL CAN'T KILL THE FORCES OF DARKNESS IF YOU CANT PASS MY COURSE—NOW GET TO IT!" Kaine shouted, but the other kids didn't blink. Dante's face was impassive, like he was used to it.

I'd joined the Marines.

Kaine's mouth grew impossibly large as he shouted, "YOU KNOW THE RULES! IF YOU FALL OR FAIL TO PASS A CHECKPOINT, YOU'RE OUT!"

Emma raised her hand, "Uh, we're new. We don't know all the rules. So, don't you think you should—I don't know, explain things to us since you are the teacher?"

The other students gasped. Some gave an impressed nod at Emma's boldness.

Kaine slowly walked over to her in his large combat boots. The gym was silent, so every step echoed. He stopped in front of her and looked down, cracking his knuckles. Dori whimpered. Emma looked up at Kaine and crossed her arms with an unwavering expression.

Emma didn't care if getting answers meant being the loudmouth or the pushy one. "…Well?"

"What was your name again, blondie?"

"Emma."

"And do you always ask this many questions?" Kaine sneered, leaning down to meet her gaze.

All of us agreed in murmurs.

Micah scratched his head. "Yeah, she kind of does…."

Killian nodded. "Never stops talking."

Galahad put his thumbs in his pockets. "She's very inquisitive…."

"Likes to get answers…" I mumbled.

"QUIET!"

We all stopped. The other kids from all corners of the gym were approaching us and standing at attention like the real work was about to start. Kaine straightened, "Since the national inquirer here is so curious, I'll explain. The course is made up of several components, built to represent some of the challenges you'll face in the field. It judges nerve, reaction time, and resourcefulness and finds out what kind of shape you're in. Kids who have been here longer have already passed it."

Uriah and his group straightened proudly. Some of the jocklooking kids fist-bumped and laughed, "Alright!" "I died the first few times!"

My mouth dropped, "Wait—what?"

Kaine went on, "But we keep them sharp between missions by making them go through it as a routine. The kids who've done it before will run through it first to show you all how it's done. Then the new kids go. If you can't pass this time, you'll get a chance in the next couple of weeks."

Emma pointed to the girl on the bench, "But what about her! We saw her vanish on the course and…."

Kaine groaned, "Oh yeah…." He held up a small metal thing with a blue jewel. "Death detection amulet –a tool that we can use thanks to our own, Professor Collins. You wear these in the obstacle course, and the minute you get hit with a death blow, they take you back to the bench."

Galahad raised a hand, "Uh, but wouldn't those save a ton of lives in the field?"

Collins threw up a hand from the bench and called excitedly, "Oh, oh! Yes, excellent question, Mr. Dyer…you see why that is…." Kaine rolled his eyes with a wave of his hand, "Magic powers, special globe, limited range…blah blah. Collins can explain it all to you later, but right now is gym time."

Dante looked strongly offended from the bleachers, and his mouth dropped like he was stopping mid-objection; his hands were open and shaking for a moment, but he threw them up, crossing his arms. That was probably the first time I'd seen him annoyed by anything.

"What do we do between the course runs?" Emma said to Kaine.

"I train you, so next time, you don't fail. There are things every Commissioned needs to be familiar with, exploding powders, weapons, witches flying at your head, swordsmanship, and combat. We'll alternate what you train with daily."

"See, that wasn't so painful, was it," Emma pointed her finger at Kaine.

Kaine made a low rumbling noise that was something like a complaint as he turned away from her and looked at the more experienced kids. "ALL RIGHT, YOU SORRY EXCUSES FOR COMMISSIONED! GET OUT THERE AND SHOW THEM HOW IT'S DONE! THE REST OF YOU GET YOUR AMULETS FROM COLLINS AND SIGN THE WAVER!"

Emma was following the line of kids going to Collins when she stopped, "Wait—a waver? But…"

"JUST DO IT!"

Emma and I were practically blown to the line for amulets by the force of his voice. Dante was handing out papers to the kids, and

Collins gave out amulets. Emma was in front of me and took a paper, mumbling, "That man should have his teaching license revoked...."

Kids who'd been there longer ran the course first. I tried to watch what they did so I could maybe have a chance. But the longer I glanced over, the more my hopes sank. The rest of us who weren't running the course did basic physical fitness—which I hated, but I promised Galahad I would try. All of us had to move in a circular fashion around the gym, stopping every few yards to do sit-ups (which I could fake), push-ups (which I couldn't do), and up-downs (which, if you count falling on my face, I could do). Uriah and the other kids were going so fast through the exercises it was embarrassing for Emma, Micah, and I. Emma wasn't out of shape (like me). She just didn't like to be physically taxed. When she was motivated, I'd seen her outwalk my brothers, but when she didn't want to, she wouldn't be moved. I noticed Uriah's group mumbling and laughing as I tried to keep up. Uriah never laughed—he simply shot me the most disapproving look I'd ever seen in my life—and that was saying something. Galahad and Killian were going just as fast as they were in the exercises, and that only made Uriah go faster. Before long, I could swear Uriah and Galahad were competing over who could drop and get back up quicker. I tried moving slower so that Kaine would pull me out of the rhythm. Kaine was about to, but then Galahad took him aside, "Isn't a group only supposed to move as fast as the slowest person in the team?"

Uriah had been standing close by and scoffed at the idea.

Thanks a lot, Galahad.

Dashiel went through the course and was back in a matter of moments. I couldn't believe how perfect his timing was, how quickly he climbed the wall. I wondered what his gift was. Uriah went next, causing gasps and defeated sighs to go the room. I was annoyed because he was almost as fast as Dashiel. His timing was ridiculous moving through the blades, and he didn't even get singed by one fireball. The way he did it made me think he'd run the course a million times. Uriah landed and walked back past Kaine. Uriah's smaller friend/servant, who'd been holding his weapons, ran up to him, holding a wet towel. Uriah took it without looking at him and wiped his face.

Dante was leaning against the wall, looking down admiring his rings, "A little slow there on the flame dodging, Hark." He glanced up at him and gave a small smile.

Uriah paused mid-step and lowered the towel from his face. He looked at Kaine.

"He's messing with you, Hark," Kaine said.

Uriah tossed the towel back to his man servant, who fumbled to catch it. "Herodotus, what was my time?"

"One minute and five seconds," the girl with the long straight brown hair, who was Uriah's carbon copy, looked at her stopwatch. "A personal best."

Uriah glanced at Dante, "Stick to your heathenistic potions, Vaniah—don't pretend like *this* is your field." He raised his arm, and Nicodemus flew to him, perching on his shoulder.

Dante chuckled, "Well, one of us has to enjoy himself at something."

Uriah ignored him and walked past Dori and Addie, glancing down, "It's easy for you to *say* you're Commissioned after three months of juvenile games. Now it's time for you to put your calling to the test."

Addie shrank back slightly. Killian snarled, stepping forward.

Galahad held out a hand to keep him back. "Cut them some slack, will you?"

Uriah dusted his shoulder off. "True Commissioned know the realm of the demonic, and the blind won't cut you any…slack. This isn't a game. It's a way of life."

"I take it you're not wishing us luck?" Dori said.

"Luck is an idol of the blind. I don't wish you anything. If you aren't truly Commissioned, you'll be sifted like wheat before the end of this term. And the Commissioned have no use for discarded chaff," Uriah walked past them and went into his group.

Emma and I exchanged glances. "I suddenly feel very selfconscious...."

"Welcome to my world...." I mumbled. When more seasoned kids had gone through the course, it was our turn. Dori was up first, and as supportive as Addie was trying to be, she wasn't excited. I could barely stand. I was leaning on the wall, trying not to throw up.

Dante walked up to me and put his hand on the wall, a little out of breath. "Not a fan of the basic training?"

Why was he talking to me? I was literally the person who had slowed the whole group down. I nodded with a half grunt. I ended up saying something between "yeah" and "Nah."

He tilted his head, "You agree, or you're not sure?"

"I...uh...I'm not one for any kind of training."

"Don't hate Kaine too much. He can't find kids' talents if he doesn't put them through the wringer," Dante ran his hand through his hair.

I looked at the ground. "What if Uriah is right? I don't have any talent," I said bluntly. Dante raised his eyebrows in slight surprise, studying me.

"Wow—already letting him get to you, huh? Look, everybody here has a gift...."

There was an explosion.

Dori was running away from the obstacle course, waving her arms, and yelling with the back of her gym shorts, smoking. There were weapons flying out from the obstacle course, and amazingly they were all missing her. "PUT IT OUT! PUT IT OUT!" she yelled, running in a circle.

Micah grabbed an ice chest full of water and threw it on her.

Splash!

Dori stopped running and closed her eyes; she was now soaked. "…Thank you."

"Anytime," Micah grinned proudly.

"Okay…maybe not everyone but most of us," Dante smiled.

"What's Uriah's problem with you?" I asked after a moment's silence. "You seem like you've been here longer." Dante glanced down thoughtfully at his hands, looking morbid for a moment before he smiled.

"He and a lot of the other kids weren't a fan of mine when I first showed up. I had some… magical talents they thought were a little too strong. Strict Commissioned, like Uriah, has a problem with kids gifted in sorcery. They think it means they might be…. dark." He looked up at me, and his eyes flashed a brighter color like they had when he'd levitated the sword the first time we met. "Now, can you imagine why they'd think that of me?" He put his hand to his chin thoughtfully. His eyes went back to normal, and he laughed, "Plus— other than Collins, I'm the only one here gifted in sorcery. It's rare, remember?"

"Uh…." I wasn't sure what to say to that. "I don't think that gives them a right to call you demonic or anything," I said at last.

"Do me a favor and don't tell anyone it's all true," he quietly put his finger to his lips before breaking into a grin. My hair stood on end, and I averted my gaze. Other kids went through the course and were dropping like flies. I learned a bit from Dante while they did, grateful that we'd be going near last. Percival was the head swordsmanship teacher, and Dashiel was his teaching assistant (much to Uriah's chagrin). Dante practiced sword fighting with Dashiel, which told me something about him. Uriah had refused to teach Dante, apparently, but Dashiel didn't mind.

"So, you train with Dashiel…doesn't that mean you're one of the best too?" I said, making him look at me in surprise. I might have overdone the flattery, but he didn't seem to mind—he smiled, glancing down.

"I admit, I can see how you would think that—but no. Dash, Uriah, and his crew have me beat at swordplay. I'm good enough to be in their class, but they don't really…acknowledge me. None of them except for Dash. He doesn't really care where you come from or what you look like. He's just interested in your skills."

"Are you guys friends?"

Dante looked over at Dashiel. "I don't know. He's never told me otherwise. Now, in a Raziel challenge where I get to use spells of levitation, fire, water, or teleportation….I'd kill those kids," he said playfully.

"What's a Raziel challenge?"

"That's like a big combat gym event where one group of kids challenges another. They compete in an arena designed by Professor Clash. Basically, it's anything goes, and both teams can use all their gifts to beat the other."

"Do you guys have a champion team?"

Dante let out a breath, "—Guess?"

"Uriah's team?"

He nodded. "Team six…they take on all challengers. And the only ones to give them a run have been the gym rats who work a lot with Kaine. But the challenge is more than fighting, its resourcefulness, speed…." I'd seen stands out there next to the baseball field, and I'd wondered what they were for. The land around the Manor was so large I was still finding new things. There was no way I could ever survive something like that. I'd just have to hope to be average at this school and not fall on my face—that was my hope. Dante saw my face fall, and his expression softened, "What is it?"

"Nothing, I just…I could never do that," I said, adding a light laugh.

"You're okay being average, right?" he raised an eyebrow.

"…Yeah," I lied.

"—Wrong," Dante stepped towards me. Naturally, I could have stayed where I was like a boss and glared up at him, but I stepped back, stumbling against the basketball rack and knocking the balls everywhere. Dante glanced at them and then down at me. "No one is comfortable being average—you weren't born to be like everyone else."

"So, everyone here reminds me…." I mumbled, rolling my eyes.

"The rest of the normal world lives in a bubble; they can't handle the things we were made to—they can live their lives blending in with the crowd because they're not capable of anything else, you are," he said. "And there's no reason somebody like Uriah should be able to do this stuff, and you can't."

I stared at him and then looked down at my oversized, overdressed body. My hair was fuzzy and covering half my face with my knit hat on to keep it in place—I was anything but impressive, and he was talking like I was some supernaturally gifted goddess. "I can't even run a lap around the track; what do I have…."

"Power—you just haven't tapped into it yet. You know that's why they pick on us? You, me, Addie…it's because we have power, and it scares them."

The whistle blew. "It's time for the rest of the new kids!" Kaine called.

Dante gestured out the open wall to the course, "I think Kaine wants you guys to get a better look. Shall we?" There was a crowd of students in front of us that weren't letting us through.

"Uh, I'm fine back here…." I began.

Dante rolled his eyes. He raised his hands and brought them together. A second later, his eyes flashed a brighter green, and he spread his hands again. The crowd parted in the center as if some invisible force were pushing them aside. A pathway parted for us, and his eyes went back to normal. He waved a hand, "Shall we?" we walked down the center of the crowd as murmurs went around.

"Freak!"

"Professor Kaine, he used magic!" He didn't seem to notice the comments or pay attention, so I didn't either. I followed him, stepping outside towards the front of the crowd into the light. No. Just—no. There was no way I could begin to cross that course. My mouth was hanging open as I looked at it. Dante stood next to me, arms crossed.

A look of horror crossed my face. "It's a death trap…"

"So is life. That's the fun of it, right?" Dante looked down at me mischievously.

"No."
He laughed. "Don't worry, Dyer; you're not up next."

Addie had gone after Dori, and she'd failed somewhere halfway through. She walked back, pulling shards of wood out of her curly hair. The boy who'd been picking on her in class was making snide remarks as she came back, but Killian growled at him.

Galahad was up next. He looked like his mind was working in overdrive. He'd been watching everyone else go through with close attention. Galahad secured the amulet to his gym shirt, looking up at Kaine, "So this takes you out if there's a killing blow?"

"That's right," Kaine nodded.

Uriah scoffed, "Not like it will make much difference. No one but myself and Dashiel has succeeded in passing this course the first time." I shot Uriah a glare, and he didn't bother to return the look.

You don't know my brother.

The cool breeze was blowing outside, and the sound of the steel swinging filled the air. Galahad poised himself to break into a run at the foot of the moving stairs on the obstacle course. Kaine stood by and blew the whistle. Galahad went up the moving stairs. He kept his balance which was already better than I could have done. My siblings and I were as tense as possible. Galahad stopped at the swinging pendulums and caught his breath; he looked like he was counting. He paused and moved through each blade as we all cheered him on.

"Go, Galahad!" Killian said.

"You are magnificent!" Micah was yelling. Galahad was onto the monkey bars, and he leaped, taking hold of them and swinging through as the fireballs began to shoot. Galahad let go of one bar hanging from one arm so he could turn aside and miss being scorched. I noticed Uriah hadn't been paying attention before, but now he stepped forward and was watching intently.

Dashiel straightened his collar approaching Emma, "How are your siblings fairing in the course?"

"WIN!" Emma yelled right in Dashiel's ear. "Oh, Dash!" she fixed her hair. "Sorry, I didn't see you there."

Dashiel tapped the side of his head as if to check if he could still hear out of that ear. "Quite alright, no permanent damage. I fail to see how all your vehemence will allow your brother to have more success."

"It's called support," Emma said.

I was trying to cheer as loudly as them, but as usual, I never quite made it. Galahad's athletics at Blech's must have helped him out a lot. I had no idea how he was moving so quickly, like he was made for it. He had to slip down on his stomach to duck the swinging sandbags to get across to the next platform. Even Kaine looked impressed. Galahad grabbed hold of the rope at the end of the platform and swung over the pool of cold water, barely reaching the rock wall at the end. He let go of the rope and nearly slid down the wall.

"AH!" Emma grabbed Micah and Killian by the arm and shook them. "HE'S NOT GONNA MAKE IT!"

"Well, why do you have to stop all my blood circulation because of it?" Killian pulled his arm free.

Galahad grabbed the rocks and scaled the wall slipping down the other side in a squat.

I let out a scream, "YEAH!"

The students looked at me in shock, probably just realizing I was there.

"No one makes it through Kaine's course the first time…" Dashiel said.

We all cheered. Emma turned to Dashiel. "YES! IN NO ONE ISNT MY BROTHER BECAUSE HE'S AWESOME!"

Dashiel pulled his head back, "If you could lower the volume, young lady…."

Galahad quietly walked over to us, clearly uncomfortable with all the attention. The Harks were staring at him, but he didn't look at them. Herodotus was smiling suddenly with interest.

Micah stepped up next, "I've got this," he grinned.

"GO, MICAH!" Emma yelled. I was jumping up and down, cheering, and noticed Dante looking at me strangely. Maybe he wasn't used to families being as whacky as ours. Call us whacky, but we were supportive. Micah ran at the stairs and tripped losing balance.

"You did your best, Micah!" Emma called.

He walked back to us. "And that's how it's done," he said slyly.

"Did you just fail so you wouldn't have to go through the whole course?" Killian said.

"Duh, you know me so well."

147

Uriah rolled his eyes, annoyed, and muttered something like, "Why don't they just leave now...." I looked down and pretended I didn't hear it. That course could kill us. It wasn't fair of him to judge us for not wanting to go through when this was our first day.

"Hair goals! You're up next," Kaine waved Killian over.

Killian rolled his eyes, annoyed, "My name is not...uurhgg! Fine, like I even care about passing this...."

The boy who'd been teasing Addie was standing near us behind her. He mumbled to his friend, "Bet you he makes it two seconds...just like voodoo girl."

Killian must have heard, which was impressive. I was standing closer to Addie, but he was in front of me. He turned his head to him, "What did you just say?"

Addie looked back and forth between the two of them. "Guys, don't..."

"How many times did it take you to pass this course, loser?" Killian marched up to the boy.

"—Three," the boy admitted.

"I'll do it in one. Take notes," Killian turned, walking towards the course. Addie spread her hands, confused.

Killian made it his goal to make the rest of us look bad (as usual). Killian shot up the moving stairs like a cat and stepped through the blades, pausing and listening for the next one. He moved through and slid under the last few blades coming up the other side. I'd never seen him move like this before; it was different than Galahad. Killian was moving like he had heard things before they hit. We were cheering loudly as Killian came close to the finish. He got to the rope and grabbed hold of it. He looked back to shoot the boy an overconfident look.

Galahad stepped forward. "Killian, look out!" Killian didn't see the flying sandbag coming right his way. It flew right by him, and he stepped off the platform losing his grip on the rope.

"Killian!" Emma and I stepped forward, concerned.

Uriah suppressed a smile, "Oh, how unfortunate."

"You shut up!" Emma said.

Uriah's eyes grew large in surprise. He stiffly exchanged glances with his sister and the rest of his crew. Killian fell into the water, and there was a loud echo of, Ooo! Killian's head popped out of the water, and he flipped his hair out of his eyes. Killian got out of the water and walked over to us, squeezing the liquid out of his shirt.

Addie stepped towards him, "Are you okay?"

Killian shrugged, "I'll get it next time."

"Why did you..." Addie began.

"What, did you think it was for you?" Killian looked up at her before walking towards us. Addie went back to Dori, confused.

"Learn anything from that, students?" Kaine looked at all of us. "Stop to enjoy your glory, and you might just lose the battle. You're the fastest kid I've seen on that course, and you could've passed it. But you cared too much about what the people watching thought. Don't do it again."

Killian hung his head slightly. Emma and I gave him an encouraging hug, and she brushed his hair out of his eyes. That brightened his mood a little.

Emma was up next. Emma didn't make it past the flames. She got up the stairs, past the blades but got hit by two fireballs as she fell from the monkey bars. Emma vanished in a blue light and appeared on the bench, dizzy, next to Collins.

Emma came back to us with her hair and shirt slightly charred, "Stupid course…burn me…the nerve…! How does my hair look?" I was quiet a moment, "It doesn't look that bad…."

Dashiel picked up a charred slice of blonde hair from her shoulder. "I think this is yours."

Emma's mouth fell open, and she put her hands on her head, "OH, MY HAIR LOOKS LIKE A CHARCOALED YELLOW CRAYON!" Emma went past us to the girl's restroom. I was there with Dashiel and Dante next to me while Kaine had gym assistants check the course. My brothers were talking, and I knew I'd be next. I was trying not to shake.

Dashiel titled his head, "I wouldn't have put it so pejoratively. Some students have burned more than their hair in this course." Dante

nudged me excitedly, "You're up, Dyer."

I realized he was talking to me.

I felt my heartbeat quicken, and I pulled down my sleeves to my palms nervously, "…What? Me?"

"Do you see me talking to anyone else?" his tone was teasingly curious.

"I…I can't."

"Why not?"

"I, I don't have the right shoes for walking those stairs. I don't have the arm strength to climb a wall, and that rope will leave rope burns if I don't have gloves…."

"You're afraid of a lot of things, aren't you?" He studied me. Jasmine walked up to us and stood by me, looking at him and Dashiel. She had her hands in the pockets of her leather jacket and was looking at her feet while we talked. "It's not impossible," Dante said.

"It kind of is," I objected. My out-of-shape self was NOT surviving that course.

"Okay, so what if it is? Aren't you dying to try it?" he smiled.

"If I try it, I'll just die," I said flatly, making Jasmine giggle.

"Impossible things are being done all the time. Dash here showed the Manor that the best swordsmen didn't have to be a knight of valor. I showed them a knight of Valor can have sorcery and that you don't have to be big or strong to be fierce."

Jasmine squinted and gave him a strange look, "I showed them that."

"But I was there so... we kind of both played the part," Dante nudged Jasmine lightly on the shoulder.

She glared down at his hand. "--Not really." Jasmine made a priceless annoyed expression.

"Now, are you gonna give it a try and show these stuff shirts you aren't scared?" He looked at me.

"Well, since you asked…no," I said. "They're gonna laugh at me!"

"So? Your brothers and sister did it. If you don't even go up there, I promise Sir Uriah and his crew will be laughing louder."

"Look, there's got to be a way I can opt out of this! It's too soon. I can barely stand right now," I complained.

Dante let out a breath, "Okay, if you won't—you won't. Here, hold this for me," he gave me a baton that he'd previously been playing with as we talked.

I took it, of course. "What do you want me to do with…."
"Oh, nothing, just hold on." Dante stepped back and flicked his hand. Oh, heavens no. He wouldn't. The baton flew, taking me with it toward the training course. I went flying and let out an ear-piercing scream.

Chapter Eleven

I'm not showing My Face After this....

"YOU LOUSE!" How did I know what a louse was? I remember hearing my mother call my father that when they fought. I heard Emma go up to Dante and yell at him, "Are you trying to kill my sister?" I heard Dante say, "She's fine." I decided Dante was a psychopath. Cute as Dante was… in that moment, I committed myself to the image of me hitting him with that baton. The baton took me to the turning stairs.

I balanced myself, nearly twisting an ankle, trying not to fall off the moving steps. My curly, tangled hair fell in front of my eyes. I could barely see with my knit hat pulled down, and my large clothes made moving even more awkward. The blades were spinning before my eyes as I got motion sickness from the moving stairs below my feet. "….I'm—so—dead."

I was there a long time staring at the swinging blades. If I moved forward, I'd be cut in half, and if I stayed, I risked falling off the stairs and breaking my neck. Which would be a quicker death? I had to trust that stupid amulet to teleport me away. I heard Emma, Killian, and Micah shouting and cheering from a distance.

My heart was hammering. I was completely torn.

My head started spinning as the floor moved beneath me. I moved a leg to step forward, and the stairs shifted. I reached out to grab something to steady myself, but the blades were the closest things to my hands. I pulled my hands back. The sudden action made me lean back and lose balance.

I fell off the moving stairs and landed flat on my back.

The world was spinning over me, and the pain in my back was deafening. I don't know how long I was there before I sat up. It couldn't have been very long because I heard my siblings' voices over me talking within a few seconds. In the background, I heard laughter and sympathetic groans. I couldn't lay there with everyone looking at me. I forced myself to sit upright. Before I realized it, Emma's hand was on my shoulder, helping me.

"Elsha, are you okay?" Galahad squatted down beside me. All the other kids had begun rushing over.

Perfect.

Uriah shook his head, walking over, "And that's how we separate the chaff from the grain."

Killian shot him a death look, "—Watch it."

"Wow! She fell off in less time than I did!" Dori exclaimed.

"What happened?" Addie ran up.

"She set the record for the shortest time on the course," Dori said casually.

"Why don't you get it on the loudspeaker and call the teachers out so they can see?" I groaned, standing up with the help of Emma and Galahad. My siblings were surprised at my snappy retort. All the kids were surrounding me in a circle murmuring, "Oh my gosh, that's so embarrassing," "I'm glad I wasn't that bad," and other things I began to block out.

I didn't look at any of them. Kaine approached me and tried to put his hand on my shoulder, "Are you okay, kid...?"

I brushed his hand off. I marched right toward all the startled kids. Dante was still standing behind them.

The crowd parted. This sort of thing never happened to me, so I must have looked like death. I stopped in front of Dante, making him come to a halt.

"What the heck was that?" My voice was clear and angry now.

"I didn't expect...."

"For me to in *no way* be ready for it and *fail miserably* exactly like I said I would?" I said, my voice rising. The crowd of kids was coming over and murmuring, but I didn't care.

Dante knit his brow at me, "The only way to get ahead in life is to *move*."

Those words sounded like Galahad, so I shouldn't have disagreed. "If I'd gotten the chance to talk to Kaine, I might have been able to put off the course till I was ready!"

He crossed his arms and stepped towards me, "And when exactly would that be? After you've put it off so long, you've lost the nerve?"

"You threw me at it!"

Dante spread his hands. "So? Kaine dragged me?"

"You figured you'd kill me then? It's easy for you to push. You can do it already," I snapped.

"I *couldn't* when I started," he said.

"Well, thanks for embarrassing me in front of everyone! Now I'm probably never gonna finish that stupid thing! I don't know why I agreed to do this in the first place!" My eyes grew moist.

He'd been about to retort, but he looked guilty. "Elsha…"

I turned away from him, nearly walking into Emma. Emma shot Dante a death glare, "You jerk!"

I hid in the girl's locker room for the rest of gym, feeling embarrassed, sad, and angry. I'd agreed to this for my brother and the rest of my family, but I'd never belonged in this place.

#

I barely ate a morsel at lunchtime. Emma tried to cheer me up by saying it wasn't that bad, but I wasn't buying it. Next was the History of the Commissioned with Tulken. I was sitting somewhere in the middle beside Emma in the slightly larger classroom. It had a sloped floor leading up to rows of seats. At the bottom of the room with a long blackboard with a desk where Tulken was standing. This was a class where I would be taking notes. Tulken went over the course curriculum and what we'd be covering. Tulken explained that long ago, Manor's had been formed because of all the children called with special abilities. God's angels were sent to form safe havens for the student's and those gifted in sorcery set up a barrier around every Manor and the outside world. The Manor of Raziel had a magical barrier around it which Collins formed with other sorcerers some time ago. The academies and schools for the Commissioned were founded after generations of them grew up and wanted to teach others. Most of it was details on what he'd told us before. Tulken explained there was a Manor for every large city and even some towns.

"Every Manor is run in a slightly different fashion where they focus on specific aspects of the Commissioned. Some focus more on education for the sake of evangelizing others, some mostly on battle tactics like our neighboring Manor."

Emma's hand shot up, "Which one is that?"

"The Manor of Samael in San Francisco. They're known as the destroyers of God to sinners," Tulken said.

Killian lifted his head, "—You're kidding?"

Tulken took off his glasses and cleaned them. "Not at all. The headmaster there prioritizes ensuring his students are educated in how to kill demons first and foremost. He finds their knowledge of history and even their education of magic to be somewhat superfluous unless they can fight."

"Sounds like a cool Manor—let's visit there," Killian said.

Tulken smiled, putting his glasses back on. "If you think Kaine is a difficult gym teacher, he'd be *kind* compared to those at Samael's Manor."

"Let's *not* visit there," Micah shook his head.

Tulken laughed and continued teaching. Emma wasn't paying as much attention. She was too busy looking at a small potted plant that was an assignment from Clary's class this morning. Each of us was supposed to grow something, and I could tell she was anxious about it. I tried to take notes for both of us. Eventually, Emma got her head in the game and wrote some in her notebook. The class finished, and we all got up, grabbing our things. Emma was frowning, looking down at her plant as she went ahead to the front of the class. She went down the list of questions for Tulken. Killian was behind her, complaining that she was keeping us.

Emma shot him a look before looking down at Tulken. "Sorry, I know I ask a lot of questions...."

Tulken knit his fingers on his desk and looked up at her. "And why would that be a problem?"

Emma blinked. "I just...I know it annoys *some people.*" She glanced over her shoulder at Killian, who crossed his arms and looked away.

"The people who ask a lot of questions are usually the ones paying enough attention to have them. You're what we call inquisitive—I respect that. Your brother should, too," he gestured to Killian, who immediately looked guilty. Emma beamed, finishing up her list. When she was done, she walked out with her plant in hand, and I followed.

Galahad was suppressing laughter. It wasn't often he'd gotten to see an adult put Killian in his place, partially because we had no adults who weren't evil back at the Boarding House.

We made it to Kaine's class, and Emma told me she was going to get special tutoring from Clary so she could help her plant. Kaine wasn't much less scary at teaching Demonology 101. He commanded attention and glared at the students from the front of the class. If we got answers wrong or acted out, he openly told us that we'd have to drop and do pushups. When Killian heard this, he smugly said, "Bring it on."

Galahad groaned, shaking his head. He was always quiet in class. Galahad tried to pay so much attention that he never had to bother the teacher with questions. That, and Galahad openly told me he felt speaking to other people was like bothering or intruding upon them—even in a classroom.

Kaine arched an eyebrow at Killian, "Don't push me, kid. It's your first day, and if you spend it with your nose to the floor, you're not gonna learn much."

Killian sat back.

The classroom was somewhat full. I guessed there were quite a few kids who hadn't yet gotten the basic Ed. I recognized Dori, Jasmine, and Addie but not most of the others. I was still silent as the grave because of my embarrassment in the gym. The last thing I needed was to be stuck with a teacher whose class I'd horribly failed. I sat in the back and slouched down so Kaine wouldn't look at me. I hoped to sharpen my pencil and look busy, but my sharpener was broken.

Perfect.

Micah must have seen my discontented expression because he held out his hand and mouthed *let me try.*

I shrugged and handed it to him quietly so as not to interrupt Kaine's lecture. Micah fiddled with it in his hands. Kaine was walking back and forth slowly before the class in his large black combat boots. His army cap was slightly turned, and his dog tags were out as he looked down at all of us.

"So….you all want to get right out there in the world and kill some demons, huh?"

Micah shook his head while he fiddled with the sharpener.

"Ya'll can't kill demons if you don't know how to recognize 'em. This world is full of ugly, horrible, freakish losers….and you've got to learn how to tell them apart from the supernatural kind," Kaine said.

Emma pulled her head back, "That's not very nice...."

Kaine arched his head at her. "You can *ask—questions—after*...till then, listen up."

Emma scrunched her nose, looking away.

"In this class, you'll learn how to spot demons, witches, goblins, and the main freaks gallery apart from other creatures. You'll learn how they're made, the difference between them, and most importantly...how to kill them. The first thing we're gonna look at is what we call *The Third*," Kaine turned to the board and pulled down a screen. He pressed a few buttons on the computer to project an image. I glanced up and froze. They were just drawings but still vivid enough to make my blood curdle. At the center of the images was a demon with red skin and horns. His skin was wrinkled, and his eyes were deep black. It was humanoid, but like it had been distorted somehow. I saw the name below the image: Asmodeus.

I swallowed.

"These guys were the first to fall in what we call the rebellion," Kaine said.

Emma's hand shot up, "You mean when Lucifer rebelled against God?"

Kaine nodded, "Right—he took a third of the angels with him. These guys are the ones we've identified as the OGs. We really can't know how many there were, but past Commissioned has seen these freaks in the flesh."

I swallowed my fear and raised a trembling hand. Kaine nodded in my direction. "Are we...gonna have to fight them?"

Kaine gave a small weak smile. "No, not unless all hell breaks loose. Most of these guys have been cast into one pit or another, bound by spells. One of the few who was free for the longest time is this ugly mug," Kaine gestured to the picture in the center. "Asmodeus."

"What do you mean *for the longest time?*" Emma said.

Kaine's expression grew in displeasure at the images. "Of all the Third...next to Lucifer as the worst of the worst was this guy. Everywhere Asmodeus went, he spread sin, chaos, and violence bringing out the worst in people. Demons jumped in line behind him. He used dark magic to get mortals to his side and screwed up some good people. A bunch of Commissioned died to get him out of the world. So now....he's no longer active."

There was something in the way Kaine said it that made me doubt. It almost sounded like he wasn't sure the demon really was out of the fight. I didn't press it. I was grateful to hear we wouldn't have to deal with him.

"Hypothetically, what would we do if we met a demon like that?" Emma said, her hand still up.

Kaine was still looking at the image. He looked down and fingered his dog tags, "The best advice I got besides praying? Demons are fallen. They prey on our weaknesses and pull us into depths we can't get out of on our own. Think about whatever it is that you got to live for— if you don't...just being around a demon like that can poison you. Greed, fear, anxiety, anger, the more you let them grow, the more power a demon can have over you."

I was frozen in fear just hearing about it. A voice snapped me back to reality.

"Hey."

I caught my breath. My pencil fell from my hands and rolled under Galahad's seat in front of me. Micah was leaning slightly out of his chair, holding my pencil sharpener.

"I fixed it for you."
I looked down. He had indeed. "...Thanks."

Micah gave a small smile looking back down at the figurine he was repairing.

Kaine was smacking the side of the projector like it was glitching.

159

He leaned out and looked down the row of seats at Micah and me. "Hey kid—"

Micah raised his head.

Kaine gestured down at the projector with his head, "Try your hand at this, will yah?"

Chapter Twelve
The Dyers Spy? Ha! Believe It

The rest of the week was like the first day. In other words: a bit of a mad house where some of my siblings excelled and I failed miserably. Ecology wasn't my speed. Emma thought her plants died? Mine were practically laughing at me. I overwatered my project, and Clary looked with a horrified expression saying, ".... You murdered it." Emma sought Clary's help after school for her plants, and surprisingly—they weren't dying anymore. In Magic 111, our first small assignment was a pop quiz at the end of the week, which I failed. The questions were far too confusing. Rules of magic, what made it light and dark, I tried, but it was all just too complicated. Every rule had a bylaw, and bylaws had footnotes. My siblings weren't great in magic either, but Emma asked enough questions to keep up. Galahad never told me how he performed in subjects, I had to peek at his quiz scores or prod him. When I managed to find out, Galahad was always getting As'. One of the only things I retained from magic was something Collins told us about dark magic. He said there were some creatures that had an attraction to darkness and were associated with evil. One of them was serpents. That shed some more light to me as to why the kids here didn't like Dante. I'd learned over the week that Cleopatra and the other snakes at the Manor took a liking to him. I asked Collins, and he said it wasn't a cold fact, simply a theory that had been occasionally reinforced.

Tulken announced to us Friday evening that the faculty would hold a meeting to see if any of the new student's gifts had been discovered. The gym was a nightmare the whole week, in which I avoided eye contact with Dante. On Tuesdays and Thursdays, we were forced to practice fencing (because Percival believed it was necessary for students to have a basic knowledge of swords).

My heart wasn't in most of the activities. Friday night was the students' party night, and I was sitting up in my room looking down at my security blanket: Bella, my doll. Emma had made her some new

161

clothes to cheer me up. That was one thing about the Manor beside the gardens that excited Emma: the maids' household magic included sewing. They had a small cottage on the land where they lived and kept a sewing workshop. They let Emma use some of their leftover material. Emma was sitting on the window seat of our room, watering her flowers. Since getting Clary's help, she had several on the window seat, blooming beautifully. I was in a large sweatshirt staring down at Bella.

My homework was by me, untouched. I'd never pass these classes. I'd never be cut out to be a demon hunter.

What was the point?

The only thing I cared about was finding out if this place and our freakish calling had anything to do with our parents leaving us. And Killian had warned me not to ask about it again. If I asked Tulken, it might get back to my siblings. And Galahad was trying to get us to move on with our lives. Still…the dreams I'd been having with that woman and that dark palace haunted me. And Tulken still didn't know why I had been able to see the witches and monsters when they were concealing themselves…

Emma got up from the window seat and sat by me on my bed. "Hey, you've been awfully quiet lately. What's… going on?" she brushed my hair behind my ears.

I looked up at her. "I'll never be a demon hunter if I can't even survive gym without making a fool of myself. I don't understand the magic business, and my plants die more than yours! I don't know why I ever agreed to this…." I whined, hanging my head.

Emma was silent for a long moment. "I do. You didn't want to disappoint Galahad, did you?"

My silence was basically like agreeing with her. I swallowed a lump in my throat and put my head on her shoulder pitifully, "No one else was complaining or saying they were scared to do this. I didn't want to be the only wimp holding us back…"

Emma put her arm around, resting her head against mine, "Don't even talk like that! You're not a wimp just because you're afraid. This is new to all of us, and we're all scared. Even Killian. And…Galahad appreciates you still holding out for our parents, he doesn't say it but he misses them too. Galahad remembers them better than any of us…so it's been the hardest on him."

I sniffled, "Did he say that?"

Emma let out a breath and grabbed a tissue box at the foot of the bed, "He doesn't have to. Galahad might not shout what he's going through from the rooftops with a megaphone like Killian, but he has feelings too. It's okay to miss our parents. But this is where we are now. You heard what Tulken said. We can go to school at the Manor and then go back to the normal world if we want. At least we'll know what's out there."

I nodded. "There's more."

Emma raised her eyebrows, "Did that weirdo do something else?"

I shook my head, knowing she spoke of Dante. "He's not a *weirdo,* Emma. He's just different, like the rest of us. No, not him. I've been having these dreams lately…." I told Emma everything about the castle, the red knight, the woman, about how they were looking for some people called The *Avengers*. Emma listened intently and jumped up when I was done.

"This is…big! We've gotta tell the boys! Maybe this has something to do with why you could see the witches and the goblin at Blech's. If you're seeing things in dreams…that might be a gift!"

I frowned, "Don't you think that's reaching a little?"

Emma rolled her eyes, getting up and rushing to the adjoining bathroom door. "Oh my gosh, Elsha, don't be such a defeatist!" She went to the door to the boys' room and opened it sticking her head inside, "BOYS! EMERGENCY FAMILY MEETING NOW!"

"Micah and I are busy! Besides, you can't call a family meeting!" Killian yelled from inside the room.

"I just did!" Emma argued.

"Tough to have a meeting by yourself!" Killian said. "Only the oldest can call a family meeting…."

"Then *I'm* calling a family meeting," Galahad came into our room. "What's going on Emma?"

Killian and Micah followed shortly after.

Micah raised a hand, "What are we having a meeting for?"

They all sat around the room. Killian lay on Emma's bed opposite mine and groaned in an annoyed fashion. Micah sat on the rug messing with one of the toys he'd gotten from the rec room and fixed it. Galahad stood in front of us and put his thumbs in his pockets, shifting back and forth slightly on his feet, awaiting what Emma and I had to say. "I think the girls are gonna tell us that."

Emma came over and sat by me, "Elsha, care to share?"

I began quietly. "I…I was telling Emma…"

"Somebody better share…." Killian said.

"SHE WOULD IF YOU COULD GO *TWO SECONDS* WITHOUT INTERRUPTING HER!" Emma turned to him. She looked back at me and put her hand on my arm encouragingly, "Go ahead, Elsha."

I told them what I told her. Killian sat up, growing invested as I spoke. Galahad and Micah only interjected to ask questions. When I was done, Galahad looked at me concerned, "Why didn't you tell us, Elsha?"

"I didn't think you guys would believe me," I admitted.

"We always believed you; it was our family rule. None of us lie, so if any of us says something, we all gotta back them, "Galahad quoted our father. For someone who didn't want to recall him, he sounded a lot like him sometimes.

"I've been seeing weird things for years, and only now are we getting any proof. And I know we always said that but be honest— you didn't really believe what I was seeing was real. And every time you guys covered for me…."

"I won't lie, it wasn't easy backing you when the stuff you saw…we thought it wasn't real. But if you'd told us about these dreams…we would have believed you," Killian sat up and looked at me. His tone had changed; he didn't like the idea that I didn't trust him to support me if worse came to worse.

"You don't listen to me; you're always too busy being upset about something else…." My voice shook a little. Killian always seemed preoccupied with his own problems. And if you mentioned yours, he would get mad that you were upset.

"I am not!" Killian raised his voice. "All of you are always blaming me for everything…."

"Killian," Galahad cautioned. "Elsha's trying to tell us something. Can you hear her out before we make this any more complicated?"

Killian swallowed. As soon as he said it, he had a look of guilt, "…But you're right, we haven't exactly listened to you the most in the past. I'm…*sorry*—about that."

165

"We all are. Trust is just words if we can't really depend on each other. No matter how crazy what we say is, we have to believe it, okay?" Galahad looked around.

"I promise I'll believe you guys," It was barely loud enough for them to hear.

"Even if we say we saw a pink unicorn dancing to single ladies on the lawn with Dori riding her in a flotation device?" Micah said.

Galahad shut his eyes, sounding forcibly calm, "Yes, Micah….even that."

"With Dori, I could believe that," Killian made all of us laugh.

"What do we do now? These dreams might be a sign of Elsha's gift, or maybe that something else is going on," Emma got us back on track. "Who are these Avengers?"

"That's exactly what we're going to find out. And the first place to look is the books. Killian, and Micah, you two check out the library and see what you can find. Emma, you, and I are going to…." Galahad began.

"I know, I know, we go to Dashiel in his late-night fencing lesson, and I flirt with him so we can learn what he knows about it," Emma said as if that were perfectly obvious.

Galahad looked at her strangely, "That's…not what I was gonna say."

"No, but that's what she wanted," Micah whispered to Killian.

They laughed.

"I'm serious—Dash might know something," Emma pressed.

"No telling the headmaster. Or anyone else, we keep this completely to ourselves. Clear?" Galahad said.

Killian hopped off the bed with a huff, "Why? You don't trust the faculty this little *safe haven* all of a sudden?"

Galahad sighed, shooting him a look, "Killian…."

Killian walked over, "I know, I know…*hands in*. Gosh, I'm sick of that tradition."

We all walked over to him and put our hands in.

Killian was the last to comply, "Fine…my hands there—yah happy?"

"As long as you don't mess this up—perfectly," Emma said.

"Alright, Dash, get ready because here we come!" Micah said.

I smiled to myself, wondering why I didn't tell my family about my problems sooner. Galahad began to tell Emma we were not going to flirt with Dashiel when he paused in the doorway. Killian walked into Galahad like he'd bumped into a rock wall and stumbled back, knocking the rest of us over like dominos. Killian growled, getting to his feet and dusting his jeans off, "What! We're not having another family meeting *now*, are we?"

Galahad didn't notice the rest of us getting up. "The faculty, they're having a meeting to talk about potential gifts. If we could listen in…."

"Faculty does meetings on the third floor. How are we supposed to get up there without being noticed?" Emma said.

Galahad's expression looked lost in thought. He looked at us, "I have an idea. But Killian, you gotta come with me. Girls, I want you hitting the books with Micah instead."

"No!" Emma said. Galahad looked at her in surprise. "Elsha and I want to know what's going on here too. Whatever you have in mind, we can help. Elsha's been having dreams, and she has a right to listen in on that meeting. They're gonna talk about what gifts we might have."

"You don't even know what the plan is…." Galahad cautioned. "You don't have to protect us from everything, Galahad. Just because we can't pass gym doesn't mean we can't…." Emma began. "Scale the wall of the Manor and make it to the third floor?" Galahad interjected.

Emma blinked. She and I exchanged glances. Emma and I went over to the window seat. We opened the window and stuck our heads out, looking up. It was cold outside. The sky was full of clouds like it was going to rain soon. The wall had terraces and a pipe with some vines and plants growing up it. On the third floor, there was a light coming out of a room illuminating a balcony. For an athletic person, it was possible. Truth be told, for an average person, it *might* have been possible. But for a below-average person like me?

Less possible.

Still, I couldn't be too scared to do this. It left all the responsibility to Galahad and Killian, and that wasn't fair.

I groaned. I expected Emma to retreat, but I was committed.

"So what!" Emma pulled her head back inside.

I followed her. "Wait—what?"

"We can take it! There're vines out there to help us make the climb. It's time you trusted your sisters to do something around here!" Emma put her hands on her hips proudly. "Right, Elsha? I'm not scared!"

"I am, "I confessed. Galahad was looking at me, waiting for an answer. "…But I can do it."

#

Micah climbed out a ledge for me at Blech's, Galahad and Killian climbed over a fence and into a dumpster for my dolls, and Emma

168

climbed up to my bunk every night so we could talk instead of letting me cry myself to sleep. I had to remind myself of all these little seemingly small acts. They were the things that got me through each day. I didn't know what other people in the world spent waking hours thinking about, what made them feel loved, but for me, it was those things. In light of all that....I zipped up my large sweatshirt and tied my sneakers, getting ready to make the climb. Galahad wanted to go last as a precaution. Emma went out more bundled than me: she had a zipped-up pink coat, fuzzy gloves, a hat, and a scarf. Mostly clothes the maids had helped her sew.

Lastly, Emma put on ear muffs and put her hands on her hips proudly, "Just....get out of my way."

Galahad was in his grey sweatshirt and jeans by the window, looking at her. "Be careful, and do exactly as I say. I did climbs like this back at Blech's, and it's all about knowing where to put your feet and what to grab."

Emma went out first. Initially, all we heard from her was, "Oh my gosh, it's freezing!" "I should have worn a bigger coat!" "My nose is numb!" She complained, but she still took hold of the thick vines on the side of the Manor. She stepped on bricks so as not to put all her weight on the plant. I followed her lead. After grabbing hold of a vine and going up two steps, I was already tired. But the third floor wasn't far. That wasn't the scary part.

I looked down to make sure Galahad was below us. That was the scary part. The yard and the gardens below seemed incredibly small; the wind was blowing harder the higher up we went. I froze with my hand on a vine. There were small figures of students below walking around; they probably couldn't see us because it was so dark. But suddenly, I was too scared to go any higher.

"Elsha," Galahad said, snapping me to reality. "I'm right here, and I'm not gonna let you fall. You're a few feet away from that balcony, just grab hold of the thickest vines and pull yourself up."

I steadied my breathing and went up a couple more feet. Emma was above me. She pulled herself against the thick vines beside the ledge. She reached out, grabbed the terrace, and strained to pull herself up. I made it next to her, and she reached out. "Take my hand!" she whispered urgently.

I was tired, and my arms ached from the small bit of exertion. I was clinging tightly to the vine, trembling. It was too late to turn back now, my face plastered against the side of the Manor. I caught my breath. Galahad was below me watching. I couldn't chicken out. "God help me…" I breathed before reaching out to Emma.

My fingers brushed the tips of hers.

I lost my footing. My life flashed before my eyes as sheer terror stopped a scream in my throat.

Chapter Thirteen

Everyone Has A Gift...Well, Almost Everyone

The feeling of your body dropping through the air isn't fun. I'd felt it when I was much younger in our old home—I was outside playing a game with Galahad. I'd climbed our treehouse and fallen flat on my back when one of the boards came loose. All the pain from that fall flashed in my mind now as I fell from the side of the Manor. Then I stopped.

Something like a rope wrapped around my waist and pulled me against the Manor. I grunted as I connected with the brick wall flattening my hands against the cold surface. It was dark, but I could see the vague shape of a vine around my waist as I looked down. Emma's hand was still out, and she was breathing hard. I gasped, "How...that didn't...what just..."

"No time to answer that. Pull her up!" Galahad climbed up next to me. He put his hand on my back to ensure I wasn't going anywhere as the vine helped lift me to the terrace. Galahad grabbed the edge of the terrace and did a chin-up pulling himself onto it. He put his hands on my shoulders and looked me in the face, "Are you okay?"

I nodded, still trembling.

Emma was in shock, but as she relaxed, the vine retreated to the wall. All our mouths were hanging open. Emma shook her head, "Did I...."

Galahad looked at her, "I don't think we'll have to listen to that faculty meeting to learn *your* gift."

#

We'd landed on the terrace of the meeting room. Not the one the faculty was in (thank God), but the lights were on. We crept out of the room and into the hallway, trying to be as quiet as possible. Emma was still in shock. Once that faded, she was amazed. Galahad told her to be amazed more quietly as we tried to figure out what room Tulken and the other professors were in.

Galahad was lightly pressing his ear to doors while Emma went on. "I mean, I can't believe I really have control over plants, me! Everything I made at Blech's died, and now I control vines by just thinking about it!"

"Shh!" Galahad said.

"Right, sorry!" Emma whispered.

"Help me check these doors and do it quietly," Galahad said.

"Got it, and no matter what happens—even if we're discovered....be cool," Emma pressed her ear to a door that opened. "AAAHHH!" she stumbled back.

Dashiel was standing in the doorway, rigid as ever. He knit his brow. "—Emma," he said as if Galahad and I weren't even standing there.

Emma's breathing quickened as she attempted to look casual and leaned on the wall, "H-hey Dash! We were just taking a tour, seeing the sights and all that...how are things?"

"Sufficient. What brings you to the third floor?" he arched an eyebrow at us.

"We were....we um...let me tell you exactly what we're doing...." Emma began.

"We're looking for our brothers. Not sure what they got themselves into, but they got a little carried away in one of their games, "Galahad said.

Dashiel nodded. He seemed to buy that excuse. "You all appear as though you've been braving the elements," he curiously gave us a once-over. "Pray tell, how did you get wet searching for your brothers inside the Manor?"

I hadn't even noticed it had sprinkled on us while we were outside. Our sweatshirts were damp. Emma took that one.

"We left our windows open," she said quickly.

Dashiel raised an eyebrow, "Why would you stay inside just to open your windows with a storm brewing?"

Emma rolled her eyes, "Well, duh! We can't open them *outside*! Use your head."

Dashiel put his fingers to his temple.

"What?" Emma said.

"My brain has difficulty adapting to your family's breed of logic," he said quietly.

I huffed, "Good luck trying."

"If you'll excuse me, there's a meeting I have to attend," Dashiel pulled at the cuffs of his dark blue shirt before walking by us down the hall.

Emma followed. "What meeting?"

"It is the concern of the administrators," he spoke quickly.

Galahad easily kept in step with Dashiel, "Why would you have to attend that? Aren't you just the assistant fencing instructor?"

Dashiel looked at him peculiarly, "Professor Percival requested me there. As Tulken announced, after the first week of study, the faculty holds a conference to see if they've discovered any of the student's gifts. We make these assessments based on the instructor's testimony, and I've been asked to report in."

"You couldn't give us a little hint as to what you're all suspecting our gifts are?" Emma smiled.

Dashiel paused at the door at the end of the hall and looked at her trying to comprehend. It was a good three seconds before he responded, "No." He opened the door and gave us one last look, "Go find your brothers, and remember the third floor is for faculty only. Don't keep yourselves here for an unnecessary amount of time, or I'll be forced to inform the Professors. And as neither of us would take pleasure in causing your family grief or punishment, I hope in the future you adhere to the rules, Emma."

And he shut the door.

"Yikes....I have to agree with Killian on this one," Galahad squatted by the door.

Emma and I dropped our mouths in alarm. Emma stuttered, "Now, Galahad, let's not go crazy...."

Galahad's eyes grew large, "I just mean, he's a stiff."

Emma frowned before getting down next to him. I pressed my ear to the door as well. I instantly recognized all the voices: Tulken, Percival, Clary, Collins, and Kaine. As always, Percival and Kaine were bickering, and Clary was trying to make peace. Eventually, Tulken quieted them down. "I trust this meeting has another purpose besides identifying the Dyer's gifts," Dashiel said.

"A few, in fact," Tulken said carefully. "Collins, what of that matter I asked you to look into?"

Collins' usually bubbly voice was tense, "I've looked...and I can't find anything on these people. It's like they never existed. That makes me think..."

"Do you believe it could be a sign of dark magic?" Tulken said after a long pause.

"It would depend on the children's reactions to it," Collins said.

"Elsha says she remembers her parents, but everything is vague, like she can't describe them. It's the same for all of them," Tulken said carefully.

"What are they saying?" Emma whispered.

It took a moment for it to sink in. I thought back to Magic 111. Collins said that what made dark magic different from light was it broke the fundamental rules. If only I remembered them all...

I racked my brain. Dante had answered that question (yes, I mostly recall some of it because he was talking). One of the rules was magic cannot alter reality. If someone does attempt to alter reality with dark magic, there are consequences and signs that something is off. Memories are altered, stories don't line up, and something won't quite make sense. Collins suspected...

I pressed my ear closer, not wanting to miss a word.

"It could be a sign, but I don't want to say anything for certain. It would take a powerful sorcerer to even *attempt* a spell like that without losing his life. Someone immersed in dark magic with proficient knowledge. No random sorcerer or demon can cast a spell over the Commissioned," Collins said.

"If there was a demon powerful enough to cast such a spell, it would be deteriorating as we speak...." Tulken mused.

There was a painfully long silence before Dashiel interjected. "With all due respect Tulken, the possibility of demonic intervention is slim at best. There are a thousand natural-world explanations for the disappearance of Mr. and Mrs. Dyer. What does this have to do with the matter that's come to Kaine's attention?"

Percival spoke next. "For the past three years, we've been getting signs and sightings from the active Knights of Valor and from Samael's Manor. Nothing concrete, but the dark forces are gathering, and it's under someone powerful. Violent crimes and the persecution of the Commissioned have spiked. You know what that means, Headmaster...."

"One of the Third," Tulken said gravely.

"We have to tell the students; it's important they know what's at stake," Clary said.

"I agree with Mads. We tell the kids and put together a force now to go find the son of a…." Kaine began.

"Just like you, Kaine—thinking with your fists and letting your brain take a vacation," Percival said condescendingly. "We don't even know which of the Third this is. And it would take the most battle-ready of all our students to even attempt a mission like this."

"I hate to be the bearer of bad news…but if these sightings started three years ago, it's perfectly possible the most likely of the Third to cause this…." Collins fumbled nervously.

"I feared as much. That's why the situation of the Dyers is of such great concern to me," Tulken said.

Silence.

Percival cleared his throat, "Surely…you don't mean *those* five?"

"After what Kaine has informed me of, it would be about time for them to surface. Nothing happens without reason, Percival."

"I know, Headmaster, but…*them*?" Percival said.

"Some of them have shown real progress. There are several gifts Galahad and Killian could have. Micah and Emma are a little more difficult to pin down, but…." Clary began positively.

"What about short stop?" Kaine said.

"She's definitely not gifted at fencing…." Percival began.

"Percival!" Clary cautioned.

"Much as I *love* to disagree with chip drama pants over here…he has a point," Kaine said through what sounded like clenched teeth. "I like the little one as much as you, H.M.T., but if she doesn't fit the bill…they can't be the ones."

"The ones to do what??" Emma whispered urgently.

"She has no gifts as far as we know," Percival said.

"Everyone has gifts. What you mean is her supernatural gifts haven't manifested yet. We don't have much time. There have been signs for three years...he wasn't truly imprisoned," Tulken said.

"You really believe..." Professor Clary said.

"Don't go tossing the name around, sweetheart. It ain't good for morale," Kaine said.

"If he really wasn't imprisoned, none of us are ready for the battle that's to come," Dashiel said.

"As always, Dashiel, you lack the ability to see the silver lining behind the clouds. We cannot alarm the students. And there is no need to tell the Dyer family of what we suspect until we're certain," Tulken said.

A thousand questions were soaring through my mind. Who was coming based on signs? My mind went back to Kaine's class. I was going to ask Galahad because he was usually better at retaining class material than me. But it seemed as if we remembered the details all at once. Emma, Galahad, and I exchanged glances. Details from my notes and memory were falling into place like a puzzle:

Only the Third can inspire chaos like killings, earthquakes, tremors, etc.

-Most of the Third had been caught or imprisoned.

-The chaos was happening for three years, and that was when Kaine said....

A look of pure horror crossed our faces as it sunk in. Asmodeus was coming back.

Chapter Fourteen

God's Timing

The details of the conversation were still sinking in. The Professors seemed to see promise in all my siblings, but I was the weak link (as usual). Collins said what happened to our parents might have been a spell, but why to our family? Was it possible *we* were these five Tulken had talked about? What were the five supposed to do? If we were, why was I such a failure? What if there was more about my family I didn't understand? Maybe they'd made a mistake with me. Maybe I wasn't Commissioned. The sound of the storm hammering on the roof grew heavier as I backed away from the door. Galahad was shocked by the news as well, but as always, he was more concerned about me.

I parted my mouth to speak. Something crashed outside.

"That sounds like it came from the garden!" Emma said. The three of us rushed to the stairs and hurried down to the second floor. Students were hanging out in the halls and the loft talking.

Dori was leaning on the wall waving her hand, "And I'm like Kaine, I was the ambassador of the Himalayan hula dancing guppy society—why do I have to pass this obstacle course to prove I'm battle ready?"

Addie shut her eyes, "You know that's not a real thing…."

"It is if I say it is…." Dori began.

We all came to a skidding halt, nearly ramming into Addie, Dori, and Jasmine.

Dori jolted back, "—AAAH!"

We all stopped an inch from her. "We heard something crash outside. Is everything okay?" Emma said.

"Yeah…. where are your other brothers?" Jasmine gestured to us.

Emma scoffed, "As if we were always together?"

Jasmine blinked.

"Okay, we kind of are…"

"I think Professor Clary's hanging garden was having trouble with the storm, so the boys went out to help," Addie said. "Her garden?" Emma exclaimed.

Galahad hurried down the stairs. "I'll go help!"

"Wait for me!" Emma adjusted her earmuffs as she scurried after him. "Back out into the storm, cold, hail, sleet, and Canadian winds…" she grumbled.

I groaned, looking at Dori, Addie, and Jasmine.

"Don't look at me! I don't care about nutty Clary's vegetable garden," Dori griped.

I followed Galahad and Emma. I darted down the stairs, and students looked at me in surprise. The living room was warm and smelled like pizza. Friday night was homemade pizza night at the Manor. I'd been spending most of the nights hiding up in Emma and I's room after my embarrassing week, so I'd planned to miss it. Now with how good it smelled, I wasn't sure I could. I only had a few seconds to take in the scent as I grabbed a raincoat by the door and hurried out into the storm. As soon as I stepped on the front porch, the wind hit me. Taking the back door would have made more sense since the garden was behind the house. I walked off the porch and hurried around to the back of the house. There were overhanging lights that had been torn and were blowing in the wind and hail. Several bodies were in long raincoats, trying to tie a tarp down and cover the garden. Galahad was tying down one end with Emma, and Dante was in a long cloak struggling to pull down the other. It must have happened suddenly because the teachers hadn't even heard. If Clary knew her garden was threatened, she might have thought the demon threat wasn't a top priority right now.

My sneakers sloshed through the mud awkwardly as I made my way to Dante. I only recognized him by his tall boots and the way the light from the lamps illuminated his rings. His boots were sliding in the mud, making it difficult for him to keep his hold on the rope. I hurried to his side and grabbed the rope beside him.

He turned, looking at me. His green eyes widened in shock, "…Elsha?" I barely heard him through the rain.

"Pull!" I said, making him refocus on his task. We both pulled and tied the rope down to the post in the ground. We all were able to cover the garden together though it took a lot of rolling in the mud and getting soaking wet. As I made sure it was secure, hail was coming down, and Dante fell in the mud. I turned, extending a hand to him as water sprayed my face.

He looked up at my hand as his hood fell back. "It's a little cold out here for you, isn't it?" he said as I helped him up.

I shrugged. I'd been hiding from the elements along with everything else most of my life. Now outside, standing in it, I felt…some freedom. I looked up at the beauty of nature storming down. "Nah, it's actually kind of…."

Dante squinted, seeing through the soaked hair that was hanging over his eyes. "Freezing and wet?"

"Nice!" I said over the storm.

He stared at me for a long moment. He broke into a blindingly white smile and shook his head. "You're…. something else, Elsha Dyer."

"WHY ARE ALL OF YOU STILL OUT HERE WHEN IT'S FREEZING? I'M GOING INSIDE! ELSHA, GET IN HERE BEFORE YOU CATCH YOUR DEATH OF COLD!" Emma said, rushing inside. Me, Killian, Galahad, and Dante all laughed as we walked back towards the house. Dante held up his cloak to block me from the hail as we ran. We went to the front door, and I let the rain hit me in the face before I walked inside. Dante did the same. I walked onto the porch and was about to go inside when Dante stopped me.

"Thanks for the help out there." He shook the water out of his hair and ran his hand through it. His eyes looked pretty in the rain, and it gave them a luminous glow. I brushed the hair out of my eyes and held my arms; I was shivering, but surprisingly… I didn't mind.

"Don't mention it."

"Look, about what I said a while back in training…" he began.

"You don't have to…"

"Don't always be the martyr, okay—I'm trying to apologize. I didn't mean to be so hard on you. I just don't want you to be afraid to take a shot at…whatever you could be."

"Why?" I said, genuinely curious. "You don't know me."

"Because…I was almost kept out of the Manor because of fear. If I never would have had a chance to practice magic… I came from a Boarding House, just like you. The kids there wanted me gone, and so did most people here. But if I hadn't tried, I'd never have been anything. I don't like to see untapped potential go to waste," he said.

I nodded, "Okay…I think you're wrong, though."

He narrowed his gaze, wringing out his black robe, "I'll bite— about what?"

"I…I don't believe you were ever nothing," my breath shook. My face was hot despite the cold, and I didn't know if I'd choked the words or gurgled them.

He met my gaze. That was all the reassurance I needed. There was something in the way he looked at me, and I could only compare it in a small way to the reassurance Galahad gave me with his gaze. It made me want to step outside my comfort zone and try to be better. To be what he believed I was. It was like that when Dante looked at me. And the thought that maybe…my family was called some great destiny, and I was the weak link stopping them….I couldn't accept that.

Dante smiled at me. I wasn't sure, but I may have turned to sugar and melted from the raindrops right there on the porch.

"Thanks, you'd be one of the few to think that." Dante walked past me and pushed open the front door. "Are you gonna stay down for dinner or…"

"Yeah," I nodded, coming back to reality. Dante nodded and gestured for me to follow him with his head. "Dante!"

He paused, looking back at me.

My heart was pounding. "I…I want to pass the combat class….I need help with my fencing and gym, I mean. If I could do that…maybe…."

"You could pass Kaine's course?"

I nodded. "Would you…would you help me?"

Dante was surprised. I didn't know if he'd suspect the other possible reasons that I would ask him for help and not Dashiel. I prayed he didn't. But if my family could be called to greatness and I was the only chink in the armor…I had to get it together. Dante crossed his arms, resting in the doorway, "You know it's gonna really stick it to Uriah that you asked me and didn't go to him or his crew…."

"Yeah…"

"I already like the idea," Dante grinned. "We start tomorrow at dawn."

"Dawn? Are we allowed to be up that early?" I followed him inside, and he laughed.

"Yes, youngest Dyer-it's just more students prefer to do things like sleep and have breakfast…" he said as if those were silly. When we were inside, he took off his cloak and shook the water from it hanging it up. I closed the front door, and Addie's mom came out of the kitchen.

"Are you guys okay?"

"Gardens all taken care of," Dante gave a slight bow.

Uriah was sitting on the couch by the fireplace reading, and he spoke without looking up, "Exhilarating—could you close the door, or do you want to get the Manor more soaked than it already is?"

I hadn't even realized we were dripping on the carpet.

Dante held out his cloak and squeezed the last drops of water from it directly before him on the carpet pettily.

One of the maids let out a scream.

Uriah's cold gaze looked up from his book.

Dante hung up his cloak, "Happy, captain righteous?"

Uriah's brow contracted before he looked back down, "…*Joyous*."

Calisto waved her hand at them, "Knock it off, you boys! Kids, thank you so much for helping Clary's Garden. All the pizzas are out of the oven, so I hope you're hungry." I took off my knit hat shaking water from my hair, and went into the kitchen with the rest of the kids to get food. The maids were on the couch watching some soap operas as we all got food. Uriah was reading *Laws and history of the Commissioned* as his falcon was perched on his arm. His sister was by him studying with the other kids from their group. Uriah's eyes flashed up when I mentioned Dante was going to train me. It ate at him just like Dante had said. That made me a little more encouraged. I knew I'd have to get up early the next day, but I didn't want to think about it then. It was my first real Friday night at the Manor. I wanted to have fun. Tomorrow, the real work started.

#

In my defense, when Dante said *at dawn*—it really wasn't that clear. So naturally....I overslept. Little did I know, Dante had enlisted my youngest brother to get me up. My face was down in my pillow when I felt someone hopping on the side of my bed saying, "You gotta get up, you gotta get up IN THE MORNING!"

After trying to kill Micah for a good five minutes, he eventually got out, "Wait, wait, Dante told me to come to wake you up! Elsha, AAAHH!" He was being overdramatic, really—like always. I was only beating him senselessly with a pillow.

The noise woke Emma up, and she started shouting, "IT'S FIVE AM! WHAT ARE YOU GUYS DOING MAKING ALL THIS NOISE? KILLIAN!" Killian really had nothing to do with it, but in Emma's mind, he had to. I let Micah scramble back to the boys' room, where Killian was now awake and blaming Emma for the noise. I forced myself to get dressed in gym clothes like a zombie (it was Dante's request if I trained, I had to dress right). I quietly went outside my room and closed the door. The loft and second floor were dead. The maids weren't even up to collect the laundry yet. I yawned and made my way down the stairs. Some of the windows in the Manor were cracked to let the cool morning air in. When I got to the bottom of the stairs, I paused. We'd gone up and down these stairs so many times that I never took time to really take in the painting on the wall that I'd noticed the first day. I stepped back against the banister and looked up at the tall wooden wall covered in art. I recognized some traditional angelic pictures, but others caught my eye. The creatures which were human-like in the paintings stood inhumanly tall; they wore combinations of white robes and knight-like armor with wings that spanned miles. A painting at the center depicted an angel with enormous white wings wearing a white and gold uniform with armor on his chest, arms, and legs. A hood covered his face, but he had a large red cross on his chest and a powerful sword that matched. At the bottom of the image, it read: The angel Raziel.

I caught my breath. That was the angel who founded this place. In other words....he was real. Did he really look like that? I had always thought of guardian angels as being small loveable baby cherubs or women in white gowns with a harp, never looking like that.

"Wow," I breathed, stepping down the stairs and passing the kitchen door. I smelled coffee and paused.

Who was up at this hour?

I peered inside to see Tulken resting against the counter, drinking a cup of Coffee. He was talking to Professor Collins, who was attempting to pour coffee into a mug while he had a stack of books tucked under one arm. He had his cartoonish wizard robe over his shoulder and was scrambling to write on some papers on the kitchen butcher block table. The number of things he tried to do at once seemed to even make Tulken nervous. As I watched, I saw the papers were flipping aside on their own as he marked them, and the small cream dish was pouring into his cup by itself.

"Try to calm yourself, Collins," Tulken tensely sipped from his mug that had a quote in block letters I couldn't read. The only thing I could make out from the doorway was the name CHARLES SPURGEON—whoever that was.

Collins glanced up at Tulken with a toothy grin beaming, "Oh, you know I always get excited when we're getting ready to announce students' gifts! This Friday is going to be big! Looking over everything the teachers have told us, it looks promising! Cream?" Collins said as the bottle of cream filled up his mug.

Tulken's eyes grew large, "Collins!"

"What? Ah! Now you stop that. Are you trying to make a mess?" Collins looked disapprovingly at the creamer, and it straightened, dropping on the table with a *thump!*

I knocked on the kitchen door lightly before sticking my head in.

Both professors looked at me. Tulken broke into a smile, "Elsha, what are you doing up so early?"

I swallowed nervously, but to be honest, I kind of wanted to tell him so he would know I wasn't slacking. "I…I'm getting fencing tutoring from Dante, and I wanted to be up bright and early."

Tulken looked pleased. "That's wonderful, and I'm so proud of you for putting in the effort. Don't push yourself too hard, though," he said with a hint of concern. "Five o clock is awfully early for someone your age to be up."

"Dante made it sound like he gets up early and stays up late to study magic, so…it won't hurt me," I said, trying to make it sound casual.

Tulken's expression grew slightly more serious, "Yes…that boy seems to prioritize those arts above all else. I trust some of his dedication won't hurt you."

Collins was fumbling to grab paper towels and clean up the spilled cream while the rags were hopping to his assistance by themselves. Tulken picked up his papers so they didn't get soaked as Collins reprimanded the creamer.

I swallowed, gesturing to the painting on the wall outside, "That…picture of Raziel, does he really look like that?"

Tulken grabbed a napkin, cleaning the cream from the table, "According to the Commissioned who founded this Manor, yes. But most likely, he was much more terrifying."

"Terrifying?" I said shocked.

Tulken nodded, "And he's only a servant." Tulken looked up at me, noticing my shock, "You're not familiar with the idea of angels as divine warriors of the Lord?"

"Uh…I guess I always imagined cherubs or women with harps," I said.

Tulken chuckled slightly, "According to the book of Isaiah, an angel of the Lord killed 180,000 Assyrian troops in *one* night. Angels don't serve as kind, cuddly protectors. Typically they only spoke to men when giving extremely grave or joyous news—or to end battles for God."

"Even guardian angels?" I asked.

Tulken shook his head, "There's no difference in the nature of the angel. Guardian angels don't merely exist to provide comfort; they're assigned to protect men from the devils' servants and many vices. Pride, greed, envy, and lust all have demonic forms, and they will seek a Commissioned's— very— *life*. When you've seen the true form of the enemy, you won't question why an angel would need to carry a cross sword."

I narrowed my gaze at Tulken's cup. "Headmaster, what does your mug say?"

His eyes grew slightly large before he glanced down, "Oh, this?" He turned it so I could see. "It says I never cease to wonder that God has elected me."

I blinked. It made perfect sense to me, but I couldn't fathom why someone like Tulken would identify with it. "Huh," I said.

Tulken smiled at my bafflement. "You're not the only one who has no idea why the almighty would choose you. Providential success with your training," he raised his mug as if toasting to me.

I nodded with a smile and hurried outside. Tulken's reassurance fueled me to go through with this. I was nervous as could be, and my heart was hammering, but I wasn't going to chicken out now. As I stepped out on the front stoop in the cold air, I was reconsidering, but it was too late now. I put my hands in the pockets of my sweatshirt to warm them and hurried around to the back of the manor. I followed the walkway to the trees and stone patio near the course. I saw a few people up, like the groundskeepers, Kaine and Clary. Clary was watering her flowers and checking on the damage to her garden from the storm. Galahad passed me on the walkway jogging.

I don't think he recognized me at first because as he passed me, he said, "On your left." He came to a skidding halt a few steps ahead of me and turned around. "...Elsha?" His expression said I could have knocked him over with a feather. He was happy to see me up early but in shock. I explained to him what I was doing, and he gave me a hug of encouragement before continuing off jogging. When he reached a small gymnasium area on the lot, he dropped to do pushups.

He was putting me to shame, and I hadn't even started exercising yet. I saw Dante in the distance sitting under a tree, reading with his legs crossed.

I was uncomfortable, as always—but I did my best not to let it be obvious for once. Dante closed his book and took me to the armory, which was on the lot in a separate building. I didn't mention that the walk to the armory was tiring me out. Inside the armory were so many kinds of weapons I was overwhelmed. It was a rust wooden building with racks on every wall of spears, axes, and swords. Dante stepped through it slowly and did a dramatic turn, facing me as he spread his hands.

"You want to learn swordplay… here are all the toys anybody could ever want."

I blinked dumbfounded, "Uh…what kind was Dashiel doing the other day?"

"Fencing," Dante held his arms shifting his weight back and forth on his feet.

"Is that what kids here mostly do?"

"No, that's just the one Percival teaches his best kids to show off how many styles they've learned. Fencing isn't only with rapiers. That's just what Percival likes best. Dashiel practices them all—the guy's super-human, I swear. Uriah would like to get to that level, but alas…." Dante grinned, "The poor soul is still…mortal."

"Okay…what's the most practical sword to start with?"

Dante arched an eyebrow, "If you're a baby step beginner?'"

"Like—below that."

"If you're, Dori?"

"If you stink."

Dante blinked in disbelief. He laughed eventually, "Uh…so, level negative one?" Dante turned and looked over the sword racks. "Hmm, let me see…*those* people use this." Dante's hand moved past the various types of swords and came to a wooden stick. Dante raised it, detaching several thick cobwebs before stepping towards me.

I looked down at the stick and back up at him in disbelief. "A stick? Can't I at least start with a wooden sword?"

Dante tossed the stick to me. I wasn't ready for it. My natural reaction kicked in, and I let out something like a squeal as I pulled my hands back. The stick hit the floor in front of me. Dante arched an eyebrow. He held out his hand and gestured with his fingers for something to come towards him. The stick on the floor radiated with green light and was slowly raised off the floor, flying into his hand. "Clearly…you're not ready for the wooden sword."

I couldn't argue after that horrible embarrassment. Dante recommended a step below the stick, but the only thing there was for that was the plunger—I said no. I was pitiful, but I had some dignity, okay? The first part of the training was Dante teaching me how to hold the stick as if it were an arming sword—he said that was what I'd probably be using most. We stayed on the field in the back of the armory for most of our training. Occasionally other kids would walk by and murmur or look, but I tried not to pay any attention to them. But I was human, so the snickers and comments made me feel like I needed to learn faster and get on the same level as these other kids.

On the second day, I begged Dante to use real swords. Dante was reading when I asked and casually agreed, taking me to the armory to gear up. In the armory was a section with sword fighting gear. I stood by, waiting for Dante to grab what I needed. As he did, my hopes sank. First, he grabbed a leather vest like a coat and strapped it onto me over my normal clothes. It was a little heavy, but I didn't mind it. Then he grabbed a fencing mask from the top row above the vests called gambesons and put it on me, and then a neck pad called a gorget for throat protection and, lastly, padded gloves. I felt like a trussed chicken who couldn't move my arms. When Dante waved to follow him going outside, I moved very slowly. We got outside, and Dante handed me an arming sword handle up.

I swallowed, straining to raise the sword, "So…now what?" I blinked behind my headgear.

Dante raised his sword with his book in the other hand, "Now, try the strikes I taught you."

"How?"

He glanced up from his reading, "Raise the sword."

I told my body to do that, but it wasn't listening.

I strained for a good long 30 seconds before getting the sword up and letting it fall directly afterward. I was panting now.

Dante was waiting when he looked up again, slapping his magic book shut. "Come on. I'm getting old over here."

I blinked, "I don't have any muscles."

"Of course you do. How do you think you walk anyplace?"

"I don't know if I can…."

"You can—you just have to use those muscles you're not used to moving. Now come on," Dante encouraged. I strained and got the sword up after some trial. We practiced the basic strikes, and I felt incredibly slowed down because of all the armor. Dante assured me it would do me good in the long run. We went at it again and again like that all morning, clear through breakfast. Dante didn't break for it, so he said I shouldn't either. I gradually learned that eating was something of an inconvenience to him that got in the way of his magical studies. I felt bad not seeing Emma and the rest of my siblings at breakfast for the next several mornings. All the "I can't, I have to train" and "I'm too sore" that kept me from rec and games made me feel terrible when I went to sleep. Occasionally I saw Galahad because he jogged around the campus in the morning, and he volunteered to practice with us. Galahad was more shocked than anyone to see me sticking with it because he'd tried to get me to be athletic for years, and I'd always said no. He was eager to assist in any activity that would get me outdoors or doing something physical. The fact that it excited him made me eager to stay with the training.

By Friday, my hands had been bruised and were growing stiff from holding the sword so much. I saw people come and go in the morning and had to keep from falling asleep in class that day; the week had been so long. That evening I got to the point where I was clashing blades in the slowest, most controlled fashion with Dante. He taught me where to step and how to move. I fought to keep up as we sparred Friday night on the same patch of grass. Dante never really looked like he was fighting me when we sparred, always deflecting me while I was trying my hardest. Dante was still reading his magic books while he deflected my blows (I thought he was doing that just to frustrate me). He'd have the magic book levitating in front of him at eye level and the pages turning on their own as he blocked my strikes. I slashed my sword at him again, and Dante raised him with one arm stopping it mid-blow. I was a little discouraged, but he told me good work, and we went inside to have dinner with the rest of the Manor. We missed most of the dinner, but Calisto left out the pizzas buffet style like always. Dante and I got ours and made our way into the living room, where all the kids were. I sat next to Emma and Galahad on the couch with my paper plate and slices of pizza. They asked me how training was going, and I told them I was getting better. Dante affirmed it. That made me smile a little brighter.

Some of the kids were playing games, and Killian was sitting against our couch on the floor by the fire. He looked as comfortable as a cat with a ball of yarn; he and Micah were deep in conversation, probably brainstorming their games and stories. Occasionally he glanced over at Addie but didn't get up to talk to her. Killian was sure of himself in most things, but I could tell when he was feigning confidence. And Addie's rebuffing him continuously must have made him want to pull back. Killian had always thought he should have had a girlfriend back when we were at Blech's, but he never could seem to form a relationship with any girls.

Still, if he really did like Addie, I felt bad she didn't seem to look his way. After a bit of eating and games, we retired to our rooms. It was announced that we'd get information on our gifts in letters. Surely enough, the next morning, we had letters from the faculty left at the mail slots by our assigned rooms. Emma called us all into the same room so we could read them aloud to each other. It was exciting. Same as I recall, Christmas morning: Emma, Micah, and Killian would be jumping for joy, itching to get up, and Galahad would be as relaxed and calm as ever. Galahad let everyone open their letters first.

Emma already knew her gift, but she wanted to see it on paper. I snuggled next to her so I could read it:

Emma Dyer. It has come to the attention of the Manor of Raziel's faculty and staff that you have been divinely gifted with a supernatural connection to plant life. We hope this allows you to narrow your field of study and fulfill your calling as God wills. We look forward to being instruments in helping you realize your full potential. Congratulations!

Respectfully, Edward Tulken

We all congratulated Emma and high-fived them. Next, we read Killian's, and the congratulatory remarks were much the same. Killian discovered he has superhuman speed, stamina, and reflexes— a unique gift for Commissioned. That didn't surprise any of us, but he was still very excited about it. Micah congratulated him and told him how cool it was, and so did the rest of us. Micah was trying to steady his breathing as he opened his letter. His mouth fell open as he read it," No way!" Micah's letter said he had an even more unique ability. He was what they called a Craftsmen—it was a gift that hadn't been seen in years. Micah could make art with his hand in any shape or form, and he could build and use tools from seemingly worthless items. I'd noticed that over the last couple of weeks, but I had no idea it was a gift. Micah could take a piece of charcoal and draw architecture; he could take a broken tool, and, in a few seconds, it was fixed. I had no idea what that meant he was capable of, but I was excited to find out. Galahad, as always, was fine going last, so I opened my letter. My palms were shaking, and my hands were sweaty. I got the letter open. Emma was next to me, leaning in to see. Killian and Micah were leaning against the twin bed with their elbows to get a look. Galahad was behind Emma and me looking over our shoulders. I was glad we'd come upstairs to do this. Addie and Dori were friends, but this felt like a family matter. I was the only one the faculty thought wasn't gifted, and now was the time I got to see if we really could be the special five they were speaking of. I'd been trying so hard not to be the only weak link. My heart was hammering as I pulled out the decorative brown paper and unfolded it.

Elsha Dyer, it's been a pleasure and a privilege to watch your progress here at the Manor of Raziel. You've grown a great deal, and we hope God allows us to continue assisting you in any way He sees fit. Unfortunately, currently, we've been unable to identify your divine gift. Please don't take this as a failure on your own part but rather as our inability to see or understand your unique talent. God has a plan for every one of us, and I look forward to being able to witness His in your life. Have patience for His timing, and keep up the good work.

Respectfully, Edward Tulken.

Chapter Fifteen

It's All Fun and Games Till Somebody Makes a Challenge

It hit me like a punch to the gut. I didn't know exactly what the five of us were supposed to be fit for, but whatever it was, we weren't if I was in the equation. Galahad didn't even open his letter that night. I was so upset he spent the time comforting me. Killian was pressing him to check it, but he said it could wait. Emma and I stayed up late talking about it. That was really when I let myself go—when the night was over, and I could tell my sister how I was feeling. Emma held me as we snuggled in the same twin and talked till late into the night. Saturday, Dante let me sleep in (meaning he didn't have Micah run in and jump on the bed).

The weekend was a nice break from all the stress of classes. Emma spent time with me, walking outside and growing plants. She and I basically were trying to find events, groups, or hobbies on the Manor that interested us, but my mood wasn't the best for it. When Sunday rolled around, Church was held in the chapel building on campus. I wondered who was supposed to be preaching, but Tulken said a friend of his was the pastor for the Manor of Raziel. He didn't spend much time in the Manor during the week, even though he had living quarters on campus. He spent most of his time street preaching, according to Tulken, and came by for Sunday service and Bible studies. I wanted to try going to them, but spoiler alert: Uriah was front row at every sermon and study. Naturally, in all my bravery...I didn't want to go anymore. However, Emma, being the brave girl she was, told me, "You're not gonna let somebody scare you out of doing something you want!" So, we all went to the service together Sunday (and sat in the back, as was Dyer tradition). Uriah was in the front row beside his sister, with the rest of his group in the same row. He stood with his hands in front of him, straight as a board, all through worship but never sang. I had a terrible singing voice and hated being heard in general, but the church was one of the only times I'd sing because no one else could hear me.

Micah was enjoying his new gifts over the weekend to great extents—he was beginning to fix anything and everything with his hands (which the maids and faculty appreciated). Killian spent most of his time either playing with Micah and the other kids or finding excuses to be where Addie was. I liked Addie too, but it wasn't easy getting to know a girl when your brother was always trying to hog the conversation. Galahad did homework, exercised, and helped us with our studies where he could. I spent most of it being silent in crowds Emma took me to and feeling sorry for myself. Eventually, I realized I couldn't quit my training with Dante just because of this. I'd have to run that course again, and there was no way I'd ever complete it if I quit now.

I knew I'd find Dante in the Library studying his books. I was walking down the wooden hallway of the Manor to the double doors when someone brushed past me. Books fell to the floor. "Oh, I'm so sorry…" I fumbled to squat down and grab them. I looked up through my hair and found myself looking dead in Uriah's eyes. "—Ah!" I pulled back.

It probably didn't seem like the nicest thing to do, but it was a gut reaction. His eyes were hazel, but it was so light they were nearly gold, calculating, and intense. I fell back on my butt. He was still squatted, looking at me with an expression of pure, unforgiving judgment. His leather book bag was across his shoulder, and his white collared shirt was tucked in like he was going to go teach a class. There was a long awkward silence, and I desperately wanted out of it.

"Let me help you with those…." I began, leaning forward to grab the books I'd knocked over.

"I've got it," he said flatly, finally looking down and grabbing his things.

"No, I knocked it over. Just let me…" I grabbed a couple and handed them to him, making him suck in a breath.

He opened his mouth to object as he stood but paused, forcing himself to appear calm, "…Thank you."

"You're welcome," I stood up and smoothed my large sweatshirt. He was still boring holes in my head with his eyes. "What are you staring at?"

"Why are you here?"

I blinked, "I'm looking for Dante…."

"I don't mean *here* in this hallway; I mean at this school. Your interest in working with that heathen says enough about your character."

"He's not a…what is that?"

Uriah scoffed, "Exactly my point. You don't even know the difference between them and us. "

"My family and I are supposed to be Commissioned, and so is Dante…."

"Supposed to be? What does that even mean to you? Do you have any idea what that calling is?" he put his books in his bag and looked down at me. "It's not something you are tossed into like a new school or a study group. And it's not for everyone."

"You think I don't know that? I didn't ask to be brought here! Your teachers found me! If commissioned are called this young, how would you expect them to be? In case you didn't notice, nobody my age knows what they're called to do."

"Exactly my point. You don't know. And bringing you and your family into this life on the hope you *might* be Commissioned is unfair to everyone. If you were really one of us, this wouldn't be a small thing to you. Do you know how many students we've brought in who never find their gifts? They don't belong here, but they stay because they like the classes, the kids, and the idea of having a purpose. But this *isn't* their purpose. If you're like that, then you're just as blind and dead as the rest of the world. And it doesn't help the Commissioned to have people who aren't one of us trying to represent us or uphold our duties."

"And how would Uriah the Great recommend finding what kids are Commissioned? Put them through questioning and tests before they even get in the door?" I snapped.

"I've submitted that idea to Tulken numerous times, but he's never green-lit it," Uriah said regrettably. "The least Tulken should do is see if they know all the commandments before we let them in the door…."

"I can't imagine why he hasn't gone for that…."

"Don't be impudent," Uriah snapped.

I blinked, "What did you call me?"

Uriah averted his gaze, annoyed. "If we tested why students wanted to be here or what they believed, then we'd weed out most of the blind and save everyone a lot of time." He turned to walk away.

I followed him. "And who exactly proved that *you* were Commissioned?" I clenched my fists.

That stopped him dead in his tracks.

He turned around and started walking back towards me. "I knew the truth when I was six years old and had already repented of my past indulgences. I began studying history, monsters, demons, and the forces of evil before I was twelve. At that age, my parents put me here as a year-round student. I've come out at the top of every single class as well as mastering all weapons. I've been on fifteen missions, and I haven't failed one. I study the history of the Commissioned every morning at 4 am and every night before I go to sleep. I don't associate with people of the world or with practitioners of the dark arts of any kind. I *don't* break commandments or laws, and I *don't* pursue frivolous pleasures."

I was backing up until I bumped into the library's double doors. "...Okay."

"If you had any charge against my character that would say I'm otherwise, I would love to hear it. If you and your family were really Commissioned, there would be a million things you'd be doing that you aren't. Everything from how much you study, what you talk about, how you dress would be more like my sister and me if the calling was yours."

"Self-important much?" I said with a frown.

He glared down at me, "—We're done here. I'm going to the gym to train, don't bother coming back and getting in the way."

"That's quite a list," someone said from behind me. I turned to see Galahad there.

Uriah stepped back from me and crossed his arms. "Thank you." In his warped brain, he might've thought Galahad was sincerely complimenting his character.

"You sound pretty wise in your own eyes. Ever read Romans 3:19?" Galahad's brow knit as he looked at him. "So that every mouth may be silenced and the whole world guilty before God..."

Uriah flexed his hands, interrupting, "--I know the book well."

"Oh, "Galahad nodded, trying not to look too surprised. "You might want to study it some more."

Uriah's expression twisted.

Galahad put his arm around me and turned away from him. He led me away into the library. I didn't understand the jab, but whatever it was, Uriah had no retort. Galahad walked me into the library, "Find Dante. After that, we're all going to the gym."

I thanked Galahad for the save and asked him what he meant by that poke. Galahad explained to me what a Pharisee was. In short, he said it was men who thought they were worthy and good enough to earn righteousness and who prioritized their own laws and standards over the commands of God. When he was done, I said, "So…they were, Uriah?" Galahad found that amusing. I went looking for Dante in the Library. As I went into the section of magic books, something came flying at my head. I ducked, letting out a small cry. Dante was up on a ladder looking through books. As he waved a hand, several of them flew down from the shelf onto a pile on the table below. Several pages were turning without him doing it, and items were floating around as he flicked his hand dismissively. "Elements, elements, come on…."

I crossed my arms, looking up at him. "Are you…using magic to get all your books?" I recalled Collins saying magic should be confined to faculty-sanctioned assignments and practices when it concerned the students. He'd also given Dante a reprimand for using magic in the gym. Collins had specifically said not to use magic to make daily life more convenient. But surely Dante had forgotten.

Dante turned, looking at me. His eyes grew slightly large, like a deer in headlights. He snapped his fingers, and all the books fell to the floor. "…No."

#

We kept at it through the next couple of weeks. To be completely honest, an excuse to see Dante continuously was a motivator to keep me training. But I didn't want to quit either. Everyone who'd seen me fail miserably at the obstacle course would see me get good at something. I tried to learn more about Dante while I was training with him, but he didn't make it easy. He never spoke of his family. I had to pick up bits and pieces from our conversations. I learned he was an only child. And that when he'd gotten here, Kaine had whipped him into shape and literally carried him to the course (he wasn't kidding about that). Naturally, I'd assumed because he was a longtime student that he had a lot of friends. I thought it would be difficult for him to take so much time to train me, but it turned out the only thing he was taking a break from was his magic studies. He never made plans with the other kids or went to any of the recreational games unless it was mandatory. I tried to figure out what he liked, but I only ever got him talking about one thing—can you guess? You guessed it: magic. Things like control of the elements, levitation, and teleportation came almost naturally to him since he was gifted in sorcery. Still, extreme control over those skills and expansion of them came with practice and study. Dante was performing some of them when he was very young (as I said, it's the only thing I got him talking about).

We'd been at the Manor for a little over a month, and the time for me to go through the course again was nearing. It weighed on my mind as I clashed blades with Dante during gym. Thursday, we were supposed to practice fencing, and Percival had let Dante teach me personally. It bothered Uriah every time, but that only fueled me to do it more. We were at the portion of practice that was something like a mid-term. Students would spar with each other in a point system at different parts of the gym while professors supervised. Emma was fighting Killian (you can imagine how much their supervisor had to step in). Jasmine and Micah were sparring, but he kept making her laugh by goofing off, so Kaine had to remind them to get to work. Dori and Galahad were supposed to be fighting, but she was doing something entirely different. Dori was hopping and dancing around Galahad, who was staring, confused.

"It's only fair to warn you…I was captain of the rubber fighting ducks of Malibu! AAAAHHH!" Dori lunged at Galahad dramatically. Galahad stepped aside, and she ran right into the basketball rack. Balls rolled across the floor past the other kids who were *actually* sword fighting. Killian broke out laughing, and Emma smacked him. Kaine stepped in to take care of the chaos when Dante and I were asked to begin a match.

Dante brought his blade down, and I blocked.

"—Good," he spun around and slashed at me again.

I stepped back, barely avoiding getting my throat cut. My shoes squeaked slightly on the gym floor, nearly making me lose my footing. He paused before delivering the next blow. He tilted his head, "You have something on your mind?"

"It's nothing," I regained footing and thrust my sword toward him. He deflected it with a light shift of his wrist, moving the angle of the blade. I attacked again, and he did a similar thing.

He raised his sword, blocking a high attack of mine.

Ching!

Uriah walked up with Dashiel beside him and sheathed his own sword. I didn't know why they were watching us. Uriah's sister and the rest of his crew were talking amongst themselves. Everyone knew I'd been the only one in my family not to get a gift. It had been a couple of weeks, and they hadn't let me forget it. I forced myself not to look at them.

I saw Emma approach with Killian. She must have finished her match. "Come on, Elsha, stab him!" Emma yelled. She looked around curiously as Dashiel arched his head to her. "…What? You know what I mean!"

"Frankly, I'm amazed the match has taken this long," Uriah said haughtily. "But then again, she is fighting reptile boy."

Dashiel turned his head slightly to Uriah and commented robotically, "Serpent's affinity for Dante doesn't negate his skill with a blade, Uriah."

"Even a heathen can hold a blade," Uriah scratched under the chin of his falcon.

Emma shot him a sneer. "Dante is in the same class as you! My sister could beat him if she wanted to! She's been training hard!" Emma clenched her fists. "Show him no mercy, Elsha!"

"What's going on?" Micah walked up, eating a granola bar.

"Elsha and Dante are sparring," Galahad approached. It was growing more and more difficult to focus as all my siblings and other kids approached. I knew I'd lose this match, but I didn't need all of them seeing. I narrowed my gaze and kept coming at Dante stronger, faster, slashing, and stabbing, but he deflected them all. The sound of my siblings rooting in the background grew louder and louder. I sidestepped a thrust of Dante's and moved in, knocking the blade from his hand.

CLANG!

The sword clattered on the floor, and Dante grabbed his hand, wincing.

Everyone, including me, was speechless. Professor Percival had been supervising a different match, but now he was watching. The sound of him clapping was the first thing to break the silence. Then the cheering broke out. "Alright, Elsha!" Killian said, rushing in as Galahad picked me up and swung me around. The gym rats of Kaine's were staring, mumbling, "I don't believe it…."

Uriah was speechless. He forced his expression not to look too surprised as my siblings congratulated me.

Even Dashiel raised an eyebrow in surprise. He suppressed a smile, "Well done, Elsha. Defeating Dante is a definite step in the right direction. You're improving."

Emma smiled at his congratulation. "Of course she is!"

Uriah let out an unimpressed sigh at last, "I have to say…beating *him* might mean you're better than you were, but it isn't exactly monumental. Everyone here knows Dante's…good, but he isn't the best."

"Oh, yeah!" Micah said.

"Great comeback, bro," Killian said.

Emma smacked Dashiel on the arm. "Dash, what is he talking about?"

"Unpleasant as it is to confess…. Uriah is correct. He and I are the finest swordsmen at the Manor. However, I wouldn't say that demerits Elsha's current victory…." Dashiel began.

"I seriously doubt you or your family could have a victory I would be forced to respect," Uriah turned away from all of us dismissively.

"If you're so amazing, why don't you prove it!" Emma snapped.

Everyone went quiet.

Dori croaked.

"Do you know how old I was when I came here…" Uriah began, and I groaned.

Not with that list again!

Emma had less patience than me. "I'm not talking about your academic record; I'm talking about here! In gym! Prove it!"

Uriah and his bird both looked at her. "Are you…challenging *me*?"

There was an echo of *Ooos* from the crowd. Percival and Kaine were now present, watching.

"Yeah! Wait, what?" Micah looked around frantically.

"We all are!" Emma said. "We've all been training for the course, and Elsha's gotten good with a blade—there's gotta be some way we can put you and your snobs to the test!" Emma crossed her arms.

Killian came forward, wiping his face with a towel. He'd been running drills in the gym, and his hair was wet with sweat. "Wait, what's a challenge again?"

Kaine briefly explained the concept. Killian nodded, "So let me get this straight… it's like the obstacle course on steroids, and we're competing against each other?"

Kaine shrugged, "Pretty much."

Killian looked at Uriah with unhidden dislike, "And anything goes?"

Kaine moved his head in thought, "You wear the death detection amulet, so…yeah."

Killian tossed the towel down and crossed his arms, "Finally…sounds like a chance for a little action around here. I'm in."

Percival stepped forward and tucked his poetry book under his arm, "It seems as if they want a Raziel challenge, Uriah."

"Uh…kids, are you sure about that?" Kaine said.

Uriah wasn't looking at any of them anymore. He was looking at me. He expected me to be the first to back out. To wimp out and say I couldn't do it. I swallowed back my fear. "Yeah…that's exactly what we want."

I stepped forward and looked up at Uriah, crossing my arms. "Our family vs. your team. Dante said your team always wins. So, the Dyers are challenging you."

"A team can't make a challenge unless a faculty member is willing to represent them," Uriah held my gaze.

Kaine raised a hand, "I'll represent their team."

Percival waved a hand with an intrigued smile, "It goes without saying I represent the Harks team." No one seemed surprised.

Herodotus flipped her hair behind her and looked down at us, "If this is a challenge, let's make it interesting. When our team wins…"

"—If," Emma corrected.

Herodotus exchanged looks with the rest of their team, and they stifled a laugh. "Okay…*if* we win, you and your family are weapons and water boys for us the whole week. We'll give Danny here the week off." She gestured to the smaller boy carrying their equipment. She flashed her gaze to Galahad with a smile, "Sound fair?"

He didn't smile back at her. "Then I take it my family gets something if they win?"

Uriah's eyes flashed up to my brother momentarily, "Name it."

Micah raised a finger, "A parking space!"

Killian nudged his brother. "We can't drive, dummy!"

Galahad looked as if he was losing patience.

"You have to be reasonable…." Dashiel began.

Galahad put two fingers to his temple. "You're asking too much."

Micah pulled out his sketch pad and flipped to a drawing of arrows and lines around the globe. The sketch had stick figures of all five Dyer children, and Killian's image had a huge mouth. I was a small body with a shag of hair covering my face, and Emma had bug eyes. "Okay…we only want…this half of the globe."

"That's more like it!" Killian said.

Uriah blinked. His mouth parted slightly, "What is wrong with you…*no*."

"How about Las Vegas?" Micah said.

Killian grunted excitedly with a fist pump.

Uriah straightened indignantly, "If I owned that den of iniquity, I'd wipe it off the face of the earth. Like *this*!" he snapped his fingers, and Micah jumped.

"Kill joy…" Killian mumbled.

"He's kidding, right?" I said quietly to Dante.

Dante shook his head.

Uriah glared at me, "—Ask, Jonah."

Galahad blinked, "I think you missed the point of that story…."

I thought and thought as my brothers tossed out every idea in the book. Money, power, the Pentagon, the Whitehouse, Dove Cameron (that was Killian's request), the Jumbo Tron…. eventually, something came to me. "I've got it," I picked up my head. They all looked at me. "Professor Clary mentioned a Homecoming dance happening in the Great Hall…Dori, Addie, and Jasmine are the only volunteers to help so far. If we win…you do all the preparations."

Uriah's expression said it all. The rest of his group groaned and argued; even his bird objected. Dori blinked in shock, "But Uriah can't stand Addie and me, and he really hates dances and…" she broke into a grin. "Oh, that's good!"

"What's the matter?" I pressed, watching Uriah's expression twist. "Are you afraid you're gonna lose to a bunch of wannabes?"

Uriah leaned down to look me in the eye. "…You're on."
Everyone was excited about the challenge. Uriah and his group walked away. Percival said he had to clear the challenge with Tulken first, and then arrangements would be made. As the students cleared away and my heart rate returned to normal, I noticed Dante being awfully quiet. I was about to go over and ask him what was up when Kaine approached us.

"You kids got guts…I'll give you that. But before you roll out any red carpets and get too cocky…have any of you seen a Raziel challenge before?"

We shook our heads.

Kaine straightened his army cap and said a word I wouldn't repeat. "Okay then…let's get you familiar with the meanest, wildest savage beast at the Manor."

"Is that…what we'll be fighting in a challenge?" I said as Kaine turned to go outside.

He paused, "No… she's the one who comes up with the course."

Chapter Sixteen

A Raziel Challenge… We May Have Pushed Things Too Far

Kaine walked us outside across the field past the obstacle course and the class buildings. We came to what looked like a large barn; beside it, on the right, was a track. As Kaine led us in, I saw it was a canal that smelled full of animals. There were horses inside, but I heard other animals too. Emma petted the horses in the stalls. Kaine led us to the back of the barn, where there was a gated sandlot.

"How many animals do you guys have here?" I asked.

"I'm not the expert on that…Clash is the one you wanna talk to," Kaine walked into a doorway at the back of the canal and crossed his arms. There was a gated area that looked like it was for rodeos or breaking animals in. We approached, and a leopard's growl broke the silence.

We froze in the doorway behind Kaine.

My gaze zeroed in on what looked like two cats wrestling in the lot. It had to be two large cats…didn't it? As I looked closer, I couldn't believe what I saw—it was a woman wrestling the cat. A person's arm wrapped the leopard around the neck and brought the animal face-first to the ground. The creature slid down in the dust before the woman stood up, dusting herself off. She wore a tan sleeveless vest, and her arms were nearly as large as Kaine's. She had dark green camo pants and hiking boots with a bandana. Her pixie haircut made it difficult for me to tell she was a woman at first. She pulled the leopard to its feet by the scruff of its neck like she was playing with a small kitten.

"Kaine…you brought some snacks for my friends?" she had a husky voice.

Micah swallowed, "On second thought, maybe a challenge isn't such a good idea...."

"No need to scare these guys, Clash. They've got enough problems," Kaine warned.

Clash looked us over while petting the leopard, "They look like they got all their limbs to me."

"Yeah...we're practically the luckiest kids in the world," Micah joked.

Kaine cracked his knuckles. "We got another challenge for you to plan."

Clash raised her eyebrows. "New kids in a challenge?"

Kaine coughed, "...Against the champions."

Clash gave a harsh laugh, "They got a death wish?"

"You make it sound like we don't have a chance," Galahad said.

"Uh, you don't. Points for trying, though," Clash shrugged, leading the large cat past us back into the canal. We all plastered ourselves against the wall as she put the cat away. Killian was following, trying to pet it.

"Look, these guys have never seen a challenge before, and they're up against the best. I want you to give them some personal tips and training before this Friday. As a favor to me," Kaine said as she latched the gate shut.

Clash looked at him curiously, "Hm...no."

"Okay... then I'll owe you one," Kaine tilted his head down to look at her.

Clash crossed her arms and rested against the canal. The Leopard was growling and snarling inside the pen. She nodded thoughtfully, "Anything I want?"

Kaine moved his head reluctantly, "Let's not lose our minds, okay…."

"Good luck wiping these kids off the floor after my challenge…" she started to walk away.

"Alright! Fine…anything." I didn't know why Kaine was helping us, but it was nice of him.

Clash grinned, "Alright then…you kids wanna know how a challenge works?" she pulled the whip that was wrapped around her torso off and walked out into the gated area. "I'll explain a little bit…oh, and feel free to back out anytime."

#

I'll confess, I wanted to back out the rest of the week. But…I didn't say a word. We'd made the challenge. And if we backed out now or complained, Uriah and his friends would never let us hear the end of it. It was a close call because Uriah looked more tense than we did. He and his group were not the kind of people to sit back and assume victory even if it was over someone as inexperienced as us. I caught glimpses of them training earlier and more than before. I probably looked scared to death but Emma said that wasn't a good face to show competition. The next time Uriah and I caught a glance at each other leaving training, I gave a winning smile.

That confused the heck out of him. He huffed, walking by, wiping the sweat from his face with a towel.

Saturday night was the dance (which all the girls had been talking about), but Friday was the challenge. Everyone had been talking about that, too, but I'd tried to drown them out. It was mostly things like,

"Those new kids are gonna get destroyed!" "Uriah will show them a lesson!" "I wonder if they'll be in good enough shape to walk out of here?" Mostly it was the jock kids, Uriah's group…and everyone but Addie, Dante, and Jasmine. My siblings and I didn't take it lightly. Clash showed us the way previous courses had been run, where the teams had failed or slipped up. She'd done courses in a forest-like maze in the fields behind the manor with wild animals, combative ones, and challenges centered mainly on speed and magic. I'd found out later Kaine was asked by Dante to try and give us an edge by letting Clash show us around. I wasn't sure why Kaine would be doing favors for Dante—he wasn't in his group of gym rats or, as Micah called them, "violent thugs."

My siblings and I exercised with Galahad out in the quad. He showed us the things he'd been doing in the Boarding House that helped him pass the first course. Swordplay, agility, and many other things we'd been training would come in handy. I asked why the team of jocks that studied under Kaine hadn't beaten Uriah in any of the challenges. Kaine said they got too focused on the combat aspect and failed the objective. Translation: the jock kids would charge and start wailing about the competition and beating the other kids up. They'd either get caught by one of the traps or lose the goal.

Friday came, and they had set up the stands and arena like it was ready for a concert/gladiator tournament. The seats were high like bleachers, only wooden, and the arena was encompassed by tall wooden walls and doors. All the Manor was outside walking to get seats. Addie and Dori were pushing through somewhere to the front of the seats holding popcorn and snacks. It was a surprisingly cheerful event for one that seemed so terrifying. Addie's mom was in a small booth near the arena giving out snacks and food. "Doughnuts, cookies, popcorn! Come on by and grab some food before you watch the challenge!"

Micah whispered to me, "Oh great, they're selling food to watch us get killed…."

"Come on, bro, we got this," Killian nudged him in the arm. "We're gonna kill these guys. Just let me at that stuck up...."

"This isn't about pulverizing Uriah; it's about working as a team. You've seen them train. It's more than just being good with weapons; it's about working as a single unit," Galahad said as we walked through the back doors to the arena. The weapons armory was right beside it. The sound of the crowd cheering filled the air as we walked by and looked up at the stands. Addie and Dori waved down at us. My eyes searched the arena for Dante. The crowd was full of students, faculty, and staff bunched together.

Eventually, my eyes settled in on a tall, lean, darkly dressed person walking through the row to sit next to Addie. Seeing them there made me feel slightly less horrified.

Across the arena, there was another entrance, double wooden doors like the ones we'd walked through. It was in the setting sun of the evening, and the arena was lined with tall torches. The Professors were in a box seat at the top of the stands overlooking us below. This seemed like a huge event for the Manor. My heart was pounding, and my palms were sweating as I knew people above were looking at us. For a challenge, we were all given matching uniforms—it was pretty unglamorous. Combat boots, camo pants, and dark brown t-shirts. Emma and I both had our hair tied back—for me, that was a real accomplishment. I hated showing my face. Drums began to sound around the arena, and flames shot up from the torches. The doors across the arena opened, and Uriah's team emerged.

Micah huffed, "Why didn't we get a drum roll...."

Their attire was much like ours. Only their combat boots were knee high with a rich chocolate brown color, expensive looking. I remembered Dori saying something that their parents are investing in all their uniforms and supplies. They wore moveable camo pants with pockets and fitted pearl-colored turtlenecks with zippers. They looked like some superstar combat polo players, while we looked like rejects from the Hunger Games. As soon as they entered the arena, the kids were cheering louder. I saw the Professors clapped equally for everyone in a polite fashion, but some kids clearly had their favorites. There were crowds of girls in the stands cheering and screaming loudly for the championship team. I'd learned over the course of the past few weeks that Herodotus was the topic of lots of boy's conversations, and Uriah was the subject of many girls. A lot of the boys from the wealthier families were envied and considered high on the popular rating. Some of the boys on Uriah's side looked like the adoration fed their confidence, and they puffed their chests out.

Emma crossed her arms, rolling her eyes, "Oh please…like they're so impressive…." She was stopped short when she saw Dashiel was on their team. He remained in a more combat-ready version of what he usually wore—the dark blue collar high shirt. He looked completely unmoved by any of it and calm as always. Emma's jaw dropped. "Dash!"

Micah closed his fist, "Don't even look at him—he's one of the enemy now!"

Uriah zeroed in on us like he could have cared less about all the cheering. His falcon rested on his shoulder and seemed to be glaring as well.

All of us had fingerless gloves, and I wondered why till I saw the structure in the arena between both of us. It was like Kaine's course, only larger, taller. It was a massive wooden tower like structure and each level held new death traps. There were stairs, hanging ropes, and at the top, stairs leading to a table with a luminous glass vase. Around the arena were doors like pens that I suspected kept animals at bay. I didn't want to think about what kind. Clash was at the center of the arena between us, waiting for the crowd to stop cheering. Clash looked around with a broad smile before she closed her eyes and calmly put one fist in her hand like she was concentrating.

Clash opened her eyes and her mouth. I thought there was no way she could scream loud enough for this crowd to be quiet. "GRRAAAAUUUUGGHH!" the sound of a lion roar echoed across the entire arena, and the cheering stopped. Clash put her hands on her hips and looked at everyone. "Do I have your attention now?" she said, causing the crowd to cheer. Clash raised her hands again, and they quieted down. "Now we all know you kids are required to train how to fight, kill and generally not die out there in the field. But let's face it—some of you do it better than others," she gestured to Uriah's team.

The crowd cheered.

"The team leader Uriah Hark—fifteen missions, all successes. Twenty-two challenges in the last three years, all wins. Number one in weapons assessment, first in survivalist exercises. His team has talked a lot of big talk over the years…but how do we tell if it's all true? Not just in the field but right here. These guys only get to keep their title if nobody's woman enough to take it from them. Somebody was gutsy enough, or *cough* * crazy to try. Now, what new kids, you're all asking—were nuts enough to challenge the champs…."

Killian smoothed his hair back proudly.

I was trying not to tremble.

"Twenty-two challenges…" Micah was mumbling like that was all he heard. "They've won all twenty-two…."

Clash gestured to us, "A little family called the Dyers wants to teach Uriah's team a lesson. Let's see if they have what it takes." The crowd cheered. I swallowed and exchanged glances with Emma. "Now, every challenge is different, so I'll briefly explain the rules and the objective. The challenge will mimic a mission you might have in the field. In my hands, I have two scrolls. One will be given to each team. Both contain a destructive spell of dark magic that is too powerful to be opened or used by the enemy. Your objective is to obtain the scroll from the other team and take both to the top of the structure and place them in the magically protected vase." Clash pointed to the top of the structure.

"There'll be obstacles, traps, and dangers—but the greatest danger you will face is each other. In a challenge, anything goes. In other words, if it's a skill or a gift you have—use it. Your opponents will use everything at their disposal to take the scroll from you and to stop you from getting to the top. None of you will begin with weapons. They'll be by the walls of the arena, and you'll have your chance at the start of the clock to take whatever you can. It will be a choice of yours to go for the weapons or to try and take the scrolls without them. I recommend getting a hold of something you can use because if you die in this game...you're out."

Micah's jaw dropped.

Clash chuckled low in her throat, "Alright, don't get excited...though injuries are likely in this game, we don't let you die- if we can help it. Built into all your uniforms is something called a death detection amulet. Cornelius will be refereeing from the box seat and have a clear view of all actions in the challenge. When you're about to receive a killing blow or you fall to your imminent death...then the amulet will transport you out of the challenge and to the side bench. If you lose or damage your detection amulet and receive a killing blow...well, that's obvious," she smiled. "Whichever team member makes it to the top and sets the scrolls in the vase...wins. Now you'll have five minutes to confer a strategy with your team and to assign a team leader. Team Six was formed a while back and has never changed leaders—Uriah Hark. Team seven, you have five minutes to pick a leader and plan a strategy."

Micah raised his hand, "Couldn't we get ten?"

"In the field, you'll have less," Clash walked past us and cracked her knuckles. She checked her watch, "Now get busy, kids."

We all got in a huddle.

"Okay, we need to pick a leader…." Galahad began.

"Galahad," the rest of us voted in unison.

Galahad gave a reluctant sigh, "…Nice how things work in this family. Let's talk strategy. They've got Uriah, Riya, Herodotus, Thomas, and Dashiel. Dashiel, Uriah, and Thomas will go straight for the weapons. The only one Uriah is gonna trust with the scroll is himself. Elsha, I want you to have ours."

My jaw dropped, "W-what?"

Killian looked at Galahad in disbelief, "You're kidding, right? I'm the fastest one among us. I should have…"

"Exactly, we need you to go hand to hand with Uriah's team. But I want Elsha to start with our scroll. It'll confuse them," Galahad's tone was a matter of fact. None of us understood that decision. It put a tremendous amount of pressure on me. I was scared, but I was determined not to be the reason we lost.

I nodded. "Okay."

Galahad went on, "Killian, you're fast, nimble—you won't need a weapon to get past the others. And you've got the best chance at getting the scrolls to the top. Elsha, if Killian has a clear run, get your scroll to him."

Killian and I exchanged glances and nodded.

"Emma, when we get to the second level, your control of plants won't help," Galahad said.

Emma bit her lip, "He's right…I can only control plant life; I can't create it. No vegetation…no powers."

Galahad met her gaze, "It's okay. Keep who you can on the ground."

Emma nodded, "Got it."

"Yeah, and don't let the fact your boyfriend is on the team make you soft," Killian teased.

Emma rolled her eyes.

"Micah, use your craftsmen skills. Trip them up. Take what tools you can use, and don't let Uriah's team catch up with us," Galahad said.

"I-I'll try," Micah said. "I still don't see why we couldn't have made our prize that they have to serve us for a week…."

"Micah!" Emma objected.

"What? If I'm risking my life, at least I want it to be for something worthwhile!" Micah said.

Emma scrunched her nose, "You know what? We're freaking out for no reason. Me, Killian, Micah, and Galahad all gave gifts! All we gotta do is use our special skills and…." Emma turned to Galahad curiously. "You still haven't told us what yours was?"

She was right. Galahad hadn't. It had been easy to overlook what his might have been because Galahad kept his thoughts to himself unless pressed. Killian, Emma, and Micah had been so busy talking about their gifts and finding outlets to use them we hadn't even thought about Galahad's. Emma and I had asked a couple of times, but when Galahad wanted to change the subject, he could.

Galahad blinked, "Oh, I didn't have one. Does everyone know their job?"

Micah's jaw dropped, "Whaaaaaat?"

Killian's expression didn't change much, as if he already knew. I sometimes forgot as the two oldest boys, they knew things about each other we didn't. He looked like he already knew Galahad didn't have one.

"WHY DID WE AGREE TO THIS THEN?" Micah said frantically.

I had several questions, but now wasn't the time.

"Keep this on, and you'll be fine," Killian poked the dark blue amulet on Micah's t-shirt.

"We'll argue about winnings later. Elsha, you've gotten pretty good with a sword, so you'll need to keep their other key fencers at bay. I'll get the scroll from Uriah. Whatever happens, keep the scrolls with our team," Galahad said.

"We've got this, and I can get those scrolls up there no problem. Uriah is mine," Killian pressed.

Galahad narrowed his gaze at him, "Don't turn this into a one man show. If you don't make it to the third floor, we need to trust each other."

Killian immediately objected. "—Micah and the girls can't…."

"—If one of them is open, you give them the scroll. *Any* of them. We don't have time for you to pick and choose who can take it. You trust your teammates," Galahad said.

Killian bit his lip fighting the urge to argue. "…*Fine*."

"Alright, let's show these guys what the Dyers are capable of!" Emma put her hand in and waited.

Killian looked at us in disbelief, "Are we seriously doing *handsin?*" Galahad shot him a warning look because my hand was already in. Killian rolled his eyes, "Alright…team Seven---hands in."

"My favorite number," Galahad smiled. "On three—together. One…"

"Two…" Micah continued.

We all put our hands down. "Three!"

We hadn't used the whole five minutes to plan our strategy. We had a minute left as we stood across the arena from the other team. Everyone was trembling with anticipation, including me. The sounds of the audience whooping and cheering were slowly drowned out as I zeroed in on the competition. The only thing I heard was Clash's countdown. I steadied my breathing as we all took a running stance. Uriah had the scroll. I could see it strapped to his side. The deafening cheering and screams faded as we looked at each other. Clash's commanding voice echoed behind us,

"—Ten, nine, eight…."

I lunged slightly forward, waiting to break into a run. If I didn't get a hold of a sword, I had no chance of not dying in the first few seconds. If I received a killing blow, I was out.

"—Seven, six, five…."

Uriah and Dashiel's eyes were both flashing to the weapons. We'd have to fight them for it. My pulse was racing. All the Manor was watching us. Every kid who'd thought the Dyer's would fail was about to be proven right or wrong. There was no turning back now. "Four, three, two…."

I caught my breath.

"—One."

And then the sound of the gong echoed in my ears.

Chapter Seventeen

You Don't Die In This Game…. Ha—Right

Initially, all my nerves exploded, and my head spun. It was really happening—and it took me a second to remember what I was supposed to do. Everything happened so fast that it was a blur. Galahad's words ran through my mind in those two seconds as the crowds' screams deafened me:

Get the scroll from Uriah.

Emma keeps them on the ground.

Killian, stop arguing….no, wait—he didn't say that this time. Did he? Elsha has the scroll. Get a sword…a sword!

That's what I needed to not die.

My eyes went to the weapons rack lining the walls of the arena. Uriah's team split in a fluid motion, half of them going for the weapons and half going for us. They were running in a strange S shaped motion when they split. Maybe they were just moving and leaping over certain parts of the arena to look fancy.

Killian darted in Uriah's direction, leaving Emma wide open, "I've got their scroll!"

"No—stick to…" Galahad began.

Uriah and Herodotus said something to each other. He folded his hands, and Herodotus stepped onto them, backflipping over Killian. She landed behind him, and Killian skid across the dirt floor into the wall. It was amazing she could dodge that fast—it was like she knew where he'd aim. Killian was nimble, so he managed to stop in a squat. Killian winced, having scraped his hands.

Uriah got hold of a sword first. The falcon took a dagger in its talons and flew it straight to Herodotus. The bird quickly returned to Uriah. Galahad rushed Thomas on the other team and managed to knock him off his feet with a shoulder throw. Thomas' arms changed shape—they looked almost stonelike for a moment as they scraped along the rough arena floor. He quickly maneuvered his way back to his feet, but that gave Galahad enough time to grab a sword. Killian scurried past the competition and grabbed a short sword.

Riya moved her hands.

A whirl of wind whipped a circle of dirt up from the ground like a sandstorm before Emma and extended to Killian, making it hard for him to see. Emma raised an arm to shield her eyes, "—Ah!"

Riya leaped off one leg and sent a front kick right at Emma through the sand. Growth-like bushes emerged from the ground in front of Emma. Riya's leg was caught in the shrubbery. That shocked everyone, including Emma. Emma's powers reacted before she did. That only stunned Riya. She kicked Emma in the shoulder with her free leg knocking her to the floor.

Micah turned to me, "I'll cover you! Get a sword!"

That was bold and out of character for Micah, but he couldn't use his gift if he didn't get a hold of some tools or weapons. I followed him as we ran for the weapons. Dashiel was blocking the weapons rack and reached to grab a sword for himself. Micah came at him with a basic few blows he'd learned in Kaine's self-defense training. Dashiel ducked and moved his head from side to side before taking Micah by the arm and throwing him over. Micah hit the floor with such force it made me wonder if Dashiel's gift was super strength. It was quick, and Dashiel fought with as little emotion as he did everything else. In those few seconds, I ran past them to the weapons. My foot landed on a lump. Something beneath me exploded.

I flew against the arena wall next to me and groaned. A puff of dark blue and black smoke emerged from the ground. Strands of hair fell beside my face. I turned and looked at the ground, which was now blurry. I was still in the arena. That meant whatever happened wasn't a killing blow. I put my hand to my death detection amulet instinctively, still intact. There was smoke coming from a patch on the ground that was now blackened like charcoal. The bumps in the ground…that's why Uriah's team had been running that way. They were avoiding mines. A magic obstacle made by Collins, no doubt.

"Don't step on the bumps in the ground! They're bombs!" I cried.

They were all at different parts of the arena, busy, but I hoped they heard me.

I tried to recall what Galahad said: stay on task. Get a sword. Herodotus was coming at Galahad with her dagger. Slashing and stabbing, protecting the way for Uriah. Uriah wasted no time in going for the kill at Killian, who was only surviving because he was so nimble. Uriah stabbed the wall behind him as Killian slipped to the floor. Killian glanced at me.

Killian rolled under a slash from Uriah and came to his feet, grabbing another sword. "Elsha!" he threw it to me.

I ran forward and slid onto my stomach to grab it before Dashiel, who was surely close behind. The sword fell into the dirt. I grabbed it just in time to turn around and block a downward strike from Dashiel. As our blades collided, the crowd cheered. I heard Addie and Dori screaming, and I couldn't tell if it was excitement, fear, or both. I could feel Dashiel's strength as the blade pressed down at me. He was so unmoved it felt like he wasn't even using full strength. I rolled aside, knowing I couldn't match him. I narrowly avoided being impaled as his sword went into the dirt next to me. The dirt sprayed in my eyes. I wiped my eyes and looked beside me. A bomb was right between Dashiel and me. That wasn't the only thing.

The scroll had fallen from the holster on my belt and was lying on the floor. Dashiel and I both looked down at the scroll and then up at each other. I grabbed it. Dashiel kicked it from my hand.

The scroll went flying in Uriah and Killian's direction. They both ran for it. Only something I couldn't explain happened. Killian ran in the wrong direction. Uriah ducked and rolled, coming up right below the scroll. He reached up, catching it. Killian ran to the structure in the middle of the course before he came to a halt. He shook his head and looked around, confused. Had he not seen where he was going? Or had one of the other teams done something? These kids were full of surprises. And they'd gone to great lengths to keep their abilities secret so we wouldn't have an advantage in the arena. I got to my feet and backed away from Dashiel with my sword. I shot my gaze around for a moment and took in what was happening. Riya was tangled up in plants. If Emma had known a way to kill her and get her out of the game, she probably would have, but that wasn't the objective. Getting both scrolls to the top was.

Thomas had gone towards the tower. Maybe Uriah had told him to go for there first, so he'd have someone higher up to pass the scroll to? I didn't know.

Micah was at the structure beneath the first floor doing something I couldn't see. Dashiel hadn't killed him—maybe he didn't think he posed enough of a threat.

Emma was coming towards Dashiel and me. Another gong sounded. I took it now the game had changed. I wasn't sure how I knew, but maybe one team getting both scrolls meant the odds would change for everyone. Clash had said every level would have obstacles. Three doors around the arena were lifted.

"GR—A-A-AUUGHH!" It was a roar, and it wasn't Clash. She was sitting from a nearby box seat by Collins with her feet up, grinning like a Cheshire cat. I darted my eyes around. Emma let out a scream. From each pen emerged a large tiger. They snarled and growled as they began to come closer to the kids in the arena. I was breathing hard. Now none of us was looking at each other now. We tried not to make any sudden movements.

Remember, you're wearing the amulet. You're wearing the amulet…

My eyes shot over my shoulder to Uriah. He was already headed to the structure with both scrolls. Galahad and Herodotus both turned and stood defensively before the cat walked slowly at them. "I hope these detection amulets can tell if we get mauled to death," Galahad said.

Herodotus shot him a look, "We? I'm three steps ahead of you, Dyer," she backflipped away twice. She was out of reach from the tiger, but the sudden movement had shocked the beast.

It growled, coming towards Galahad. The cat stopped and snarled. The tiger looked back—Killian had grabbed its tail. Galahad rushed for the weapons and grabbed a long sword. The tiger turned, trying to leap at Killian, but he was staying behind it. Amulet or not, that was brave. He was forced to let go of the tail. The tiger leaped at him. Killian rolled out of the way with an inch of his life. Dashiel was keeping the tiger before us at bay with his sword. Galahad went at the one by Killian getting its attention. The last tiger was going after Herodotus, who was running straight for the tower. She grabbed hold of a beam below it and pulled herself up in a chin, narrowly avoiding being eaten. I couldn't fight those cats or even keep them busy. I ran straight for the structure. There was no chance of Killian or Galahad getting the scrolls now.

The tiger that had been after Herodotus emerged from below the structure and growled at me low in its throat. I stepped back, swallowing hard. "Oh no…"

"HERE, KITTY, KITTY!" Micah screamed from below the structure. He was a few yards away waving a steak. I had no idea how he got a hold of it; maybe he'd brought it into the arena to pacify Killian (I never knew with Micah). The tiger turned, sniffing, and went towards Micah. Micah ran to the arena wall and threw the meat in the air. The tiger leaped at it, and Micah pulled a rope that was connected to the pen door in the wall. There had been ropes on the structure. Maybe he'd found a way to unfasten and use them, and he did have the craftsman gift after all. The tiger leapt for the meat catching it in midair and running back into the pen. Micah let go of the rope, and the door to the pen dropped, closing the cat in. I had already started up the stairs to the structure.

Thank you, Micah!

I glanced over my shoulder to see Dashiel coming at me.

Emma leapt on his back, making him grunt. "Oh no, you don't!" Emma wrapped her arms around his neck.

A tiger leapt at Killian while he grabbed a weapon. Killian turned around. He didn't have a sword in his hand anymore. I froze on the stairs, "—Killian!"

As the tiger came upon him, Killian gasped. He vanished in a shockwave of blue light. Killian appeared on the wooden bench seat behind a small gate with the number 7 in front of it.

Across from the other bench, I saw Riya was there. They had both died in the game. Killian was muttering under his breath. Emma was choking Dashiel while Micah was trying to get up the structure from the opposite stairway and avoid the other cat. Dashiel threw Emma off him and came at her with his sword. His slashes were wicked fast, but every time he struck, a plant, a vine, emerged, protecting her. Emma still went, "Ah!" with every strike.

Dashiel cut through every vine, plant, and shrubbery closing in on her. He cut away at the last vine whipping around and poising the sword at her throat. Emma blinked. "You wouldn't," she cautioned innocently.

Dashiel had been about to strike when he paused. A plant wrapped around his leg, pulling him down to one knee. He shook his head as if snapping back to his senses and lunged at Emma with his sword. Emma stepped aside, avoiding the strike, and grabbed his wrist, now fighting with him over the sword. An arrow came flying at Emma, and she let out a shriek. Thomas had fired a crossbow at her from across the arena. She vanished in a blue light. Galahad was keeping the remaining tiger back, "Elsha—go! Get those scrolls!"

I hurried up the steps.

Creak!

I turned, looking to my left. A hanging wooden beam with a bag of sand tied to it came swinging down before my face. I stepped back and grabbed the sides of the stairwell so I wouldn't fall. It swung before my eyes, much like the pendulum from Kaine's course. I counted as it swung back, "One…two…" it came again. When it swung back, I stepped through. I did the same thing with the swinging sandbags after that one. I came to the second staircase. I could see Uriah through a web of ropes tied across in X shapes at the stair of the next stairs. It would be tricky to get through those, but I didn't have a choice. I put my sword in the sheath on my belt and grabbed hold of a rope, trying to get through without tripping. Someone grabbed my hair from behind. I grunted, being pulled out of the ropes and onto the floor. I put my hands up to protect my face as I fell.

Herodotus stood over me and came down in a squat attempting to stab me with her dagger. I reached up, grabbing her wrist. She may have been nimble, but I didn't want to die. She grit her teeth, pushing down on me. I shifted my weight, turning and hitting her in the face with my elbow.

Herodotus grunted and nearly fell off the structure. She flipped off her back onto her feet. I slashed my sword at her, but Herodotus' eyes flashed as she met mine, and she moved aside, dodging every attack. After a few moments, it got annoying—how was she able to predict each move?

Herodotus smiled, leaping off one foot and kicking me in the gut. I fell back to the ropes. I grabbed hold of them trying not to fall. I tried to get through. Herodotus was above me now. I hadn't even seen the monkey bars above the ropes. I could never have gotten across that way anyway. I stumbled through the ropes, but she was ahead. She let go of the monkey bars and landed on the other side, flashing a proud grin at me, "Did you really think you first-timers were gonna do anything but embarrass yourselves in a challenge?"

As soon as I stepped out, she'd kill me. I was the only one on the structure, and if I was out, we didn't have much hope of catching up with Uriah. Herodotus saw I was trapped between the ropes and her dagger—it was either go back or step out and get killed. She lunged with her knife.

Creak!

The boards beneath her broke. "—Ah!" Herodotus fell through the floor, dropping her dagger. Uriah paused at her scream. She was struggling to hold herself up. "Forget about me! Go!" she called to him. Uriah did as she said. I saw his figure disappear onto the next level. I didn't know what he was dealing with up there, but he couldn't get to the vase that easily.

I heard Micah's voice below the structure, "These things just aren't made the way they used to be!" he called out. I didn't know where he was now, but he was doing a good job of keeping himself unseen and alive. I grabbed her dagger and cut a rope loose. With the floorboards gone, I'd have to swing to the stairs on the other side. I gripped the rope and stepped back to get momentum before jumping across the stairs across the missing boards. I hurried up to the next floor and came to a skidding halt. Something hot and green flashed before my face. I brought up my arm and winced in pain. Hot liquid singed my arm. I looked down and saw something green burning my skin. I glanced back up.

Uriah was at the center of the second level cutting through the acid that shot at him from different directions. Nicodemus was flying around dodging the green acid when Uriah called to him, "Go—find Herodotus." The falcon flew below. I was tempted to crawl by him on my hands and knees to avoid it, but there was hot acid on the floor. Uriah was wicked fast with his blade. He stepped around quickly, and even his footwork had me watching. But I'd never get across just watching. I got to my feet and took a stance cutting at the acid that shot in balls at me from different corners. Uriah shot his gaze at me. He was clearly shocked I'd made it this far.

"What is this stuff?" I asked, ducking another flying green bomb.

"Ghoul acid, used in dark magic but also made by the fowl creatures as a weapon," He ducked and came up, cutting through another bomb.

Another bomb was shot by my arm, and I let out a cry falling to one knee. Uriah ran at the wall adjacent to where the ghoul acid was firing and jumped off it. He cut through a black tube that was glowing. When he did, one final blast of acid shot out, and then it slowly dripped from the tube. Uriah landed in a squat beside me, still holding his sword that was steaming with green acid. I was looking up at the wall through my hair.

"Thanks," I breathed.

Uriah rose. "That wasn't for you. It was for the mission. Now stay here, and you're siblings won't have to see you go to the bench."

I stood up, still holding my sword. My shoes and pants had ghoul acid-burning small charred spots on them, I'd been hit more than him, but I wasn't ready to quit yet. "This is a simulation—not a real mission. What's wrong with…"

"And the fact you see it that way is exactly why you're going to fail," he stepped before me, looking down. His hair was slightly out of place, which was strange for him. His expensive white turtleneck scuffed slightly, but not nearly as much as I was. He flexed his hand around the hilt of his sword, and his brow contracted as he looked down at me. His hand was so tense I could hear the leather from his gloves stretch. "Take my advice Dyer…choose a calling you're more suited for."

"I'm glad I don't have your calling—to be a massive jerk," I held his gaze.

"At least I'm not a helpless victim masquerading as Commissioned. I could bench you right now if I wanted. The fact that I haven't is a pure act of *mercy, "* he said the word like he didn't like it. "You're too weak to fight—beating you would be an embarrassment more than a credit." He turned away from me and put a foot on the stairs starting up to the final floor.

My face grew hot. I glared after him, "Then why don't you take your best shot?"

He paused, "I'm trying to do you a service of *gallantry,* Dyer. Don't push my limits…."

I came at him, lunging with my sword. Uriah turned and blocked with a quick motion of the wrist.

Ching!

He looked down at me in curious surprise when the blades collided. I attacked him again. He raised his blade in a block. "This is getting sad. Stop now before I…"

I kept coming. I slashed and stabbed, but he continued to block. After a few seconds, he had to start defending more vigorously. Uriah was on the stairwell, so in terms of footwork, he was at a disadvantage. I whipped the blade at his head, and he ducked, lunging at me. I deflected and reached for one of the scrolls on his belt. He stepped to the side. My fingers brushed the side of a scroll. His eyes grew large. I slashed at him again, but my sword stuck in the railing of the stairwell. I paused. I could have sworn he was standing right there…

I turned, and Uriah was behind me. He slashed at my head. I ducked, coming up with another strike, but once again, he wasn't where I thought. "What the…"

Uriah was on the stairs above me. "It's called a gift."

"Some kind of cheap parlor trick!" I stepped forward after him.

"No, imagery. I can make you see things where they aren't. I did the same thing to your brother. With his super senses, he should have smelled it wasn't real, but I guess that was asking too much. The truth is, I don't even need that to beat you."

I nearly growled like Killian as I struck at him the next time. I knew it wasn't good to be angry when you confronted your opponent, but right now, it gave me a shot of energy. Uriah was backing up the stairs, now fighting more fiercely. He wasn't working as hard as I was, but I could see him putting in some effort. I back him up the stairs all the way to the top level. I slashed at his legs, and Uriah leaped over the blade. He landed and thrust with his sword.

I hurriedly blocked.

I backed up against the railing of the top floor. I could hear the crowd screaming now. I glanced back over my shoulder as Uriah was pressing his sword against mine. The students were getting more excited, and the yelling was deafening my ears. The top floor was the most open on the tower—the crowd could see us because it was only lined with railing. The vase was at the very top on a decorative stand glowing. My arms grew heavy and were aching from holding up my sword against his.

"Ready to quit?" he breathed as he felt my hands trembling.

I brought my foot down on his as hard as I could.

Uriah winced, and I shoved him off me. The crowd screamed with every change in events. I reached out and grabbed the scroll from his belt. He swung at me again, and I ducked, stumbling to the floor. I stepped back, avoiding his next slash. I brought my sword forward, blocking his downward strike. "You need both scrolls to win, Dyer…and I've never lost a challenge yet."

"There's a first time for everything!" I slipped my blade out from under his and turned, sending a side strike. Uriah blocked, raising an arm, and side-kicked me in the gut. I grunted and fell back on the floor.

The crowd went *Oooo!*

I groaned, sitting up.

Uriah looked at his blade casually as he strolled towards me. "You're committed…I'll give you that. But I've seen more zealous men fall away. You're a blind…you might not be one of the worst …but you're still one of them."

He had me at the end of the line, but I wouldn't quit. I wouldn't let all the Manor see me go down without a fight. I struggled to hold my sword up and kept the scroll behind me. He must not have realized I snatched it from his belt, it was a chance I could get him off guard…"Y-you need both scrolls…to win…remember?"

I panted and brought the scroll out from behind my back.

Uriah's eyes went down to his belt in shock. His surprise quickly shifted to a mix of outrage and determination. "You…." He said like he was about to curse but took a sharp breath and stopped himself. "…. For a blind girl to beat me, God would have to cause a tremor. So long, Dyer." He thrust at me with his sword.

The blade came at me in a split second. My amulet would take me out of the game. The edge of the sword came to a hair length from my chest. I closed my eyes when I felt the tower beneath me shake violently. I was jolted violently like the beams of the tower were being pushed. I grabbed at my amulet instinctively, wondering why I hadn't been teleported out. Immediately I regretted it.

Snap!

The small dark blue amulet fell from my t-shirt. A cry stopped in my throat as Uriah brought his blade down, and the tower shook. "— Wai…."

THWICK!

Chapter Eighteen

If there's anyone not fighting for their lives....
GET BUSY!

When I got to the pearly gates, I was telling on Uriah. He thinks he has a good list. Ha— wait till I tell the Lord he killed a helpless pitiful orphan girl. I didn't recall much from my catechism, but I remembered God saying *whatever you do for the least of these, you also do for me.* A pitiful sad orphan was definitely the *least,* and he wasn't being nice by killing me. Everything I'd tell the Lord and all the things I hadn't done flashed before my eyes the second his blade came down. His sword stabbed between the floorboards next to me.

I caught my breath.

Uriah was on one knee, holding onto the hilt of the sword as the building shook. "Hang onto me!" It took me a second to realize he was talking to me. I grabbed hold of his arm, dropping my sword. My weapon and the scroll rolled off the edge of the tower as I heard loud steps below.

I looked up at Uriah, whose chin was tucked as he struggled to hold on, "I didn't do that!"

"I know!"

I looked below at the walls of the arena. Part of them had been blown away like an explosion hit. Smoke was coming from them, but that wasn't the most shocking thing. Over the charred wood on the floor stepped a tall red figure in armor. I felt my heart stop in my chest. It was the armored creature from my dream.

"Oh my, Go…" I said.

Uriah turned his head to me slightly, "Watch your mouth!"

I pulled my head back, not liking how close this life-and-death situation was forcing us to be. "I've seen that thing!"

Uriah looked down, "How is that possible—I don't even recognize it...."

Down below, beside the beams that held up the structure, were some large creatures it took me a second to make out. They were height of the second floor or taller. The creatures were a greenishbrown color and bald but not like the ghoul in the window— it had broad shoulders and was less wrinkled. It wore a leather vest of some kind with fur. They'd broken through the arena doors somehow and now people below were running screaming. Uriah's gaze intensified. "....Trolls."

"That's what's shaking this thing?" I said frantically, loosening my grip slightly on his arm. I didn't like clinging to anyone this way which wasn't one of my brothers and especially not him.

"We need to get off this tower," Uriah nearly lost his footing as the tower tilted and shook. The tower was leaning in a slant now with gravity against us. He was holding onto the sword, but I wasn't holding onto him tightly enough. Uriah looked at my hands, noticing the change in my grip, "What are you...."

The tower rocked.

"I'm fi—" I tried to argue, but my arm slipped from his. "AHH!" I slid down the stairs into the tangled mess of ropes which cushioned my fall. But not for long; the tower was still rocking. The vase flew from the stand it was on and came flying toward me. I screamed (I'd like to say I did something at that moment more helpful than screaming, but I'd be a liar, okay?).

"Elsha, look out!"

I ducked my head, and the vase flew past me, shattering against another beam.

Uriah hung his head and let out a breath before pulling the sword free from the boards. He came sliding down in my direction as I slipped through the ropes.

"AHH!" (You try falling from a web of ropes on a slanted tower with a troll trying to shake you to your death and *not* scream, okay?)

Uriah dropped his sword on the way down and caught hold of a rope. He caught my hand with his other, gripping my fingers so tight I thought they'd tear off.

I winced in pain from the weight pulling at my limb. He was holding me by my arm alone. The tower was going down. Uriah's face was in pain from holding me. He grit his teeth. "I need you...to listen to me..."

"Okay...what do we do?"

"W-e....need to jump..." his breath was strained.

"Oka....WHAT?" I looked up at him wide-eyed. "Are you crazy!"

"Just do—as I say. On my word....now!" the tower was tipping closer to the ground. Uriah let go of the rope and pushed himself from the structure. I fell/jumped as it tumbled horizontally with a loud CRASH! Uriah and I rolled onto the floor, skidding across the dirt, and coming to a halt near the arena wall. I landed face-down and my whole body shook. Everything ached. I heard students and people screaming and rushing around me.

I forced myself onto all fours and looked up. "What the..." my eyes shot around. It was a chaotic mess of students running from their seats. Calisto was trying to lead everyone away safely. I heard Clash yell, "Get the weapons!" and saw her running towards one of the trolls with an axe. The other professors likewise grabbed their tools of the trade and rushed forward. The older long-time students followed, grabbing from the row of weapons that had been lined up for the challenge. Kaine had a crossbow and shotgun on his back and was following close behind. Students were running from the stands like crazy, and some of them were going to the armory. Collins levitated himself out of the teacher's box in his long dark blue dress coat and scarf that he'd worn for the occasion. He landed in the arena before the troll. Emma, Dashiel, and Riya were attempting to fend off the armored red knight. That was the most painful to see. The red knight lifted a forearm, and deep red flames flew from his armguard, shooting around the arena. That explained the charred smell. Riya tossed Dashiel a shield, and he squatted down, blocking Emma from the flames. Dante was in the arena now too. He was near the troll that had taken down the tower. There was too much to see and...

"Uriah!" He was on the ground next to me, not moving. I crawled over to him. I had no idea how to revive someone, so I hoped he wasn't dead. "Come on, I...I don't know how to...." I slammed my hands on his ribs, trying to remember how you woke someone up. "Please don't be dead!"

Uriah smacked my hand away, "What are you doing...cough* I'm not choking, and if I were, you'd have killed me by now..." he sat up, wincing in pain.

I blinked in shock, "You...you saved my life."

"It's commanded of me. Don't get personal," he touched his belt instinctively, grabbing for a weapon. "Oh, for heaven's sake..."

"We don't have weapons," I cried.

"I know. I lost mine saving you!" he said regrettably. "Get out of here to safety!" he ran towards the weapons rack.

I jogged after him.

Uriah looked annoyed at me, "What are you doing—I told you to go?"

"My family's out there! I'm not leaving!"

We got to the weapons rack. I grabbed another sword, and Uriah strapped on as much as he could wear. I ran towards the troll that Galahad and Herodotus were fighting. He was huge. Every step he took seemed to shake the dust on the ground forcing us to shield our eyes. Galahad had a larger sword than me—it was more medieval than mine. He stepped back out of the troll's stomp and stabbed at its legs with his weapon. I came to a halt behind him and forced my fear down. "G-Galahad, where did these things come from?"

Galahad glanced back at me, "Elsha—thank God you're okay. They just broke down the walls around the arena and started smashing things!"

"Death to the filthy Commissioned!" the troll grunted and growled.

"What does it matter where the un-Godly creatures came from— all that matters now is killing them," Uriah aimed a crossbow and fired, hitting the troll in the collarbone.

That seemed to only make him angrier. The troll brought both fists down in front of us, causing the ground to shake. All of us fell like dominos. Galahad crouched, holding me down so I wouldn't be tossed aside. He stood and brought his sword down on the creatures' wrists. The troll roared as blood shot from its wrist.

Galahad stepped back, pushing me behind him. "Got any ideas on how to kill this one?"

Uriah met the troll's gaze, and his expression strained.

The troll grunted, turning to the arena wall, "Kill!" he growled, walking over.

"Why is he going over there?" Galahad said.

"Shh—I can fake images, but I can't give illusions of sound or smell," Uriah's brow was straining as he stayed focused. "Galahad...how good are you with that sword?"

Herodotus shot her brother a surprised glance, "I can predict the monsters' movements, why don't I...."

I shot her a look. Was that her gift? Seeing what would happen next? It would make her actions in the arena make more sense.

"No—I need someone to get close and throw the sword like a javelin. You're not strong enough," Uriah asserted. The way he spoke to her was like the way Galahad talked to me.

Galahad and Uriah held each other's gaze for a second like they had an understanding. "I'll do it. Where do I throw it?"

"Just aim for the body, it's risky but if we can slow him down..." Uriah said.

"....Make him stumble onto Collins minefield," Galahad finished his sentence.

I looked between the two of them and put my hands to my head, "This is so weird...."

"We'll need to close the distance," Galahad said and Uriah nodded. Uriah's brow strained like he was concentrating as the troll walked closer to us. I didn't know what he was making him see but the creature was walking towards us blindly. Galahad moved in.

Uriah drew in a sharp breath and the troll began to turn around blindly, shaking the ground with every step. Galahad avoided the bombs on the floor and threw the sword at the troll's chest. I squinted, looking at the blade travel. It looked like it changed to a warm golden color for an instant there as he held it. There was no way he was going to make a shot like that. I put my hand to my mouth, praying the blade would at least wound him. My heart hammered. The blade went flying into the creature's chest, and he let out a loud cry. Galahad looked as shocked as I did. He was panting from the exertion as the creature stumbled towards us. The sword hadn't hit the heart, but something was happening as the troll stumbled into the mines. His body was crumbling apart like dust in layers till I could see his skull below his skin.

Uriah's mouth dropped along with the rest of us. None of us had expected that.

Galahad backed away and came running at us. Herodotus was staring, mouth agape when he grabbed her by the arm, "Get back!"

Collins explosions in blue and black powder were erupting all over the place as the creature crumpled from skin to bones falling on the mines. What was left of the troll fell face-first on the floor, and we all leapt to avoid getting crushed by the large skeleton. I looked up through my hair to see Clash was commanding the tigers in an assault on another troll. Commissioned were hanging on the creatures' arms, and Kaine was on it's back. The troll threw the students one by one off and grabbed Kaine, tossing him aside like he was a ragdoll. Kaine flew past Clash and skidded across the floor.

Collins was walking towards the beast creating blue flames in his hands and lunging at it. Fire shot from his hands in a powerful stream so bright I had to shield my eyes. The troll was throwing pieces of debris from the tower at him, and Collins raised hands catching them with levitation and tossing them aside.

Yikes, he was whacky in class but on a battlefield I was glad he was one of ours.

Tulken swung at it with a sword like Galahad's. My eyes darted around for the rest of my family. The Dark blood warrior from my dream was shooting a row of fire before Emma and Dashiel burning up any plants she put in his way. Riya had been scorched and was on the ground behind them.

"Give me the avengers for the glory of the dark master!" the warrior in red yelled devotedly.

My eyes looked around for my other brothers, "Where are Micah and Killian?!" I grew worried and frantic. Loud stomping came from the other side of the toppled structure.

"MAKE WAY!" Micah ran by with Killian next to him. Micah was holding an armful of tools that had been left out at the start of the challenge. Close behind them was Dante, and the biggest troll of them all was following. They were running directly at us. Dante turned and moved his hands like he was gripping the air. A long beam from the tower was covered in the luminous green and dragged out in front of the troll causing the large creature to fall on its face. The fall sent a wave of dirt blowing our way. It slowed the creature down.

Uriah was looking over Herodotus (who still seemed annoyed he hadn't let her kill the troll), through strands of brown hair that had fallen out of place and were now full of dirt. His expression turned distasteful as he saw my brothers and Dante coming, "Leave it to the black magic boy to bring the worst our way."

Dante and my brothers came to a skidding halt. "Hey—nice job going the distance with Uriah Elsha," Dante grinned at me, out of breath. "If I'd had Collins' replay crystal, I would have recorded it and taped it to my mirror…."

Where did he get the energy to joke right now?

"The challenge—wasn't—over." Uriah asserted, fixing his hair.

"Keep telling yourself that Hark…" Dante glanced over his shoulder at the troll still coming. "Trolls—who knew, right?"

Uriah glared at him disdainfully. "You heathenistic magic-using warlock…."

"Hey!" I objected.

"I'll bet you had something to do with this. Warlocks attract trouble wherever they go…." Uriah stepped towards Dante.

Dante tilted his head curiously at him. "I prefer more common terms, sorcerer, magic user, servant of darkness…." Dante spread his hands teasingly.

"Heretic!" Uriah snarled, raising his sword.

"Enough! Can we argue about this later, Killian!" Galahad snapped.

Killian raised his hands, frustrated, "Uh—for once, it's not me, okay?"

Galahad shook his head, "Right…. everyone weapons ready. It's getting up."

Uriah did as he was told and then shot Galahad a look as his falcon flew back to his shoulder.

Killian took a spare dagger from Uriah, and Micah was building something. "I hate to say this…but Emma's over there, and she's gonna be charcoal if we don't help her! Now I don't wanna ditch you guys, but she's our sister!"

I shot Galahad a desperate look. He was right.

Uriah looked at Herodotus before looking at Galahad. "Go. We've got this. More Commissioned are coming."

"That's nice and all, but how do we get over there in time? Emma's halfway across the arena," Micah tightened a screw on a unique crossbow he'd probably just made.

Dante broke into a smile as Uriah's expression grew wary. "I can fix that…everyone gets close." He pulled a small pouch from his black belt and took a handful of orange sand. He brought his hands together and made some symbols I'd seen in the magic books he read. His eyes flashed a brighter green as he said some words I couldn't understand. Uriah and Herodotus stepped back like they didn't want to be anywhere near him as the sand around us began to shift. Dante brought his hands together and then apart.

241

"Dante w…" I was cut short when the world around me faded in a flash like someone had turned the lights off. My stomach flipped, and my head spun. When the lights flashed back on, I wasn't in the same place. I was across the arena, and Uriah and Herodotus were far away. The world was spinning as I put my hand to my head and registered at the new place. We were with Emma across the arena. The world was hazy, and a green mist around us was leaving.

I nearly fell off my feet from dizziness when Dante's hand caught my arm, "Careful there—it's not a fun trip for first-timers. Teleporting that is." I blinked, looking up at him. Dante wiped a small amount of blood from his nose. I looked in front of me. Emma and Dashiel were sweating, backing away from the Dark blood warrior.

Micah gave Dashiel the crossbow he'd been tinkering with, "Here, try this."

It had two arrows lodged instead of one. Dashiel looked at it curiously. "Hm—much appreciated." He aimed and fired at the Dark blood, but the arrows hit his armor and were burned up. I didn't want to think what he'd do to human skin if we touched him.

Killian sniffed and then frowned, covering his nose, "That guy smells like smoke I've never known… it's like it's poisonous…."

"He's too hot for any of us to get close," Galahad shook his head, trying to reorient himself. "What do you want here?" Galahad moved protectively before Emma, who Killian was now holding up.

"TO DESTROY THE AVENGERS AND ALLOW THE DARK LORD TO RULE ONCE MORE! TO FREE MY BRETHREN AND BRING THE BLOOD OF THE COMMISSIONED TO EVERY DOORSTEP!" All the things from my dream were coming back.

Micah frowned, "I'm sorry we asked."

"Who are these avengers you keep talking about?" Emma struggled not to pass out. Using that much energy to call on plants must have drained her.

Dante took a deep breath, and his eyes flashed green as he made hand symbols, pulled a hand back and lurched forward with it at the Dark blood warrior. A stream of frost came from Dante's hands and shot at the monster as he swung at us with his long sword. The cold was enough to slow his blow, so we could step out of the way. But the thick layers of jagged frost which Dante formed on him melted and cracked away as the Dark blood warrior moved. Galahad slashed at him and lunged, stabbing, but the armor was barely scratched. The Dark blood broke through the last thin layer of ice holding his arms and swung at Galahad. My brother ducked. Galahad moved his head from side to side, avoiding his strikes till the Dark blood raised his arm and shot fire again. We all dropped to the floor. I had to pull Dante to the ground because he was so drained. Galahad clutched his arm. The Dark blood had scorched him.

"Galahad!" I was shaking as the warrior approached us.

"ALL OF THE COMMISSIONED WILL FALL TO THEIR KNEES, AND ALL WILL BURN! PERISH MISERABLE RIGHTEOUS ONES!" he aimed his forearm down at us and was about to release a stream of flames. Galahad struggled to raise his scorched arm and defend us. Emma had passed out. There was now a thin stream of blood coming from Dante's nose as his eyes rolled up into his head dizzily. Dante raised a trembling hand to try and use magic. Most likely, he wanted to push the warrior back, but his hands and rings were scuffed with dirt and blood from wiping his nose.

I stood up before the rest of them, holding my sword tightly. "Leave—them—alone!" I didn't know what I could do, but I wouldn't let him burn all of us alive. I brought my sword forward, holding the hilt with both hands, and struck the warrior coming at us on the side where I could reach. As my weapon connected with him, a shockwave of white light went out across the arena, sending the Dark Blood Warrior and me flying in different directions. The shock of light blinded me. I flew on my back and felt pain course through me. And something else…it was like my energy had been drained all at once. I groaned as the sky above me and the shadows of my family faded into a blur.

Chapter Nineteen

I *Almost* Have My First Dance

I awoke to the smell of a freshly cleaned room and cotton sheets. There were flowers on the window seat and other beds near me. I'd only been in the room once before, and it was during our tour. There was a pitcher of orange juice on the bedside table and a single rose beside it. It didn't match the rest of the flowers on the window seat. My siblings were sitting at different seats around me. I sat up, and Emma rushed to my side first. I asked what happened, but none of my family was a hundred percent certain. Emma said the teachers had killed the last ogre, Uriah, and his sister killed the other. The Dark blood warrior from my dreams had disappeared.

That was what I had the most questions about. Galahad said the teachers were in a meeting now while Collins strove to reconstruct the magical barrier that had kept the Manor protected and hidden from Demonic forces. Somehow, they got through it. Tulken was in the doorway, speaking to Kaine in hushed tones. When he saw I was awake, he entered the room.

"Headmaster…what…what happened back there?"

Tulken put his hands in his pockets and looked down at me, "How are you feeling, little one?"

"Better, except my head weighs a ton," I groaned, running my hand through my tangled hair. Emma handed me a glass of orange juice that was on the bedside table. "Who were those things after?"

Tulken looked out the window at the garden team cleaning up the arena. His face was scuffed, and he had a cut above his eye. I guessed he got it in the fight with the troll. "All questions are to be answered in due time. My fellow Professors want to be certain before we give you answers. That Dark Blood warrior couldn't have been stopped without you. You saved the life of everyone in that arena Elsha."

I blinked, "—Me? I couldn't have…I don't even know how that happened…Dante could have made that blast."

Tulken shook his head, "No, it was you."

"Are you saying…." Killian began darting his gaze around at all of us. "Elsha's gifted too?"

Emma shot him a sideways glance, "Try not to sound so surprised, knucklehead!"

"Your sister has an extremely rare gift. Light magic. Congratulations, Elsha, it's an ability all dark powers fear," Tulken said. "That's how you saw those creatures at the orphanage that your siblings couldn't. It was also how your brother Galahad managed to throw the sword directly into the troll's chest from that distance. Your magic guided the tool because your emotions were pushed."

I was paralyzed.

What? Me? Gifted?

Three of my siblings jumped up and ran to my side, giving me congratulatory hugs and high-fives. Killian remained at a distance where he was--his expression went from surprised to bothered. Galahad shot him a glance as he noticed but said nothing. Emma hugged me, "Wow, that's so cool!" "Awesome!" Micah was jumping up and down.

Galahad asked the question that was on my mind. "If you know her gift…what is it you and the Professors have to discuss?"

Tulken looked down a moment before giving a small smile at us. "That will be an announcement for tomorrow night. After all, we promised you, children, a Homecoming dance. And with how hard you've worked along with the other students… you've earned a night to celebrate. By tomorrow night, the faculty should have come to a decision on how to handle the troll's infiltration." Tulken went to the door where Kaine was waiting with his arms crossed. He paused and looked back at me, "Oh, and Elsha...."

I arched my head.

"In the future, try not to keep secrets from me. Your brother told me of your dreams. They were visions. Somehow you were able to see the Dark blood Warrior rise. If we'd known sooner, we would have tried to help you," Tulken said sympathetically. He softened his tone, "You need to trust us. Everyone here may not be your blood relative, but we are brothers and sisters in our calling." He walked out of sight with Kaine, and I immediately felt guilty. I'd been so used to people not listening to me or thinking I was crazy it was difficult to let anyone in. I hung my head.

Emma put her head on my shoulder, "Hey—don't look so down. You've found your gift!"

"You don't think I could have prevented this...." I began.

Galahad sat on the edge of the bed next to me and tousled my hair. "—Don't even think like that. Just because you saw the dark blood warrior doesn't mean you had any idea it was coming for us or that it could get through the barrier. What worries me is what that means for the Manor."

Killian crossed his arms, sitting on the window seat. He wasn't happy. That wasn't new, but I didn't get what the cause was this time. "If you ask me, Tulken isn't being the fairest guy in the world. He wants Elsha and us to trust them, but we don't know everything they know."

"They're the teachers. They're supposed to know more than us," Emma retorted. "Whatever is going on, they think it best we don't know yet. I say we let them handle this problem for now and do like Tulken said. Celebrate. We can't do anything more now, and he said they'd have an answer tomorrow night."

The rest of my siblings murmured assent.

Emma crossed her arms, looking at Galahad accusingly, "And speaking of keeping secrets...why didn't you tell us you didn't get a gift?"

Galahad shrugged, "I didn't want to make it about me."

"But you couldn't have been happy with it!" Emma said.

Galahad cast a gaze up at her. It was like he was trying to sort through what to say to that. "*And?* I wasn't happy about it, but I could live with it. I knew how much stock Elsha was putting in it, so I was more concerned about how she'd react, but I should have been more honest with you guys."

I looked at Killian, "You knew?"

Killian nodded, "I knew whether he got a gift or not, we wouldn't hear about it. Either way, he probably thought it would make you feel worse, so as usual, *Mr. Perfect* kept it to himself."

Galahad turned to me, changing the subject, "But now that you know what your gift is..." he smiled brightly. "We really have something to celebrate. I'm so proud of you."

I smiled, but Killian's resentful expression didn't change.

Emma beamed, "You know what that means...."

We all looked at her.

Emma smoothed Killian's hair teasingly. "Time to dress up!" He

swatted her hand away, "Ah, heck no!"

#

News traveled fast in the Manor of Raziel. As soon as I got out of the infirmary, Emma and I found out that word of my light magic had already been passed around. I asked if the rest of the kids were okay, and Emma said none of them had sustained any major injuries. Dante had been by to see me while I was unconscious but had been ushered away by the nurse outside. My siblings had been allowed to stay. I didn't' see why the nurse had sent him off if he'd helped fight off the trolls, but I guess some biases existed even here at the Manor. Emma and I talked with Cheryl, Joyce, and Leanne about the dresses we wanted (Emma *wanted,* and I forcibly conceded to wearing them). The maids' household magic included sewing, and they'd made dresses for the kids who didn't have any from home as well as suits for the boys. Galahad and Killian thought suits were torture—Micah surprisingly didn't mind. He had Joyce make him a pin-strip suit (Micah had a closet love of gangsters. Don't ask me why). Eventually, he talked Killian into being okay with a suit because he said they could look like mobsters together (they'd seen one gangster movie at the Boarding House, and now it was a thing, okay?)

Emma had the maids design her a pink dress that looked straight out of Jane Austen's times. It wasn't surprising since Pride and Prejudice was her favorite book. Galahad rented it for her many times, along with comics for the boys (a.k.a. Micah and Killian). Emma's dress had short, artfully wrinkled sleeves and was straight below the ribs with a small ribbon. Emma had input with my dress (I told her nothing would help, but she insisted). A blue dress with small ¾ length sleeves that had slight ruffles and a fitted waist like a princess corset but not as painful, along with small flat blue shoes, and my hair was curled slightly, held back by a blue ribbon. I was afraid our dresses would look too old-fashioned or something, but when we got to the dance, we were the least strangely dressed people.

Everyone in the grand hall had their own style. Oh yeah…the Hall. Let's talk about that first. The grand hall was where the Manor had banquets, parties, and such. It was like a large, nice, decorated warehouse. There were long buffet tables with food. Lights hung in streams from the rafters, and the dance floor was at the center of the room. The faculty table was at the head where Clary, Clash, and Kaine were. Tiki torches were outside in the Hall's doorway leading into the yard. There was a gazebo out in the yard with a small wooden dance floor beside it and lights there as well. It looked amazing. Even if I stood in a corner the whole time, listening to the music and watching would be fun. Calisto was by the dessert table, arranging things with Addie, Dori, and Jasmine. Dori was wearing a poofy pink dress and had her hair curled like a princess. Her crazy grin made it difficult for her to look innocent, though. Addie wore a purple skirt to her calves and a loose white shoulder-bearing shirt with long beads, with a bandana like a fortune teller. Jasmine had a purple dress but kept her small biker boots and leather jacket.

Emma and I went right for them.

Social occasions were never comfortable for me. I never knew what to do besides stand there and watch people talk, but Emma insisted we should go. I was determined to at least try to have a good time. As I walked past the student, I brushed someone's arm.

I stepped back, looking up, and a look of horror crossed my face.

"Forgive me miss…" Uriah stepped back with a slight nod of his head when he froze. His eyes grew large as he gave me a once over like he didn't recognize me. He was in a pricey-looking dark suit with gold cufflinks and a white collared shirt—most likely, his family had provided the attire. I recalled he saved my life in the challenge, but honestly, I still wasn't totally comfortable with him. "—Elsha," his brow contracted.

I wasn't sure what to say but I didn't want to be rude. I was surprised he was even acknowledging me. "Uriah—how's your sister?"

His expression almost softened. "She's fine."

Awkward silence.

"Did you hear," Emma put her arm in mine. "Elsha has light magic," she said proudly.

I was tempted to put it in his face too, but he'd think it was petty. Emma, as usual, didn't care what anyone thought. Uriah's expression twisted slightly as he glanced down at his shoes before looking up at me, "Yes...I *heard*," he said the words like cracking glass. He gestured towards me with his head stiffly, "—Congratulations. If a Commissioned is going to be gifted in the arts, we should at least have proof the magic is the good kind."

"Thanks," I held his gaze. It was killing him to accept I had a gift. Because that meant he couldn't tell me I didn't belong here anymore.

"—You're welcome," he said like he may as well have been cursing me. "....Excuse me." He crossed the room to Thomas, Riya, and Herodotus, who was all expensively attired. He walked around people like they didn't exist and only nodded at teachers and students I'd seen sitting with him.

Emma shot me a look. "Burr! He's about as jealous as they come...."

"Of me?" I said incredulously as we walked over to Addie.

"You heard Tulken. Because of you, everyone in the arena was saved, that includes Uriah. I'm guessing he doesn't like being saved by someone he called a blind minutes earlier," Emma shrugged. Dori straightened her tiara, "I tell you, the boys had better be able to control themselves with how good we're looking tonight...."

Addie rolled her eyes, setting out a plate of benign and fixing her bandana. "I doubt we're having trouble getting too many names on our dance card."

Dori fixed her dress, "Speak for yourself—I've already seen many a stallion giving me the eye..." she waved at some boys across the hall and grinned. She winked in Uriah's direction, and he averted his gaze, annoyed. Dori nodded, "Oh yeah—he likes me."

Addie frowned.

"What? He might be stuck up, but he's cute!" Dori objected.

Addie looked up as Emma, and I approached and broke into a smile, "Wow! You guys look amazing!" she approached Emma and took her hands, looking at her dress.

"Thank you, and so do you," Emma said. "Have you seen my mischievous brothers around?"

Our brothers came up, talking amongst themselves. Galahad was speaking to Killian in a hushed tone. Killian's was a simple black suit, and Galahad's was dark blue. They paused before they reached us, and Galahad said a few words to Killian before Emma closed the gap.

"What are you guys whispering about? Look who we found?"

Galahad smiled, complimenting Emma and me. He pulled at his suit collar, and I could see he was no more comfortable than I was.

Micah was grinning like a Cheshire cat in his pin strip suit and hat with a piece of licorice in place of a cigar. One of the boys from our class Chamberlin had come over and was talking to Jasmine.

Killian's eyes fell on Addie, and his slightly irritated expression changed to wide-eyed. Addie looked up at him, "…What?"

"You look….uh…" Killian cleared his throat and put his hands in the pockets of his pants. "You…look okay, Addie."

"Thanks. My mom was a fortune teller before she was a cook. I used to dress up, and... you can guess what my Halloween costume was," Addie laughed, glancing down.

Killian nodded with a small smile, and Addie's expression shifted, "Are you okay?"

Killian shrugged, "I'm fine."

Everyone else at the party made me a little more relaxed. Some boys were in Viking outfits (Kaine's class), suits, Greek dresses, and prom-style dresses. The Manor embraced differences.

Killian was looking at me like he barely realized I'd dressed up. "You're in a dress..."

I immediately wished I'd come in jeans. Whenever I did things out of character for me, like speak up, joke, the boys never let me forget it. "Yeah, I uh…" I knew it—it looked bad. "It was Emma's idea…" I began to say.

"You look nice. A little out of character but...nice," Killian said finally.

"Thanks," I smiled.

Killian relaxed against the table and put one foot over the other. "Well…the kids at the Manor can't dance. Not that it's a big deal to me; dancing is for losers."

Addie moved her head thoughtfully, "I like it."

Killian looked at her in shock, "You do?" His expression strained, "I guess it doesn't completely suck..."

"Galahad, why don't you ask someone to dance?" Emma smacked him lightly on the arm.

"Okay…Emma, do you wanna dance?" Emma laughed and grabbed Galahad's hand taking him out on the floor.

Jasmine was talking to Chamberlin while Killian and I drank punch and chatted with Micah and Addie. "And they had me fence with this little kid. He was short, like shorter than me…."

Killian looked at Jasmine, who was about 4'11, in all sincerity. "Was he a dwarf?"

"And I was…." Jasmine turned her head to Killian, and her brows knit into a deep frown. "Watch it, pretty boy. I might not be big, but I know jujitsu."

Killian laughed before he realized she wasn't joking. "…. Seriously?"

Jasmine nodded, crossing her arms. "Just give me a reason…"
"Okay…one of us should be dancing," Micah extended his hand to
Dori. "My lady…." Dori grinned and took his hand out to the dance
floor. Killian turned his attention to Addie, and Jasmine danced with
Chamberlin. I was beginning to feel like a third wheel standing there,
but I tried to be happy for them. Killian was getting Addie to talk to
him, and Micah was having fun. As I stood there, the party music
seemed to fade as my thought weighed heavily. I was glad I had a
gift, but I had no idea what it meant I was capable of. All the
consequences of that gift…. I'd have to go to magic classes. Would
that make the other kids look at me differently? They already picked
on Dante and Addie. Suddenly, I felt like kids in the room were
looking at me, murmuring to themselves. I slipped away from the
conversation between Addie and Killian. They didn't notice. I slipped
through some students and passed dancing couples to find a new
corner of the room to catch my breath. I came to a halt at a pair of
curtains and looked down at my hands. Everything made sense
now—the plate flying into the jerk at the orphanage, the car flying
out the gate when I was scared, and Kaine saving us from the witches;
even being here…having magic meant I really belonged. But
somehow…I didn't feel better.

I didn't know what this meant for me, if I'd have to study to be a
teacher like Collins if I'd ever find our parents…. I'd seen the
sorceress in my dream at our first home. It had gone up in flames, and
she was there. Tulken said my dreams were visions, so that had to
mean something, but what? I heard Herodotus and Riya walking up
and chatting. I slowly backed up and put my hand on the red curtain
behind me when I realized there was no wall behind it.

I slipped behind the curtain until I backed into someone.

"Ah!" I nearly jumped out of my skin. I turned around. I'd bumped
into Dante, who'd been sitting on the arm of a lounge in the fireplace-
lit room. Dante dropped a book he'd been holding and something
small and metal. My heart stopped with embarrassment as we stood

and looked at each other. Dante was dressed up slightly for the occasion, wearing his good, less worn black leather knee-high boots and a new black dress shirt under his vest that had silver buckles keeping it shut.

"Elsha," he said as if it took a moment to recognize me. In the firelight and in my dress, it was probably difficult. He broke into one of his disarming smiles that looked so innocent but mischievous; somehow, at the same time, he didn't say anything, but I knew he was smiling at the dress. Clearly, he found it amusing that I'd worn one—I couldn't blame him; it was so unlike me.

I opened my mouth to speak when I realized I'd caused him to drop all the books he was holding. It was typical of Dante. There was a party going on outside with food, dancing, and gossip—but he was hiding and reading magic stuff.

"Hey, I'm so sorry about knocking that over...." I squatted instantly to pick it up. He did the same, and both of our hands fell on a dark brown leather-bound book. My hand touched his, and my nerves did a dance on my goosebumps, making me shiver. His hand was cold and long, unlike my small round hands. My eyes fell on the label on the book *The Art of Magical Immunization.* I could've sworn that was one of the black magic books from class they told us not to touch, but then—Dante wouldn't be touching it if it were wrong somehow. A small metal coin he'd dropped rolled into the fireplace, and I panicked.

"Elsha what are you..."

I reached out my hand. The coin came out of the ashes and flew into my hand, slightly scorched now. I winced from the pain since the coin was hot now, I blew the ash from it, but it was still burned. "I'm really sorry, it's a little burned, but I'm sure you can shine it...." I was afraid I'd ruined a family trinket.

Dante stood holding the book. "It's just a piece of tin, a coin—it's *not* worth a fortune. And what's more, it doesn't have any magical properties, so…pretty much useless."

I looked down at the coin. I recognized a Celtic cross engraved on it with a flower at the center. It was old and faded but nice. I guessed for a Manor based on an angel; Christian art was everywhere. I felt silly being so worried about it, but it was nice. "It's uh…still really pretty."

He stared at me blankly before gently taking back the coin. I nearly dropped it because I was trying hard not to let my hand touch his. I didn't want the physical reaction it gave my nerves to make me embarrass myself anymore.

"The Professors at the Manor use these as book markers," he said, flipping through the book to show me. There were coins of various sizes, leaving indentations of various Christian designs in the book. "We've literally got thousands of them," he flipped the coin through his ringed fingers so I could hear the metal *clink* before slipping it into his pocket.

"I don't remember that book being in the main Library," I tried to change the subject.

"It wasn't," he put it into a black leather-bound bag with buckles that sat on the couch. He cast his gaze up to me, "Did you get my flower?"

I flushed, "Th-that was from you?"

Dante smiled. "When I was sick at my Boarding House, I spent a week in bed with the flu, measles, and chicken pox before anyone came to check on me. Usually, it was to see if I died so they could use the bed. So, I figure people appreciate getting *get-well* gifts and all that."

I blinked. I couldn't tell if he was kidding because he was smiling as he said it, but then—it sounded too horrible to make up, and Dante wasn't a liar. "Did that…really happen to you?"

Dante laughed half-heartedly before a solemn expression crossed his face, "…I was sick a lot as a kid."

I rested my hands on the back of the couch, looking down, "And I thought Blech's was bad…how old were you?"

"Eleven. Kaine found me not much longer after that," Dante looked down at the buckles on his book bag. The firelight cast a shadow on his face as a memory seemed to fade in his eyes. "I'm sorry," I said. "At least you've found good people here."

He didn't respond.

"I can go…did I interrupt your reading?"

"Nah, I'd just rather be doing…pretty much anything else besides talking, dancing, and…all that. All the parties and recreation Tulken makes me do just take time away from my studying magic," he put the books in his bag.

"I guess you and Uriah have that in common…being book smart," I sat on the back of the couch and put my hands in my lap, looking down.

Dante laughed briefly, "Uriah likes to know it all because he's Commissioned, and he's gotta be the best at everything. I eat, sleep, and breathe magic because it's the only thing that's given me power my whole life. And being powerless… it's not something I'd wish on anyone. Can you keep a secret, Dyer?"

"Of course," I couldn't disagree when he looked at me.

He pulled out the book from the bag and held it out, "This book was in the forbidden room."

"The one Dashiel tells me every time we pass it that it's offlimits?"

"That's the one. Tulken tries to keep it from us, but all the interesting books are in there. Go ahead, look through it," he said casually. Nothing about this should have been casual—we'd learned in class that books we were forbidden to learn from were dark magic. And dark magic was unstable and dangerous; my hand trembled even at the prospect of touching it. Like hot coal, I didn't want it anywhere near me; Dante could sense it.

"It won't hurt you," he said.

"But Tulken said…."

"Tulken's being careful, but if he's never let anyone up there, how does he know that the books are dangerous? They haven't been used in years."

I nodded. If Dante said that they were okay, they couldn't have been that bad. I took the book—it didn't burn me. I let out a breath of relief and flipped it open, looking through the cracked brown pages. There were spells about being immune to poisons, counterspells, aging, and sickness; none of that seemed bad. "Why wouldn't Tulken want us having spells like this? They look like they might come in handy."

Dante shrugged and took the book back, "I don't know, he somehow thinks that these defy the *natural order* of things, and anything that does that is dark."

"But that interests you?" I rested my hands on the back of the couch.

Dante's face grew solemn in the firelight, "I think there's a reason we have special gifts. You, your brothers, and your sister, we can do things mortals can't because we were meant for more. Anything we want to know that normal people couldn't learn, don't have access to, we should be able to have it. If we can't, what good are all these gifts?"

"There are things you really want to know," I guessed.

"Is it any different for you?"

"No," I said honestly. I still wanted to know who my parents were and why they split up, to remember how happy life was when I had them, for it to be more than a vague dream. "I've always wanted to know more about my parents, their lives, what we were like as a family when we were happy."

"And there's no reason you shouldn't," he said. "It's not wrong to want to know more about our lives in this twisted, messy, screwed-up world. But Tulken doesn't see it that way right now," he said, putting the book away. Suddenly his expression grew concerned," Elsha, you can't tell anyone about this, *especially* not Tulken. Promise me."

"Okay, calm down, Dante. I wouldn't do that. I promise," I said, making him relax. I didn't want him not to trust me, and if I could keep this to myself, he'd consider me more of a friend. He'd rely on me.

He straightened on the arm of the couch, still taller than me, and crossed his arms," So, you're not one for parties?"

I stared at him. The answer to that question should have been obvious, "I'm not really."

"Every pretty girl should feel welcome at a party..." he tilted his head.

"Pretty? You think...I look pretty in this?" I gestured to the outfit. I could hear the music from the party going on outside.

"You should be out there waiting for some sad sappy boy to ask you to dance," he gestured outside the curtain with a hand, not answering my question.

"I don't even know how to dance."

He shrugged unenthusiastically, "I can teach you."

"I...I don't want to embarrass myself..."

Dante rolled his eyes with a smile, "We've been over this, Dyer...how are you gonna excel at anything if you're too scared to start? The girl sticking it to Uriah in that challenge wasn't afraid to embarrass herself."

I laughed, "Oh, I was mortified."

Dante snapped his fingers, pointing one at me, "But you still did it, right? I didn't care about dancing because it had nothing to do with my magic and, therefore, was kind of a waste of time. But you....how are you gonna have fun at a party if you don't dance?" he stood up and stepped towards me. I wanted to. I had the image of dancing by the fireplace like a princess in a movie and getting to feel magical for the first time in my life. There might not be any harm in learning. I raised my hand, hoping it wasn't shaking. His eyes sparked as he saw I was almost willing to step out of my comfort zone.

Before our hands touched, the curtains to the room were pulled open.

We both turned to see Kaine standing in the doorway with his usual expression. His eyes went to Dante and then to me curiously. "H.M.T. wants to see everyone out front for an announcement in a bit. What have you two been up to?"

For a moment, I thought he was concerned in a protective way. But anyone who thought I needed a chaperone with a boy had eye trouble. But shockingly, when my eyes went back to Dante, he looked

260

a little disappointed at the interruption. But he lowered his head a moment before looking back up at Kaine respectfully.

"Just telling her about some of these books, Kaine, nothing nefarious."

"Hall—now," Kaine asserted.

Dante let out a breath, "Never a moment when I'm not needed….shall we?" he extended a hand. I stared at it stupidly. Kaine's glares at us deepened, and I suddenly felt self-conscious and held my arms. Dante retracted his hand more from my reaction than Kaine's gaze. I held my arms and walked out of the room beside Dante, who let out a disappointed breath. Dante and I walked over to my siblings, who were gathered around the punch table. Emma was talking to Dashiel a few feet away, and Uriah stood by him. Uriah shot Dante and me an offhanded look as we approached together.

Dashiel looked like he was trying to listen to my sister, making eye contact and nodding. Emma was telling him about our stories. I think he was shocked by how much thought we put into our *games*. "That's…very expanding for the imagination," he commented. "I don't meet many young ladies able to do so much with their minds." Emma beamed.

Uriah was standing by him, holding a glass of punch he casually examined, "It's not very becoming of a Commissioned young lady to waste her time. My sister Herodotus as an accomplished young woman, spends her time gaining a thorough knowledge of history, doctrine, music, the arts, combat, gymnastics, singing, and dancing."

Emma scrunched her nose, "And I guess someday you'll marry an *accomplished commissioned* like your sister?"

Uriah sipped his drink. "I plan to be wed before the age of five and twenty. When I am, an accomplished Commissioned will bear me ten children at least."

Emma raised an eyebrow at Uriah, "If you find a woman who knows *all* that stuff *and* wants to bear you ten kids, let me know."

"If you'd like to receive her tutelage on how to be an acceptable wife, I'd applaud your submission," Uriah said condescendingly. "No, I'd like to know why of all the boys she could have married, she picked you!" Emma said flatly. Dashiel suppressed a laugh. He seemed surprised at himself for nearly releasing the emotion and cleared his throat. Uriah shot him a glare. Emma excused herself and followed Dante and me away from Uriah's group, going off on how he'd ruined her talk with Dashiel.

As we all started talking at once and having three different conversations when Kaine started telling the room to be quiet. The rest of the kids didn't listen. Kaine yelled, "QUUUUUIIIIEEEETTTT!"

As the room silenced, the only person left talking was Dori, "And I said, Professor, I don't see why I can't use the chemistry set to burn a hole into the boys' locker room…."

We all looked at her.

"Okay, that tells us something," Emma said.

Micah huffed, "Yeah, I'm putting acid-proof walls in the boys' locker room."

Tulken walked up to the dark brown wooden podium and silenced everyone. A pen could drop, and you would have heard it when he stood up there. "Students, a matter of great importance has come to my attention. And while my instinct is to protect you from it, it is you who will be called upon to face it."

I saw Dante watching him fixedly while Jasmine did her best to look calm. Clearly, these kids had faced their fair share of troubles in the past—they were on pins and needles, wondering what it would be. Uriah narrowed his gaze and listened intently with his sister by his side.

Tulken's expression grew grave, "The fate of the world is at stake."

Murmurs and whispers went around the room. Some were saying, "What?" "How?" "Not again…" Kaine let out a groan and ran his hand through his hair. Professor Maddison started to hyperventilate. Dashiel blinked, acknowledging the fact. Galahad held Tulken's gaze, and Emma's mouth fell open.

"And as all of you know, when the safety of mankind is threatened, it's once again time to gather a team and form a mission," Tulken said.

Uriah let out a breath and looked at his sister. He started telling his group what they needed to gather and how to prepare. It made sense. After all, he and his team had won twenty-two matches. I wouldn't be surprised if he got sent off to handle whatever this was.

"Is he serious?" Micah said.

"I think he is," Galahad said as if he knew more about this than me.

Emma's face grew white right alongside mine. "The...the *world*? That's...how...this is awful! What could be worse?"

"Normally, we send teams based on individual skill, experience, and gifts fitting the task. In this case, however, the warriors we've been waiting for have finally been called. The Dyer family are the only ones who can save it. They…. are the Avengers of Light," Tulken said.

All of our mouths fell open.

Killian looked the most shocked of my siblings, aside from me. He couldn't form words, "We're...what?"

Uriah's glass fell from his hand and shattered on the floor. He was staring, mouth agape like the rest of us. Even Dante couldn't hide his surprise as his mouth parted and his eyes grew large. Dori fainted. One student started crying.

Micah let out a breath, "Oh look—it got worse."

Chapter Twenty

We're off to Save the World

Tulken said something after that, but my mind was stuck at *Avengers of Light*, the *fate of the world,* and *the Dyers are our only hope*…that was the hardest to believe. All the students had an expression like they knew what that was. Uriah's expression was twisting as he parted his mouth to speak, but nothing came out.

Eventually, he stepped forward and spread his hands, "Headmaster, there *must* be some mistake. The Avengers of Light are supposed to be formidable warriors, the kind of Commissioned others respect and admire. Selfless, reverent, meek tempered, gifted, educated…." As he continued talking, my siblings turned their heads to him. I felt like telling him all of that was insulting, but something told me he already knew.

Micah crossed his arms and arched an eyebrow, "—Just *what* are you getting at Uriah?"

Galahad shook his head, stepping forward, "What do you mean the fate of the world is at stake?"

"And who are the Avengers of Light?" I asked.

"You are," Tulken gestured to us. "Ages ago, it was prophesied that five warriors of the elect would be gifted to face one of the third. We've generally believed that Asmodeus, one of the worst of them— was locked away three years ago. But signs have said otherwise. Now I have word from the other Manor's; they believe forces are gathering under him. Asmodeus… wasn't fully imprisoned. That Dark Blood warrior who you saw in your dream Elsha, he has an army like him on the other side."

"The *other side*?" Killian said.

"Hell—exactly where Asmodeus is supposed to be. What your sister witnessed in her dream was one of the Dark blood being brought into this world. Their sole mission is to serve one of the third and plunge the world into darkness," Tulken said. "The five of you are the sorceress of light," Tulken looked at me. He turned to Emma and then to Micah, "…the empress, the craftsmen…" he settled his gaze on Galahad. "And the warrior."

Galahad knit his brow confused, "Wait…I thought I didn't have a gift?"

"We couldn't identify it until recently. I didn't want to say anything till I was certain, but there's more than one reason you and your sister were able to kill that troll. As the warrior of light, you have the gift of endowing weapons you use with righteous justice. The ordinary sword you used was blessed to harm a demon, ghoul, monster, and any other servant of the fallen one. After all of you were sent to the infirmary, we confiscated it. You're the only one who can use that blade now."

Killian's expression was the most dumbfounded (second to mine). "The sorceress, empress, craftsmen, he's the warrior—what's my title?"

Tulken exchanged glances with Collins, who nodded. "The beast."

Killian opened his mouth to object, but Tulken continued. "I don't understand the terminology in all of your titles, but as of now, we can only attribute it to your supernatural enhanced senses and strength. Professor Clash has the gift of being able to temporarily take on any animal's ability, but she can't have one more than one at a time, and it doesn't last. We thought yours was something similar, but your senses and speed are enhanced all the time without you having to borrow any creature's strength."

Killian was speechless.

Galahad shook his head, "But we can't be…."

Tulken raised a hand, "It's not me who's saying you are—your calling has come from an *infinitely* higher place than my opinions. Only you and you're family can stop Asmodeus."

I was trying to find words, but they weren't coming. "But…you said he was in hell. How can he be in two places at once? I saw a man on a throne in my dream with a sorceress. He didn't look like Asmodeus from Kaine's class."

"A seer at the head council for the Commissioned believes Asmodeus has a link to the mortal world. He may have inhabited a host. If that Dark Blood Warrior you saw in your vision was pledging allegiance to the man on the throne, that must have been Asmodeus' vessel. His…mouthpiece, if you will. The third and other demons can possess a willing host if they are of the world."

"So Asmodeus wasn't completely imprisoned, and now he's using someone to gather forces and destroy the world?" Galahad summed it up.

"Enslave it, most likely," Dashiel corrected calmly.

Killian huffed, "Thanks, sunshine, we get the picture. Is that why the Dark Blood came here? Because it somehow knew we were the Avengers?"

"Asmodeus has eyes of his own in many places…he must have known five of the Commissioned were chosen. The Avengers of Light are the only ones to stand between the third and the world. He wants you destroyed," Tulken said. "This won't be easy, but now that we know who the five of you are…." His expression looked heavy. "We've had so little time to train you…we'd understand if you aren't ready for this... But I have to warn you, even if you don't take this mission and remain at the Manor....it won't be safe here anymore. The trolls were just the beginning. Someone must take this mission, whether or not that's the five of you..." he exhaled. "I'll be waiting for

267

your decision in my office. If you accept, you'll have to leave immediately."

Uriah went after Tulken, arguing for him and his sister to go in our stead.

Galahad turned around to face us and opened his mouth.

"Family meeting," we said in unison.

As usual, a family meeting was more like a heated debate with us. And before we even got into voting (we took the democratic approach to everything, okay?), apologies had to go around for everything we said during the debate *cough** argument. Killian and Emma apologized (not that they were the ones who started it, but I'm just saying), Micah said sorry, and so did Galahad and I (even though he wasn't really at fault). Eventually, we looked at all angles, but no matter how insane what Tulken was saying sounded, it all came back to one thing: the fate of the world. If we didn't try to stop Asmodeus, then more monsters would come here. The lives of everyone in the Manor and the rest of the world were at stake.

Killian (like always) was the first to speak. "Are you seriously thinking of letting this family be responsible for the fate of the world? If Tulken thinks it's some divine prophecy, the powers that be have had their heads in the clouds. Fighting one of the third? We've been learning about them, and Kaine says most Commissioned don't have a prayer! You can't think we're responsible...."

"It's not about what *I* think. According to Tulken, we *are* responsible. Kind of like how we've never had a choice about being responsible for each other," Galahad said.

We all went silent. We all remembered our father telling us that no matter where we went or what we did, we didn't have a choice in being responsible for each other.

"Galahad is right. We all agreed to train with these kids to give this place a shot. Now they need us, and we're just gonna walk away?" Emma stood.

Killian shook his head, "Is this family going to make another really bad decision that I have to go along with?"

"We promised we'd stay together, and if fighting some host to an ancient fallen is the only way to protect this family....I'll do it. What choice do we have?" He had a point. Tulken had told us what the *end of the world* meant (because Micah had asked for clarification). Exactly what it sounded like. If Asmodeus' host wasn't stopped, there would be earthquakes, tremors, and violent outbursts in society that would make what I heard on the news look like little skirmishes. And that was only the build-up--if Asmodeus was released at full power with all his demons, humanity would be overrun and destroyed.

I walked up to Galahad and put my head on his shoulder like I was used to doing when I was scared or unsure. My heart was pounding with fear, but if we sat here, we were waiting to be victims. "...He's right."

"You loyal, faithful, preachy chump...." Killian cursed. His expression was twisting like it did when he wanted to argue but didn't have any points to support his view at the moment.

Micah shrugged, forcing a shaky laugh, "Hey, if we can't...what have we got to lose?"

Galahad gave him a grave look, "This...each other, everything. Losing isn't an option here." It was one of the most spontaneous votes I'd ever made. Uriah was itching and begging to go risk his life, and it wasn't even his mission. Despite his arrogance and my general dislike for him, that was still a noble effort. Another thing itched at the back of my mind as we voted. It was the timing of Asmodeus' imprisonment.

Three years ago.

That was when our parents disappeared. And now we learned we were the Avengers of Light destined to stop him…. it couldn't be a mere coincidence. I didn't pose the idea to Galahad because Killian had warned me not to. Maybe some other time, if we talked alone, I could bring it up. But I'd seen the sorceress in our old home. It was possible she or Asmodeus knew something about what happened to our family. We all agreed to go on the quest. We went to Tulken's office, where he was speaking with Professor Collins. Collins had a book open on his desk and was quickly flipping through pages when we walked in.

"I see you've all come to a decision," Tulken took his glasses off.

Galahad looked at all of us to be sure we agreed, "We'll take the mission."

"…Very well. Your mission—is to retrieve an artifact. Old and so powerful that Lucifer himself was trying to find it in his days roaming the earth. Lucifer wanted to be at full power again, but the angels who served God ensured he would never have it. They couldn't destroy it, but they managed to break it into three pieces and scatter them across what is now Sacramento. It's known as the demon's stone," Tulken said. "Not only can the stone return a demon to full power, but it's also capable of latching onto their power. With the proper dark sorcery, it could be used to open a doorway into the depths of hell itself and free Asmodeus."

"What would happen to the host if he got out?" Galahad said.

"Most likely? They would perish," Tulken said.

Collins pulled a purple cloth bag off his shoulder and reached inside, "All of the faculty will have different equipment for you, but I know you'll be needing this…let me see..." He pulled out everything from books, a teapot, a broom, a rabbit, etc. "Ah ha!" Collins finally pulled out a turquoise globe that looked like a small storm was whirling around inside it. "This is what we in the magic world call a seeking globe. It was used back in the day for Commissioned to be alerted of strong magical artifacts of a demonic nature. The demon's stone will be the most powerful artifact anywhere within range, so this will help you see where to find the pieces."

"Everything else you need the other faculty, and I will provide you with. You may choose one other Commissioned to go on the mission with you as a guide," Tulken said.

"Well, we have to take Dashiel," Emma said like it was a no-brainer.

My brothers and I looked at her.

"Why, exactly?" Killian huffed.

"Duh! He and I are practically a couple!" Emma waved her hand dismissively at Killian.

"Dashiel is a fine member of the Commissioned, but I think it should be a decision you make together," Tulken said.

"Seeing as how light magic is a rare gift and Elsha has had the least training with her gift, I think sending someone with a knowledge of magic with them," Collins ventured cautiously.

Tulken set his glasses on the desk carefully as if considering what Collins was posing. Tulken knit his fingers, and his eyes averted to a corner of the room. Eventually, he spoke up, "—Are you suggesting Dante accompanies them?"

"Yes Headmaster. Elsha's had no training in magic, and if she goes without someone who's experienced. She'll be going in blind," Collins said.

Tulken looked up at us carefully, "Is that choice acceptable to all of you?"

It was more than acceptable to me. Dante had taught me swordplay and was one of the only friends I'd made here. I was nodding when I caught a glimpse of indecision on Galahad's face. I didn't know why it was such a tough choice. My other siblings murmured in assent.

Galahad nodded, "If it helps Elsha, we're for it."

Tulken let out a reluctant breath. His face showed concern, his eyes indecision. I wondered if he looked this tense at every Commissioned he sent into the field. "It's time to get you everything you'll need. All of us here will be praying for your safe return as we prepare for the enemy's next move."

I nodded, "Thanks…but just us going on a mission this big…it's a little…."

"—Terrifying?" Micah interjected.

Tulken was about to say something, but he put his hand to his mouth a moment as if in silent debate. We all probably looked scared, even though we were doing our best to fake it. "….What does Joshua 1:9 say?" he said at last.

Micah's expression fell, "Oh no, it's *another do you know your catechism* quiz…."

Tulken let out an exasperated breath putting his fingers to his temple, "I've told you all these *many times* now. One of you has to remember…."

Had he? I was so bad at remembering class information I didn't know. And it had been years since our parents taught us the catechism. We all looked at Galahad. If anyone knew, he would.

"…Have I not commanded you to be strong and have courage, for the Lord your God is with you wherever you go," Galahad said.

Tulken fixed his gaze at my eldest brother strangely, "…. Correct. God won't test you beyond what you're capable of handling. He won't put more on your shoulders than what each of you can bear. If you are called to this, it's because you can achieve it. I have faith in all of you. It's time you had faith in yourselves."

Galahad gave a respectful nod. "Yes, sir. Now what do we need?"

Chapter Twenty-One

We Get a Family Car

When we told the other Commissioned we were taking Dante, there were audible gasps. One girl pulled out a rosary and started chanting next to us. Uriah was the most shocked. He didn't say anything at first when we announced who was going to be our guide. He just stared at us with a blank expression while the other kids freaked out and chatted away. His sister was complaining she would have been better suited to go, and Uriah was still in shock when the teachers led us away to get our equipment. As we followed Kaine, the other professors were getting the rest of the Manor prepared to set up a defense.

Kaine gave us weapons. Not so many that we'd be laden down, but enough that each of us had something we could use along with the basics: three swords, a crossbow, a dagger, and a bag of tools for Micah. Other students at the Manor were in line being given weapons after us. They expected more attacks like the one in the arena. Seeing them prepare so boldly gave me courage to not show fear as I strapped on my own sword. Clash gave us camping equipment (while we each got an allowance for food in case of emergency, Tulken said most likely we wouldn't be staying indoors). Collins provided Dante with some powders, potions, and a basic spell book to teach me as we went along.

Next, the maids helped us pack practical clothes for the trip. Emma wore her pink t-shirt with a denim jacket, jeans, and slip-on tennis shoes. Killian got a leather jacket made by the maids with a black t-shirt and combat boots. Galahad took a dark blue windbreaker with running shoes and jeans. Micah never liked to change attire much. A red t-shirt, jeans, and gym shoes—he was good to go. We were led by Kaine into the large garage beside the main parking area at the Manor. The outdoor parking was lined by trees, and the air was chilling as we walked into the garage. I didn't know who would be here to see us off.

I was trying not to think too much as I followed my siblings into the garage.

When I stepped inside, I immediately registered the tall ceiling and bright lights illuminating the building. There were vehicles of every shape and size at different corners of the building. Some of them looked like they'd come out of old movies, while others were new and fancy. It smelled surprisingly fresh and clean for a garage. Tulken was somewhere in the center, speaking to Dante and Dashiel. Dashiel was standing with his hands behind his back and head slightly tilted down, listening to the headmaster, rigid as ever. He turned when we walked in. Addie was there holding a white paper bag and smiled when she saw us. Dori and Jasmine were with her.

Emma brightened instantly, "Dashiel came to see me off!"

Killian gave her a look, "Right....it wouldn't have anything to do with him talking to the headmaster?"

"Be quiet and come on!" Emma hurried, carrying her equipment over to the center of the garage where they stood. My brothers followed her quickly. Galahad called after her, but she ran right up to Dashiel and grabbed his ear as always. Dashiel tensed slightly when she approached. Dante was trying not to grin like a Cheshire cat as Tulken took him aside and spoke to him. He must have been excited. I took a step towards them when a hand fell on my shoulder.

"Hyah!" I whipped around, raising a flat hand. My bag slid off my shoulder, and Uriah's arm blocked my raised hand. My eyes grew slightly large, "...Uriah?"

He looked down at my open hand, unimpressed. "Is *this* supposed to be some kind of attack?"

I frowned. "It was a gut reaction!"

"If I were a demon, you'd be dead," he looked at my arm. "Typically, the Commissioned arms are supposed to be trained for battle. He pulled his arm away quickly, and the cuff of his shirt scraped my wrist.

"Ow!" I complained, rubbing my hand.

Uriah's expression fell miserably. "You're too soft."

I rolled my eyes, "Unless the demons are wearing well pressed collared shirts, I think I'll be fine! Who irons your clothes? They feel stiff…."

"I need to talk to you. Outside. *Now*."

I pulled my head back in shock. "I'm not talking with you outside alone! It's getting dark!"

He looked indignant. "Is that supposed to be an insult to my personal conduct? How dare you…." The more he used that condescending tone the more I was ready to walk away. Uriah released a forcible breath and choked out the words as calmly as he could. "May I…*please*—have a word with you outside before your mission?"

I glanced over at my family. Galahad and Emma were watching me curiously from the center of the garage. I huffed, "Fine…one minute! That's it," I held my arms and stepped outside the garage doorway. The cold breeze blew against me as the pine trees moved in the distance. The sky was turning a rich dark blue and purple color. Uriah was still in his suit, but he didn't look cold. He crossed his arms and looked off in the distance a moment at the lamps lining the walkways around the Manor.

"Well?" I shifted my weight back and forth on my feet to try and stay warm.

"Take me with you," he said after a pause.

I scoffed, "I knew you'd say that I just didn't think you'd be stuck up enough to pull it as we're leaving…."

He stepped towards me, "—I'm serious. Dante's never been on a mission before, and I've been on several. I'd be more useful to all of you, and you know it. You just didn't pick me because you don't *like* me—admit it."

He was good. I knew it from the challenge and his history in the field. But I hadn't suggested Dante. Collins did. Dante was the only one who could help me with my magic. And something told me one of the reasons Dante hadn't been on a mission was because of the gossip about him being dark or the reptile boy. It wasn't fair to judge someone by appearances and Uriah had done that with Dante and my family. My frown deepened at him, "Why don't you admit it!"

He pulled his head back.

"You don't want Dante to go because you don't trust him! Because he doesn't meet your standards of being commissioned! You don't think he belongs here anymore than you thought my family did! I hate to tell you this but who's called to this isn't up to you! So why don't you get off your high horse and…."

"—My family *expects* me to defend the world. If I did anything less, they'd think *I* don't belong here. I prove I'm Commissioned to them, and everyone here daily," his tone grew grave. "I want to go on this mission because it's what I live for. Why don't you ask Vaniah if it's the same for him?"

As bothered as he made me, hearing what a fine line he had to toe almost made me sad. "My family's not perfect…but there are some things I never question. Your family should trust you enough to do the same. Dante's never going to get a chance if no one gives him one. Just like me. You were wrong about us not having gifts, and you're wrong about him."

Uriah averted his gaze from me a moment, "Then…you won't take me with you instead of him?" he didn't merely look bothered. He looked wounded. Worried. Like he feared repercussions from his family or how others would look at him if he didn't go. That made me feel sorry for him. I didn't have my parents, but if I ever got them back I hoped I wouldn't spend every day proving my worth to them. Tulken supported my siblings and I and he'd only known us a short while. If Uriah went to school here, I wondered how he could feel like he had to meet such a high bar. But then, I didn't know what kind of treatment he got at home.

"No….I'm sorry," I used a slightly softer tone.

Uriah looked at me quizzically. He must not have expected me to apologize. "—It should be me on that quest. But seeing as how I'm the only one who sees that….be careful." He looked down at me shifting more quickly in the cold. "And get inside. If you freeze to death to won't be able to fight anything." He turned walking out of the lot.

I couldn't believe him. He never quit. I hurried inside the garage and walked quickly to my siblings who were looking at me.

"What did Uriah have to say?" Tulken asked curiously.

"He just…wished me luck."

Dashiel looked up calmly in thought, "Unlikely. Uriah principally believes luck to be a fictitious tool of the unbelievers and the blind. He'll never use that expression. Providentially he may wish you success, but never luck."

I swallowed. Dante was watching me and so were my siblings.

"Uh…he…"

"The stuttering leads me to believe you're taking time to arrive at a slight prevarication to conceal the true nature of your conversation with Uriah. If that is the case it would most likely be the most considerate action to not inquire further," Dashiel said affirmatively with a methodic nod.

Emma raised an eyebrow, "A little too much information there, Dashiel."

Dashiel looked genuinely oblivious as he returned Emma's gaze. "Hm—I'll consider that the next time your sister and Uriah hold a private conversation."

I raised a hand, "Trust me that will be the last. So how does this transportation thing work? None of us know how to drive except for Galahad and Killian a little bit."

"Everyone's got a vehicle that speaks to them, these ain't normal transporters. They've been passed down, found over centuries by Tulken and the other faculty. One of these hunks of metal will be your guy's transporter for all your quests," Kaine said.

"Each method of transportation is magically enabled to be drawn to the right Commissioned," Tulken said as my siblings and I walked around the different vehicles. Tulken explained that we'd be getting a mission allowance as it were, enough money for each of us to eat and get whatever we may need while on duty. We didn't get phones because technology that wasn't specifically made by the Commissioned tended to be vulnerable to the enemy as a means to track us. I didn't understand that but Dante said he'd explain it later.

Killian walked over to a sleek black Maserati with flames on the sides, "Oh—wow—yes."

"You wish," Addie said.

"So we can drive this one, right?" Killian said.

"Ha—no," Kaine said. "Nice try, kid, but the vehicle has to say something to you."

"Well, it's saying something to me right now," Micah drooled over the car.

"That car only holds two people—what are we going to do, run alongside?" Emma said.

"What about that one?" Galahad said pointing to a large slightly beat up red Durango in the corner. It was rusted and older, maybe 1995 or 2001. Killian frowned. Micah shook his head. Galahad turned to them, "It might not be pretty but it looks like it would fit us all."

"That car is for soccer moms and kids who can't afford real cars but don't want to be seen in it," Killian said. "That old thing wouldn't be our car."

I kind of liked the red car, but Tulken said the old thing hadn't moved in years. Before Killian said anything else, the sound of a car coming towards us filled the garage. We all pulled our weapons, but Dante didn't move like he'd seen this before. The lights from the Durango lit up, and Killian's mouth fell open.

"No…" Killian said.

The Durango revved up and drove straight at us with no one inside it.

"IT'S ALIVE!!!" Micah cried as the car came at us.

The car came to a halt pulling up alongside us. We all stared. Dante cracked his knuckles. "I think you've got your car for missions…if you let me, I could make some magical improvements…."

Tulken shot him a look.

Dante raised his hands in surrender, "But then again, it's not my place…."

I put my hand on the vehicle, walking alongside it. Dante looked at my amazed expression curiously, "Are you okay?"

"Yeah, I just…we haven't had a car since we had parents. This is….a really big deal," I smiled. Dante stared at me like he didn't understand my amazement. I didn't care what he or Killian said. This was our new car and I loved it.

"Right…. I'm glad you like it," Dante said at last.

"It's ugly," Killian huffed, crossing his arms.

"Materialistically it could be more pleasing to the eye, yes," Dashiel said logically. "Its functionality however is what you should prioritize."

We loaded the car with our supplies. Addie gave us a batch of freshly baked oatmeal raisin cookies and hugged Emma and I goodbye. Tulken explained as soon as we were off, he had to make preparations for defense at the manor because the enemy would have forced coming back after the trolls. Knowing that we wouldn't be spared from danger even there encouraged me to swallow my fear and do this. Like Galahad said, we didn't really have a choice. We all said farewell. I noticed Dante looking at Kaine like he was waiting for something, but Kaine simply stood back with his large arms crossed in an unchanged expression.

Dante cast his eyes down a moment before breaking into a grin and looking at us, "Okay, Avengers….the forces of darkness and hell await—who's driving?"

"I am," Galahad and Killian said at once.

Tulken chuckled lightly under his breath, "The car is magically guided. Each vehicle has a help guide to allow you to control it. It isn't like a normal vehicle, it's capable of many things: impossible speed, camouflage and heaven only knows what else. You'll have to learn the individual vehicles abilities as you go along. One of you needs basic driving skills to operate it. Galahad, Killian—as the two oldest I'd prefer you both drive."

Either Galahad was trying to be humble or he had a temporary lapse in judgement because he let Killian in the driver's seat first. There were six seats so plenty of room for all of us. Galahad got in the front passenger's seat and Micah crawled in the back. The back of the car was the smallest space, so it only made sense for Micah and Emma to go there. Dante stepped in the middle seat and took one last look at Dashiel, "Farewell, old friend—if I die don't let the kids hurt Cleopatra."

Dashiel studied him, "Since the Dyers are the Avengers of light and pivotal in stopping Asmodeus, your life is technically the most expendable. However, if you were to pass, I fear I'd be too disoriented to think of Clash's serpent as the first priority."

My siblings exchanged glances.

Dante looked at us, 'That's his way of saying he cares." He got in the car and took a seat.

Emma got in last. She leaned out and looked at Dashiel, "In case I don't make it back…..I'll never forget you."

"Oh, you've got to be kidding me…." Killian rolled his eyes.

Dashiel's mouth parted, and he looked at her quizzically, like even he didn't know what to say to that. Dante was staring, in shock at her guts—I'll admit I was doing the same.

Dashiel was still poised to speak but hadn't. "….Emma….."

"Yes?" she said pleadingly, leaning out of the car and holding onto Dante's arm to keep her from falling out.

"Emma…"

Micah stuck his head out from the far backseat. "Want to try for double or nothing on her last name?"

"If you say her name three times and wave a charm, I can turn her into a cat…." Dante spread his hands, making my brothers laugh.

Emma shot them death looks, "Alright already! Enough with the jokes, HA HA!" Emma frowned and got in the back. "Alright, driver man—get us going. Dante, where's the first stop?"

We closed the car doors and waved goodbye to the teachers as Dante pulled the globe out of his bag. The rings on his fingers clinked with the glass as he laced his hand around the globe. His eyes flashed green, and something in the globe began spinning. Dante let out a small breath. I leaned forward from behind his and Emma's seat. "Are you okay?"

Dante smiled forcibly, "Yeah, it just…takes a little magic to get this thing going. It's basic 101 of the Commisioneds gifts, they're like using any physical ability, it takes its toll on you. Remember Collins class? You can't make something from nothing. I'm gifted in magic so I can use it to start this thing but it takes my power. Thankfully…I've got a bit on reserve."

An image appeared in the globe and all of us in the backseat leaned forward to see it. "…Sacramento Airport….the first piece is there."

"Alright!" Micah sat back excited. "Where's our magical guide?"

A human figure appeared in the car like a ghost, it was blue and smoky and right on the dashboard making Killian jump slightly. The smoky figure looked female and smiled, she had a voice like a GPS system. "Hello! I'm your magical travel helper designed to be patient and meet all your needs for your journey."

Killian groaned looking around the inside of the vehicle, "Can you make this car less ugly?

The spirit sizzled, "No...the exterior of the vehicle can't change. Now please buckle up—are you buckled up?" Emma nodded, "Yes."

"Are you sure?" the spirit said cheerfully.

"Look, spirit lady, if you could cut the cheery clap trap and let me drive, it'd be great. Now, do you have a map of this airport? Because I'll bet I could find it without your stupid directions...." Killian said.

"I've been helping students of Raziel for centuries on missions, and you'll need my expertise...."

"I just need you to shut up and tell me where I step to go fast," Killian interrupted.

"Yes, I..." the spirit began.

"And don't tell me where to go unless I ask? Unless you play rock music just stay in the carburetor where you belong...." Killian buckled himself in adjusting his hair in the mirror.

The small spirit sizzled and steamed as the woman sneered, "LOOK BUSTER! I DIDN'T TAKE THIS JOB TO GET TOLD ABOUT DIRECTIONS FROM SOME PUNK WHO WEARS TOO MUCH HAIR GEL! DO YOU THINK I LIKE THIS JOB?!"

Killian raised an eyebrow, shocked, "I'm guessing, no."

"NO! I'VE HEARD ALL THE JOKES BY ALL THE KIDS AND I'M SICK OF IT! YOU THINK YOU CAN DRIVE THIS THING YOURSELF? WELL GO AHEAD! I QUIT!" she yelled disappearing into a puff of smoke that filled the whole car.

We all coughed and looked around. Emma was speechless, "I don't believe it...you angered the magical help out of helping us." Dante was laughing uproariously in the middle seat. He put his hand to his mouth, trying to suppress it as Emma and Killian began to argue. I hung my head and pretended my name wasn't Dyer.

Galahad was trying to tell them to settle down and instruct Killian when, once again, my middle brother interrupted, "We don't need her, and you should trust me with something for once! I can drive this thing," Killian said, starting the car.

It began to shake vigorously, and Emma put her hands on me and Dante to steady herself. The car was shaking violently before the doors to the garage opened and Code Red (that's what I'm calling our car now) shot out in a burst of speed. We cleared the large garage and drove out of the main lot past the trees. I cracked my window letting the cold air cool my face. I took in the smell of the Manor, the air, the trees, the lot, and the land—I wouldn't be seeing it again for a while. I turned and looked out my open window to see flames on the ground beneath us mixed with the tire tracks we left behind. Tulken and Kaine were in the lot watching us leave. The Manor of Raziel got smaller and smaller in the distance as smoke shot out behind us. I felt a tap on the shoulder and turned to see Dante holding a black leather bag on his lap.

I blinked, "What's that?"

He gave a small smile, "Collins said you were taking me along to help you with magic...so—lesson number one begins now."

#

Part of me thought Killian didn't want to drive. He had to know Galahad would make him pull over if he kept up like this. Killian shot out of the country roads that led to the Manor and drove into the middle of town. That genuinely terrified me. If you've ever been on the Sacramento highway, you know there are six lanes, and it's impossible for normal cars to know which one they need to be in or when to change. For a magically charged vehicle that had a mind of its own (and no help spirit thanks to my brother), it was borderline impossible. Galahad made Killian pull over so he could drive.

Dante was leaning back in his chair, arms crossed, and eyes closed like he was asleep the whole time. He'd brought his black hooded coat he'd worn in the rain, and he had the hood pulled down over his eyes.

He'd given me a section of a book on a sorcerer's primary abilities and their rules after we'd talked for several minutes. But everything he said was so confusing that he said it might help if I just read definitions.

Emma had been yelling at Killian the entire drive, making it very hard for me to focus.

Right now, she and Micah were exchanging last will and testaments. "So, Killian gets all my artwork, he'll carry on the legacy. You and Emma can use my clothes for your dolls and Galahad…"

Emma smacked the back of Dante's chair, since she was unable to reach Killian's. "Do you want to kill us before the demons get a chance?!"

Killian huffed, "Funny—all I'd have to do is give them you, and they'd leave us alone, big mouth!"

Galahad looked over his shoulder back at us, "—Nobody is dying, okay? Now everyone pipe down—Elsha's trying to study and you're making it impossible."

"Oh, sorry, Elsha, go ahead," Emma encouraged.

"How far is the Sacramento airport?" Dante said without opening his eyes. He may as well have inserted *Galahad* into the end of the question because it was clearly addressed to him.

Galahad adjusted the mirrors to his height and looked behind him (I hadn't even known that was a thing while Killian drove). "Not much farther. Thankfully, our helpmate left a map in the car."

Killian strapped himself in the passenger's seat. He slouched, crossing his arms, "It's amazing and lame you know how to read that."

"Unlike the rest of you, I remember paying attention when Dad needed help with directions on our family road trips," Galahad slowed the vehicle down and took an exit.

Emma leaned forward, accidentally smacking Dante with her arm.

"Oof!" Dante grunted, pulling his hood back slightly to see who'd smacked him.

"And how old were you during these family road trips?" Emma said.

Galahad thought about it, "Eleven."

"And what would that make Elsha and I?" Emma pressed. I knew where this was going. Emma and Galahad constantly got into it when he expected her and us to recall things that we weren't old enough to. Galahad recalled everything from our Bible studies, homeschooling, the movies we saw as kids...

"Ten and eight," Galahad said.

Emma sat back and crossed her arms. "Humph, see? This is like when you want us to remember movies we saw when you were six and Elsha was three...."

My family chatted away and I wondered how it didn't drive Dante nuts. I even saw him release a strained sigh. Then his expression went blank, and I thought he might have gone to sleep again. "How can you sleep while my family is in the car?" I really meant how can you sleep while my family yells at each other?

"First of all—I'm not asleep. Secondly, I slept while Jasmine tried to axe ghouls around the training room last summer with Kaine and he blasted 80's rock," Dante sat up and pulled his hood down, letting out a breath, "Until they nearly got ghoul blood on my boots anyway." He turned to me. "How's the reading? Making any more sense?"

I closed the book. "I got that sorcerers are supposed to have telekinesis and control over the elements...but why haven't I been able to do any of those things yet?"

"You haven't practiced them. Why hasn't Emma turned a little sapling into a giant tree, yet? She hasn't tried. Your gift is like a physical trait you haven't trained, your big brother, the gym rat, could probably tell you about that. If you don't jog, you're never gonna run.

You have a connection to the elements; you just gotta focus. Watch…" Dante took a quill out of his bag and set it in my open hand. "Concentrate. There's water in the air, and with the windows cracked there's more cold. As a sorceress you have a connection to the natural world more than most—pull those elements in and control them. Freeze the quill."

I raised one eyebrow. "I can't just make ice?"

Dante laughed, "One of the rules of magic, Dyer, something can't come from nothing. Sadly, nobody but God has figured out how to do that. When I froze the Dark blood warrior, I had to manipulate what was around me, I can't just create things." I looked at the pen and concentrated, but nothing was happening. It took several moments but nothing happened. Eventually, Dante requested all the windows to be rolled down to make the car even colder, apparently that was supposed to help. I breathed and was made more nervous by the fact Dante was watching intently. In another few moments the quill grew cold in my hand. The quill frosted over and my siblings who could see were gasping. Emma started sneezing and demanded we roll up the windows. Dante clapped moving onto the next thing. Galahad said we weren't practicing fire in the car, so Dante begrudgingly moved on to telekinesis. That took me less time. I was able to make the quill float and that made Dante more excited. When I levitated something, the thin layer of energy around it was gold, different than Dante's and Collins. He explained to me that basic element manipulation and levitation would become my primary skill in combat till time allowed me to study more spells and incantations. Something like shooting fire was one skill, but if I wanted to set a permanent or lasting blaze somewhere that would call for an incantation. As I breezed through rules of light magic, I saw that in places of pure darkness my powers would be more suppressed. I didn't understand that and neither did Dante completely. We read through and practiced till Galahad approached the Airport.

We were here. We parked on the second floor of the parking lot. It was bustling with people and the air had gotten colder. We all got out of the car and tried to look normal walking into the Airport. Six kids carrying bags and weapons didn't look natural. If we didn't try to get on a plane or pass security Galahad said we'd be fine. Galahad told us how to split up. We searched the Airport high and low. Emma and I searched the baggage terminal, the lady's room, the Starbucks (and we may have bought some treats in the process). Galahad and Micah searched the crowds and Dante went with Killian to the second floor. We were running out of options and regrouped in front of the Starbucks café area.

Galahad let out a breath, "This is getting pointless. Dante, what's the globe saying?"

Micah snapped his fingers, "Oh—I know! Dang, it's dark in that bag!"

We all looked at him. Micah shrugged, "What? Oh, like I was the only one who had that on the tip of his tongue?" Emma scrunched her nose, "Yes—you were."

Galahad looked at Dante.

"I thought you'd never ask," Dante pulled the globe from his black bag. It flashed brightly and he had to look away. The rest of us shielded our eyes. Dante looked back into the globe and ran his fingers over it trying to clear the image. His eyes flashed like they did when he released power. Words appeared in the globe, but they weren't clear. We all gathered round.

Micah squinted, "How can you read that? It doesn't even look written in English!"

"The power of gods wasn't meant for people who weren't willing to make sacrifices for it." Dante's eyes strained as the color in them shifted. His fingers pressed around the globe. "Clavis….Inferni is the name of the first piece, and it'll be between the heavens and the earth…." Dante's eyes went back to normal. "That's what it said."

Emma looked around. "What does that mean?" Galahad squinted, "Clavis Inferni…hell key."

Killian huffed, "Of course…."

Galahad turned to him, "You don't remember our Latin lessons…."

"No!" All of us said in unison.

Galahad shook his head. "Between the heavens and the earth…the first piece is in the sky."

Micah spread his hands, "That should make this easy-we just look for the first piece of an artifact that's floating around in the sky and tell it: hey, get down here!"

Galahad rolled his eyes, "I don't think that's what it means."

Killian nudged Micah on the arm, "We're at an Airport! Between the heavens and the earth? The piece is probably on a…."

We all turned our heads to see a pearl-colored plane with a black strip along the side that had written on it, ANCIENT FLIGHTS OF WRATH parked on the landing strip.

No, it couldn't be. I choked. "But…that plane is parked, the piece has to be in the sky…"

Galahad interrupted pointing to the flight schedule. "It's going to take off."

Dante cursed and Emma shot him a look. Emma snarled at Killian, "…You just had to say it."

Killian raised his hands, "So what? We're here before Asmodeus' people and we can get it first!"

Emma covered his mouth.

The echo of footsteps was behind us. I looked behind us to see a woman in black and purple. I recognized her, she was from my dream. My siblings didn't know what she looked like, but they saw the expression on my face. She had an air about her as she walked, like she wasn't of the normal mortal world. She had a glass vase with green fire in it in one hand—it was glowing. Her nails were long sharp and purple, and her thick black hair fell about her back in waves as she walked towards us in leather thigh high boots. She wore a long velvet cloak with a silver clasp at the neck. She tilted her head at us and broke into a small smile, "Hello, Avengers of Light...it's amazing your headmaster never minds sending his students to their deaths."

Chapter Twenty-Two

My Family Chases an Airplane

We all tensed up. People and crowds were walking around and by us like they didn't notice anything off. The woman strolled in front of us with confidence looking at the glowing vase in her hand. Galahad and I pulled swords. Micah grabbed the crossbow from his bag, Emma and Killian readied themselves. Dante put the globe away and had his hand by his bag prepared to pull spells or weapons most likely.

Galahad stepped forward, "Who are you?"

"She's the woman from my vision," I said quietly to Galahad.

Emma glared at the woman. "If she works for Asmodeus, what else do we need to know?"

Micah blinked innocently. "She's pretty,"

We shot him a look.

"And absolutely evil….." Micah quickly tried to recover.

The woman knit her brow, "You little ones must be the Avengers of Light…..and siblings no less. How sweet."

Dante tensed, "What she's got in her hand…."

"Oh this?" she looked at the glass vase in her hand. The green firelight reflected off her pale skin. "This is a gift for you, you see— my master wants the Clavis Inferni. And the only thing in the way— well, it's supposed to be the five of you." She looked back up at us, "You're all such young persons…thriving with potential. Do yourselves a favor—let the blindly faithful fight their own battles."

Galahad was just staring at her. Not in the same way the rest of us were, we were untrusting and scared. But he was looking at her like he knew her somehow. She seemed to notice and hold his gaze a moment. Something red flickered in her eyes and she looked back at the rest of us. It was almost like I heard someone whispering to her. I heard it, but none of my siblings seemed to.

"You're gonna kill us with one fireball, lady?" Micah said.

"No—they are," she threw the vase on the ground causing a large explosion of fire to come up from the ground. Galahad shielded his eyes. The blast had gotten the closest to him because he seemed distracted. The people in the airport began to clear and scream like a real fire had just broken out and I wondered how much of this they were seeing. As the fire cleared, I saw small slimy long green hands coming up from the ground that now looked like molten acid. "And I'm no lady—my name is Darkfire and there's no reason to bloody my own hands with your lives. Long live Asmodeus."

Dante breathed tensely, "Goblins."

Out of the fire crawled long gangly creatures with ridges on their bald heads, scaly skin, and large fangs with clawed fingers. They couldn't speak well, but I heard vague pieces of words and garbled speech as they crawled out. They were slobbering and snarling as they struggled to get onto two feet, but every time they did, they fell down on all fours as if that was their natural state. Something was off about them, though; they seemed too human to me, like distorted figures of what used to be humans. They looked at Darkfire, who didn't appear afraid of them at all.

"Don't let them have the piece at any cost. Do that, and you can have all the gold your filthy hands can grasp," she said.

"What kills these things again?" I said.

"Were you *not* paying attention in class?" Dante said.

"Blunt force, water, beheading," Galahad said. "But be careful, there's too many people around and we don't want anyone else getting hurt."

The goblins came scampering towards us like a pack of hungry fire ants crawling on top of each other. Dante wasted no time in pulling his sword to cut them down. He slashed away at them but unless the sword got a direct hit the blade would slide off their slippery leatherlike skin. Micah was firing at them with his crossbow and backing up as the creatures closed in. Killian was tearing them off him and ducking their advances. They were violent small creatures grabbing at our legs and arms. I felt teeth sink into my pant leg and let out a cry looking down. There was a goblin holding onto my leg. I stabbed it in the skull with the edge of my sword shaking it from my leg. Galahad took his sword and went at them. A goblin came at Micah and Galahad sent a downward chop to its head—I could tell he was a little nervous fighting these things but he quickly got over it when his protective instincts kicked in.

Two came at Emma, and she stepped back, telling me to get behind her.

"What are you going to…" I began.

She pulled a small pot from the ammunition bag we had with us and held her hand shakily over it, "Keep them back. I'm working on something Professor Clary taught me!"

The goblin's clawed hands were reaching for me and took hold of my other pant leg tearing effortlessly through my jeans—I picked my other leg up and stepped on his head as hard as I could crushing it.

More were coming.

It was like a thick wall of tree branches that the goblins immediately tried to start fighting their way through. It kept them back and that was a huge help because we were outnumbered. Micah came over and was working on his weapon.

"What are you doing…" I began frantically. In my defense, goblins were crawling though the cracks of the tree branches and Emma was kicking them back while my other brothers stabbed at them. Micah tinkered with the tool, grabbed some things from the bag and wired it, turned a couple wrenches, and aimed it.

"New and improved," he said. Micah aimed the crossbow which now had a rapid-fire mechanism. With that he probably didn't even have to be a good shot. Micah open fired at the creatures and started sending arrows into their heads and shoulders.

"Micah you're awesome!" I said as the goblin shrieks filled the air.

"I know, but feel free to keep reminding me," Micah said.

Killian was stabbing at the creatures with the dagger when one's claws slashed him. Killian clutched his arm in pain. Airport security was starting to come over.

Galahad cut down another goblin, splashing green blood on his shirt. The creatures were screeching and turning to dust crumbling much faster than the troll had. Every time his blade connected with one of them, they fell to pieces in a similar way. He looked out at the landing strip. "Dark fire's going after the plane! Dante, can you get us to Code Red?"

Dante opened his hand levitating a writhing goblin. He closed his fist as his expression strained. The creature's skull exploded sending green goo across the floor. "To *who*?"

"Our car!" I shouted backing away from the howling creatures.

"I don't have unlimited placement powder so are you sure…." Dante backed away towards us as we gathered in a huddle. The goblins were closing in and we were running out of ideas. People at the airport were rushing over. I didn't know what they were seeing but it couldn't have been good.

"Do it on my mark," Galahad darted his eyes around.

"What about the goblins? We can't leave them here with the people!" I said.

"Oh, they'll be fine…" Dante waved off that concern.

"—What!" Emma snapped.

"The goblins were called by Darkfire and told to stop us to get payment, they won't hurt these people. They only want to kill us. If we leave, they'll follow," Dante said.

The goblins leaped at us, crawling on top of each other like locusts. They licked their crooked lips with blood lust in their eyes.

"—Now!" Dante looked over at the parking garage. Dante spread his hands after throwing down a small handful of powder. The goblins and the inside of the airport faded around me. My stomach did a double take like last time and my head spun as the world went blank. We appeared on the second level of the parking garage right next to the edge. Micah let out a scream and Galahad caught him by the back of his shirt to keep him from falling. Two teleportation's in two days was a bit much for me. I threw up by the edge of the parking garage and Emma held my hair back. As soon as I got whatever was in my system out Galahad hurried us to Code Red. We didn't have much time so for once I was grateful for Killian's driving. We raced out of the garage and went onto the landing strip. I really hoped we got the artifact and got out of here because if we didn't, we were probably going to jail for all the laws we were breaking. When we got to the landing strip, the goblins were still coming after us so Galahad told Dante and Emma to stay on the ground and kept them back. Emma's powers wouldn't be of much use if she wasn't on land. Micah had his crossbow in hand and window rolled down as Killian sped up to Darkfire who was on the airplane's trail. I was beside him and Galahad was in the passenger's seat.

Darkfire had created a purple horse out of flames and was riding it like lighting after the plane. Her hair and cloak whipped behind her, and on her face was pure determination. It was more than following orders. She looked intent on getting the piece the same as we did. With the windows down, my hair was whipping in my face.

Micah was trying to get a clear shot at Darkfire but we were too far away. "Uh guys, how do we even know where this artifact piece is going to be?"

"Elsha knows," Galahad said.

"I do?"

"You're a sorceress of light—magic is your gift. If this thing is a piece to a dark artifact, then you should be able to sense it. That's what we learned in our magic class," Galahad said as Killian pressing on the gas to catch up to Darkfire.

I'd heard something like that, and when the Dark Blood warrior had attacked my light magic emerged without training. But I still didn't see how I could figure out where it was…Dante's books. I crawled into the back seat where some of our equipment was and rifled through the books. Dante had only been able to bring a few. One of them was labeled *Use of Light and Dark in Magic*. That had to help. I flipped through it searching for some information on how to sense dark magic if you were gifted in light. Surprisingly, it was a common thing in a few chapters. There was a constant opposition between light and dark, and both sides could sense each other: When dark and light collide they're incapable of mixing, one will either overcome the other or both would be destroyed. The light can sense the darkness like flames in the night, as the darkness can see light like a lamp. That didn't help me. It wasn't specific, it said merely to reach out with my power and make my mind a blank. I had to search for the evil in the area. That sounded simple—ha. I closed my eyes as the wind from the rolled down windows hit my face. I tried to make my mind a blank. Flashes crossed my mind much like in my dreams. I closed290my eyes and tried to sense the darkness. It was everywhere—I got an overwhelming tingling like I couldn't distinguish one thing from another. Like noise, I felt it—pain, sadness, envy, selfishness, ambition, anger.....it all came flooding to me like sounds. I tried to zero in like a memory, I saw flashes, Darkfire in blurs, a man in red suit, the goblins—but they weren't just goblins, I saw flashes of people.I felt something like a wave across my mind and there were colors. Red, black, and gold were lingering in my mind over so many people and thins in the area but the colors weren't as strong. I saw flashes of strong red, black, and gold lingering over Darkfire. In my mind I saw my siblings in hews of gold as well as Emma, Dante was under a shade of black and gold combatting like fire and water. As my mind strained, I saw something in the cargo hold of the plane…in a wooden box being shipped away somewhere it was black as the abyss.

My eyes shot open, and I panted. "…Wow."

"Where is it?" Galahad said, bringing me back to reality.

"The cargo hold…" I said, feeling drained.

Galahad slipped out the open driver's window crawling over Killian who objected loudly, and the car began to swerve.

I got into the front seat--I'd have to get close, that meant leaning out the window and using magic...I didn't like that idea. I crawled over leaning out the window past Killian whop grunted in annoyance, I looked up at the top of Code Red as the wind whipped the hair in my face.

"Watch it!" Killian said trying to see through me and my hair.

Galahad was on one knee on top of the car and had his sword poised as we came up alongside Darkfire. She turned in shock. Darkfire formed a purple fire ball in her hand and threw it. Galahad ducked. He slashed at her but her horse was too fast. "Get me closer!"

Killian steered the car towards her, "I'm trying to see through our sister in case you didn't notice!" Galahad slashed at the head of her horse. It was made of fire so to be honest I didn't expect it to do anything—but I was wrong. Darkfire was as shocked as I was when the Horse's flames deteriorated in the spot where he'd slashed. The horse's body reshaped quickly but was forced to slow down behind us. Galahad caught his breath as our vehicle pulled up underneath the plane's cargo hold. I got an idea how he could get it out.

"Killian, I need your help!" I said ducking my head back inside the car and glancing down at my middle brother.

"Micah, take the wheel!" Killian said with a groan as he moved into the passengers seat not giving my little brother a choice. Micah let out a quick cry reaching up and grabbing the wheel to steady the now swerving car. Micah climbed up to the front seat setting his tool bag in the backseat behind him. "But I can't drive!"

"You'll be fine—just keep it centered and don't get Galahad killed," Killian said.

"I love how responsibility is passed down in this family," Micah said with large eyes.

I would never get a clear shot crawling over Micah. Too sloppy and too risky. Galahad was right below the cargo hold. His sword was glowing white as he balanced himself hanging onto the kayak bars on top of the vehicle. Killian crawled into the back seat with me and held my arm as I asked him. I hung slightly out the side of the car and focused on Galahad's sword. This had happened in the challenge. Tulken said my magic flamed up with my emotions. I'd somehow levitated or directed Galahad's sword in the challenge to go directly into the troll's chest.

I was focusing now on his weapon as he slashed at Darkfire. "Galahad, throw the sword at the hold!" I cried out over the blaring wind.

"Quit now, boy, and no one has to die!" Darkfire extended a hand, creating another ball of flame. I could feel the supernatural heat coming from it even with the cold wind against my face, I squinted trying to see. Killian's fingers were boring into my arm trying to hold me tightly enough so I wouldn't fall out the window.

Galahad's eyes went to me and then to the cargo hold. He looked back at Darkfire, "I'm sorry about this."

Darkfire squinted at him incredulous. She threw the fireball at Galahad and he blocked it with the glowing sword. I didn't know where the light was coming from because I hadn't made it. The flames encompassed the sword like the dark was battling the light. Darkfire shielded her eyes with a shriek. She shook her head as the horse beneath her began to fade with her concentration. Galahad threw the sword up into the hold and I concentrated on it. I increased the sword's speed in the throw and it stuck there along with the combatting flames and light. The back of the cargo hold exploded with a burst of energy from the light and the flames Darkfire had made like two fireworks going off at once.

The luggage and bags flew out and tumbled onto the landing strip. Galahad slipped back inside the passenger window of Code Red breathing quickly. Darkfire tumbled to the ground and rolled aside as the luggage was strewn everywhere.

"Killian now!" Galahad grabbed the wheel helping Micah swerve the vehicle around to the wooden artifact box on the landing strip. Killian pulled me inside and buckled my seat belt. He opened his door and rolled out of the car onto the lot grabbing the box. Darkfire got to her feet and in seconds streams of purple flame were coming in his direction. Killian was fast. Ducking and rolling like a cat avoiding water when he ran back at Code Red. I reached out my hand to pull him in and he gripped my palm tightly.

I pulled him inside as Darkfire shot one final blast of flame in our direction with both hands.

Chapter Twenty-Three

Prodigal's Progress

As the car door slammed behind him I felt Code Red get unbearably hot and sweat drip down my forehead. Killian narrowly avoided having his legs torn off. We both ducked our heads below the window and rolled up the glass shielding ourselves from her attack. Galahad took the wheel back from Micah (who was all too happy to surrender it) and swerved the car in a circle driving past Darkfire towards Emma and Dante. As Killian and I sat up I put my hand on his arm, "Are you okay?"

"Yeah…" he nodded with trembling hands. His hands were sweating. I reached in the backseat and grabbed a cold bottle of water from the cooler and put it in his slightly scorched hands. He winced before making a face of slight relief, "Thanks."

I nodded, taking the box and sitting on the floor of the car.

Micah stuck his head out the window, "Guys, we have a slight problem!"

"What now?" I was sorry I asked when we drove up to the airport and saw Emma and Dante being taken aside by security. They were soaking wet; a fire hydrant by the sidewalk near them had burst. Amidst the water was a pool of green liquid that was smoking like acid. An ambulance was parked and a fire truck was approaching. We could drive up but there was no way we could get out of the car and get them in fast enough.

Killian put his hand to his head, "What are you doing, bro…trying to make everyone else lose their lunch like Elsha?"

I frowned at Killian.

Galahad turned the wheel to get us closer. "Dante can transport them in here as long as he can see where he's going!"

Dante saw us coming and managed to reach a hand into the pouch on his belt. His nose was already bleeding from exertion but his eyes flashed green and he threw the powder on the floor as officers tried to pull him and Emma away.

He and Emma vanished in a puff of green smoke before my eyes.

I shot my gaze around when the vehicle filled with green smoke. We all coughed and Galahad rolled the windows down to release the smell, letting fresh air fill the car. I turned around to see Dante with his head hung back on the seat next to me, his face was inches from mine.

I jumped. "—Ah!"

Dante's nose was bleeding down his jaw and his eyes were glazed over. Emma had appeared behind him in the back seat. Dante gave a halfhearted laugh, "We're o-officially…out of placement powder…" his head fell to the side and he was out. Emma was asleep in the back of the vehicle as well. I recall Dante saying water was a weakness to goblins. They must have found some way to burst the hydrant and flood them. Galahad was driving to get us as far away from the airport as possible. We were speeding along the highway before I knew it. Emma woke up before Dante and I gave her some water. Galahad told everyone to drink and get themselves together before the next stop. We'd gotten the first piece but it was by the skin of our teeth and I didn't see us being in great shape for piece number 2.

I looked at Galahad in his rearview mirror as the car sped along; everyone else was out. Killian's head was in my lap; he was fast asleep. I brushed his hair back consolingly with my hand. Micah was asleep on the passenger's side by Galahad. "

"Can you get a look at Collins globe and see where we're going? I think Dante's gonna be a little drained for a while."

I carefully opened Dante's bag next to him. I took out Collin's globe and looked at it. I had to magically charge it, but Dante knew how to do that, and I wasn't so sure. Micah yawned and stretched, sitting forward. He looked behind his seat at me, "Why don't you ask it to show you the next piece?"

I narrowed my gaze into the whirling wind in the globe. Eventually, an image formed of an old building in what looked like the Old town of Sacramento. "It's...a church," I said, as the image of a wooden cross on top of the building came into view. "We have to go to church."

Dante's hand twitched in his sleep. He sat up and groaned, "Wwhat's happening?"

Killian sat up and cracked his neck. "This family, go to church? I thought that idea died when our parents left...."

"Next stop, Church," Galahad spoke more firmly.

"Shouldn't we stop somewhere first? To eat or rest, I mean? We've been going non-stop," Emma said.

"We don't have time to..." Dante began ringing out the end of his cloak, which was still damp.

"That's a good idea. We should stop somewhere to eat with whatever money we have left and then find a place to make camp. The sun is setting, and it's going to be dark before long," Galahad said.

Dante didn't argue with him. I fingered the box that had been in the cargo. I opened the wooden box and saw a mess of brown paper inside. I pulled it aside, and there was a black rock shaped like a curved claw. It was incomplete—like a puzzle piece. It felt like if charcoal could be cemented and turned into a deep black glass-like structure, this would be it. Dante's eyes were fixed on it.

"Put that in one of the bags in the back," Galahad said.

"Okay," I did as he said. I didn't want to look at it anymore. Anything that was a hell key, I probably didn't want it.

"How did you find where the piece would be on the plane?" Dante asked me.

I told him. As I did, the flashes of faces and monsters I saw came back—I cleared my throat, "Dante…when I was sensing darkness, I saw faces behind the goblins. Like they were *people*…they weren't right?"

"Not anymore, no," he shook the water from his hair.

"What do you mean not anymore?" Emma said.

"Goblins are demons that were made by the fallen ones, like every other monster. Either that or they were released from hell or some dark dimension. But after the original Goblins, they made more by preying upon weak and sinful humans. The Goblins have a tree they lure people with selfish desires towards and feed them the fruit. If you eat it, you give in to your wicked desires, and you keep coming back for more till…."

"You become one of them," I said, feeling a chill run down my spine. Those creatures had been people once.

"Those people sold their souls. It's possible for you to get free if you haven't become a full Goblin yet, but the more evil you do, the faster you change. After they become full goblins, their slaves to one thing—gold, they'll do anything for it. Every creature we killed wasn't a person—they were monsters. Trust me," Dante said.

"Like vampires?" Killian said.

"Killian…" Emma rolled her eyes.

"No, he's not wrong," Dante said.

"What?" Me and Emma both said at once.

"Vampires are one of the only other kinds of demons that are made from humans. There were the originals, but then they made their armies by turning people. Same as Werewolves," Dante said.

"I didn't know that," I said. "I always thought these monsters were some myth made up to teach people lessons."

"The best lessons and myths have the most truth. And every real monster is born of some kind of selfish human desire. Heck, Lucifer fell because he liked himself too much," Dante said.

"You hear that, Killian!" Emma teased, leaning forward from the backseat and putting her arms around his neck affectionately. Killian told her to knock it off, but he was laughing. He smiled as Emma laughed, and then Dante's expression changed to solemn. He watched them like the affection was foreign to him. We pulled up in front of a diner-type place in Old town that had a few cars but not many. Galahad got out, and my nerves were brought to life by the smell of the breakfast food coming from the building.

#

We all got a large table to ourselves—the waitress was very nice because she didn't question a bunch of kids coming to a diner without an adult. We ordered a reasonable amount since our funds were limited. Chicken strips and fries, biscuits and hash browns, sausage and bacon, we all ate like hungry wolves once we got started. Emma was smacking hands to make everyone share, so she and Killian butted heads throughout the meal. But still, everything that had happened that night aside—it was a nice family dinner. When paying time came, we were all grateful for the allowances provided by the faculty.

After dinner, we drove out to a field that was only about a mile away from the Church to set up camp. Galahad didn't want us to stay in Old Town because it was more dangerous (I didn't know why he was worried about criminals and the homeless when we were fighting

306

demons, but who was I to question Galahad?). There wasn't much greenery near the town, but enough so that if we parked our car and put up one tent beside it, no cops or adults would pester us. Since Code Red was a Commissioned vehicle, it had cloaking abilities to the blind. I couldn't tell, but we took Dante's word. Emma and I set up pillows in the back seat with a blanket to share. Micah took the middle and Galahad the front because it gave him the best view to keep watch. Dante sat in the passenger seat with his eyes closed (that was his version of sleeping comfortably). Killian set up a small area to sleep outside on the ground because he said he preferred it. I wondered what was going through his mind. He'd been against all of this from the start. I slipped out the car door and sat next to Killian on the small blanket he had out.

"Are you doing okay?"

"Is anybody really *okay* with how all of this has turned out? We've been commissioned by some whack job school to go find an artifact that opens the door to hell, to save a world of people who never knew we existed and treated us like trash. Who are we doing this for, Elsha? The people at the Boarding House who thought we were losers and wasted space?"

Wow—I'd forgotten what I was getting into by asking Killian how he was. But he was my brother, and I wanted him to talk to me. I guess I didn't say it often enough, though, because whenever we did talk, he had a lot bottled up inside. So did I, but I tried to keep it to myself. "It's not about them. It's about the rest of the world."

"And what have they ever done for us?"

"Are you saying you don't want to do this?" I sat next to him on the ground, holding my knees. I pulled my sleeves down to my wrists and adjusted my knit cap so it covered my ears.

"I wanted a lot of things. But our parents skipping out made them impossible. I wanted friends, a school, a girlfriend, a life…."

"The people at the Manor can be a lot of that for us," I argued.

"As long as we live by their rules and protect the world without getting a single thank you? Yeah—sounds great. This might be better than Blech's, and I went along with it because of...."

"Cool weapons and a girl?" I interjected.

Killian let out a breath, "Yeah...but being commissioned... We got a whole list of rules to follow and classes to take, people like Uriah have standards for what we're supposed to be, and I'm not sure I want it. What if I don't want to be a righteous avenger of light? I hated Blech's because it was like being in a prison. How is this going to be any different?"

I didn't know what to tell him. We'd just begun our first quest, and we knew now we had the gifts, but living up to them was a personal choice. I hadn't stopped to wonder if Killian's heart was in it. It had been the same way with Killian growing up. Galahad would try and get him to read his Bible when he was angry, frustrated, or depressed. Killian would tell us sometimes he didn't even think he was a Christian. Considering all that, I saw how frustrating all the teaching and conduct at the Manor must have been for him.

"Why didn't you say any of this?" I said quietly.

"Because Galahad always expects the best from me...he thinks the rest of us are as itching to be *selfless servants* like him. He does everything for you girls and people besides himself. It's kind of sickening, to be honest. If I were to argue, he'd tell me I'm being selfish, but I'm telling you, I'm not sure this is right for me. Do I like the idea of learning how to fight and kill stuff like Kaine? Yeah. But do I want to live like some martyr? No."

I nodded. I'd tried advising in the past, but if Galahad couldn't counsel him, I was less qualified. Killian put his arm around me as he saw my expression fall. "But that doesn't mean I don't still care about you guys. Even if I am this…Avenger of light or not, I'll always look out for you."

The way he said it both encouraged and concerned me. I didn't want to say that, though, so I forced a small smile, "Thanks. But you never know, when I turn 14, I might do something really dumb, and you'll stop liking me."

"I'll never stop caring about you, little sis," he put his head to mine. "Your brother may be a selfish knucklehead, but he'll never be that stupid."

I laughed, and Emma stuck her head out the back window, "Someone talking about Killian?"

Killian looked over his shoulder at her, "Eavesdropper."

Emma waved off his comment, "Don't be silly…I just woke up, so I didn't hear everything."

"What's going on?" Micah sat up in the middle seat and opened the door, looking out at us.

"You couldn't sleep, bro?" Killian said.

"Nah, it's kind of hard to in a car unless I twist myself like a pretzel." We laughed. Micah could always be counted on to improve the mood no matter what. "So…anybody remembers this one time when we were little kids and went to the sheep Church?"

"What are you talking about?" Killian sat back.

"The pastor guy was like, 'sheep are God's people because they're so wise and brilliant,' and I'm like—their fat lazy biddies—what's the deal?" Micah spread his hands.

We all couldn't help but chuckle at that because, surprisingly, we did remember it. Micah hated the sermon so much that after that when we wanted to scare him, we mentioned sheep. "Don't worry, Micah, there were no sheep at this Church," Galahad said from the front seat. "Good—because if I see sheep, I want to go on record that I'm out of here."

"Do you Dyers never sleep..." Dante said in a drowsy voice putting his boots on the dashboard and leaning his chair back. He turned his head aside and was seemingly out again.

Galahad smiled, looking out the driver's window at us, "Usually no...but I think you guys had better settle in if you're gonna have energy for tomorrow."

We all talked a little longer before going back to our designated sleeping spots. Micah and Killian stayed up the longest talking. Emma and I squirmed under our blanket, trying to get into a comfortable position before we fell into a deep sleep, and the sound of the city faded into the background.

Chapter Twenty-Four

We Go to Church together to Fight Temptation

When we were all awake and had our weapons in hand, we loaded up in the car and headed out to the Church. Old Town wasn't terribly busy. We passed a lot of shops, restaurants, and buildings that looked straight out of a western as we came to the end of the road and turned a corner. It took a little asking around to find the Church, but eventually, we made it. The building was on the corner of town on a dead plot of grass that seemed to be separate from the other buildings. There was a sign on it that said it was soon to be demolished. Orange wooden barriers were around the building, but there weren't any construction workers on it yet.

The Church was tall and had wooden steps leading up to it. There was a bell tower above and two tall wooden doors at the entrance. I had my sword in hand, and Galahad's was sheathed at his side. Micah held his crossbow, and Killian's dagger was sheathed. Galahad looked around at the vines as he climbed the stairs. When he reached the doors, they were also covered in vines and branches.

Micah looked around the empty lot, "I don't see any sheep...we're good so far."

"Emma, do you think you can give us some space here?" Galahad gestured to the vines.

Emma outstretched her hand, but nothing happened. The vines didn't move. "They're not responding to me. My powers must only work on living vegetation...here...it's all dead."

As I climbed the steps, I saw a flash—like last time in the Airport. It was darkness. Worse than darkness, it was evil. Some strong kind of evil, and it was here in the Church somewhere.

Galahad's eyes shot around the building. "Killian and I will check the perimeter. Emma, you, and Dante go inside with Elsha and Micah.

Elsha and Dante might be able to sense the piece first, so we need them inside the building. Is the globe showing us anything?"

Dante pulled out the globe and frowned. "I know black is my favorite color…but in this case, I'm thinking it doesn't mean something good." The globe was swirling with color like before, but it was different. It was blacker than what I pictured the abyss looking like. The globe occasionally flashed red but then returned to its prior color. "There's something very dark and powerful in there…."

Galahad's expression grew serious. "New plan. I'm going in with the girls and Dante. Micah, you and Killian check the perimeter."

Killian scoffed, "Why do you have to…."

"—No arguments. Just do it," Galahad took the sword from his belt and cut down the dead vines on the door. We were down to two swords and a dagger. Our last sword was left at the airport (security must have had a field day). Galahad pushed the tall wooden door open.

Creak!

The door slowly moved open, and a puff of dust blew across the floor. We were standing in what used to be the greeter's lobby; only the walls had faded, and the floor was rotted wood. There were two staircases leading in opposite directions up to the second level. Directly in front of us through two more doors was the sanctuary. There was a hallway to the right with closed doors that had most likely been pastors' offices or study rooms.

"Emma and I will check upstairs. In a building like this, there are only so many places it could be. Dante, you, and Elsha search the ground floor. If you run into any trouble…." Galahad began.

I raised my eyebrows, "Scream?"

Galahad nodded encouragingly, "Right. I'm only a holler away." He and Emma started carefully up the stairs to the left. Emma was going on as they went up, "This is so dusty!"

When they were gone, Dante and I exchanged looks. "Okay…the safest place in a church has got to be the…." He moved his hand as if the word was on the tip of his tongue.

"—Sanctuary?" I said. He could remember everything about spells and magic but not what the main room in a church was called.

He snapped his fingers, "Right—you go there. I'll check the back hallway and meet you inside. Practice your levitation and the elements. It might come in handy since we don't know what's in here."

"We're supposed to be looking together…." I began walking after him as he started down the hall and came to a stop.

Dante paused and turned around, facing me. "And if anything happens to you, Sir Galahad has already told me he'll break my neck, so I'm leaving you the safest job, okay?"

"Galahad said that?"

"Not in so many words. But you'd be amazed what two guys can talk about on watch," Dante averted his gaze.

Now that was a conversation I wanted to hear. Why was Galahad talking to Dante about me? Who brought me up?

"But…"

He pointed, "The sanctuary."

"I don't want to stay in there alone!" I complained as he went down the hall.

He turned around while walking backward and spread his hands, "What do the Christians say….God's always with you? Keep that in mind." The sound of his boots on the wood slowly grew more distant as he disappeared into shadows.

#

The pews were dust-covered, and the communion table was rusted. At the head of the Church was a large wooden crucifix that had a white cloth hung on it like I'd seen at many Churches. Someone should have kept it up; it must have been a beautiful place once. I looked above me at the ceiling and climbed the small steps to the Church podium. I stood there, opening my hands, and breathed. I was trying to create something as simple as a ball of frost in my hand. It was cold in here, and a draft was blowing through the cracks on the wooden boards. It should have been easy. I'd made one in the car before with Dante. Something was stopping me, though, I was straining to do it, but nothing came. This place… it gave me chills. I hadn't been to Church with my family in so long, not since we had parents, and I was too small to remember it. I didn't expect this to be the way I came back. One of my dreams was to have a home Church— to belong somewhere and know people who knew my name and my family, who cared about us.

"Yeah, like that'll happen now," I said to myself.

"Yes, it is very hard to go home again," someone said behind me.

A chill ran down my spine.

I spun around and caught my breath. There was a man sitting in the pews. He was tall with short blonde hair combed back and a long deep hunter-green coat with black embroidery on it. His boots were tall and black leather, like the sleeves of his coat. His green leather vest with buckles on it looked more expensive than anything I'd seen at the Manor. He didn't look like a demon or a goblin—a Prince maybe, but not a monster. The feeling I got from him, though... it was like what I'd felt outside but stronger. I hadn't even realized my hands were shaking. I stared at them, mentally screaming for them to stop. I wasn't in any danger-not so far.

"Who…who are you, and how did you get here?"

"I walked—same as you," he crossed his arms and looked at me quizzically.

"My brothers and my sister, we didn't see you," I tried not to sound shaky.

"Oh, you might not have seen me, but I was there."

"You didn't answer my question."

"Who am I? Hm—inquisitive girl, aren't you? My name is Verrine," he stood up and let his coat sweep behind him.

"Are you some kind of royalty?" I walked around the pulpit. I didn't feel safe standing still.

"*I* think so, yes," he smiled. "As for you…I know who you are, Elsha Dyer. You are one of the Avengers of Light—and you've come to this… place of *worship* to find the second piece to the Demon Stone."

"How do you know that? Do you work with…"

"Darkfire? Yes, she's quite the aspiring sorceress," he stood before the Church stage. He was about to walk up, but he looked at something behind me and stopped himself. "Only she can't seem to stop a handful of children so that duty is now left to me."

"Are you some kind of sorcerer?" The closer he walked, the stronger the sense of darkness I got from him. Like he was something worse than the goblins, if I stalled him long enough, then one of my family would come and save me.

He laughed quietly, "No child, I'm not a sorcerer. Magic is for mortals who want to become like the forces of darkness… I'm already there. The Demon's Stone is not for your family to have. The key to hell should be used by someone who isn't afraid of what lies there.

Not people of the light. Do you want your family to die defending this key?"

"No, we won't," I said. "Tulken said…."

He huffed at the name, "Oh, I'm tired of hearing about him from Dark Fire…he'll perish along with the rest of Raziel's Manor in the end."

"You work for Asmodeus?" I breathed.

"I serve no one. Everyone and everything in this Godless world serves me. Now there's a riddle for you—what am I?" he smiled, looking up at me.

"….You're selfish desire," I said, taking him by surprise.

"Tulken must have taught you something. More specifically, I'm temptation. And as such…." He disappeared, and I spun in circles, looking for him. He appeared next to me at the corner of the Church stage. "*Everyone* is a slave to me. Every weak, selfish, emotiondriven person must do whatever I ask of them because I am who they truly serve. Your brother serves me every time he gives in to his desire to fight, be prideful, and be contentious. Your sister serves me with her harsh words and impatient spirit, and you…." he stepped towards me, and I moved back, nearly stumbling off the Church stage. "You serve me every time fear keeps you from serving my Father. Because like the rest of the world… you give in."

I tried not to quiver. He wasn't doing anything to me, but if he wasn't even human, I had no idea how I was supposed to fight him. As I stood there, I sensed something else dark—nearby. Like I'd done with the first piece. But with him so close, it was impossible to tell. "N-no…I don't…"

"Yes, you do. Now drop your sword," he ordered.

My fingers were pried loose like my body was acting without me wanting it to. The blade fell from my hands, clattering down the steps of the stage.

He smiled, "Now do you see who serves whom? There's no shame in admitting it. Fear of hellfire and condemnation—yes. Shame…no. Now…give me the artifact piece." I felt every limb in my body wanting to walk over to where I sensed it. I knew where the artifact was. I could sense the darkness, and it was on the podium. But I couldn't tell him. Still, as he looked at me, I felt everything in my brain screaming it, like I had no choice. I tried to calm my mind as he waited patiently for the answer. I couldn't tell him lives were at stake, my family… I remembered Tulken giving me the flower—he said it could grow into anything, but only if I nurtured it. And that would define what I grew into. I wasn't going to betray him like this after he'd reached out to me. I tried to remember what Dante, Galahad, and Tulken had said. "*God is with you everywhere….*" My body was quivering and screaming in a battle not to do as he said. My nerves stung as I forced my eyes shut and put my hands over my ears, trying to block out the sound. I thought one thing repeatedly and prayed to God: *Help me say no, help me say no, please help me say no….!*

Finally, the words came. "….N-no!"

"Finally, you see sense…*what*?" he said, completely taken aback.

"I would never give it to you—you're going to use it to hurt thousands of innocent people!"

"Billions, but who's counting?" he said casually. "This is a strange turn of events, conveniently—I'm not discouraged. Maybe you don't want to do what I ask because you think other Commissioned will never forgive you for the sin? My partner Asmodeus committed a *small* outburst, and his Father didn't forgive him…"

"He led a revolt with Satan against all of heaven and poisoned mankind against God!"

He shrugged, "Everyone must leave their parents' ways for their own eventually. When all of you return, Tulken won't have mercy for you. Not after you fail the world, oh—and after what you do to each other."

"What do you..." I began.

Dante hurried into the sanctuary and came to a halt. "Elsha—who..."

"He's a demon!" I cried.

Dante moved his open hands, one over the other, creating a ball of frozen jagged icicles. The cold air from outside seemed to be sucked in through the boards, tearing through the wood to form the ice floating between his hands. His eyes flashed green, "Why haven't you used your magic?"

I looked at my hands helplessly. "Something's blocking it!"

"Move!"

I plastered myself to the nearest wall as Dante shot dozens of razor-sharp ice blades directly at Verrine. Verrine vanished in a whiff of green and black smoke as the shards stabbed into the wall behind the podium.

He reappeared a few feet away and straightened his coat. "A little sorcerer, eh? Well, that's annoying...." Verrine turned to him, "Dante—if you're going to be trouble, I'll have you drag Elsha off this stage and kill her?" Dante froze mid-step, and his expression strained like he went into a daze.

My mouth fell open. "Dante...no! Fight it! You can..." Before I finished, Dante outstretched a hand, and I felt myself being lifted from the stage. "Dante! Let me go...."

Micah and Killian came into the sanctuary from the side door and took in the scene with horrified expressions. "What the heck are you doing!" Killian ran for Dante, leaping over the pews, and took him to the floor. Killian and Dante were wrestling now. I fell to the floor in front of the church stage and put my hands up for protection. Killian was stronger than Dante. He got hold of his wrists and held him down.

Dante's eyes flashed green, and a chair from across the sanctuary came flying and hit Killian in the body, knocking him off.

I groaned, forcing myself to my feet.

"Micah, put that crossbow to your chest and pull the trigger," Verrine waved his hand at him casually.

Micah had been aiming the crossbow at Verrine, but his expression strained like Dante's had. Micah slowly turned the weapon around pointing the arrow at his chest.

"No!" I reached out, and the weapon flew from Micah's hands. It went crashing into the plate glass windows above the pews. I looked down at my hands—they radiated warmth now like Galahad's sword had done. What had been holding my magic back before? Fear? The demon Verrine? I wasn't sure, but it wasn't stopping me now.

Dante was levitating flaming vases from the entryway and sending them flying at me. I screamed, ducking behind the podium as the glass shattered above me. Dante lurched forward, pushing both open hands in my direction, and an icy gust of wind whipped inside the church, tearing through the boards and glass on the walls. I pressed my hands over my head, shielding my face from the glass that was flying at me. "Dante, stop!"

Verrine adjusted his cuffs calmly, "All of this could stop if you tell me where the artifact piece is."

I crawled as quickly as I could to the podium, "I'm sorry, Dante." I pressed my hands to the podium, and it glowed. A surge of power went through me. The podium flew from the stage in Dante's direction and he ducked, rolling out of the way. Verrine's eyes settled on an artifact piece that was under the podium. It looked like it connected to the one we had: it was a curved dark hand that looked like it was meant to be laced around a stone. That must have been the third and centerpiece. I hadn't meant to show it to him, but at that moment, I didn't have another way of stopping Dante. I looked up to see that Verrine had taken hold of it.

"Even the well-intentioned bring about the worst ends for themselves," he said, looking at the piece.

Courage welled up within me, "—Give me that!"

He looked at me in slight surprise, pulling his head back, "You really are one of the Commissioned, aren't you? Insane and delusional for your cause—oh, you'll be a perfect martyr."

As he said it, I felt something grab me by the throat. I felt my limbs freeze and looked to see Dante's outstretched hand levitating me. He pulled me towards him and off the stage. I shook and clenched my fist, but it was no good, "You don't want to do this….it's me, Elsha—fight it!"

"You don't want to fight it. You *want* to kill her," Verrine said, casually examining the artifact. He glanced behind him at the tall wooden crucifix and noticeably shuddered, stepping away from it.

"Dante…" I choked, as I felt myself losing air. His hand was out and shaking as I clasped my hands to my throat, trying to breathe. His expression twisted, but his eyes softened like he could see what he was doing.

Galahad came up behind Dante and slipped his arms under his, taking him in a choke hold. Dante was forced to lose his grip on me and I fell, gasping for air. Galahad was holding Dante down but his hands were free; he reached out, covering the torn curtains above the sanctuary windows with green energy. They ripped free from the windows and flew at Galahad. He dropped to the floor, forcing

320

Dante's face down. Galahad groaned, "Sorry about this…" he threw Dante to the side where his head hit the side of a pew. Galahad rushed over to me, "Elsha, are you okay?"

I nodded, clearing my throat. "Galahad, leave! He can make anyone do whatever he says! We can't fight him…"

Verrine nodded in agreement. "The girl has some knowledge. And I… have what I came for…." He looked at the artifact hungrily and I heard a low growl deep in his throat.

"I'm not letting you make my family hurt each other," Galahad slowly walked down the pews.

I hoped he had a plan. Because putting himself out in the open in front of this guy was like offering yourself as a tool to be used. Verrine looked at Galahad and knitted his brow. "Hm…I know you… Galahad Rainard Dyer… and not in the pleasant sense. You do your damnedest to fight me… it's very annoying."

Galahad flexed his hand around his sword as his eyes took in the situation. "Sorry to be such a bother."

Killian groaned, sitting up across the sanctuary, and Micah shook his head like he was barely coming to. We all were looking at our eldest brother and then at Verrine.

"Oh, how heartwarming …all you're doing is prolonging your subjugation. Now that I have the piece, the only thing left for me to do is finish what Darkfire couldn't—I command all of you to…."

"—Wait," Galahad said, standing at the end of the Church aisle across from Verrine.

Verrine rolled his eyes, "This isn't a *wedding* where you can object, child. *Weddings,* I *hate* those almost as much as Churches…."

"Leave them alone," Galahad readied his sword.

"Or—*what?*" Verrine taunted. "Do you think I'm honestly afraid of any of you? Small, weak, pathetic children who work for a thankless tyrant—every time one of your kind sins against our maker, I add a jewel to my hand or a gold threat to my coat. As you can see, I'm very well-dressed," he gestured to himself. "And I have closets *full* of such garments."

"You might not be afraid of us, but I know what you are afraid of," Galahad said, making Verrine's expression twist curiously. "Emma—now!"

I'd been watching Verrine and Galahad, so I hadn't even seen my sister sneak up to the stage from behind us. Emma was hiding near the tall wooden cross directly behind Verrine. Emma gritted her teeth and pushed it over. As Verrine turned to see it, I saw his face change in a flash—it went from classical and handsome to blistering red, his hands went crouched to his chest, and his fingers quickly flashed to being long claws. His eyes changed to a devilish red, and he let out a shriek that made all of us cover our ears. The glass in the Church shattered, sending shards flying across the sanctuary and showering the pews with fractured pieces. The cross hit the floor, crushing him in a large puff of red and black smoke.

Chapter Twenty-Five

We Follow the Sheep

When the smoke cleared, we were all coughing and waving dust from our faces. Galahad rushed to my side and steadied me. "Elsha…." He put his hand gently to my throat, and I immediately felt the bruising. I winced and put my hand to my neck. Galahad's expression grew more serious as he looked at Dante.

I tried to say it wasn't his fault, but my voice was hoarse.

"Don't talk. Your throat's been hurt," Galahad encouraged.

Emma was coming down off the stage to check on Micah, who was an inch away from firing the crossbow at himself again. He shook his head with his hand on the trigger. Micah made a horrified expression and dropped the weapon. Dante sat up and put his hand to his head with a groan. Killian didn't let Galahad intervene. He was on Dante with inhuman speed. Killian grabbed Dante by the front of his vest and lifted him off the floor, slamming him into the wall.

Dust shook from the wall on impact, and the building creaked.

Emma was checking over Micah when she looked up. "Killian, no!"

"I didn't…m-mean to hurt her…" Dante choked out as Killian tightened his grip on him.

"But you did! You nearly killed her!"

Galahad let go of me, walking towards Killian and Dante. He arched his head to my middle brother. "Let him go! You heard Elsha, that was a demon who can control anyone he talks to. God only knows what all of us would have done if he'd given us commands. You and I included. Fighting amongst ourselves isn't going to help us right now."

Killian fought back a low snarl as his grip tightened, nearly tearing through the leather in Dante's vest.

Galahad snapped. "Killian!"

Killian let go, stepping back. Dante fell, steadying himself by grabbing onto the back of the pews. He looked up with his tangled hair half covering his green eyes. "I…would never…hurt…Elsha. I didn't mean to…"

Killian turned away from him, "It doesn't matter if you *meant* it or not—if you did, I'd kill you."

Dante straightened. "Like you're gonna pretend you haven't hurt the people you love…."

Killian spun around, throwing a punch. Galahad grabbed his arm mid-throw and held him back. "What the heck are you…" Killian snarled.

Galahad turned Killian around to face him. "Enough! Or are you gonna fight me too? I don't want any more of this bickering-why do you think that demon has so much power over us? Because being selfish and stupid helps the enemy-not our mission! Now get it together." Galahad shot a gaze around the room at our ashamed faces.

Galahad looked angry, more than I'd seen. Whenever this family fought, though, the only thing at stake was our relationship, not the world. Galahad sighed with a guilty expression.

Killian shrugged his grip off. He and Galahad held each other's gaze and for a moment I was afraid they would fight. They'd never fought for real, only wrestled briefly, and it always ended with Killian face first on the floor. Galahad was bigger than him, so it wasn't fair. Galahad looked around. "Is anyone hurt?" No one was severely injured. Damage to feelings and dignity had been done more than anything else. Galahad walked over to the stage and searched around the pews. He squatted down checking the floor for the piece and frowned. He stood up.

Emma walked over eagerly. "Did he drop the piece?"

Galahad's expression wearied. "No, he got away with it."

I was about to start apologizing for letting Verrine get the piece. Emma and Killian looked at each other and opened their mouths. Knowing my family like I did, blame would start getting tossed around in another second.

Before anyone could say anything, Galahad spoke up. "We weren't prepared for this….any of us. I should have known if Darkfire failed Asmodeus would send bigger guns. And Elsha, I should have stayed with you. This isn't on any of you. This is on me. Understand?"

We all exchanged glances and mumbled assent. Galahad looked at me last, "This wasn't your fault—understand?"

I cleared my throat and said barely above a whisper, "…Yes Galahad."

"Good," Galahad scooped me up and I put my arms around his neck holding on. My throat hurt and so did my whole body, though I couldn't explain why. It was like saying no to Verrine took something out of me. I hid my face in the collar of his coat as he carried me out.

#

I felt bad for Killian as Galahad carried me back to Code Red. I didn't know why he'd lashed out at Dante like that but in his own way he was trying to protect me. Galahad was right, we'd been controlled to do the things we did. Code Red was parked by Waverly Park in Old Town. It would have been a nice place to walk around with gazebo's, trees, and pathways. It was getting dark by the time we got food in town and then came back to the car, settling in. We ate at Slice of Old town Pizza house and got a combination to share. My throat wasn't feeling the best but thankfully Galahad took leftovers, so we'd have something to eat later when I felt better. The town might have been nice to look at but when it was dark enough anything looked scary. Most cars cleared out of the park and it was just ours by a pathway and trees. Killian got out to walk around and be alone. He said he'd rather sleep outside anyway (I swore sometimes he was more comfortable outdoors than a wild dog). Micah was in the back of the car taking a nap. Galahad had gone walking around the park area with Dante.

I sat in the middle seat with the car door open, chewing some of the leftover pizza as Emma sorted through the clean clothes we had left. The sun was setting across the park, and the cool breeze was hitting us both, tangling our hair slightly. "I tell you something about boys…they always want us to look nice, but then they're like, *why do you need to bring so many clothes? We are not gonna be gone for a year!* Ha! Now, look—I barely have a couple of clean shirts left!"

I swallowed a bit of pizza and set the to-go container aside in the car seat. "Emma…about what happened in the church…."

"Don't even go there," Emma nudged me in the arm commandingly with her hand. "You heard what Galahad said—it wasn't your fault. We were all controlled to do things we would never normally do."

"But you didn't hear what Verrine said…every time one of us does something selfish, gives in to what we want, we don't fight it…we serve *him*. I never thought much about giving in to bad things like fighting, being greedy, insensitive—but now that I've met who we're helping when we do that…"

"You feel guilty about all the times we've been selfish," Emma rested against the car, holding her shirt at her waist dejectedly. She was silent a moment as she brushed her blonde hair from her eyes, "…I know. Me too." We were both quiet a good long while, watching leaves blow from the trees and scatter across the park. "You're not the only one who struggles with thinking you're too weak, Elsha. I feel like…I talk a lot but I don't help. I've never been a leader like Galahad, super athletic or passionate like Killian, or an artist like Micah. And sometimes, I'm scared that it will always be the boys looking out for us. When I should be looking out for them too, and you."

I looked up at her, "You do look out for me. You always have. Just because you didn't shoulder everything Galahad and Killian did doesn't mean I needed you any less. You're my best friend."

"But didn't you ever wonder why I wasn't biking to the library or trying to get you involved in games with other kids like Killian?" Emma said.

I shook my head.

"I was…afraid. I've never set foot in the real world and I've never had friends who weren't you guys. The idea of making some at the Manor is exciting and…scary at the same time. But I don't ever want to hold you back because I'm afraid to do something." She smiled. "Just don't tell Killian—I'd never hear the end of it." Emma put her arm around me in a hug.

Micah stuck his head out from the back of the car, "Aw! Group hug!"

Emma and I jumped. "Ah!"

We both giggled as the boys came back to Code Red from across the path. Galahad was walking up with Dante and Killian came stomping up with his hands in his pockets.

"The globe Collins gave us still hasn't cleared up. We need to get away from here. If it's still black, then that might mean we're in for another demon encounter," Galahad said.

Emma frowned, "You mean we gotta drive at night? We don't even know where we're headed next!"

"Sorry, Emma, but we don't have much of a choice," Galahad went to the driver's door. "Put your things away and we'll get moving."

Killian sniffed the air, "Something doesn't smell right…."

Micah sniffed his shirt sleeve, "Well, I haven't showered in three days…."

Emma went to the back of the vehicle to open it. "Just let me put my things…. AAAHHH!" Emma's scream made everyone jump to their senses.

"Emma, what's wrong?" We all rushed over and came to a skidding halt. Galahad instantly put his arm out, keeping me at a distance behind him. But I still saw it. We were inches away from a small bear-sized creature with ridges on its head, hooves, large bloody fangs, and a row of spines reaching from its neck to the base of its tail.

Killian covered his nose, "That's what I smelled…what the…."

"…HECK IS THAT!?" Emma said, stepping back.

"Chupacabra," Dante said.

"Bless you," Micah said.

"It's a demon that prowls on humans and livestock in the deep heart of the forests. I thought most of them had left this area, but…." Dante said.

"WELL, CLEARLY, THEIR NEIGHBORS DECIDED TO STICK AROUND!" Emma said, getting behind Killian and Dante.

Galahad unsheathed his sword.

"We need to get in the car…." Galahad said.

"Small problem with that," Dante said.

"What?"

"Chupacabras don't travel alone, they travel in…."

"Don't say it!" Micah said.

"—Groups," Dante said. As he said it I turned to see three more creatures almost exactly like the one before us prowling around Code Red. We froze like deer in the headlights. The creatures were moving slowly as the area around us grew darker. They seemed to step forward more readily as the sun grew completely out of view.

"No—sudden—movements," Dante spoke slowly and tensely, "They're pack hunters—they prey on fear and react to loud noises, quick motions…so whatever you do, don't…."

Low growls formed in the creatures' throats. Micah slowly slipped out of the car and stood by us holding his crossbow. As he did, the to-go container hit the grass. The creatures sniffed and moved slightly at the sound. "Whoops," Micah said tensely.

One of the creatures leapt on top of Code Red and snarled, causing the car to creak from the weight. "CRRRAAAUUGHKKK!" The sound echoed like a dinosaur from a monster movie.

That was it. "AAAHHH!" I wasn't sure which among us screamed, but it was more than Emma and I.

Galahad held the creature's gaze, stepping back, "—Drop everything but the weapons, the artifact, and run!"

We all didn't need to be told twice as we turned, taking off down the paved walkway past the trees. It got darker the deeper we went across the park, and we all tried to stay together, but I heard the beasts behind us. We passed tall trees and came to the field section of the park. Emma had my hand, and Dante was behind us, trying to keep them back. Galahad was keeping up the rear.

Micah was running, holding his crossbow to his chest, "What do these things want with us!"

"I told you, they kill livestock!" Dante said.

Killian was leading the way, moving faster than all of us. "Then that explains why they smell like goat's blood!"

Dante stopped, turning around. He levitated a stone bird bath in the park and pushed an open hand forward, throwing it at a creature. He caught the creature mid-air, leaping at him. It yelped, rolling to the floor, and Dante continued after us. Galahad flipped his sword facing down and stabbed the Chupacabra in the body. It let out a cry and slowly crumbled to dust from skin to bone as soon as he removed his blade. Galahad hurried, running after us.

"Galahad!" I paused, watching him, but Emma was pulling my arm.

"Come on, Elsha, keep moving!"

Galahad slashed at the creature coming after us, keeping them back. "I'm coming, just go!"

I looked ahead to see we'd run to a row of trees with hanging flowers and vines. The moon was our only light now. I struggled to run faster and keep up with Killian who made his way out of the park first. I made my way through the trees with Emma beside me following Killian's lead, next Micah, and lastly Galahad. The Chupacabra's were within feet of us and our only transportation lay behind them. Dante had no placement powder left and even if he did, we couldn't see the car. My heart was hammering like it would explode out of my chest. I was already feeling like I couldn't go further.

I heard their snarls grow louder and turned. It was bounding toward me and Dante. We both raised our hands at the same time; the freezing night air sucked towards us in a whirl, creating a blast of frost in our hands. We both lurched forward, blasting the creature. The frost froze its face and snout, making it yelp and fall to the grass in pain. I breathed quickly, turning to Dante who was staring at me impressed, "…Wow. It's like you read what spell I was gonna use…."

"Dante!" I interrupted him as the creature growled, shaking off the cold, and kept coming.

Dante panted, "If we make it to a populated area…past this field….they'll stop for other prey or retreat with the pack." Killian sniffed the air. As little kids we had a running joke that Killian could smell food from miles away (it was true, okay? Restaurant searching on vacations with mom and Dad was easier if his head was outside the window). But now with his gift of heightened senses I guessed he really did have a special nose.

Killian looked around quickly, "There's a road nearby…in this direction….if we can get to it they'll probably stop there! We just need to cross this field."

Micah raised his hands, "We are trusting your nose with our lives!"

"Listen to Killian! Emma give us some cover," Galahad stabbed at a lunging Chupacabra. It pulled its head back with a snarl. Emma raised her hands and her expression writhed. The hanging vines from the trees grew longer and tangled in a web. The Chupacabra's were held back for the moment. They clawed at the vines but as Emma focused the plants grew thicker. Soon there was a wall of greenery between us and them.

Emma lowered her trembling hands and released a breath. We hurried, trying to avoid potholes and thorny bushes. We kept moving till the sound of growls grew faint behind us. I brought down one foot after another as fast as I could, but my chest was hurting from all the running. We came to a small patch of land with a few scattered trees. We were nearing the end of the field. I could hear the cars on the road passing nearby. Headlights were in the distance, occasionally illuminating the trees.

I looked behind us and back ahead. "What now? If we go to the road we could get hit by a car!"

Galahad paced, running his hand through his hair tensely, "If you all have any bright ideas, I'd like...."

Micah opened his mouth. "BAAAAAAA," echoed behind him, and Micah froze. Micah turned to see a large flock of fat sheep standing by with mouths full of grass and completely stupefied expressions. "—It—is—sheep!"

Galahad stopped, "This is no time for jokes, Micah!"

Micah held up a fat baby lamb that was chewing grass with a totally uninterested expression. Chupacabra ate sheep and goats so it had every reason to be scared. "Ah ha! We can give them the sheep!"

Dante stepped towards Micah, "Are you insane? Duttur was the Sumerian Pagan goddess associated with sheep, ewes, milk, and arts of dairy."

"Oh, the dairy queen, huh?"

"I'm serious—the sorcerers in Sumer...."

Emma rolled her eyes and shot Dante a look, "Oh, now you're just making things up! Look Mr. 'I know random magical facts about weird stuff' I don't believe you know as much as you say!"

Dante looked down at her, "If you don't want to trust me, fine—but if it gets someone killed or cursed, don't blame me. I don't make the rules of magic."

"What goddess are we talking about?" Galahad stepped into the argument.

"She was the mother of Tammuz, the Shepard god of birth and new growth. If Commissioned kill or intentionally allow a sheep to be harmed without undergoing the proper ritual, you will be cursed for life," Dante said.

"Isn't she a little late for that?" Micah said.

"Do you want hooves and a rams head?" Dante said.

"So, what now, because he wanted to let them have the sheep if it dies…." Killian began.

"The chupacabra will be the least of our problems," Dante said.

Micah gave the small baby sheep to me and waved his arms to clear the others, "MOVE, YOU STUPID BALLS OF WOOL!" "BAAAA!"

"Yeah, yeah, your mother was a mattress," Micah pushed through them. I ran after my family with Killian leading the way and a fat ball of wool pressed to my chest. This was officially the strangest thing we've ever done. We hurried to the road as I heard vines tearing behind us. We all nearly fell into the street but we stopped ourselves as a vehicle drove by. The wind from the speed of the truck passing hit us in the face. Galahad leaned out, looking down the street to ensure no cars were coming.

"Come on!" Galahad ran across the street and we followed quickly behind, crossing to the field on the other side. I still had the sheep in my arms but its legs were kicking, making it tough to keep hold of. We stopped as a series of cars flew by us. I looked around at my sibling's worried faces.

"Did we…make it? Are they gone?" I breathed. Killian was right next to me and close to the street. Emma and Micah were out of breath. Galahad still held his sword and hadn't relaxed yet. In the moonlight, I saw his sword smeared with liquid and felt my stomach grow sick.

Dante leaned forward, putting his hands on his knees and breathed. "Yeah….we should be…."

A single Chupacabra came bounding across the street and leapt right at us.

Emma and I shrieked.

Galahad stepped forward, but Killian was the closest to the street.

"—Killian!"

But the creature had already taken him down.

Chapter Twenty-Six

The Dyers—Stoop To Hitchhiking! Never!
Well…Stranger Things Have Happened

I was screaming so loudly I couldn't hear what anyone else was saying. The creature was on top of Killian and they were fighting. The Chupacabra had Killian trapped beneath its four legs. Killian was holding its jaws closed, keeping it from biting his head off. There was no way he should have been that strong…it wasn't possible. Emma stretched out a hand and a plant sprouted from the ground. It grew and wrapped around the Chupacabra's neck, tightening till it was pulled from Killian. Micah aimed his crossbow shakily at the creature, but its jaws closed on the weapon snapping it into shards.

It was dark and we were all around the creature trying to stay a safe enough distance to kill it. Galahad stepped forward, swinging down on the creature with his sword. It let out a final cry and its body turned into a pile of ash and bones. I rushed to help Killian. Even in the moonlight I could see his shirt was torn—I wondered if the creature had been able to get at him with those fangs. My hands were trembling for fear of seeing blood, but his shirt wasn't wet as I helped him to his feet. Galahad shook his head at Killian, "That was…insane."

Micah looked down at his crossbow, "I'm gonna have to fix this again…."

"Are you okay, Killian? Are you hurt?" I squinted to try and see but he looked fine.

Killian shrugged with a wince. He must have been in some pain. "I guess that superhuman thing comes with its perks…"

"Now what? We can't go back to our car with those things around, and we can't stay here on the side of the road!" Emma said.

"She's right. This one followed us across the street, it's only a matter of time till his friends show up," Galahad said. "Where's the globe sending us for the last piece?"

Dante laced his hand around the globe. The image inside was whirling in a blur. A picture cleared and he groaned. "Great....it's across the Sacramento Suspension Bridge. In the forest. It's a hiking trail in upper Sac and that means...it's a long way from here."

Micah let out a breath and walked to the edge of the field right by the road. He held out his thumb. "You've all got perfectly good thumbs, come on!"

Killian huffed, crossing his arms, "If a car stops for him, I won't argue with anyone the rest of the night."

Emma arched an incredulous eyebrow, "Killian, I'm not prepared for the world to come to an end."

I walked over standing by Micah. The sheep trotted over next to us with a mouth full of grass. Headlights in the distance began to slow down. It looked like one of those vehicles carrying livestock. They stopped right in front of Micah.

Killian's mouth dropped open. "There's no way..."

"I've got the magic touch!" Micah spread his hands excitedly.

Dante looked indignant, "I resent that remark...."

The car door opened, and an older man with a beard and cap stepped out. He dusted off his hands on his pants and looked down at us.

"Hi, uh, sir, we'd be really grateful if you could give us a ride to the Sacramento River trail," I said.

He shrugged, "As long as you don't mind the company—but by the looks of your little friend here, you shouldn't." He gestured to the sheep between us.

"What do you…" Micah began before his eyes settled on the balls of cotton in the back of the truck. Micah's expression was petrified, "No…. more sheep…."

#

There was no room in a livestock truck to hold six kids except with the cargo. We told the man the Chupacabra remains were roadkill. He nodded as if that was what he saw. I guessed he wasn't a believer so he couldn't see it. The back was lined with wooden boards, making it easier for us to breathe, but my allergies were still killing me. I know Micah was being a little overdramatic with the sheep thing, but in his defense the creatures did not smell good. There were small heaps of grass in the back of the truck where we sat. Micah was messing with the crossbow trying to fix it without tools. Sheep were crowded around him more than us chewing and watching him work. I doubted he'd have any luck. Even Micah needed duck-tape, screw drivers or something. Emma and I were sneezing up a storm for the first part till she fell asleep on a pile of grass. Killian was sleeping next to Emma resting his head back against the shaking wall of the vehicle. Killian had already nearly broken his promise to not argue as soon as we stepped in the car. First it was with Galahad, then Emma. Galahad suggested he get some sleep to make keeping his word easier (even Killian couldn't argue in his sleep). Galahad was at the back end of the vehicle, sitting upright with his arms on his knees watching the highway go by, sword still in hand. I was sitting against a pile of grass feeding Clementine (that's what Micah had named the baby lamb). I brushed my hair behind my ears as I sat forward and held my knees.

Dante walked over and slid into a seating position next to me. He pulled up one knee to rest his arm on and let his head fall back with a groan.

"How do you like your first mission so far?" I asked weakly.

337

Dante cracked a half-hearted smile, "Oh, this isn't the way I saw it going...but I can't complain. So, what's the deal with your family and the sheep? I didn't really get the inside joke." He gestured to Micah with his head. I laughed and explained to him our experience with churches and how the pastor said sheep were wise. One of the sheep next to us had its head against another sheep's butt. The sheep in front of it was chewing uninterested. They both waddled to a different part of the vehicle and plopped down. Dante laughed, "Okay...I get the point. Not...what's the word? Biblically accurate huh?"

I turned, looking at him curiously, "Did you read the Bible before coming to the Manor?"

Dante shrugged, "Never really saw the point. I was more focused on, you know—staying alive."

I looked down at my hands, "When did you...know you had magic?"

Dante's eyes flashed green and he opened his hand, turning it in the moonlight. A green light that moved like mist floated between his fingers, curling and coiling as he slowly moved his hand. "This...happened a lot when I was a kid. Other kids at my Boarding House were like the ones at the Manor. They would get scared, call me evil. I tried to steal contact lenses one time because I got so many cracks about having serpents' eyes."

I flushed as he flashed a glance at me. In the dark, I hoped he couldn't see. "I...I like green eyes."

What the heck am I doing—he's gonna know I like him!

Dante simply stared at me in slight disbelief. He cracked a small smile, "Thanks...I wouldn't want normal colored eyes anyway. So boring."

"No one at the Manor has ever...hurt you or anything?"

"No, kids at the Manor judge with their eyes and if they want to kick my tail, they do it in gym where its allowed. I've gotten into the occasional tussle but nothing severe. At the Boarding House the kids were less forgiving. I got stuffed in lockers, locked in broom closets, jumped…" he turned his hand and the green mist formed a thin snake that coiled around his hand. "—Till I learned to control this," he grinned. "Then, they were too busy screaming."

"How did Kaine find you?"

"All of my…retaliation got me on the Manor's radar. They started wondering if my Boarding House was haunted because of all the strange happenings. Kaine shows up like Rambo and tells me I'm Commissioned; he wants to take me away from there. I'm not one to argue, so I go along. They tell me my magic is my gift and not a curse. But some people still aren't convinced."

"I'm sorry you had to go through that. But you're so good with magic now…"

His expression hardened a little, "I know…but not good enough. There's all kinds of powers and manipulation I haven't even tapped into yet. I don't wanna be, a sorcerer like anyone else. I want to be…better."

I studied him. He continued before I could ask what he meant.

Dante's frown shifted to a smile, "Speaking of which…your powers have just been a ball of joy this trip, huh?"

I released a breath and ran my hands through my hair, "I've done a couple things but…. I'm not sure how to control it."

"You need a little help? It's okay, that's what I'm here for," Dante held out his hand. "Take my hand."

My eyes grew large, "W-what?"

"It's okay, I don't bite—much." My hand was shaking so much I was afraid he'd laugh at me, but his expression was serious. I put my hand in his and swallowed. I was clammy and sweaty now, but he didn't seem to notice. He opened his hand right below mine and a green light emerged that looked like pure energy.

My open hand was trembling, but nothing was happening. I frowned, "What am I supposed to be focusing on?"

"If sorcery is your gift it's tied to you. Your motives, your heart, your feelings. If those things are all scattered than its more likely your magic will come out in bursts. You need to control your emotions, find what drives you—focus on it. You have light magic so you should be able to produce light at any time."

Dante leaned his head down to meet my gaze, "Why did you agree to take this mission?"

I blinked, "To save the Manor and everyone…."

"No, I don't mean why you should've taken the mission. Why did you? Saving the world isn't a bad reason but there's always more to it."

I looked at my family in different corners of the vehicle. "Because…. Asmodeus was supposed to have been put away three years ago. We're the Avengers of Light, the only people who can stop him, and we still don't know what happened to our parents. It can't be a coincidence."

Dante nodded, "You want to find out what happened to your family."

I nodded.

"If you find them…, are you gonna go home, or are you gonna stay at the Manor like Commissioned?" he asked more quietly.

"I…. I don't know."

"Okay, then focus on them. Think about your parents. That's what's motivating you, then center your mind on it, try..."

Dante kept his hand underneath mine, and I stretched my fingers. I thought about everything I remembered. My Dad's voice, our mom in the kitchen while the five of us played in the living room, all our games we played home schooling, the birthdays, Christmas when we had a home…. I wanted all of that back. I closed my eyes.

Dante called me out of my memories, "Elsha…look."

I opened my eyes, and a small ball of light had formed in my hand above his. It was bright and fluid, like a ray of sunshine illuminating our faces. I looked at Dante's face in the light both of us were making. Dante smiled, "You're a natural, Dyer."

I glanced over to see Galahad was watching us. When I looked back, my light and Dante's were combatting like two flames that couldn't mix. As they tried, the flame between us grew. Dante and I both pulled our heads back as an explosion of light like a small firework erupted. I raised my arm to shield my face, and Galahad came to my side.

Dante stood up and looked at his hands, "…. That's new."

"That's enough magic lessons for now," Galahad led me to the back of the vehicle. "You need to get some sleep," he sat down next to me.

I rested my head on Galahad's shoulder, trying to find a comfortable position. "You saw?"

"And heard," Galahad tousled my hair lightly.

I was silent a long moment. "You don't think it's wrong…me wanting our family to go back to the way it was?"

Now it was Galahad's turn to not talk for a while. The only sound was the rustling of the car and the sheep. Galahad put his arm around me to keep me warm. "There's nothing wrong with wanting our parents back."

"Killian told me not to tell you."

Galahad chuckled lightly, "Killian doesn't know me as well as he thinks."

"So…he's wrong?"

"You have to be more specific."

"He thinks…you don't care about our parents anymore, that you want us to forget them."

Galahad shook his head, "I don't not talk about them because I don't care. I think about our parents every day. But sometimes…there's things in life you can't change. Because of them leaving, nobody was there to teach you guys how to handle the real world. I went outside the Boarding House more than any of us because I wanted to protect you. But I can't do that forever, and someday you're not gonna want me to."

"Why wouldn't I want you to protect me?" I picked my head up and looked at him.

"I know the real-world scares you. But living in fear…that's not something I'd wish on anyone. And waiting for our parents to come back, it makes you dependent on a slim hope. No calling is bigger than you, but you need to believe that."

"I'm scared…"

"Things won't get easier. But you can't let that stop you from living. And as to me protecting you, things aren't meant to be one way forever. Everything has its time and season…"

"Your favorite book of the Bible?" I recalled.

Galahad exhaled, "…Ecclesiastes. Enjoy everything in its time because we won't always have it."

I thought about something a while back. "Why did Verrine know you?"

Galahad was looking down at his hands as the vehicle rumbled along on the road. "If he's temptation, I guess we've had a lot of runins with each other."

I looked at him, surprised, "You don't struggle with temptation."

Galahad laughed weakly. "I don't know where you get this opinion of me, Elsha…the things the Manor's pastor says we're supposed to have, kindness, patience, meekness—none of it has ever come easily to me."

"…Then how do you do it all the time?"

Galahad let out a strained frustrated breath, "I…. have no idea." He turned, looking out the cracks in the wood of the truck as scenery flew by. The truck grew colder. "Nothing tries my patience like this family…" he began.

My expression must have looked concerned because he softened his tone, glancing back down at me.

"Still…. it's what keeps me from being selfish. If I take care of you, I can't wallow in self-pity or get angry whenever I feel like it. I'm not happy about the way our lives turned out either….but it's no excuse for me to quit," he ruffled my hair. I never thought about it that way. Maybe Killian was always angry because he was in his own head and focused on what he wanted and needed. I was depressed because all I ever thought about were the things I didn't have. If I spent more time focusing on Killian, Micah, Galahad, and Emma I'd be too concerned with them to be sad. I put my head back into his shoulder to try and sleep. I wasn't sure I was as capable as he believed. I wanted to be the person my big brother believed I was, but I was just…me. As I let my hair hide my face and began to drift into sleep, I felt Galahad hug me tighter and put his head to mine. I remembered Galahad saying three words, "Don't be afraid, don't be afraid…" and the rustling of the vehicle rocked me to sleep beside my brother.

Chapter Twenty-Seven

The Beasts of the Field

The sound of the vehicle door opening woke me up. I sat up and put my hand to my face, shielding my eyes. I was still next to Galahad. He sat up and my other siblings were coming to as well. We'd stopped in a small town with maybe 40 people that was right before the hike up to the trail. Most likely for people on vacations to stop and eat. Our money had been left back in Code Red so we couldn't get ourselves food. Micah let out a breath, putting his hands on his hips.

"So—I have a plan for how we get money."

"What is it?" Emma combed through her hair with her fingers.

"It's a way that's practical, brilliant, and above all...dignified," Micah puffed his chest out. "...But we're gonna need the sheep."

Micah rattled a small tin cup. "Alms! Alms for the poor!" Emma stood by the side of the road with her arms crossed, criticizing Micah for his brilliant and dignified plan. I was sitting on a box with a blanket on me (to make me look old, apparently) with a small rope around my sheep who sat beside me.

"This is ridiculous! Emma Dyer does not pan handle!" Micah

raised an eyebrow, "Does Emma Dyer want to eat?"

"Isn't this like conning people?" I asked.

"Yes, Elsha, that is exactly what this is like. If Dashiel ever saw me doing this he'd never date me...." Emma said to herself.

"He isn't dating you now," Micah commented, receiving a glare from Emma.

Someone walked by Micah and kept walking. He turned and whispered to Emma, "Watch and learn." He walked up to the woman who passed him, "Alms for the poor ma'am!"

"No, I don't want to give," she said.

"PLEASE! PLEASE, I BEG OF YOU! WE HAVE NO FOOD, MY SISTER'S HUSBAND IS A BUM WHO'S NEVER WORKED A DAY IN HIS LIFE! AND THE CHILDREN! PLEASE! MY OTHER BROTHER SPENDS ALL MY HARD EARNED MONEY ON HAIR GEL!" Micah said, falling on his knees and taking hold of the woman's pant leg.

Everyone was staring now. No surprise there. Killian shot Micah a scowl. Dante and Galahad looked up from the map they seemed to be arguing over and stared open-mouthed.

"Alright! Here are five dollars. Just stop making a scene, little boy," she said, walking by. Micah grinned broadly as he walked back to us.

Emma rolled her eyes. "Stunning."

I pulled the blanket off my head and grabbed Clementine, "There's gotta be a better way to do this."

Galahad opened his mouth like he was about to say something in haste; he stopped himself, putting his hand to his head, releasing a breath. In the moment he'd been about to speak, he reminded me of Killian. "...We don't–have–time. We have to reach the suspension bridge and we're so far away it'll take the whole day to get there on foot."

All of us were in a huddle when an elderly woman on a bench in a cloak called to us. "Psst! Over here children..." she waved a wrinkled finger to us. I couldn't see her face, just a long hooked nose. But there was no green skin or anything so I assumed she was human.

We all exchanged glances before walking over. She had a small tin cup and was shaking it.

Micah whispered to me, "This lady knows what she's doing! Elsha come here—I'll draw some wrinkles on you…"

"Micah...." Galahad cautioned, making Micah retreat, raising his hands. "What is it you wanted to tell us, ma'am?"

"You all want to get to the suspension bridge…I know a shortcut…." She coughed before breaking into a crooked grin.

"Great, let's take it!" Micah said.

"Unless you'd rather take the long way," she posed.

Emma spread her hands, not following."Why would we want to take the long way?"

"Because the short way is known to have La Ciguapa…."

Micah perked up, "Oh great, I'm starving. Anybody else like beef tacos?"

Killian shook his head, "I don't think that's a Mexican restaurant."

"Oh no, children, it's an evil spirit of a woman who died centuries ago howling in the woods….. Her killers never met justice from mortal men, so she stole their lives and left their bodies to the birds and the beasts of the field. Many have gone the short way and never lived to tell the tale," the woman smiled.

Micah shook his head, "Let's not take the short way."

Galahad looked up the long road we'd have to walk. By the time we made that hike Asmodeus might have the third piece. I knew what he was thinking. To my big brother obstacles weren't excuses. I could see in his eyes he'd already made up his mind. "No time for doubters. Which way do we go?"

#

It was still a hike but the old woman promised it would be a shorter one. The trees blocked the sun that normally would have been streaming down on us if we'd taken the road. We passed through a creek that was full of uneven rocks with Galahad leading the way. I could have sworn I was getting bruised up from ankle to knee as the current beat down against us.

"Come on, we can't afford to get tired," Galahad pressed forward as Emma and I struggled somewhere near the back. Killian was even having trouble not slipping and getting pushed by the current.

Micah rolled his jeans up to his knees and was wading through the water, trying not to trip. "Let me just get one thing straight…this thousand-year-old lady tells us an evil spirit is at the end of the rough creek, through the jagged rocks, splinters, and basically no man's land…so we go—that's the way for us! Am I on track so far?"

Galahad caught hold of a branch from an overhanging tree and steadied himself, "That's right."

"Okay, I'm just checking…I thought we didn't want to make choices that would get us killed, but you know—that's just me," Micah shrugged.

Emma grunted as she hiked, bringing up the rear. "I mean…this wasn't my idea–but I'd rather not run the risk or an ancient monster coming for us. What are we going to do if we do run into them, Galahad?" she said his name accusingly.

Galahad was looking ahead, scanning the area carefully with his nerves on alert. "We'll cross that bridge when we get to it."

Micah was breathing heavily as Killian helped him over awkward steps, "Literally, since we are, in fact, crossing a bridge."

"I'm just saying I would have taken the longer safe way...." Emma began.

Galahad arched his head turning back to her, "Emma–we're here. We can't risk losing that much time and complaining doesn't help." Emma stopped next to me. Her expression was a mix of guilty and hurt. I looked at her and then at Galahad accusingly. "She just meant..." I began.

Galahad closed his eyes, "I know. But we need to keep going. Everyone watch your step." He looked around at all of us and then kept going forward.

Killian put an arm around Emma encouragingly and she mumbled, "I just mean this is dangerous..."

"I know, I know," Killian said. "He's just a little uptight as usual, don't take it personally." Killian encouraged. This was familiar too. Despite the crazy situation, there were times when the four younger siblings bunched together because Galahad was turning into a drill sergeant or dealing with things we didn't understand. The four of us talked for a little bit, and Micah tried to improve the mood.

Emma looked back over her shoulder at Dante. "And I suppose you know about this evil spirit she mentioned, magic boy?"

"As a matter of fact...yes I do. I've heard the legend, and La Ciguapa was said to have been killed ages ago, and now her spirit lingers in darkness and by the light of the full moon. She targets trespassers and is said to sway men to her control if you look her in the eye. The only way some travelers were able to distinguish her from a human being was her backward feet."

"That's...weird," I said.

"So why would anybody be dumb enough to look at her?" Killian made it to the end of the stream with my eldest brother.

"Because La Ciguapa has been said to appear as a beautiful woman and weak-willed humans find it impossible to resist staring at her," Dante shook the water from the edge of his sleeves.

"How do you kill it?" Killian said.

Dante knit his brow, "You rob her of her beauty."

We all looked at him.

Micah made a confused expression, "You want us to put a bag over hear head?"

Dante laughed, "No."

Micah blinked, "…You want us to take her make-up?"

Emma scoffed, fixing her hair, "If she was naturally beautiful, she wouldn't need make-up…."

Dante put his fingers to his temple, chuckling, "You guys….that's not what it means."

Emma put her hands on her hips, "Well, magic boy, what does it mean?"

Dante checked his hands to ensure his rings hadn't slipped off, "….I haven't a clue. It wasn't a super interesting part of class for me."

We all stepped out of the water and squeezed out the end of our wet clothes. We weren't carrying much anymore. Galahad had his sword, Dante his magic bag with the globe, Micah had his crossbow he'd fixed since the Chupacabra's. But that was it. Honestly, I was trying not to be too scared. We were massively unprepared and flying blind. The bridge was in view. Trees were on each side, blowing in the wind. They seemed to be taller than the others and they kept the sun back, making the bridge look like it was veiled in shadow. At the other side was the only sunlight. Where we stood was shaded like an eclipse had passed over.

I felt a strange chill. "Uh, guys…." I began. My gaze flashed around at the leaves falling from the trees. The trees hadn't been this thick before. I couldn't even see below the bridge. It was almost like the trees had closed in around us. I looked behind us. An eerie whistle filled the air as the breeze whipped around us. I looked ahead at the bridge again and swallowed hard.

Galahad flexed his hands around his sword, "I'll go first. Everyone stay close."

We all walked up to the bridge. Galahad set foot on it. The water beneath us rustled. We'd all barely stepped on when the whistling echoed. We all turned, forming a circle, and looked around.

Emma tried to keep a steady voice. "W-what was that?"

Micah swallowed, "It…was probably just the wind. Right?"

Killian huffed, "Is it ever with us?"

I looked at Dante and then back ahead of us. A scream stopped in my throat. At the center of the bridge was a woman—something about her wasn't human. She had jet black hair that was like a cloak covering her whole body, only her arms and legs were visible. I couldn't even tell if she had clothes beneath it because her lustrous hair was intertwined with her pale blueish skin. She had large almond grey eyes and gaunt cheek bones. Her nails were long and midnight blue, and around her eyes were liquid looking lashes that gave her inhuman cat eyes. She held her hands in front of her at her waist. The way her appearance moved in the shade was like a reflection of moonlight, but it had been day when we left. "Hello, children, what are you doing crossing a bridge out here by yourselves?" she had a melodious voice that sounded much like the whistling in the wind.

Killian's jaw was hanging slightly open. "Who…is that?"

Galahad's gaze flickered down to the ground where she stood. A look of horror crossed his expression, he arched his head down. "Don't look in her eyes!"

Killian must have already done that because his eyes flashed white like a storm cloud. Dante's had done the same.

"Come towards me," La Ciguapa gestured with her hand. Micah had his arm over his eyes, being extra careful. Dante and Killian began walking towards her.

Emma grabbed Killian by the arm, trying not to look ahead, "No! Don't do it, you big dummy! If you get yourself killed, I'm gonna murder you!" Killian was stronger than Emma so he shrugged her off easily.

Galahad arched his head, still trying not to look up, "Emma! Use the hanging branches behind you to keep him back!"

As Emma struggled with Killian, the branches on the tree behind her grew out and grabbed at Killian's arms. He was pulled slowly back, though he fought tooth and nail. Emma was breathing quickly as she cast her gaze up to Galahad, "What now?"

Galahad was trying to pull Dante back by the arm while still looking down. La Ciguapa stood at the center of the bridge, her bewitching gaze unmoved. "Micah—shoot her!"

Micah aimed the crossbow and fired off a couple arrows. They both flew by her head. He couldn't even look at her. How was he supposed to hit her?

"Why do all of you persist so much? I only want to lead you back to my cave," she titled her head. I looked down at the bottom of the bridge where her hair was arrayed like silk touching the floor. Her feet…they were backwards. It was the only thing about her appearance unpleasant. It must have been how Galahad noticed she was a demon.

"You're not going anywhere with our brother!" Emma exclaimed as Killian shook and struggled in the branches that had grown out behind her.

"Elsha, take the bow from Micah!"

I'd been standing there paralyzed. I didn't know how to kill this thing. I took the bow from Micah. La Ciguapa raised a delicate hand. The wind whistled louder and shook the bridge where we stood. I stumbled to the left and then to the right steadying myself on the railing. I caught a flash of the rocks and water below and my heart flipped in my chest. I screamed and grabbed for the side of the bridge. The crossbow fell from my hands.

"No!" I leaned out to grab it as the wind shook the bridge again.

I fell forward.

Emma was stumbling, trying to steady herself, "Elsha!"

"Hang onto me, Elsha!" Galahad caught me by the end of my hand and I winced in pain. He squeezed my hand so hard my arm yanked in my socket, and I let out a scream. It hurt, but better I have a dislocated arm than be dead. Galahad's teeth were clenched as he struggled to pull me up. It was a good thing he did all those chin ups because otherwise this story would stop here. The veins on his arms and neck strained as he pulled my up with his arm. I grabbed a hold of the bridge with my free arm as soon as I could to take some weight off him. Dante had already walked to La Ciguapa's side and Killian was fighting to follow as well.

"Pull yourself up!" Galahad called to me.

I struggled, trying to get my elbows onto the bridge so I was no longer hanging by a hand. As I did, Galahad let go and I held myself there. I got my leg up next and rolled over onto my back, releasing a tired breath. Galahad got to his knees and reached for his weapon when a gust of wind blew at us. The whistling in the wind grew louder and louder.

We covered our ears as the whistling became earsplittingly ghoulish.

Emma's hands were pressed to her ears, and Micah was still covering his eyes.

Emma called to Galahad, "How do we kill her!"

"You've been getting A's in Kaine's class. You've gotta know how to get us out of this!" I said. Galahad must have figured it out. I could see the trains of thought running through his mind a mile a minute.

Galahad nodded, "I think I do– I just need an opening."

Micah smiled, "Maybe we'll survive this!"

Galahad's expression shifted. He had an idea. He opened his mouth standing up. "Guys—we have to...."

The wind whipped at us again and a loud screech, much like the whistling before, echoed across the bridge. Galahad flipped his sword in his hand, turning to attack. La Ciguapa appeared before him. He'd had his head arched down so as not to look in her eyes, but she appeared at eye level.

Emma and I gasped.

No, no, she won't be able to get Galahad. Galahad beat Verrine, he was temptation itself. There was no way she...

Galahad's eyes flashed stormy white and his hand, which held the sword, opened.

He blade fell to the floor.

La Ciguapa straightened, "Follow me."

Galahad took a step after her.

Emma and I exchanged looks.

Micah still had his arm over his eyes. "What's happening! I still can't see!"

Emma's voice rose with panic. "Galahad's under her control!"

Micah's expression sank, "...Oh, we're dead."

Chapter Twenty-Eight

Do we really have a choice?

Killian was tearing free from Emma's branches. He pushed past us. Micah dropped to the floor and grabbed him by the leg, trying to keep him back. "If it's all the same to you ladies, I don't want to save the world without my best friend!"

Emma was chewing her nails with stress as the wind beat against us. Dante, Killian, and Galahad were walking by La Ciguapa to the other side and slowly disappearing in the distance. Emma grabbed the sword and went at La Ciguapa but she moved like wind. She disappeared and reappeared in a flash. I was doing my best not to panic. Right now I was crawling and begging after the boys with Micah, trying to make them stop. But stopping Galahad…Emma and I were both scared to try because he was twice our size but we loved him too much to let him leave. We both debated the risk in our minds before running after him. Emma jumped on Galahad's back and he turned, taking her arms off of him with little effort and throwing her behind him on the bridge.

Emma rolled across the bridge and few boards broke. She nearly slipped through the hole and screamed, grabbing onto the weak boards in front of her. Emma steadied herself on the swaying bridge.

"Emma!" I ran after Galahad. Micah was wrestling with Killian and failing. I didn't want to hurt Galahad, but truth be told I had little hope of doing that at all. I grabbed his sword off the bridge and swung the blunt end at him. "I'm sorry, Galahad!" I didn't want to kill him, just knock him down or stop him.

Galahad moved his head aside and raised a hand, catching the flat end of the sword mid-swing. I pulled, trying to move it back but couldn't budge it an inch. Galahad's expression was blank, like he wasn't even in there. His eyes were still stormy white under Ciguapa's control.

Galahad pulled the sword aside, taking me with it. I stumbled against the side of the bridge and steadied myself as he now held the sword.

Micah was rolling around with Killian, struggling under his strength. "Great! You gave him a weapon!"

Galahad swung the sword with far more force and accuracy than I had and I yelped, dropping to the floor. He raised his arm again to deliver another strike. I raised my hands, concentrating on the sword; it became covered in light and I pushed my open hands up, trying to force the blade from his hands. I grit my teeth as the dark sky clouded above us and pushed with all my strength.

Galahad pushed down against my strength. My arms were pained as I struggled to keep the blade away.

I cried out, rolling aside, unable to keep him back anymore.

Galahad brought the sword down beside me, breaking through the board in the bridge.

I groaned in pain, sitting up and clutching my arm.

La ciguapa's voice bellowed, "Come with me…."

Galahad threw the sword down, and it slid across the bridge, but I squatted, grabbing it. That was my brother's weapon, and when he woke up, he'd be bothered that we lost it. He was going to wake up. Emma, Micah, and I weren't going to lose them that easily.

La Ciguapa was screeching. The wind was beating against our faces, pushing us back. I tried to see through the blinding dust. When I slit my eyes open, I was staring right down at her backward feet. Her thick black hair was like liquid all around the floor, partially concealing them.

To beat her, you must take her beauty….

I looked back over my shoulder at Micah who was crouched, covering his eyes as leaves and dirt flew at him. "Micah! I need some cover!" I called over the whaling demon. My other brothers and Dante were disappearing in the distance at the other side and La Ciguapa wasn't halting. "We have to steal her beauty!"

"I thought we agreed nobody knew what that meant?!" Micah yelled.

"Just do what I say!" I demanded. The fear of losing them was driving me to make a choice, some decision. Anything had to be better than screaming and crying while they walked away into God only knew what kind of fate. "Aim high and don't look at her!"

Micah did as I said. If he aimed low at all, he'd shoot Emma or me. The arrows began flying, and La Ciguapa was forced to halt her screeching. She couldn't howl when she was in motion. Her howls halted like gusts of wind as she moved around the bridge. She was getting closer to Emma, and I. Emma still had the sword and was swinging at her head but missing. I grabbed Emma by the arm and pulled her down to the floor beside me. No matter where La Ciguapa moved, her hair was always on the floor like a long sheet, within easy reach. I hoped I'd interpreted what Dante said correctly.

"We have to cut the hair!" I yelled over the screeching at Emma.

Emma processed it a moment and nodded, "It's worth a try!" La Ciguapa was going towards Micah as the wind howled, and he was stepping back, covering his eyes. The demon's hair was swept across the floor as she moved. Emma raised up Galahad's sword with both hands; it was heavy for her. She brought it down on a thick sheet of the demon's hair.

CRACK!

The sword connected with the wooden bridge cutting right through the liquid-like hair. The demon's head did a 360, turning all the way around, and her eyes flashed white. Micah had been pressed to the railing, nearly falling off, trying not to look at her.

"….What have you done!" La Ciguapa's thick luscious black hair began to wither and turn gray like a hag. Her skin wrinkled, beginning to hang on her face like it was falling off her bones, and her body hunched and shriveled as the wind whipped around us. She let out a blood-curdling shriek that made all of us cover our ears and duck our heads. "AIIIIGGHHHHHHHH! WRETCHED CREATURES!" her body withered to dust and was blown away by one last sweep of wind. When I lifted my head, the clouds had cleared, the sky was blue again, and I could see clearly to the other side.

Micah pulled his arm down from his eyes and realized how close he was to the edge, "—AH!" he stepped forward.

"Killian, Dante, and Galahad!" Emma looked at me. We looked ahead at the other end of the bridge. The three of them were slightly in view, blocked by a few trees. Emma and I ran so fast across the bridge that our feet barely touched the boards. Micah followed close behind. The three of them were standing there, shaking their heads like they'd just come out of a daze.

Galahad arched his head towards us, "The girls…" he began in a concerned tone, but I stopped him mid-sentence.

"Galahad!" I leaped at him and wrapped my arms around his neck in a hug. If he hadn't been as strong or large as he was, he probably would have fallen over, but Galahad didn't.

He hugged me tightly before pulling back, confused. "What…happened?"

Emma had tackled Killian mid-objection (don't ask me why it's Killian's business to object to everything). Micah wrapped his arms around both and closed his eyes with a smile. It took me a second to realize Dante was staring at us with an expression I couldn't read. It was confusion, and not just at what had happened but at our small family reunion. I forgot that maybe he wasn't used to family interaction. There was even a hint of sadness in his eyes. I stepped back from Galahad and looked at the three of them. I would have hugged Killian, but Micah was still squishing him.

Emma put her hands on her hips proudly, looking at our brothers, "Who's not strong enough to look out for you guys?" she grinned.

Killian looked at her strangely while Micah still hugged him, "…You guys. Now you wanna explain how you didn't die without us helping you?"

#

So, you can imagine what happened next. We had to gather everything we had left (which wasn't much in the range of weapons or supplies) and keep moving forward. But amidst that, there was a lot of arguing. We were walking through the hiking trail now as Dante studied Collin's globe, trying to lead the way. Galahad was beside him, being extremely quiet. Emma had explained at length how he'd been controlled. Something in Galahad's face was like the look he'd had when he'd snapped at Emma earlier. Guilt. Galahad thanked us for saving them and forced a small smile, but I could see he hadn't planned for that to happen.

Emma was walking beside Killian, arguing with him because he hadn't liked being saved, but he wasn't handling it the same way as Galahad.

"Just because you saved us this time doesn't mean you have before! So at least admit I'm right to doubt you!" Killian said.

Dante rolled his eyes, lacing his hands around the globe, "Making it really hard to concentrate…."

Galahad's expression was sullen as he looked back ahead and kept going. I frowned. It wasn't his fault he was controlled. Granted, I was a little shocked any demon could get in his head. But I didn't blame him for it any more than I blamed Dante for what he did under Verrine's control. I pushed my hair behind my ears, "I hope Galahad's okay."

Dante looked up to meet my gaze, "If I've learned anything about your brother, he'll know how to deal. I wouldn't worry."

I nodded. "Yeah…he's got a lot on his plate. You might not believe this, but as little kids, we used to fight a lot."

Dante raised an eyebrow, "You're siblings? No."

I laughed, "You're not…bothered we saved you, are you?"

Dante waved a hand, "Nah, my pride is a little wounded, but other than that, I'll live."

"Then…what is it?" I knew something was bothering him. He glanced over his shoulder at my siblings.

Hopefully, the fight was over. "This….is just a little different for me. You, your family….I've never had anything like that."

My eyes widened, "You can't possibly tell me you're jealous? In times like this?"

Dante shook his head, coming to a halt, the evening was waning, and the trees shaded us in the twilight. "Do you wanna know one of the reasons your brother annoys me?" I pulled my head back in surprise.

"—Killian?" I said, not even needing to think about it.

"Your family's not perfect. I mean, you guys have serious issues…."

I raised a hand, "Okay, I know that—moving on…."

"Sorry, you know what I mean. But fighting about who was right when or who's gonna take credit, I never had siblings to argue with. Anytime I get close to people…they pull back. You guys are so close it's annoying. I know he's got stuff to complain about. We all do. But if I were him…I guess I'd spend less time complaining."

"You have Kaine," I ventured carefully.

"Kaine's like everyone else. When there's no one around, he might even encourage me a little—but he's not… family. I've wanted him to be… but something keeps him at a distance from…." Dante looked at his reflection in the globe in his hand. "…me."

I stopped and looked up at him meeting his gaze, "Maybe he just has a different way of showing his feelings."

"Maybe. Or maybe, like everyone else in the Manor, he has a different idea of what Commissioned are supposed to be. I've never been allowed on a mission before now, Elsha, not once. Even when I was a perfect fit, Tulken said I wasn't ready. He'd never explain it, but I always saw him and Kaine talking in corners. Not one person in the Manor wanted me here. They don't trust me."

"I trust you. I want you here," I forced out. My voice was shaky from nerves, but the assertion was still there. The world might be ending, and suddenly it was important to me that I said what I had to. Dante's expression shifted as he looked down at me. His eyes flashed slightly intrigued, and I probably looked terrified. I swallowed hard as he stepped towards me and parted his mouth like he was about to ask a question.

"—Well, I'm not sure I approve of that."

We both turned to see Darkfire resting against a tree with her arms crossed. Her thick curly hair was slightly over her shoulders, and she had a new dark purple long leather coat. Her expression was genuinely curious as she watched us and tapped her long purple nails.

I froze like a deer in headlights. The arguing of my siblings stopped behind us.

There was a moment of debate all around as she looked at us. It was a painfully long few seconds of silence. The silence was split like a twig as we all whipped into action.

Dante raised his hands, forming a ball of green flame in his hands. Galahad pulled his sword and stepped forward. Killian was posed, ready to fight. Emma raised up vines from the trees beside her, and Micah aimed his crossbow.

Darkfire's mouth curled into a smile as she clapped, "Excellent response time, much better than the first time we fought. Fortunately for you...I'm not here to fight." She stepped towards us with her hands raised.

"Sorry if we don't believe you. The last time we met, it was hard to see through all the goblins you had trying to kill us!" Killian snapped.

Galahad was quiet while all of us began to argue and protest. Darkfire was looking at him like she was waiting for him to talk or to hear her out. I can't imagine why she expected him to. She'd tried to kill him too.

"What do you want?" Galahad said.

Darkfire's lovely expression twisted, "I want what I had before the Commissioned ruined my life. I want to clean the blood off my hands and go back to being a normal human being with family and friends.... I want to be as far away from these devils as the East is from the West....but God doesn't always make what we want an option. Sometimes He closes doors that we'd kill every living thing on the face of the earth to open. God wants to see what we're willing to do when he takes our options away."

Galahad's brow contracted, "You want revenge on the Commissioned...for something they did to you?"

Darkfire looked down at her hand, and her hair fell, concealing half of her face. "I wanted love once…but thanks to your Headmaster, I've settled on revenge. There's no reason all of you should be forced to pay the price for that."

I blinked incredulously, "Wait…are you—offering us a way out?"

Dante looked at Galahad, "This has gotta be a trick."

"What did Tulken ever do to you?" I said defensively. He'd never mentioned her.

Darkfire's expression grew darker as she looked at me, "Why don't you ask him that? Now stop trying to understand grown-ups' problems and listen well: I brought you two options. In one, you choose to live; in the other—not so much." Darkfire held out both her hands, and in a flash of purple light, a small baseball-sized glass orb was in each. One was white, and the other was black.

Micah raised his hand, "Uh…if one kills us and the other doesn't, is it really much of a choice?"

"Wait," Galahad said. He looked back at Darkfire, "Go on."

A small, almost proud smile crossed her face. "Both of these orbs contain an enchantment. Your little sorcerer in training probably recognizes them. The black orb contains an enchantment that can transport all of you back to where you were before you ever began this quest. You'll have no memory or knowledge of anything you've learned in the past couple of months."

"You can do that?" Dante said, more curious than concerned. "That's powerful magic…"

"—And it wasn't easy to come by," she looked at him. "Verrine knows nothing of this; neither does Asmodeus. They ordered I take care of you, and this will."

I couldn't believe that. "It sends us back in time?"

"No, it simply alters what you know now so that you'll never remember having left. This time, I'll tell Asmodeus not to send his minions. No one will come to kill you. But no Commissioned will come to tell you of your destiny either. There's a chance you could have a normal life again or the next best thing," Darkfire shrugged. "If you destroy either orb, obviously, it won't work. To enact it, all that's required is for someone gifted in magic to empower it. And all of you must be holding it."

"But won't the people at the Manor look for us?" Emma said.

"By the time you're back to the Boarding house, we'll have taken care of them," Darkfire said. "Oh, and just so we're clear— yes, I have every intention of helping Asmodeus destroy the Manor of Raziel and the order of the Commissioned. As for your headmaster…he's mine."

"There's no way we're agreeing to that!" I snapped. "You'll kill Tulken and everyone else!"

"I don't have a vendetta with everyone else–just him. And if it makes you feel better…you won't remember him," Darkfire shrugged.

"What does the other orb do?" Galahad gestured to it with his head.

Darkfire released a breath, "This…it will take you to the last piece. But that's also where Verrine, an army—and myself will be waiting. You have no vehicle, a slim armory, and an even smaller hope of surviving. If you come to meet us in battle…we will end you." There was almost a hint of regret in her voice. Her eyes were filled with several emotions that seemed to be fighting each other. She stepped toward Galahad with both orbs in hand and held them up to him. "Take my word on this…being Commissioned is a curse far more than a gift.

And knowing about it, seeing who's chosen and who's not... makes the world so much more unfair. One day you'll wish...that you didn't have to know the truth. Because it will separate you from those you love."

I glanced at my eldest brother. I didn't trust her; they could be magical explosives, curses—anything. But if she'd wanted to fight us, we were weak and ill-prepared right now. Against my better judgment, I believed her.

Galahad sheathed his sword and slowly took the orbs from her.

As Galahad took them from her, they both paused. He looked up at her curiously like he had before. Her expression softened as she searched his. "Take your lives back—stay out of this fight. Because if you make me choose between the five of you and what I want....I've come too far to stop sinning now." She stepped back and made signs with her hands creating a purple smoke screen. She brought them together, and her eyes flashed purple. "—Think about it."

There was a thick mist that appeared, causing us to cough and step back. When I lowered my arm from my eyes, she was gone. The way her magic had a color to it and the way her eyes changed color when she used ....it made me think of Dante. I couldn't help it. That was kind of like the sorcery he used. I wondered if it was a habit with all people gifted in magic to have eyes that matched their powers in color.

Galahad looked down at the orbs in his hands.

Micah slowly stepped back, "For the record, if they blow up...it wasn't me."

Chapter Twenty-Nine

When God Closes A Door....

The time after that was extremely uncomfortable. Galahad set the orbs on the ground in between all of us. Killian was leaning against a tree with his arms crossed, fighting the urge to spit out whatever was on his mind. Galahad was sitting in front of the orbs, silently looking at them while the rest of us debated. Micah paced around but came to a halt, sitting in the dirt by Emma and I. Dante was pacing. There was a hill before us and the bridge behind us. Nighttime was coming fast, and the sun had practically set. We were down to one sword, a crossbow, and Collins globe. Code Red was miles behind us back with the sheep. Even if we had a button to bring us directly to the piece...it would be walking into a death trap.

Micah titled his head, looking at the two orbs, "How do we know it's not a trick? What if they explode and turn us into Guinea pigs or something?"

Galahad knit his fingers and rested his mouth against them in thought. "If she'd have wanted to kill us, she would have tried. Dante, you know magic."

Dante stopped pacing and looked at Galahad, "I'm a little insulted that you're just noticing that...so what?"

Galahad gestured to the orb. "Are these legit?"

Dante squatted down in front of them and rested his arms on his knees, "....As far as I know, yes. The kind of magic she's talking about is a form of reality-altering curse. It's powerful, rare, and to work on a big scale like that...I wonder what she paid to get it."

Galahad looked up at him, "What do you mean?"

"Changing reality is a rule on the don'ts of magic. A big one. It's said to be a lesson for those tampering with the will of God. The castors pay with a piece of themselves. Curses and spells like that... don't come cheap. I've never understood it myself, but it's the way it is," Dante's eyes were peaked with a little too much interest for my brother's taste.

Galahad reached out and pulled the orbs towards him, making Dante shoot him a curious look. "Okay, if it's dark, it's not an option."

Dante cleared his throat, putting a hand to his mouth tensely before speaking, "Now, let's not be hasty...we could find a way to use their dark energy to our advantage."

Emma looked at Dante, "You could do that?"

Galahad interrupted Dante, who was about to speak. "If he can, he's not going to. No dark magic—it's a strict rule at the Manor, or have all of you forgotten?"

Killian looked at Galahad.

Galahad raised an eyebrow, "You're not gonna argue with me on this too?"

"I'm not saying we take the black orb and run away, but look at us. There's no way we can fight Verrine or Darkfire right now. Let alone an army. And what if she's right? How well do we really know these people? What if Tulken and the others end up being just like our parents?"

Galahad stood up, "We haven't proved our parents didn't have a reason for leaving."

"I remember they left. No trace. And none of us got to have normal lives because of them!" Killian snapped, stepping towards my eldest brother.

Emma stood up, getting between them, "Wait! Maybe these aren't our only options! If we head back to find Code Red and get our weapons, we have one piece. Verrine and Darkfire can't get Asmodeus back to full strength unless they have all three pieces, right?"

"Look, if we're not gonna try and use their power for ourselves, then there's no reason to consider it. We can't use the dark orb to change reality. If all of you go back, I probably won't remember anything either!" Dante asserted. Dante slowed his breathing. He brought his hands together before looking back up at us with a desperate expression. "This…is my once chance. If not for you guys, I might never have left the Manor. No one else has ever wanted me with them on a mission. If you leave, I'm back where I was…..please."

"Nobody's losing their memory, okay?" I looked at him urgently. On many accounts, I didn't want to take the black orb, but forgetting him wasn't an option.

Galahad looked between the two of us uncomfortably, and Killian rolled his eyes.

Galahad pressed a fist to his mouth, "Why didn't she try to take the piece from us?"

"Maybe if we took the black orb…the piece would stay here, and we'd go back?" I guessed. I didn't know. But whatever her plan was, it got us out of the way long enough for her and Verrine to open the portal and destroy the Manor.

Galahad looked at me, "That's not an option."

Killian shoved him in the shoulder, "Then what the heck is this meeting about? We either go to our deaths, or we run home and wait till the next suicide mission. We don't even know why Darkfire hates Tulken! Maybe she has a reason."

"How can you say that? He's done nothing but help us this entire time!" I snapped, making all of them look at me in surprise. "Calisto has been like a mom to all of us. Tulken and the others have tried to house and teach us, and no adults have done that since our parents! And I've had it up to here with you bashing them too!"

Killian was staring at me in shock, he was growing more agitated as I spoke, but that usually happened when others had a good point. "You stay out of…"

"No! I won't!" I objected. "There's a reason we're not supposed to use dark spells, or tamper with things only God can do! Some things haven't happened because they weren't meant to! It's not just the Manor, it's the world that's at stake. Whether you want this this or not that has to mean something!"

Killian averted his gaze.

"We have to come up with something else…." Emma began.

"We're outnumbered, and I want to help everyone at the Manor too, but…." Micah tried, but Killian talked over him.

"What aren't they telling us? How do we really know…" Killian argued.

Dante stepped forward so now all of them were in a huddle arguing. "I'm not giving up my one chance at this because all of you can't agree…."

I looked around at all their faces. Darkfire had poured gasoline on a fire that was my middle brother, and the rest of my family didn't have a way to respond. There were so many questions, fears, I knew there was no easy answer to our predicament. "Stop it all of you! Stop!" I tried, but no one heard me. I put my hands over my ears and shook my head, wanting to drown out the fighting.

Gift or curse, call it what you wanted—but there was no turning back. I looked down at the two orbs on the ground. Killian might hate me for it but I didn't care. I marched over to them, and my siblings didn't notice. Dante's eyes turned as I grabbed the black orb. He hadn't wanted to use it but he'd found it fascinating. I could see his expression change like he was watching me burn money or destroy a priceless object.

"Elsha! What are you...."

He didn't finish as I threw the orb on the floor and stepped on it.

Chapter Thirty

Okay…. Finally Killian Has an Excuse for Being So Difficult

When I crushed the orb, black energy shot out in all directions throwing us all back (okay, I'll admit I should have thought before I destroyed a super powerful curse). I flew back and collided with a thick tree. Pain shot through my back as I fell forward on my face. Everyone was shocked, but there was no point in arguing now. We all gathered around the white orb. Killian looked like he'd felt guilty for arguing, so he didn't complain as Galahad told us to put our hands in. We couldn't go back to the Manor or find Code Red. If we did, they could send more after us, and we'd be just as weak running away as we would meeting them in battle.

"Everyone, hands in at the moment Dante and Elsha enable the orb," Galahad said.

Micah was fumbling through his pocket and pulled out a pair of ear buds. Galahad was shooting him a disapproving look.

"We all have to be holding onto each other when the orb goes off, or else some of us could be left behind, understand?"

Micah nodded.

Galahad went on, "When we get there, wherever we appear—getting the piece is the priority. We get it and get away. We're not looking to take them head-on. This is just like the challenge back at the Manor…."

"You mean Emma's boyfriend will be fighting us, and Uriah is kicking our butts?" Micah said.

Galahad looked at him, "No…it means mission takes priority." Micah nodded, "Oh, that makes a lot more sense. Do we have a plan to deal with Mr. Alibaba of the 47 designer outfits if he shows up again?"

Galahad's expression intensified. "Fight it. Elsha did it, so can we. This is about more than skills we trained at the Manor; this is about ourselves. You heard Verrine: every time we give in to our anger, selfishness, pride…we make him stronger. We can't do that tonight. We must fight what we *want* to do, for what we should do."

Micah blinked, "Huh?"

Galahad released a breath, "Block Verrine out, try not to listen, cover your ears, do whatever you have to do. But we can't—let—him win. Remember what Kaine said if we meet one of the third?"

"Pray?" I recalled.

Dante shot his gaze around us in the huddle like he was worried Galahad was going to make us pray. If we ever did pray as a family, it was always Galahad who led. None of us had the will or ambition to take the reins. No one looked more disconcerted than Dante who shifted continuously as he spoke. It was amazing it took an oncoming apocalypse for our family to gather and bow our heads. When we finished, Galahad took one last look at all of us, "Hands in."

Dante and I held the orb first so we could empower it with magical energy. We both focused like he instructed, and I closed my eyes. I felt something moving around me like wind, it reminded me of when Dante had used the placement powder only much stronger. My mind was flashing with fears. What if Darkfire had tricked us? What if she'd told us the orb to take us to the piece was the white one but it wasn't? Would I lose my memory right now? She couldn't have known which we would choose when we didn't know ourselves. I held on tight as the world shook and tore around me, it was like being in a small whirlpool.

Suddenly, the motion stopped.

The orb left my grasp, and I grabbed someone else's hand. As all our bodies hit the ground, I opened my eyes. We weren't in the same place anymore. We must have been miles ahead of the bridge. We were farther up the trail and closer to the river. I heard the water gushing beside us, the grass beneath my hands was moist. My vision was blurry at first, but as it cleared I saw my siblings rolling around in the grass coming to. I glanced down to see my fingers were intertwined with Dante's. The cold silver of his rings snapped me into reality. I looked up at him with large eyes and despite how dark it was, I saw his pale face flush.

I pulled my hand back, "S-sorry."

Dante cleared his throat before giving a small smile, "No....don't apologize."

There were thorns and small shrubbery everywhere, many rocks, and some moist ground where I was. I could feel the moisture seeping through my jeans. Galahad was next to me with his hand on his head, blinking. Killian was crouched like a cat and shook his head, trying to see straight. Emma was beside him, sitting down with her hair tousled.

Killian turned to her, "Emma, are you okay?"

She nodded, putting her hand on his shoulder to steady herself. "Yeah...did that work?"

"It didn't kill us," Galahad stood up and cracked his neck, looking around. A look of horror crossed his face, "...Where's Micah?"

My mouth fell open. He wasn't with us. We'd all been transported to the same place so he should have been there. Galahad put his face in his hand and mumbled a word he probably wouldn't want me to repeat. "He was probably playing with those things again....I told him..." Galahad shook his head and mumbled but Emma raised an eyebrow at him.

"Big brother…how is using the language Dad did when he was *really* angry gonna help anything now?" Emma pulled twigs out of her hair.

"I'm going back for him!" Killian was about to turn around. He froze. All of us did. The familiar cackle of witches filled the air as wind whipped around us. They were on their brooms, flying in circles above. Micah's crossbow wasn't here. He must have been holding onto it when he was left behind. In front of us, before a rocky hill, stood Verrine in a jade-colored coat with golden thread and sapphires as buttons. Blackfire stood behind him unable to hide her shock. She hadn't expected us to come.

I swallowed, "Uh…I think Micah is safer than us right now."

Verrine held up a circular stone piece that had flames engraved on it. "Looking for this? We got here some time before you. I didn't expect to see you at all but then…I guess letting walk right into your demise is as good a way to kill you as any. And not even all the avengers are present…" he shook his head condescendingly. "That's a pity. An orphan should at least have the solace of dying with his family."

"Everyone take defensive position," Galahad said. But he was the only one with a sword. We all exchanged hopeless looks.

"Maybe it wasn't clear enough by your inferior numbers, weapons, and non-existent plan—but we've won. All we need is to take that last piece from you," Verrine gestured to the bag Dante had over his shoulder.

Killian looked around at all of us, "If we don't make it out of this…I…I just want you guys to know, I'm sorry for everything."

All of us looked at Killian in unison, "—*What?*" Him apologizing was more shocking than anything we'd encountered on this whole mission.

"For all of it, the fighting, and the arguing....I...I don't want those to be the last words I have with you guys. I can be brash, and stupid, I know......"

Galahad's shocked expression was priceless, "Now might not be the best time, Killian..."

Emma's expression softened, "Oh, Killian, you don't have to...."

Verrine rolled his eyes, "This is sickening—kill them now. Dante, give me the piece."

The witches didn't need to be told twice. They flew around us and opened their hands, forming balls of green ooze that looked a lot like the ghoul's blood we had shot at us in the challenge. They cackled, throwing it from their hands. Killian ducked and rolled, letting the acid like substance hit a tree behind him. The green liquid melted right through the wood. Galahad blocked the acid with his sword and ducked onto one knee. Emma reached out her hand and plants grew up wrapping around Dante's boots to halt him. I was one step ahead of Verrine. I had snatched the bag off Dante's shoulder before Verrine finished asking for it. I knew what he would do, and as far as we knew he'd failed to control me once.

Verrine's scowl deepened. "Darkfire, open a doorway so our friend is able to assist us."

Darkfire walked a few steps up the hill and began to do some sorcery. Her expression was straining with the magic she used. As she moved her hands, purple energy began to whirl around like a portal. Through the portal walked the Dark blood warrior. He was taller than I remembered, seven feet, completely covered in red armor like he may as well have been a robot or a hollow shell. His eyes were hollow and black. He stood at attention by Verrine who jumped at his abruptness.

"I AM HERE TO SERVE MY LORD ASMODEUS!"

Verrine looked annoyed. "Yes, we know...it's about time you prove your worth,"

"WHAT DOES ASMODEUS WISH?!" the Dark blood warrior's voice was passionate but hoarse.

"Take the final piece of the demon's stone from the Avengers of Light. Without it, we cannot open the door that will release your brothers Tomek," Darkfire said.

"FOR ASMODEUS!" Tomek slashed his long blood colored broad sword in the air left and right. He cut down two witches by accident and they fell before him, sending green blood across the ground.

Verrine raised an eyebrow, "Those are on *our* side, you idiot...."

Dante was coming after me.

I caught my breath as a green fire ball flew from his hand right at my head.

I dropped and felt the heat singe my hair. I looked up at him off the ground through my tangled hair. "We gotta do this again...." I mumbled.

His eyes flashed green as he made other hand signs and formed a whip of green energy.

"I guess so!" I breathed before rolling out of the way of the first lash. My hands scraped the hard ground as I scuffled out of the way. I heard the lash of energy before it hit. I rolled over and the green whip charred the dirt next to me. I turned my face away.

I opened my eyes, scrambling back and raised my hands. I had to be stronger than this...wait—yes! Maybe...

Nothing was happening so far. I yelped, scrambling back in terror as Dante kept coming. The green whip destroyed the ground and burned bushes next to me as I tried to get away. It wasn't him doing this; I had to remember that.

Tulken had said light magic was stronger than traditional sorcery. That meant I was stronger than Dante. I had to believe that. I remembered what happened in the truck with the sheep, our two magics collided, and then there were the fireworks…. Collins said one kind of magic had to overcome the other. I didn't know if Dante being controlled made his magic dark or if maybe I couldn't be controlled before because I had light.

I couldn't be afraid of Dante's magic; mine was stronger.

I bit my lip as sweat trickled down my forehead. "Here goes nothing…."

I reached out and grabbed the whip of green energy and concentrated, I thought about what Dante had said. I saw my hands begin to glow white and encompass the whip. The light travelled up the whip he'd created and flashed like a firework throwing him back.

Dante connected with a tree and grunted before rubbing his head, "What the…."

"Verrine," I said, stepping towards him.

He groaned, "I've gotta stop letting that happen. What's the plan?" Witches were flying around us and throwing down acid bombs. Dante and I ducked two as we stood there. Dante formed a ball of green fire in his hand and threw it at one of the witches on her broom. She spun in a circle before flying right into a tree. I raised my hands, stopping a witch who flew at us in midair. I pushed my open hands back in her direction, sending her flying into another hag with a shriek. Tomek was charging at us. I saw Verrine talking to him several yards away. It was a good thing there was so much chaos and Verrine was so far away. If we'd been able to hear him clearly, we might have just handed the artifact over.

Galahad blocked another ball of acid with his sword and got beside us. Emma and Killian backed up near us as well as Tomek ran in our direction.

"We protect the piece. Does anyone remember what Kaine taught us in the Demonology mid-term? Galahad looked at us.

"No!" we all said in unison.

Tomek charged and slashed down at Galahad.

Galahad raised his sword, and the two weapons collided.

Tomek's sword was about as long as me, I was amazed Galahad could stop it but he did. "Don't—touch—my sister," Galahad pushed back against the huge creature and his sword seemed to radiate light. In terms of strength, my brother was outmatched. But his weapon was magically endowed, I could see it as Tomek's armor began to sizzle like it was being charred. The energy from Galahad's sword was hurting him. I wasn't going to be helpless anymore either. I raised my hands as light shone from my palms. The light formed into a flame in my hands but I felt my strength straining to keep it there. I pushed my open hands forward as I'd seen Dante do with his fireballs. The golden flame shot at Tomek.

Tomek was thrown from Galahad and his chest plate burned. Tomek came at us again, swinging his sword. It was so long it could have cut us all down in one swipe.

Dante's eyes flashed green as he made hand signs; the long sword in Tomek's hands stopped mid-swing. Dante pulled an open hand towards himself as his expression grew weary. The sword was torn from Tomek's hands and stabbed into the earth behind Dante.

We all screamed, ducking as the blade went over our heads.

378

Tomek brought up and armored leg and front kicked Dante right in the chest.

"Dante!"

Dante went flying back into a tree several yards away before he fell face first in the ground. He trembled as he forced himself onto all fours, in the moonlight I saw blood drip from the corner of his mouth. Killian caught Tomek's next blow and was struggling to keep him back. Tomek shook him free and was swinging many blows, but Killian was too fast. Emma tried to help but was being bombarded by witches.

I stepped back and focused on the witches' brooms. As I did, light flashed from my hands and two of them snapped in mid-air. The witches came tumbling out of the sky, still alive. Emma stretched her hands out and plants overtook them, tying them to the ground.

Dante got to his feet and was coming back towards the fight when he called to me. "Elsha, look out!"

"Wh-"

"This is taking far too long," someone said behind me. I turned around just in time to see the back of Verrine's jeweled hand smacking me across the face. I let out a small yelp from the pain as I fell to the ground. "Give—me—that!" Verrine ripped the artifact from my hands while the world was still spinning.

"Give it back!" I looked up at him through my hair. The portal was still open in the distance and now Darkfire had turned and she was watching us.

He turned to face me, "And what are you going to do if I *don't*?"

I focused my thoughts and feelings, it was hard in the moment but I did it. I remembered what Dante said about feeling whatever motivates you the most strongly; I looked at Verrine and raised my

379

hand. He flew against a tree ten yards away and grunted, falling down. He looked up at me in complete surprise. I doubted he was used to being touched, let alone hurt. "How dare you…"

"Want to stop me? Then get up," I said, clenching my fists.

Verrine stood, "Darkfire, please show this miserable little girl who the real sorceress is."

Darkfire's eyes flashed and she shook her head; she formed a purple sword of flame in her hand and slashed at me. I ducked and rolled out of the way. Darkfire stepped back and opened both hands. A second flaming sword formed in her free hand and she made a motion, lunging forward. They both shot towards me. I dropped flat on my stomach and the two blades flew into the trees behind me, setting them ablaze. The purple lights and flames were blinding. I raised my arm to shield my eyes. The ground was cold and wet, despite the flames, the wind blowing was freezing.

I came up on one knee and concentrated on pulling the elements towards myself, it happened in a flash unlike when I'd been trying to freeze the pen in Code Red. A large razor sharp blast of icicles flew from my hands. It shot Darkfire and she raised her hands, forming a blockade of purple flames. The ice still frosted the sides of her arms, forcing her to fall back with a shudder.

I glanced back over my shoulder to see Killian and Dante trying to hold Tomek back. Killian was avoiding him and Dante was throwing everything he could come up with at him. Dante formed the green whip of energy and was lashing at him. I looked ahead of me again, Verrine had appeared. He grabbed me by the throat.

I choked under the pressure.

"Leave her alone!" Galahad came at Verrine with his sword and was thrusting to stab him in the side. His sword was vibrant with energy. Verrine's eyes flashed red as they shot to the blade. If his weapon connected, there was a chance we could kill him. Galahad's

380

weapon was empowered to kill dark creatures and I could see Verrine feared it.

"—*Stop*," Verrine commanded, turning to look my eldest brother in the eye.

Galahad's blow was halted, the tip of the sword was an inch away from the demon. He looked like he'd pulled something painful in his muscles. His expression was straining as he clutched the hilt of the sword. Verrine didn't like that Galahad was fighting the control; his expression intensified. "One of these days' you'll have to stop fighting me and accept the inevitable, Dyer—now, do you want to keep struggling or shall I crush your sister's throat now?"

I was fighting to breathe. I grasped at Verrine's steely hands, trying to pry them away, but it was no use.

"You let her go!" Killian started towards me when he grabbed his chest in pain.

"Killian!" Emma yelled.

The thick clouds overhead were parting, and the moon was coming into light so I could see more clearly. The world was still shaking because I was losing air. I saw Darkfire's fists clenched behind Verrine, her expression was twisting in some way.

"Verrine!" Darkfire cried at last. "The portal won't stay open forever! Not without the artifact!"

Verrine let go of me. I fell on all fours panting, "What…what's happening to Killian…."

"The Commissioned, just like the crusades—all your missions are so ill prepared," Verrine looked at the piece in his hand as he slowly walked back over to the portal with Darkfire. "Every piece of the Demon's stone plays a role in Asmodeus' plan. The first, opens the gate to hell. The second, allows Asmodeus to resume control of one body and no longer be tethered between this world and the next. The third….it restores him to his original power. When that happens…only a legion of angels could kill him. *Not*—a group of weak children."

"We're never going to let that happen!" Emma wrapped a vine around a witch's neck and threw her aside across the rocks.

"I don't see what choice you have. The demons' stone requires that a demon activate it, one of the fallen. I'll have to do the honors, so unfortunately, that means I won't be the one killing you, Avengers of Light," Verrine said, beginning to put the pieces together.

No. No. He can't…if he puts the demons' stone together, we're all doomed.

I didn't see any way this could possibly get worse.

Killian was still writhing on the ground, and he wasn't bleeding that I could see. I didn't understand it. I crawled over to him and shook his shoulder, "Killian! Killian, look at me!"

The witches and Tomek all began to move back. I didn't understand why since they were winning. Verrine was watching Killian like he'd expected this would happen. As the moonlight illuminated Killian on the floor, his eyes changed. They were deep yellow in a flash. He began to snarl and growl as his fingers stretched and curled into clawed paws. I let go of him, moving back. "What…how…Killian…."

"Has had something dark inside of him this entire time, foolish child," Verrine locked the artifact pieces into place before Darkfire's portal. As he did, thick black smoke came from the piece and howls of what sounded like demons and monsters in torment filled the air. The wind beat around us more fiercely as the witches began to howl and cackle. Killian was still changing on the floor in front of me, despite how hard I screamed for him to control it. "Your brother may have been gifted but he was also cursed.....I don't know why it took so long to come out. But I must say

I'm glad he'll give us a hand in killing all of you."

Chapter Thirty-One

The Beast, The Sorceress, The warrior, The Empress, and The Craftsmen

When Killian fully transformed I saw the *thing inside him* Verrine was talking about: my middle brother was a werewolf. We'd heard about them at the Manor. It was something the kids in upper classes studied so I'd heard Uriah talking about them for an assignment. Werewolves weren't demons, and they weren't exclusively monsters because they regained their human minds and characteristics most of the month. That was all I remembered when Uriah briefly spoke of it. Now I wished I'd taken notes. Killian snapped his jaws at me. I fell back crawling away. "Killian! What are you doing…s-stop!"

Verrine walked over to the fast-closing portal Darkfire had opened and held up the artifact. Red and black lightning cracked around it. Verrine's face shifted back and forth from demon to human. Red energy came off the artifact and a bright red flame shot from it into Darkfire's portal. The flames tore through the purple energy consuming it and the portal grew slowly. The light from the portal showed how completely destroyed the field we'd been fighting in now was: charred grass, tattered plants and destroyed trees from Tomek's sword were strewn everywhere. I didn't have but a second to take it in. The howls and demon screams grew louder, and the witches flew near it cackling with laughter. Darkfire stepped back and her mouth parted in shock. She and Verrine didn't seem concerned with us anymore.

The voices of my siblings faded. This was it. Asmodeus had won. We'd come so far and now… My mind went to all the things I'd never see us do. I'd never turn fourteen, we'd never see our parents again. We'd never be as close a family as we should have been all these years. I'd never know if me and Dante would ever have the same last name. All the time I had wasted sulking dawned on me. All the days wasted fighting came back to me. In that moment I would have given anything for another shot at the crazy drama ridden ride that was being the youngest Dyer.

Verrine chuckled as his face shifted from human to monster in the red light of the portal. "It was a shame I didn't sense it sooner....but my sorceress sensed great conflict of dark and light in your middle brother. His...*colorful* personality probably hasn't made it easier to keep the animal back. But someone must have put a powerful enchantment on Killian to suppress the transformation every full moon."

"None of us made any enchantment!" I backed away slowly as Killian snarled. He was about as tall as my chest. His nose was long, and he was a thick shaggy black wolf with blue eyes. It had all happened so fast, but in a strange way—I could see Killian's face in the wolfs.

"No, it must have been a powerful enchantment by a strong sorcerer," Darkfire said like she was trying to figure it out herself. Somehow, it made a lot of sense to me. A beast was striving to get out all these years....no wonder he'd always had outbursts. How and when Verrine knew that was a mystery to me.

"Dante...you've got to know something about this...is Killian still in there?" I pleaded. All of us were now opposite to Killian and slowly backing away.

Dante opened his mouth, confused. Killian lunged at him. Dante brought down the whip of green energy before the wolf and it snarled moving back. "According to my studies....yes, but the wolf is in control. That's why it came out, whatever he was cursed with...the animal was fed by the persons selfish feral emotions. Your brother has had a lot of those so it must have been some seal..."

Galahad was keeping Killian back with his sword and Emma was raising bushes and greenery for protection as the river rustled behind us. "One of us has to talk him down!" She said.

Galahad huffed, keeping his blade poised to hold the wolf back, "Right—listening to me made human Killian angry. I don't think the beast is gonna listen!"

"We can't hurt him!" Emma shouted over the sound of the portal growing behind us and the screeching witches. Killian leapt at Galahad, snapping down. Galahad rolled out of the way and came up on one knee pulling his sword back to strike. The wolf nearly ran into a tree.

"You're afraid we're gonna hurt him? We've gotta stop Verrine from letting the army out or we're all gonna die! Dante, your magic is the best chance at getting the piece!"

Killian turned around and snapped at Dante, who rolled out of the way just in time to spare his arm, but I still heard him cry out in pain. Killian slashed in Emma's direction with his paw but she side stepped it, catching her breath. Killian hadn't attacked for real yet, I could tell—when he did, something told me it wouldn't be a very fair fight. Killian was about to slash at Emma again when Dante focused his eyes on a large stone.

Dante's hand was shaking as he forced the stone to come free and fly, hitting Killian in the side. The wolf was knocked back but not finished.

"We can't do this without all five of us! You heard what Tulken said, the Avengers of Light were destined to stop Asmodeus! If Killian is fighting us, we can't do this!" I said as they tried to keep him back.

"There's less than five now! And even if we get Killian to back down we're outnumbered!" Galahad said.

Verrine glanced back over his shoulder at us, "Why don't you just accept your fate? The Avenger's of light are dwindling hopelessly. Half of you are already injured, and your one brother couldn't even be counted on to stay with the team. Maybe he ran home and left you to die."

"Micah wouldn't do that!" I said.

"Then where is he?" Verrine spread his hands. The echo of voices like Tomek's were coming from inside the flaming portal. I heard the howls and screams of souls in agony, shouting and clamoring. The wolf wasn't tired, and we were all at the end of our rope, and had few to no weapons left.

Emma swallowed, 'Micah is...he's...."

"*He* is preparing you for a world of awesome!"

We all turned to look. There was a familiar rev of an engine. It was Code Red. No one was in the car but Micah was on it and so was something else but he had it covered by a sheet. Micah pulled the sheet off and everyone's jaws dropped—including Verrine and Darkfire. There was a wooden structure holding up all our crossbows from the equipment bag, only he'd made them rapid fire.

I broke into a smile. I don't think I'd ever been happier to see him. "Micah!"

I saw the help spirit who Killian had ticked off sitting in the drivers' seat with a determined look. "I knew I'd end up picking up after you children sooner or later," she said.

"Where did the wolf come from!" Micah said.

"That's Killian!" Dante lashed at him trying to keep the beast back.

Micah's eyes grew large, "Oh...that explains *a lot*."

"—Right?" Emma said like it was obvious.

Darkfire's expression was almost impressed. "Oh my, Go…"

Verrine's eyes flashed red as he shot her a look, "*Don't*—say it." He looked at Micah over his shoulder, "You can't use that. All I have to do is tell you not to…"

Micah pulled out ear pods and put them in turning on music. That was so Micah. If we couldn't hear Verrine than we didn't have to do what he said.

Verrine looked offended and glared, "Why you miserable….."

Micah grinned as he took a match and lit the crossbows. The witches froze in fear in mid-air on their brooms. "Let's light these ladies up!"

Verrine snarled, "I *hate* children."

#

Odds changed drastically with Micah on our side. The witches flew right at him, but he was shooting them out of the air like flies yelling, "DIE, MY PRETTIES! DIE!" The help spirit drove Code Red so he got the right aim; she had the radio blaring so amongst the chaos hearing Verrine wasn't an issue. He hadn't really been able to order us around as soon as he started the process of opening the portal because, amidst the screeching and shouting, we couldn't hear him. But now with Micah's ear pods, the music, and the distance, there was nothing he could do. Dante used magic to open the car doors and brought weapons into our hands. A sword flew into mine and the dagger to Emma. Galahad went at Tomek while Micah gave him cover. Killian came after Emma and I, but that was what I wanted. We had to get him back with us or we'd never make it. I convinced Emma to follow me; we ran alongside the bustling river away from the main fight. I felt bad about leaving them, but Dante and Galahad seemed to be the ones Killian was snapping at the most. That meant Emma and I were the best shot at getting through to him.

Emma and I ran, splashing through the shallow river, avoiding rocks, till we came to a jagged spot and tripped. We both got to our feet as Killian came running through the water, growling. We halted in the shallow area though my legs were freezing. Emma and I were determined, like always, to get through to my middle brother. This was no different than all the other times Killian had let his anger get the better of him, and I wanted to stop him before he did something he couldn't take back. The wolf had my brothers' eyes. He was still in there. I called to Killian, "You may be the beast on the team, fine— but that doesn't make you a monster! You're fierce, Killian. You always have been. Some demon says you're cursed, and you're gonna let that define you?"

Emma caught on to what I was doing and stepped in, "She's right. You're a wolf because you've always been protective. Maybe the curse is a gift in disguise! You feel more strongly than all of us. You're passionate—hot-headed and stupid sometimes— but you're a fighter, all that can be used for good!"

"But don't let this thing inside you turn you against your family…no one is ever going to love you more than we do. But don't let some dark curse ruin it! Control it! Make it your own! Because if you hurt me like this…we'll still love you, I'll forgive you, but you won't forgive yourself…" I pleaded.

The wolf's growling was low, like he was about to strike.

"We're not the enemy…your family…our family…isn't the enemy," Emma said calmingly.

Killian's growling grew lower. It slowed. He wasn't snarling anymore. He slowly stepped toward us and I saw in his brow the same regret I saw in my brother's face when he hurt my feelings or insulted us. Killian slowed down and stood before us. For a moment, I was afraid he would pounce. I stepped towards him and held out my hand. Killian lowered his head so that I could pet him. I closed my eyes and let out a breath. Emma walked up and pet him as well, "It's okay brother, we've got you."

Killian cast his gaze up to us.

Emma tousled his hair lovingly, "Come on...let's get the real enemy."

I felt sweat trickle down my head as I rubbed Killian's head. *Thank God that worked!*

We returned to the fight and Killian acted on instinct. A witch flew right at us. Killian snapped the witches broom in half with his teeth and sent her flying. He took the second in his jaws, after avoiding her poison blasts. Killian shook his head with the witch in his mouth till she stopped moving. Killian spit her out and the witch rolled in front of Darkfire.

Galahad stared open-mouthed.

"That's impossible!" Darkfire said. She looked weak from using magic to open the portal. Even someone like her had limits. She was weakly deflecting Dante's magic attacks. He was creating green fire and throwing it at her while she deflected with purple energy.

"So is *everything* our family's done recently—get with the program!" Emma said.

Micah raised a fist and cheered, "Killian's back!" I went at the witches with my sword, ducking their flying attacks and swinging. Galahad was fighting Tomek. Demons were emerging from the portal, horrible looking creatures I didn't recognize. The artifact was now floating in the air before the portal and burning with purple energy. Now that it was together, I could clearly see the curved claw like shapes were stone colored hands holding the center piece: a purple stone. Verrine looked drained but he didn't have to be holding it anymore. Things were already in motion.

"It doesn't matter what you do…how many of us you kill….as long as this door is open, every dark demonic creature my father longed to keep in hell will be brought forth…" Verrine straightened with a smile.

I was rushing through the crowd, cutting down small goblin like creatures as they came through. Emma was right beside me while Killian provided cover. Galahad blocked a downward strike from Tomek and stepped aside before stabbing the Dark Blood warrior in a chink in his leg armor. As the blade went in, light shone from Galahad's weapon, like my magic—Galahad empowered what he used with light magic. Every time his weapon connected with a demon they were cut open or destroyed. Tomek let out a cry and Verrine turned his head to him. Verrine pulled a long thing jeweled dagger from inside his coat and frowned before he disappeared.

I knew that trick. He'd pulled it with me. I ran right to Galahad while he was fighting Tomek. Emma followed me close behind. The wind from the portal was beating in our faces and the sound made it difficult to call to him. Verrine appeared behind my brother and grinned, flipping the dagger in his hand. I stretched out my hand to stop him, to make the dagger fly from his fingers, but it was too late. Verrine lunged with the weapon.

Emma screamed and roots emerged from the ground, shooting up around Verrine, knocking him back from our oldest brother.

Thorns were on all of them and they wrapped around his legs, freezing him where he stood. "Leave our brother alone!" Emma screamed as she raised her hands, forming a thicker layer of greenery around Verrine.

He disappeared from where she had him and reappeared near us, catching his breath. "This is futile…unless you can close that portal, they won't stop coming…." As he spoke more and more creatures were emerging from the portal. Emma, Galahad and I were fighting them off as best as we could. "But your light magic…could present a real problem." Verrine stepped towards me and took my arm. "Oh," he snapped his fingers, "and I almost forgot."

"What are you…" I began. Verrine's grip was tight; I tried to pull away. I knew what he was going to do.

"You're going to hell," Verrine leaned down to meet my gaze as his fingers shifted to being long and goblin-like. As he pulled me towards him, I felt the portal sucking me in. The whirlwind was pulling at me with such force my feet were lifting off the floor. Every other demon was coming out, but the power was pulling me in.

"No!" Emma lunged forward, stabbing Verrine in the gut with her dagger. His eyes flashed red, and his expression contorted as he let go of me. He swatted Emma aside into the air, and she was pulled by the whirlwind.

"Emma!" I raised my hand to shield my eyes from the bright light. No. Not Emma.

But she was gone.

Verrine shrugged. "She'll do."

I grabbed Verrine by his coat and pulled him closer to me, "Where is she? Where did it take her?!"

"She is—where my kind is mostly trapped. I'm currently on leave as you might call it, but in there….nothing good survives—trust me. Now, if you'll excuse me…there's a vessel where Asmodeus' spirit currently resides, and I'll have to inform him he'll be joined with his real body shortly. Have fun dealing with all my brethren," Verrine disappeared in black smoke, taking Darkfire with him. I felt tears well up in my eyes, the black hole was growing and I could hear marching on the other side.

Galahad cut down a goblin and came forward, "I'm going after her."

"No...." I used light magic to push Galahad and Dante back.

"Elsha, what are you doing!" Dante objected.

"You heard Verrine, my light magic is a threat to demons, and that means I'm he safest one down there. That's my best friend and I'm getting her. When I get back, we close that portal!"

"Asmodeus is down there!" Galahad said. "He could already be free!"

"Then I have to get out and close the door before he can come through," I took one last look at all of them. I ran in the direction of the portal and jumped as my siblings voices faded into the background. The last words I heard before I went in were Galahad saying "we keep that portal open until they come out!" My eyes stung as I was pulled into the dark portal—when I got to the other side the only thing that registered was heat, fire, red, and pain.

Chapter Thirty-Two

I Keep My Eyes on Heaven in Hell

I came flying through the portal and landed on what felt like steaming hot rocks. I rolled a few feet before stopping myself at the edge of what looked like a deep cavern. I forced my eyes open and saw lava at the bottom of the cavern, out of it was rising more soldiers like Tomek. They all wore red armor which looked steaming hot like the rocks I was on. As soon as their heads were out they began to chant loudly like Tomek, "WE RISE FOR THE EVIL OF ASMODEUS!" I rolled my eyes.

"Great—more of them," I groaned, standing up. Everything was painfully hot, and the air itself even seemed poisonous. The place was so large it was like an endless canyon. I saw different creatures at every corner, some were wailing in pain and others were half alive. A lake of acid was to my right and there were creatures in it. I wasn't sure whether they were ghouls or goblins but they were burning alive, releasing screams of agony. Verrine wasn't wrong: it was a place of torment where no good person belonged.

That was why I had to get my sister out.

"Emma!" my voice echoed off the hollow walls. Something else came flying through the portal and landed near me skidding off the edge of the red rocks—Dante. I ran to his side and took his hand before he lost his grip on the edge. "Hold on!" I pulled him up. Dante's face twisted in pain—I realized I was holding his bad arm and it must have hurt like crazy.

Dante managed to get solid footing after I pulled him up," The girl who wouldn't do gym jumps through a magic portal into hell— think you can explain that?"

"What are you doing here?"

"I'm a Knight of Valor in training and I was assigned to watch you and your family. Did you think I'd let you do something insane like this without me?" he said. "Besides…your brothers never would have forgiven me if I didn't."

My face was sweating as I looked at him, "You're not stopping me."

"Wasn't planning on it. Did you find Emma?"

"No, but I found the Darkblood Army."

"We need to get your sister out before that army makes it to the portal. It's chaos out there. If the monsters keep coming out your family won't be able to contain it. We're a good distance from civilians out here on the hiking trail but not for long."

"My brothers can handle what's out there," I said.

"Yes, but can you handle what's in here?" a voice like acid echoed. Dante and I turned to see a large demon with red skin and cloven hooves; he had blood colored hair on top of his head and out of it came tall sharp horns. He wore a tattered robe and had long clawed hands. His face wasn't human, there were ridges on his head and stared straight art us. Everything I felt around Verrine, the ghosts, Darkfire, and everything else we had faced till now was multiplied as I looked at him. His eyes were on us, but not really with us, as if his mind was in many places at once. He was hideous, and he couldn't hide it like Verrine.

"Who are you?" I said.

"I am the one you strive to defeat, Elsha Dyer. I am darkness, the sin that has been in men's hearts since the dawn of man. Hate, envy, greed, anger, I once loved to walk among you and watch it all fall into place."

"You're…you're Asmodeus," I tried to steady my voice.

As I stood before him I saw the shadows of chains all over him, long, large links of metal that were miles behind him and went down the cavern into the lava. They faded from sight and came back as I looked at him—he was imprisoned here—just like Tulken had said. Verrine somehow got a "get out of jail free" card, but Asmodeus didn't. Asmodeus' power inhabited a mortal host on earth, his spirit, but he couldn't walk the earth again, he was stripped of power like our books had taught us. Still…if the Dark blood army took the world, who knew what Asmodeus could do.

"Yes, and you're one of the Avengers of light. Your master and I are quite acquainted…or at least we were," he growled lowly.

"My master?" I said.

"It's well known among the demon world who calls the Commissioned, but you won't have the power to defeat me. The Dark blood army will take the world, and you will remain here—forever," he hissed.

A question plagued my mind. I knew we didn't have much time. He didn't look like he was going anywhere, without returning to his full power he couldn't break free of those chains. How had Verrine planned on freeing him? How did Asmodeus plan on getting out? "How long…have you known my family were the Avengers of Light?"

Asmodeus chuckled. Even when he cracked a smile it was like agony filled his eyes. Every limb he moved or breath he took seemed to be painful. *"I've known for three years….I swore to destroy you then…and by the looks of it I've done my part."*

"You haven't destroyed us! We're still here, and we're still together!" I said.

"Oh child….the greatest enemies are within ourselves. I paid a great price three years ago to destroy your family, because I knew you

were the only ones capable of defeating me. All the Commissioned were convinced they had chained me permanently, but I'd only sacrificed my freedom temporarily in exchange for a permanent victory."

"What…what do you mean you sacrificed it? You let yourself be put in here?" I said.

"I had a name….one name engraved in my mind as the only family capable of stopping me: the Dyers. In order to ensure they'd never be able to….I cast a curse more powerful than any other. The effects of it have been slowly poisoning your life for the past three years and its only beginning. All the turmoil, the pain, the chaos, the loss…. if you think your family has had hardship, has known pain….you know nothing of what's to come," he chuckled tensely.

"You cursed the Dyer family…what kind of curse?" Dante demanded.

"What did you do to my family! My parents!" I screamed.

"It's only begun. Your little fight against my powers is pointless, the Dyers will be destroyed, and I will return—it has been written," he snarled. "The forces of darkness in this world overshadow the light like a thunderstorm does to a small candle, if you side with the righteous, you're choosing to lose. You'll never have the power to defeat me when I am freed," Asmodeus said. "My spirit is in one among you as we speak, and he will kill you all."

"You can't be freed, you're stuck here," I said.

"No, not forever. You see, our maker has a strange way of punishing me. The only key to my freedom, is also the sole method to my demise," Asmodeus said. I wanted to know what he meant but the marching behind us grew louder. The Dark blood army was marching out of the cavern and towards the portal.

Dante stepped forward, "What are you talking about?"

"The only one who can remove my bonds, and allow me to once again walk the earth in my true form, is one of the Commissioned. One pure of heart....and an Avenger of light."

My eyes went to the blonde hair on the floor beside Asmodeus. Emma was sprawled out next to his chain unconscious. I couldn't believe his words. Why would one of us be the ones to free a demon?

Emma stirred on the ground, "What....Elsha?"

"It's okay Emma, we're gonna get you out," I said.

"No, you're going to free me—if not now, then when the armies of this dark realm take the world!"

"That will never happen—we're going to fight you, and all the forces you have in our world, no matter what it takes," I went to Emma's side and helped her up. On the walls, goblins, ghouls, and other monsters crawled down like spiders in the hundreds, snarling and shrieking horribly. Dante formed a green whip of energy with his good arm and tried to keep them back as Emma stood with me.

"Fight me? With what? All the forces of darkness have waited centuries for something to wander in here they can kill, you'll never leave this realm alive, let alone save your world. And what do you have, Elsha Dyer?" he said.

I swallowed hard as fear crept into my mind, we were surrounded. The army was leaving the portal and that meant my brothers were fighting for dear life outside. Who's to say we hadn't already lost?

Asmodeus growled low in his throat, *"This whole world is dark. You have no power against it, no direction, no parents, no purpose, no gifts that can defeat me. What do you have to face this army?"*

"I…I have…" I stumbled over my words. The me back at the Boarding House might have broken down and cried. I would have fallen on my face and said he was right and waited for Galahad to save me. Or Emma to stand up for me. All my life I'd spent thinking about the things I didn't have, parents, friends, toys, a life, good grades, a normal school, everything I didn't have was all I thought about. Now, standing on the brink of death—I knew what I did have.

"—No. That's what I thought…but it's wrong. I have so much….I have….family. I *love* my big brother, Galahad, I love Emma, and Killian, and Micah…." my voice grew stronger. I felt energy in my hands as they began to glow white like Galahad's sword. "You haven't destroyed us by giving us a life of pain and fighting…it's made us stronger."

"FREE ME!" Asmodeus bellowed as the dark realm shook from his anger. But the chains were still on. *"IF NOT NOW, SOMEDAY, YOU WILL REMOVE THESE BONDS AND I WILL ANNIHILATE EVERY LIFE YOU HOLD DEAR! I WILL DESTROY YOU!"*

Dante pointed to my hands, and I looked at them. My hands were glowing with light.

"YOUR WORLD WILL BELONG TO ME AND ALL THE FORCES OF HELL!" Asmodeus said as his face burned with anger and his chains shook.

"Not while the Dyers are in it," I said. Light shot from my hands that blinded the monsters crawling down the walls. Light shot from my hands that blinded the goblins and monsters crawling down the walls. Even Dante shielded himself with his arm and winced from the light. Emma just stepped back. She raised her hands but nothing happened. I forgot–her powers wouldn't work with plants or vegetation that wasn't alive. Nothing in this cursed place was living. She put her hand to her head and strained, "What do we do?"

I looked down at my hands. Escape ideas and problems with each one was racing through my mind. What were the sorceress' main abilities? Elements? None were in here except fire and it was of the dark demonic kind. I couldn't manipulate it. The only thing I'd successfully used here was my light magic….

Levitation. I'd never lifted something as large as people and I didn't know if Dante had either, but if we didn't try–we'd be overwhelmed.

Two long flaming green whips emerged from Dante's hands; he was lashing at the creatures crawling up the corners of the cavern, keeping them back. Emma was scrambling to get away from them, but there were millions.

I turned to Dante, "We have to use telekinesis to get ourselves out of here!"

Dante glanced at me surprised, "I'm not sure I can get all of us…"

"I can!" I exclaimed. I wasn't sure, but we had no choice. I wasn't staying in hell. The howls and screams around me motivated me to focus harder on the only door leading out of that torture chamber: the portal above us. I held out my hand to Dante and he took it, we both concentrated. Emma stood close by. I understood the basic principles of levitation but I'd never tried to use it on people before. I felt energy going out from me, light began to encircle the three of us. Before I knew it my feet were no longer touching the rocky red floor. I looked up, focusing on the doorway above. The image of all the monsters and Asmodeus in chains grew smaller below us.

He screamed below, the army was coming and I was shooting them down with light blasts from my hand. My head was hammering in pain from the use of all this magic. I felt blood trickle down from my nose. Dante was shooting down goblins and creatures leaping off the wall at us with green flame faster than I'd ever seen. I realized that meant I was the only one keeping us moving towards the portal with levitation. As we reached the portal, I could see my brothers on the other side. Emma glanced at me. My body was trembling, and for a moment, I feared I'd fall below into the army of creatures and be killed.

"Dante, push us through! She can't keep us here much longer!" Emma said.

All three of us held hands, and I felt my magic stop. For a split second, our bodies weren't being suspended anymore–we were about to fall back down. Dante brought his hands together and green energy shot around us, pushing us through. We tumbled to the ground and rolled across the destroyed field with a shock of force.

Micah shouted, "We gotta close the portal!" Galahad and Micah were fighting creatures and Killian had a goblin in his jaws like a chew toy. Galahad threw his sword at the artifact. His sword glowed with light and enflamed the artifact before it broke into several pieces, falling in the grass like a worthless clump of cement. Galahad and the rest of them rushed to our side.

"Are you girls okay?" Galahad squatted beside us. He wrapped his arms around us so tight my body hurt. "Elsha, what were you thinking? You shouldn't have…."

"Saved *you* for once?" Emma picked up her head slowly. "Sorry to break it to you big brother, but you're not gonna be the only one making sacrifices for this family anymore."

I sat up as the world came into focus and I put my hand to the cold blood that had trickled down my face. My sister was the first thing that came into focus, "Emma….thank God you're okay!" I took her in a tight hug. "I was so worried I'd never see you again."

"I'm not leaving you, Elsha, ever," Emma used her sleeve to wipe the blood from my nose.

"We did it…" Micah breathed, "We saved the world."

Dante looked genuinely surprised, "I legitimately thought we'd die back there….I've been afraid I'd go to hell sometimes but not while I was still—you know, alive."

I punched him in the arm, "You didn't think we could do it?"

"I knew it was *destined,* but I've had my doubts about grand design before, okay?" Dante sat up and held his arm. "Congratulations, Avengers of Light, you did it. You have no idea the kind of fame you are going to get from the Manor for…."

Micah pushed through and hugged Emma and me.

"Sisters! Thank goodness, I thought I'd be stuck with Killian for the rest of my life!" Micah said.

We all laughed and Killian huffed. Galahad took all of us in a hug, and Killian knelt to be part of it. "We're alive, and we're all together— that's what matters."

I looked at their faces. I'd never been more grateful to see them.

Dante stood up and backed away.

Emma rolled her eyes. She grabbed Dante by his good arm and pulled him down next to us, "You're in this too, magic boy."

Dante was shocked and very uncomfortable. But eventually he smiled and shook his head, "I think I'm starting to like this family."

"You better watch it—if you get close to us, you might lose your mind," Micah said.

Dante shrugged, "Sounds like fun."

I smiled and held them tightly. "…Let's go home."

Chapter Thirty-Three

There's No Place like Home

Just being in Code Red again on the way back to the Manor was a massive comfort. I slept in the very back seat, slipping in and out of deep dreams, while my family talked and argued about directions. We had to put the seat down so Killian could fit in the back; he'd only be a wolf for the night, so we'd have time to get back to the Manor before he changed again. Whatever seal was on him had been broken, and that meant we'd have to keep watch every full moon. I was going to tell them everything Asmodeus had said, but I wanted to share it with Tulken first. I didn't want my family to be as worried as I was. Did Verrine expect me to let Asmodeus out? Why would they ever imagine I'd do that? To know the secret of my family's disappearance? What did happen to our parents? I shuddered to think what his dark curse had done. But he said it was ongoing, that the affects were still close by. Was that why Killian was a wolf? It was too much to consider in the moment. We'd closed the portal, stopped the army, and for the moment, Asmodeus was still where he belonged. I smelled the familiar moisture in the air as we drove on the highway back to the Manor with the windows rolled down. There are a lot of comforts I'm sure I'll know when I'm older, but one of the most consoling to me then was falling asleep in a car with the windows down to the sound of my family's voices.

I was awake when we pulled up to the Manor. As soon as I took a look at the place, I knew they hadn't been having it easy while we were away. Some of the trees were scorched, the parking area looked like a bomb went off, and there was noise bustling from inside. In the distance, I could see the challenge arena was still being repaired. I'd never been so eager to shuffle out of a car and get inside since our first home with our parents. The helping spirit was driving and let us out while she promised to take the car back to the garage. We all had our bags and hurried out to the arena behind the Manor. That was where everyone looked like they were gathered. My siblings and I exchanged worried glances.

"Let's go," Galahad ran forward first, and we followed. We were prepared for anything at this point. Killian was wearing a spare pair of Galahad's clothes because his wolf form had ruined his last ones. They were a little big on him, but for once, he wasn't complaining. We came around the corner wall that lined the arena, and Galahad halted us. There was green blood staining the grass and creatures still turning to dust all around the lot as we approached.

Tulken held a long sword in one hand and was wiping sweat from his brow. He was breathing heavily, and Dori was running in circles like a chicken without her head. Dashiel stood by, holding a sword like he'd just left a fight.

Uriah looked exhausted in a blood-stained dark brown turtleneck sweater armed with a bow and arrows. His arm trembled as he fired one last arrow at a goblin that leaped through the air at his face. The creature yelped, being impaled with the arrow through the neck, and fell to the ground. Uriah stepped on it, squashing its head like a melon with a grunt. He breathed heavily before turning to Tulken as Nicodemus landed on his shoulder. "Why have the assaults stopped? Is Asmodeus free? Have the Avengers been killed?"

Dashiel's expression tensed and he tilted his head slightly, "I wouldn't make such.... horrific suggestions without evidence. The consequences of such an outcome would be…beyond dire."

"Have a little faith Uriah, they must have defeated Asmodeus' forces or else the world would look very different," Tulken's tone was forcibly calm. "The assailments have stopped..."

"But if Dante has failed to protect Em….the Dyer family," Dashiel's voice was more concerned than I'd ever heard it.

"Dori, please tell Dashiel there's reason to be hopeful," Tulken said.

"WE'RE DOOMED! DEAD! ASMODEUS HAS TAKEN OVER THE WORLD AND WE DON'T KNOW BECAUSE HES CONTROLLING US RIGHT NOW!" Dori screamed. Tulken let out a breath, "Never mind…."

Uriah cursed.

Herodotus and the others from his group who were standing by, gasped. "Brother!"

"Forgive me, sister, but I should have been the one to oversee this mission. We should form a rescue party right now to retrieve them," Uriah argued, standing before Tulken.

I looked at Galahad, surprised he hadn't let us walk into the arena and tell them we were okay yet. He still had his hand out, holding us back as he listened curiously. My other siblings wouldn't complain; they liked eavesdropping too much. Micah's mouth hung open, "Is he actually concerned about us?"

Emma smiled hopefully, "Maybe we misjudged him."

Killian frowned as all of us peered through the windows, "Maybe he's been possessed."

"Uriah, we've discussed this." Tulken was controlling his temper. "I'm as worried for them as you are, but their calling is clear..."

Uriah clenched his fists. "Respectfully, Headmaster, this was a mistake. You know I'd never dare impose my judgment on your decisions..."

Galahad choked. "Does he want to be hit by lightning?"

Emma shushed him. "I want to hear!"

Uriah's expression twisted as he looked at the destroyed tower from the challenge, "We could have sent five completely useless, ungifted blind to their deaths under the mistake of believing they were Commissioned! And even if they are average and ungodly, it was our sacred duty to protect them."

I frowned.

Dante laughed.

Galahad released an annoyed breath, "No, it's still him."

Addie was trembling on one of the seats of the arena with her mother beside her, "I hope they're okay…."

"Addie's worried about you, man!" Micah nudged Killian encouragingly.

Killian's expression grew calmer, "I've seen enough."

Galahad met my middle brother's gaze before lowering his hand. "Okay, let's go."

We all rushed into the arena as Uriah was arguing with Tulken. As soon as we did, gasps and murmurs went about the crowd, and then silence. Everyone stared at us.

Micah spread his hands, "We're back—hold your applause till…aw heck, you can clap now!"

"Emma," Dashiel hurried towards her, dropping his weapon, 'You and your family…you're…alive…." He smiled in relief.

Emma hurried to him, "Dashiel! You don't have to miss me anymore because…I'm right here!"

"I…" Dashiel began.

Emma spoke quickly. "We should totally hang out now that I'm back. What do you think? I'm glad you agree!"

Micah made imitation sick noises and a grossed out face. Dori and Addie rushed over, asking if we were okay and talking at once.

Uriah's mouth was hanging open. He was speechless as the crowd in the arena clamored about. I waved to him with a weak smile through the crowd and his face turned white.

Addie hugged us before she turned and looked at Killian. He looked a little disappointed but controlled his expression, "It's okay, you don't have to hug…."

Addie wrapped her arms around him tightly for a moment and Killian turned bright red. "I'm so glad you guys are okay!"

That brought Uriah back to reality, "The *indecency*…." He looked away from them, bringing his gaze to me. Uriah stormed over, pushing aside other students muttering, "Out of my way, you insignificant...." They cleared when they realized he was walking through. Uriah ignored my other siblings and stood before me, looking down to meet my gaze. "You actually did it? You defeated Asmodeus?"

I nodded, "Sort of. Asmodeus is where he belongs, and the army is trapped down there with him."

"And the artifact is destroyed," Galahad said, forcing Uriah to look at him. "But it looks like things haven't exactly been peaceful here…." Students were carrying weapons. Percival and his swordsmen were standing nearby like they'd just come from fighting. Clash was with him holding an axe.

Tulken looked at all of us proudly. "Collins sensed when the portal opened, and the disturbances reached us here in all kinds of ways…if you hadn't prevailed, we'd never have been able to protect the Manor. All of us owe you thanks."

"Where's Dante?" Dashiel said.

I was about to open my mouth when I saw Dante at the corner of the wall, out of Dashiel's view. He shook his head. "He, um…didn't make it."

Uriah looked unmoved. "—Oh," he moved back from me a step and crossed his arms.

"Uriah!" Addie snapped.

Kaine was in the corner of the arena and looked concerned for a moment but then wasn't buying it.

Dashiel's expression twisted in a fight against emotion, "He…didn't?"

"Yeah, good guy—but we'll get over it. After all, *we* were the priority," Micah said, using Dashiel's own past words. Tulken put a hand to his mouth, covering a smile as he understood the ruse immediately.

Dashiel narrowed his gaze at Micah, "Well, why did you let him die? You could have done something!"

"Why? Because he's a valuable member of the Commissioned?" I said.

"No, because he's my *friend*. Now get back out there and find him!" Dashiel said.

"Oh, Dash, I didn't know you cared that much," Dante stepped out.

Kaine was standing by Tulken, and his head went up. He gave a small, proud smile, "Kid…you made it."

Dante nodded with a mischievous grin, "Thanks….but I can't take credit for saving the world. That goes to these guys."

Tulken's smile was so proud I thought he might cry. "Ladies and gentlemen—the Avengers of Light," he raised a hand to us before clapping. Everyone else clapped in return, Kaine's gym rats, even Uriah's group (though they started clapping last). Uriah remained still for the longest time. Eventually, he brought his hands together with an unchanged expression. Galahad signaled us to walk up to Tulken. We'd have to explain what happened and ask some questions of our own soon. Galahad set the pieces of the broken artifact in front of him, "Not sure what you want to do with this... but without it the doorway to the dark realm stays closed…. hopefully for good."

"Collins will see that the pieces are secured with a seal. If any of you need medical attention, the the Manor Nurses will take you to the infirmary now," Tulken said. Several students were being led away as he said it and even a couple professors. All of us were sore and probably damaged in ways we were too busy to tell. Dante's arm was the main issue and Tulken took notice of it, quickly telling the nurses to check him. He turned back to us, "I want to hear all about your adventure, but first, it appears to me Killian will need some new attention. Why are you in your brother's clothes?" he gestured to him with his sword.

Despite Killian trying to look casual, Tulken didn't miss a thing.

Killian explained briefly, and Tulken did his best to control his shock. He exchanged glances with Collins before asking Clary to take Killian to medical and have him checked. Killian looked tousled and bruised from all the running through the woods. Professor Clary led him away. "That's...quite a story. All of you will need food and rest; the faculty will see you get what you need."

I tugged on Tulken's sleeve, "Headmaster, would it be alright if I stayed with Killian a while? I don't want to leave him alone. He's been through…a lot," I said.

Tulken squatted down to be at my height. "This little one is always thinking of someone else. Of course you can. Is that what all of you want?" We all gave various forms of agreement and Tulken smiled. "Alright, Calisto and the others will prepare anything you'd like as a victory feast, and we can have it in the Great Hall. We'll talk about your mission in detail then."

"That sounds great!" Emma said.

"I'm so proud of all of you. The Manor of Raziel and the world owe you a great debt," Tulken said. He looked at me, "I knew you had gifts. I'm sorry I wasn't there to see you discover all of them. I'll bet it saved your family's life."

"I don't know about…" I began.

"She totally did! She was awesome out there!" Micah said. Emma agreed.

"And you, Empress of Light, I think you've tapped into more gifts than you know. You've done very well. Keep your sister strong. And use that bold tongue to speak for her," Tulken encouraged.

"Yes, sir," Emma smiled, ruffling my hair.

Tulken looked at Galahad, "And as for you…. I'd tell you to take care of them, but it's clear I don't have to."

Micah puffed his chest out, waiting for his recognition. Tulken smiled down at him, "All your spontaneous ideas and wit—they've saved your life, so keep honing your skills. Your family needs you."

"I made a rapid-fire crossbow machine," Micah said proudly.

"I'll have to see that—I can't wait to see what you make next," Tulken said. Dante stood there a moment, waiting for something to be said to him. After a second, he turned and began to walk out of the arena. Tulken picked his head up from looking at me, "Dante."

Dante froze. He turned around slowly, "*Yes*—headmaster?"

"Thank you for watching them for me," Tulken said. "They only mean you the best, just like the rest of us—don't ever forget that."

Dante paused.

Tulken's expression grew slightly solemn, "You've done very well."

Dante gently pulled his arm from the Manor nurse, as she was getting ready to unwrap his wound. He bowed lowly at the waist, "Thank you."

Tulken studied him but didn't say anything. Tulken's tone grew lighter when he turned back to me, "Now, what would the heroes like for their victory meal?"

"Let Elsha choose," Galahad said.

"Alright, little one, what would you like?" Tulken said.

"Pizza," I said, afraid someone would object. Instead, they cheered.

"So it is then," Tulken said.

"Did you miss us?" I asked, genuinely curious. He was the closest thing I had to a Dad figure in my life. I'd never had an adult ask me what I wanted or do things for me, not for a long time, at least.

His expression softened, "The Manor wasn't the same without you."

I laughed. "You don't know what you're getting into, letting my family live here—but I really appreciate it. We might burn the place down someday."

Tulken laughed lightly before coughing into his hand. "Perhaps some collateral damage will be involved..." He looked around at the mess the Manor was in. "...but I trust you'll do great things, Elsha. From the day I met you, I haven't been disappointed."

My eyes grew moist. I hugged Tulken.

Everyone in the room caught their breath.

Uriah choked like he'd been about to object.

Dori whispered to Addie, "Can she do that?" and Addie shrugged. Tulken was only surprised momentarily before he smiled and hugged me back. It was like being thrown back in time somehow, to a time when I had a parent; even the smell of his suit reminded me of my old home. I didn't care that everyone was shocked. Tulken stood up and kept his arm around me protectively. No one objected.

"Would you like to tell me all about your adventure?" I told Tulken everything as he walked me out of the arena, and my siblings followed. It was good to finally be home.

#

In the next couple of days, the Manor of Raziel planned a bonfire to celebrate. We had to wait another night because, well, Killian was a wolf again. After two full moons, he was done and back to himself (Micah said there wasn't much difference). He and Tulken had a long talk in his office. I'm sure it was about all the work Collins would have to do now that we knew Killian was cursed. But I didn't want to bring it up. The danger had passed, and once again, we were safe.

Micah was building a fireworks machine on the back lawn of the Manor. I was walking with my hands in the pockets of my denim jacket to where the bonfire was.

Collins and the maids were using magic to send some of the fireworks flying higher into the sky. It was hard to distinguish anyone's voice over the music and the talking. Calisto's amazing food filled the air with a rich scent. I was walking past the gazebo with the hanging lights when I saw someone resting their elbows on the railing away from everyone. I wouldn't have been able to tell who it was, except for the hawk on his shoulder looking just as stoic as him. I could have walked on by and said nothing to him. But for some reason, I felt led to talk to him. I walked slowly up the steps to the gazebo.

Uriah had one leg thoughtfully crossed over the other in dark jeans and a brown turtleneck with his hands on the railing, looking down at the other students. I saw a thin silver necklace hanging around his neck and wondered what it was.

I cleared my throat as I walked up. "You're not planning on enjoying the fun with, you know…people?"

He barely turned his head towards me. It stayed there a second, and he was silent. After looking back down in front of him, he responded. "I don't derive joy from unfruitful trivial frivolous things."

I walked up next to him and rested my elbows on the railing. "Okay…in American teenager, please?"

Uriah almost cracked a smile. "I don't like silly games."

"You don't *like* them, or you don't *do* them?"

"My parents never let me play games, so I assumed there was nothing edifying in them."

"Aw, is that why you never smile?" I teased, leaning forward. Somehow Uriah wasn't the scariest thing in the world after what I'd faced the past few weeks. It was different now, and I think he sensed it. I wasn't afraid of him anymore.

His hands tensed around the railing and he arched his head, looking down at me. "It never ceases to amaze me who God allows to be Commissioned."

I huffed. "Because you would be able to make much better choices, right?"

"You and your family just saved the world, Elsha Dyer. Before this, you were nothing, meaningless. None of you had done anything that people would acclaim or notice…."

Wow. This was what being nice got you. "You know you're not scoring any points here."

"—But *now* you're the Avengers of Light, and you are one of the only Commissioned who've been able to face one of the third. Hasn't that changed you at all?" he looked down at me.

I blinked. "Uh…how?"

Uriah's mouth parted in confusion. "If I were you, I would be so proud I'd…." he hung his head.

"You'd what?'

"I probably wouldn't be handling this as well as you," he said barely above a whisper.

"Was that just…a genuine compliment?" I was confused.

"Don't, ever, repeat it to anyone….you may not have noticed, but I struggle with…some pride."

Laughing was rude, so I held back, "…You? No."

"I wasn't finished," he brought his gaze to mine. I crossed my arms stubbornly. He looked at me a moment with an expression I couldn't read before he turned away. "You didn't have anything to present yourself as Commissioned, but you've saved the world…and you're not even talking about it. These past three days, I haven't heard anything from anyone here except the Dyers this and the Dyers that…but not a word from you. How do you do something like that and not even want to mark it as an achievement?" he looked at me, genuinely confused. "I have all the things you didn't, and I wasn't chosen to do that. If I had been…"

"I don't know…I guess….I don't have anything that wasn't a gift. So I'm grateful…. not really proud of myself."

I looked up from my shoes to see he was staring at me. He wasn't talking, and that made me uncomfortable. I nodded awkwardly and started to walk away when I stopped.

"So, after tonight, we can go back to hating each other and competing and all that…but do you wanna, I don't know, attempt to play kids' games for one night?"

He averted his gaze and pet his hawk under its chin thoughtfully. "I have other more edifying things to pursue, thank you."

I nodded and walked down to meet a couple of my siblings by the fire. Dante sat in fresh new clothes with his arms resting on his knees. His eyes were a luminous color in the firelight. He looked very handsome, but I didn't dare say anything. I wasn't that brave, even after our insane journey. Killian was with Micah and Dante; the three of them were talking. As I approached, I saw Emma walking with Dashiel. I paused in slight surprise. Maybe he really had missed her. Killian talking to Dante and Emma walking with Dashiel...wow. A lot had changed over the past few months.

I sat on the log next to Killian and Micah, rubbing my arms from the chill in the air.

"Are my eyes playing tricks or..." I began.

The three boys looked at me, and Killian spoke first. "Nope, they're really talking."

I looked at Killian. "Where's Galahad?"

Killian looked down at his hands, which he closed into fists before opening them. "Talking with Tulken."

"Were he and the faculty able to help you with the wolf thing?" I asked carefully. Killian looked a little tense, more than usual, and I wanted to be sure it wasn't a touchy subject.

Killian ran a hand through his hair, "Yeah, we talked about a lot, but there's not much they know right now. I told them what Verrine said. Collins is going to see if he can find the seal which I had on me before. Dante says it might give us an idea into who cast it."

"Are you gonna be able to control it? Like you did at the portal?" I asked.

Killian looked at Dante.

Dante knit his fingers below his chin in thought. "I don't know the conditions of the seal or if it was made from light or dark magic. Collins should be able to tell us but until then...I've never heard of a Commissioned being a werewolf. Typically, that's the result of being bitten by one or a curse, and after what Asmodeus said...."

He didn't need to finish. I knew what he meant. Asmodeus said he cursed our family, and we had no idea how deep that ran. Was it that we were put in Blech's? Was it Killian's wolf? Was it the disappearance of our parents?

Killian spoke up before I could. "I don't care if it is a curse. I controlled it then, and I can do it again. If I hadn't turned into a wolf, then we wouldn't have been able to survive back there. I don't know what Tulken and our great leader are talking about, but I know this thing...it could be an extension of my power. I can use it against the enemy; I won't let it control me."

I nodded. Maybe he was right; it had saved us back there. It could be a gift, not a curse. I wasn't sure, but I saw how determined Killian was. Did he like that he had a wolf now? "Okay," I said at last.

Killian cracked a small smile, nudging me in the arm with his fist. "Maybe Galahad won't have to be the one protecting us all the time anymore? You can actually start looking at me too."

I brightened at that prospect. Galahad walked up with his hands in the pockets of his sweatshirt and a burdensome expression in the firelight. Emma and Dashiel caught up with him before he reached us, and in a second, his expression shifted to more pleased. They walked up to us and sat around the fire as a few other students approached. Emma sat, but Dashiel excused himself, returning to the Manor. Dori and Addie came over arm in arm with Jasmine and sat by the fire with us in the grass. Killian noticeably changed expression and posture when Addie approached, trying to seem less daunted than he really was. Galahad sat by Emma across from us.

"Anything new?" Killian ventured.

Galahad arched his head slightly away. "The faculty are doing what they can. Tulken's alerting the other Manors. They all had attacks made on them, and their defenses were breached when Verrine and Darkfire started searching for the pieces of the demon's stone. They're going to have a conference, so Tulken will be gone for a little while."

"Asmodeus is locked up, the stone is taken apart-what else is there to worry about?" Micah raised his hands.

Emma held her knees, resting her head on Galahad's shoulder, "Darkfire and Verrine are still out there."

"So is Asmodeus' host," I said.

Addie looked around at us, "You guys shouldn't be worrying about that yet. You've done enough for now. Give yourselves a little time to rest."

Dori leapt with a fist. "And celebrate! You've just barely become the most popular people in the school, and now the rest of the Commissioned will be at your feet, begging for your attention!"

Jasmine nudged her with a laugh. I hadn't even realized that, but students had been talking to us more and asking about what our plans were. It was weird, but honestly, I didn't care about the attention. The people who'd liked us when we were the weird orphans were the ones I still wanted to be around. I didn't need anyone else's attention. "I'm good with who we've got here."

Micah moved his head, "Let's not be hasty...now that we're the heroes who saved the world, we could start asking tribute...."

Dante, who'd been sitting back staring into the flames with his legs out in front of him, raised a finger. "You're kid brother has a point...." Killian laughed, and everyone started talking with each other. I pulled my sleeves down to be warm from the cold. Dante rested one foot over the other and turned to us. "So the faculty has their deal going on. What's next for the great Dyers as the Avengers of Light?"

Killian tossed stones into the fire. "He's got a point, guys. What's next?"

"I say we go back to the boarding house and we make them eat dirt!" Micah said.

Dashiel emerged beside us, "I would find that action highly unproductive considering your recent duties."

Emma beamed at him, "Decided to join the festivities?"

Dashiel nodded, standing behind Dante. "I had business to discuss with Uriah, but it was completed more briefly than I had expected." Addie looked at Killian. "You guys all lived in a boarding house?"

"That must have been tough," Jasmine said.

"Not as tough as fighting goblins," Galahad said.

"Or witches," Micah said.

Emma huffed, "Or temptation."

We all laughed, "Good points."

"I guess we have a good excuse for being freaks now, a sacred calling, demon hunters and all," Micah said.

"You guys aren't freaks," Jasmine said, supportively.

"No, he doesn't mean it in a bad way. Weirdly enough—Micah's right. It could take a group of freaks to stop one of the third," Killian said.

Galahad was moving his knee up and down in thought, partially to keep warm as he stared into the flickering flames. "That's what's next. I talked to Tulken. Since we're the Avengers of Light, this mission was just a first. Anytime one of the third emerges, or a creature we think is connected to Asmodeus' host or his plan...it'll be our job. The big missions, demons, it's our territory now."

I stared up at the star-ridden sky above the Manor. We'd been thinking about the fandom, plusses of saving the world and being liked. Galahad was thinking about the responsibility our newfound favor meant. I let out a breath, "...We can handle it."

They all looked at me in slight surprise.

Dante smiled.

"Asmodeus will have his time. For now, I say we celebrate," Emma said.

Micah set off his fireworks. Tulken eventually came out of his office to watch the festivities. When I caught a glimpse of him, his expression was grave- it shifted to congenial the moment he realized I'd been watching. Addie and Killian talked. Emma learned how to dance from Jasmine. Dashiel pretended not to be looking at my sister.

The night waned on, and for the first time in a while, I felt like I belonged somewhere. My family wasn't like everyone else. Nothing I ever said or did would change that. But as I looked out at all of them, playing games, telling jokes, and getting into little fights, I felt like I wasn't just on the outside looking in. I was part of something. What was coming next still scared me, but I could face it. We could. The words rang in my head: don't be afraid. I'd be scared in the coming days, we all would—but that wouldn't stop me from doing what I had to. It never stopped Galahad. I looked down at the valley behind the Manor while listening to my family and friends' voices. Asmodeus wouldn't scare me out of living or fighting. Fear wouldn't control me. I was a Dyer. And trust me…it takes more than that to stop us.

End of Book One

Enemy Index

The third: Speaks of the original percentage of angels which followed Lucifer in rebelling against God. Specific numbers are unknown to Commissioned as many are still being discovered. The chief of whom was Lucifer. All other demons followed his example and sought to win the world to his side before the second coming. Lucifer's servants seek to corrupt and enslave the world before they're cast into hell and then have no means to harm God's creation.

Asmodeus: Second to Lucifer only in influence and power among the demons. He's been the next one to wage war on God's creation after the power of Lucifer/Satan was taken. Allegedly cast into hell by Commissioned through their divinely given gifts but still has a human tether to the world, allowing him to gather forces.

Verrine: A demon of The Third and the embodiment of temptation. Verrine's true appearance is a hairless goblin with long fangs and wrinkled clawed hands. He has two sharp jagged horns on his head and stands hunched. Because of his sway over mankind, and their complete submission to him, he's able to appear as a normal wealthily dressed man. Verrine can command humans to do his will based on their inclination to give in to selfish desires. All Commissioned are strongly encouraged to flee if this demon is encountered.

Footnote: Very few Commissioned who've encountered The Third have lived to tell the tale. Commissioned have no hope of fighting them unless they are the Avengers of Light. Many Commissioned have lost their lives to the demons, so if one is encountered, prayer is the encouraged course of action.

Creatures subordinate to The Third

Ghouls: A creature believed to only be the subject of Arabian folklore by the blind. Ghouls are a deep greenish-grey color and have rotted, wrinkled faces with long teeth and sunken eyes. They're demons that roam the darkest places, like graveyards, alleys, in search of consuming human flesh. They enter homes through dark cracks and crevices because they despise the light.

Vulnerabilities: A ghoul must eat human flesh on a regular basis to stay strong and maintain any form of sanity. If they're starved or endure long periods of time without feeding, they'll grow sickly, weak, and insane. Easier to kill through beheading or dismemberment. Sunlight is also a weakness.

Witches: Unlike ghouls, witches were human once and sold their souls to forces of darkness to acquire black magic. Their use of black magic has distorted their appearance over the years to resemble the hideous nature of their souls. They remain alive far longer than normal humans because they wish to prolong their eternity in hell as much as possible. Witches despise all things Godly, all Commissioned and specifically children. Witches mostly travel by use of brooms and are extremely fast and agile.

Vulnerabilities: Witches are susceptible to beheading and burning. Hanging was a common method but proved ineffective as a broken neck could be repaired by the use of dark magic or spells. They dislike the daylight, but it isn't fatal.

Original Goblin: The original goblins were demons straight from the pit who established a tree with alluring fruit that lured people to it. They wished to grow in numbers and run rampant uncontrolled over the world in search of wealth. Humans who were dominated by their lusts ate the fruit and indulged their selfish, sinful desires, gradually becoming distorted into figures and goblins themselves. Goblins are light green with long fingers, claws, and slim bodies that look weak but are, in fact, quite strong and fast. Not very intelligent and typically rabid and insatiable.

Vulnerabilities: Original goblins are vulnerable to water and complete dismemberment. If the body is dismembered and destroyed, they can't recover.

Copy Goblins: Also human at one point in time though they were dominated by desires of the flesh. They were turned into copy goblins gradually by eating the cursed fruit the original goblins made. Any human who did so had to be given over completely to whatever their desire was: money, power, etc.

Vulnerabilities: The same as an original goblin.

Footnote: Copy goblins should not be killed unless established there is no trace of the human remaining. If they completely resemble an original goblin in appearance and lost all humanity, then eliminate them. At that point, since the creature has lost all humanity, it's a mercy killing it before it can kill anyone else.

Trolls: Trolls are giant humanoid monsters of varying sizes with a typically dirty grey skin tone and little to no hair with large teeth or tusks. Believed by the blind only to be part of Scandinavian myth as large creatures dwelling in caves and mountains that consume humans. They're superhumanly strong due to their size and not very intelligent. Trolls typically carry large weapons made of stone, like axes or clubs. They have night vision and can see perfectly in the dark.

Footnote: There are many subspecies of trolls with different abilities, such as ice troll, mountain troll, etc.

Vulnerabilities: Trolls are weak to acid and fire, as well as other forms of heat or divine light.

Chupacabra (Meaning "goat-sucker"): A creature typically known to inhabit South America, though some of the beasts have moved and procreated into sub-species that now inhabit Northern California. It feeds on livestock (which is where it derived its name) by draining their blood. Chupacabra are typically the size of a small bear with a long-fanged snout and a jagged spine reaching down from the shoulders to the tail. They're pack animals and rather cowardly on their own. A Chupacabra will hunt if it's with its pack but not alone.

Vulnerabilities: Beheading will kill a Chupacabra, but it's extremely difficult because their bones are very durable. Recommended means of killing are fire or crushing the body completely.

La Ciguapa: A female demon found in the Dominican Republic who bears the appearance of a beautiful woman with blueish skin and dark hair that reaches past her feet. They live in forests and mountains near hiking trails, away from towns and villages. La Ciguapa is known to prey on men using her voice and appearance to lead them away into her home cave. Once captured, La Ciguapa drains the life of her victims to sustain herself. A signature sign of her demon hood is the creature's backward feet and skin.

Vulnerabilities: La Ciguapa can be hunted down with a white purebred dog because animals are not susceptible to her voice and appearance. To kill La Ciguapa, Commissioned must rob the creature of her beauty.

Micah's Drawings

Asmodeus

Chupacabra

Darkblood Warrior

Ghoul

Goblin

La Ciguapa

Verrine

Witch

Sneak peak into Author's next book

Avengers of Light

Book Two

Tournament of the Commissioned

(1)

The last day of the Dyer's Summer

What set this day apart as being the last in the Dyers summer? I'll tell you one thing, it had nothing to do with the calendar. You know that feeling when things have just become different and you can't put your finger on how, but it's just the end of something? I'm talking about the last day where things were what I considered *normal*. I know what you're thinking. How normal could the lives of five commissioned teenagers who also happen to be the Avengers of Lightbe? Not very normal I'll be real.But—there are certain things even with the life-threatening scenarios, monsters, witches, demons, and ghouls that I never questioned. Things I always thought would be the same way. But like my hero always told me, things aren't meant to be one way forever. Maybe I had just gotten too used to the way things were at the Manor of Raziel to tell how much was changing right before my eyes—too slowly for me to notice and too fast for me to appreciate it.

Fast.

That was how we were driving on that mission compared to how my oldest brother normally handled the wheel. Truth be told I found it reassuring for him to be in the front seat driving us around again. I was in the middle of Code Red (our vehicle for missions that had been tried and true through many a perilous journey). Galahad had been supervising so many missions with other students from the Manor that he didn't get to be with us as much as before. For the most part it had been me, Emma, Micah and Killian. Galahad was the oldest—that made me suspect Headmaster Tulken expected more from him and Killian always thought that too. Occasionally we'd go out with him or a couple of us depending on whose skills fit the bill—today was supposed to be an all-hands-on deck situation.

Tournament of the Commissioned

I don't know why Headmaster Tulken uses that expression because, as far as I know, he was never in the Navy.

We'd done all kinds of missions since we'd found out we were the Avengers of Light: stopping goblin theft, finding other Commissioned, hunting witches, tracking down servants of the Third. But this mission was different. Tulken and Professor Collins couldn't stress the importance of this one enough, but they didn't give us all the details. Only that we were recovering an extremely powerful forbidden artifact that had been long lost. It belonged to a sorcerer called Asher the Penitent who'd been protecting it for years. We'd had separate missions before this, but they all took a back seat tonight. Dante was extremely excited for this one and wanted to go with us, but Tulken had assigned us.... *other* teammates. I hadn't been a happy camper about bringing the stiff neck Uriah sitting next to me. Emma didn't have it much better; she was in the far back seat beside Herodotus.

Who are Uriah and Herodotus? Good question. Maybe you know those people in church that never swear or drink, they think they're better than you because they're in church six times a week, have the Bible memorized, and they've kept all twelve commandments—there's only ten, but they add two of their own for good measure.

Well, Uriah would never associate with people like that—they're not religious enough for him. I'm pretty sure he shook the dust from himself every time we were forced to interact just so my stench wouldn't get on him.

Herodotus was like a carbon copy being made in his image only she was mixed with Regina George—initially, I'd been afraid putting Emma in the back with her would result in a catfight, but Galahad had given both of us a talking to and ordered us to behave. I'd already fought with him and argued for us to bring Dante instead, but it was hopeless. What's worse, Uriah had overheard me begging Galahad not to bring him, and I could swear his shoulder was colder than usual. I spent most of the drive staring out my cracked window as the clouds hovered over us; the cold air blew in, hitting my face and helping me not to grow red from the irritation of being seated next to Uriah. The chill in the air was proof to me that we were in the last days of summer.

Micah had called a shotgun before the rest of us and was by Galahad in the front seat as we drove through Loomis Sacramento, passing through the suburban areas. Micah had the map flattened out in front of him, trying to communicate with our vehicle's help spirit (yes, our car was Commissioned property, and we had a magic help spirit inside it that told us where to go). Micah smoothed the wrinkled paper as the blue, hazy image of the spirit was before him, arms crossed, coming out of the dashboard. She looked like some kind of teacher; only her image was blue, and only the top half of her body was visible.

"You know what lady, I don't see why if you're our directional help you can't just teleport us to this old house," Micah squinted at the paper. "Why do we need a map anyway…"

Our help rolled her eyes. "I am here to assist you—but because it is not Commissioned policy to provide technology to our students who are under eighteen…you must—use—the map! I have enough trouble with your middle brother. I will not take attitude from you!"

Galahad flexed his fingers around the steering wheel with a sigh. "Killian's tracking on foot."

Uriah crossed his legs and arched his head, looking out the opposite window rigidly in his dark brown turtleneck. "—Don't you mean *four legs*?"

I sucked in my cheeks and let out a strong breath through my nose, turning to look at him. "Why did we bring you again?"

He didn't even look at me. "Most likely because the headmaster wanted *efficient* Commissioned to ensure the artifact was acquired and that you were spared further embarrassment. I've seen your mission reports when your oldest brother isn't heading them: sloppy, unoriginal, calamitous—and those are the *best* you manage to do."

"Why you....!" I sat forward in my seat, and Emma snapped at Herodotus, who stifled a laugh in the back seat.

"It's unbecoming for a lady to swear," Uriah said haughtily, smoothing his sweater.

That was one time, okay? It was one of those moments where Uriah and I were arguing, and the noise was bustling around us everywhere on the quad. Uriah asked me to tell him exactly what I thought of him, and I did…it was just my luck; Kaine blew his whistle, and the whole quad got quiet as I screamed it. Tulken had a *long* talk with me about that one.

"That's enough—my family is learning to do just fine without me on missions," Galahad said, glancing back over his shoulder. "Where next, Micah?"

"Left!" Micah said.

"Right!" The help said frantically, pointing to a line on the map, implying Micah was holding it crookedly.

"Micah!" Emma cried.

"Galahad!" I yelled as we approached the fork in the road.

"Good Lord…" Uriah grumbled.

"*—Right!*" Micah corrected.

Galahad swerved into the right turn lane just ahead of another vehicle and stepped the gas, lurching us forward. All of us fell to the left side of the vehicle, Emma fell against Herodotus and yelled in protest, and Uriah fell against me and grunted. I grabbed the handle above my door and turned to see Uriah's face an inch from mine.

"Aaah!" I screamed and he made an equally horrified expression pulling back as the car was once again driving straight.

Uriah fixed his hair and scoffed, crossing his arms. "Are we there yet?"

The help spirit looked frazzled too and blinked like she had stars in her eyes. "I don't know…what happened?"

Micah straightened in his seat. "Galahad decided to drive like Killian for a second…."

Galahad pulled up alongside a curb across from an older home. It was a bit away from the other homes on a small plot of land. It was too dark to be day but enough light that it wasn't nighttime. The house was two stories, a faded red brick color with an old gate around it. Several tall trees with almost no leaves grew around it and their long branches stretched out like gangly fingers covering part of the building. The leaves blew across the building and scattered down the street, and the clouds seemed thicker around that house. Several cats of all shapes and sizes were sitting around and, on the gate, staring dead ahead like they were watching for intruders.

Micah sat back. "That's inviting."

Emma groaned. "No less than usual."

Uriah looked at my oldest brother. "What's the plan?"

"Wait," Galahad said, turning off the car and looking out the window. Out of the corner of my eye, something went by in a dark flash.

Killian.

A deep colored, rich dark fur, almost black, was settled by the front of the car next to Galahad's window. His blue eyes looked up at us as he turned his head. It was hard to believe he could function on his own in wolf form now, even change at will and keep it under control…. mostly. I looked at my hands, pulling my sleeves down to my palms— I'd outgrown the desire to wear so many layers of clothing all the time, but messing with my sleeves was still a nervous habit. I looked up to see Uriah staring at me curiously.

"What?" I snapped.

He looked back ahead at my brother. "We move out now?"

Galahad spoke to Killian. "Circle the house, check for any threats. Stay on the outside and howl if anything comes our way."

Killian nodded with a snort. He took off down the street, circling the house, and snarled at the cats that hissed in response.

Galahad opened the driver's door. "Now—we head out."

Milton Keynes UK
Ingram Content Group UK Ltd.
UKHW020048151124
451074UK00003B/20